Blood

Blood

stories

Matthew
Cheney

Black
Lawrence
Press

Black Lawrence Press

www.blacklawrence.com

Executive Editor: Diane Goettel
Book design: Amy Freels
Cover design: Matthew Cheney

Copyright © Matthew Cheney 2016
ISBN: 978-1-62557-941-6

Published 2016 by Black Lawrence Press.
Printed in the United States.

PUBLICATION HISTORY

"How to Play with Dolls" *Weird Tales*, no. 352, November/December 2008
"Blood" *One Story*, no. 81, 2006
"Revelations" *Sunday Salon*, November 2009
"Getting a Date for Amelia" *Failbetter*, no 4, 2001
"Prague" *Ideomancer*, 2004
"In Exile" *Mythic*, edited by Mike Allen. Mythic Delirium Books, 2006
"The Lake" *Lady Churchill's Rosebud Wristlet*, no. 21, November 2007
"Lonesome Road" *Icarus*, Winter 2010.
"How Far to Englishman's Bay" *Nightmare*, August 2013
"The Voice" *The Flash*, edited by Peter Wild, Social Disease, 2007
"New Practical Physics" *Say...What's the Combination*, 2007
"The Last Elegy" *Logorrhea*, edited by John Klima. Bantam Books, 2007
"The Art of Comedy" Web *Conjunctions*, 2006
"Walk in the Light While There Is Light" *Failbetter*, no. 42, 2012
"A Map of the Everywhere" *Interfictions*, edited by Delia Sherman & Theodora Goss, Small Beer Press/ Interstitial Arts Foundation, 2007
"Lacuna" *Where Thy Dark Eye Glances*, edited by Steve Berman. Lethe Press, 2013
"The Island Unknown" *Unstuck 2*, 2012

Contents

For my mothers,
Elizabeth Cheney & Ann Thurston

and in memory of my father,
David D. Cheney
(1943–2007)

How to Play with Dolls

Jenny's father spent a year making a dollhouse for her, a three-storey mansion with four gables and six chimneys and secret passageways and a dumbwaiter and a tiny television that, thanks to a microchip, actually worked. He gave it to her on her seventh birthday. Jenny thanked him and kissed him and told him she had always wanted an asylum for her dolls.

Though he wanted her to make the house into a pleasant place for tea parties and soirees, Jenny's father stayed silent as he watched his daughter restrain her dolls with straightjackets fashioned from toilet paper. He kept his silence as she built prison bars with toothpicks and secured every door with duck tape. But as she placed the dolls into their cells and set a group of them to stare at the television, he could not observe quietly any longer, and so he went to his workshop and reorganized his impressive collection of antique awls, adzes, augers, and axes.

Jenny continued in his absence. She created schedules for the patients, times when they could wander through the halls or make origami birds or rant and rave without reproach, or sleep in the cots she had built out of matchboxes stolen from her late mother's private stash. She had considered appointing some of the dolls to be doctors, but she did not trust them, and so retained all supervisory duties for herself. She did not sleep, for fear that were she not to keep a vigilant watch, the dolls would revolt or, worse, harm themselves. She despaired, though, because none of the patients seemed to be making any progress. Instead, they were all becoming recalcitrant, and they did not want to wander or create anything, they stopped ranting, they let the television slip to a channel of grey static, they slept and slept and slept. Jenny tried extreme measures: water dunking, severe lighting, simulated earthquakes, and even, with a contraption made from spoons and Christmas tree lights, electrocution. Nothing got better, and the dolls might as well have been dead.

After a month, Jenny's father returned from his workshop with delicately-detailed miniature hot air balloons, and as Jenny sat beside her asylum and wept over the helpless despair of the dolls, her father orchestrated clever escapes for each of the patients, who proved to be masterful balloonists, each and every one. They flew to the paradise of Jenny's bed, where they waited until she returned one night, the asylum having been abandoned, and they embraced her in their tiny arms and sang ancient songs in lost languages while she slept, her face wet with tears from her dreams.

Blood

The man who (my mother said) cried at my birth was the same man who gave me a rifle for my first birthday, a .22 he had built himself. The man who taught me to shoot that rifle as soon as I was able to walk was also the man who taught me to tell deer tracks from bear tracks and bear tracks from moose tracks, to tell poplar from hemlock and oak from pine. The man who screamed at the television every night, as if the politicians and legislators could hear his rants, was the man who night after night through my childhood, and especially in the long cold of each winter, told me stories of good rabbits and bad foxes in the forests, with the good rabbits outwitting the foxes, and the owls overseeing it all.

During the nights now, I remember his stories. And I remember him sitting in a wooden chair in our front yard, shotgun across his lap, head held in his hands, saying to me as I sat beside him, my arm around his leg and my fingers in love with the roughness of his jeans, "I just want them all to leave me alone. It's the only thing I want in the world." He looked at me, he ran his giant hand through my hair, he kissed my forehead. I remember his lips were dry and sharp, and the long whiskers of his beard tickled my skin.

§

I was a homely girl: freckled and scrawny, with thick, stiff hair, sunken eyes, and large front teeth. My father told me I should be glad to be homely, because boys would leave me alone that way, and I could mind my own life. This was certainly true most of the time when I was growing up, when we lived in the big house in the woods on a hill outside of town. My four brothers hardly knew I was there at all, and I usually kept to myself, observing; waiting.

The only one I had ever wanted to notice me was our mother. She went away when I was seven, during the winter, during a storm, when you could hardly see three feet in any direction because snow filled the air. I remember staring out the window, looking at big flakes highlighted by shafts of moonlight, white butterflies in the wind. And then a yellow light, thin and bobbing: my mother, flashlight in one hand and cardboard suitcase in the other, running down the hill. I didn't realize it was her or what had happened until I heard my father's voice, cursing and crying, and my eldest brother Win saying to him, "It doesn't matter." John said, "It's a terrible storm out there." Win said, "She doesn't matter."

My mother returned three (almost four) years later, when she came for us after everything had happened. Her hair was short and dyed dark red; she wore eyeliner and lipstick, but her eyes were hollow and she could not smile. Though I lived with my mother in town until I went to college, there was a distance we couldn't cross, a coldness to us both. She cooked me dinner every night, and no matter how small the portions, every night I left much uneaten. Later, I sent her letters and once or twice each year called her on the phone as I pushed north after college, settling first in Maine, then Montreal, then Halifax, now St. Lunaire, Newfoundland, until today one of my letters was returned, unopened, with stamped in red on the front of the envelope: *Deceased.*

Three of my brothers may still be alive. I talked on the phone with Nathan a few years ago, after he was arrested again.

Death does not horrify me, and dying is not a concept I've had to reconcile with any sort of belief or doubt; I give it as much thought as I give to clouds and rocks. Yet, it is the events around my father's death that I struggle to portray for myself, to wrap a story around and save as something more than fragments of fact, shards of memory, fractured dreams. In college, I studied evolutionary biology, and tried to find in nature analogues to what happened in my life. I moved to Maine to paint pictures and teach high school science, to meld Monet and Darwin, to find myself and to discard myself. I loathed my body (skin, eyes, shape) and I gave it to any man who asked, and each time I hoped with all the hope I had left in me that he would not give it back. I kept moving. In Montreal, I bought a camera and took pictures of objects for commercial catalogs and junk mail. In Halifax, I told stories to tourists. Now I have fallen in love with the ocean. Here, there is an old man with a white beard down to his waist who wears a tattered jacket and skullcap when he sits each dawn on a rock just beyond the reach of the morning waves, and the first time I saw him, and perhaps even after, I was sure it was my father there amidst the rotted threads of fishing nets, listening to the sea and the sky and the clouds.

§

My parents met in high school and got married soon after, my father nineteen and my mother eighteen. His parents had died, and he and my mother lived for seven years in the house in town that he had grown up in. She worked at the town library and he worked at the lumber mill. He had collected guns all through high school, learned to fix up the mangled and broken ones and sell them for twice or three times what he paid. After a while, enough people had heard of him that he was able to cut down on his hours at the mill and spend most of his time gunsmithing. He named his first son Winchester, his second son Colt.

People from around the country, even the world, began to bring their guns to my father to fix, to adjust, to beautify and preserve. He had the luxury of choosing only the guns he most wanted to work on, and the money he made allowed him to build his dreamhouse on a densely-wooded hill ten miles from any neighbors. It was a giant log cabin—six bedrooms, three bathrooms, a living room the size of most other people's whole houses, a dining room, a kitchen with space enough to cook for thirty people, and a basement with two sections: one heated and furnished to serve as a workshop and showroom for my father, another left bare and cold for storage. A dirt driveway snaked up through the woods and ended at the house. The steep embankment around the driveway made it seem like a ramp leading to a castle, and served a similarly protective purpose: it was impossible for anyone to sneak up on the house without being seen. Our father's black pick-up truck sat there like a sentry, and sometimes on dreary nights I would sneak outside and climb into the truck and pretend I was in a spaceship flying away.

There was a spot behind the house for my mother to have a garden, which is all she said she wanted. After we moved to the new house, she stopped working at the library and started tutoring Win, Colt, and eventually the rest of us at home, because our father said it would be a crime if we went to school now. Now, he said, we were all free.

§

What happened, happened three years after our mother left. There's no way to tell, though, when it began. It was an accumulation. It was night after night of shouting growing louder, lasting longer. It was weekly target practice turning to twice-weekly, then daily, then twice-daily. It was the pantry filling with canned food and dried milk. It was a generator in the basement and the remnants of a savings account stuffed into a sock hidden in a hollowed-out Bible. It was banks of trees planted in the front yard, a steel gate built at the bottom of the hill; it was rifles in the bedrooms and pistols in the kitchen and a crossbow on the dining room table; it was Army-issue ammo boxes in the corners, black shades on the windows, trap doors cut into the floor of the living room and kitchen, a secret passage in the attic leading to the roof where rope ladders waited; it was barrels to catch rainwater, and my brothers disappearing into the woods for hours every day to set booby traps, and our father standing on the porch of the house, shotgun in hand, revolver in his belt, staring, waiting.

And then the day he said, "We're ready now," and he sat us all down around the dining room table, pointed the shotgun at us, and said, "No-one leaves. We'll wait for them here."

Despite being an incurable rationalist, I tend to pay attention to numbers and dates, to coincidences and correlations and patterns, and so those words began what I've come to think of as Day One. There were six days after it. A week of lifetimes. I was ten years old, a decade completed. Win was seventeen, a year away from being able to buy a rifle legally or to enter the military. Colt had just turned sixteen and wanted to get a driver's license, but our father told him we would have nothing to do with the government anymore, that licenses and Social Security cards and birth certificates were ways the government numbered you, tracked you, trapped you. John was thirteen; unlucky. Nathan was twelve, a year lived for every month of a year. There were five of us, a prime number, divisible only by one and itself. There were four brothers, an even number, divisible by two. The word "divisible" contains nine letters; nine is the last single-digit number, a sacred number, lucky to the Chinese, unlucky to the Japanese because, or so I've heard, when pronounced, it sounds like the word for pain.

§

One fall night, a few months after our mother's departure, while we were all watching a game show, our father picked the little television up, jerked it away from the wall, and carried it outside. "Come on," he said to us as we sat still on the couch and chairs, staring at the place where the television had been. He picked up his shotgun and we followed him outside. The television sat on the ground like a lost or chastised animal, I thought, something naked and cowering. Our father shot it three times, its guts flaring on the first shot, its shell collapsing, pulverized on the second and third. "Clean it up," he said to my brothers. For the next few nights, he insisted on telling us all stories of the rabbits and the fox and the owl, but he gave up when my brothers started whispering during the stories and kicking or elbowing each other. He got distracted, and he couldn't remember an ending. "Go to bed," he told us, his eyes fierce and red.

Yet it wasn't until a few days before Day One that I had any sense something was wrong, any sense of foreboding, of true danger. I doubt if my brothers were more perceptive than I. We were used to our father, his sudden temper, his moods. I remember him in the days leading up to everything that happened saying more than once, "They won't take me alive, Jill. You neither, I hope."

They were a constant presence in our lives, because *they* were the persistent enemy and tormentor of our father. Who *they* were shifted, but in general *they* were the government, sometimes the police, occasionally any authority whatsoever, from the anonymous pests at the post office to a clerk at a store to an airplane flying too low. Always, *they* were a force beyond us and in opposition to us.

§

There are things I will never know about what happened, even as I try to filter the voices and images of remembered dreams from the voices and images of more substantial memories. I remember 16mm movies of Win and Colt as toddlers wearing cowboy hats, and I remember the sound of the projector clicking and clicking and the dust motes hovering in the light, and then I remember the film stopping on one frame and the light burning it, an amoebic hole growing massive on the screen, but I cannot imagine when we would have sat down to watch home movies, nor do I ever remember seeing a projector or a camera anywhere around the house.

I hear phrases and sentences in my brothers' voices, but where did they come from, when did I hear them? Win says, "Don't be like the girl, John," and John says, perhaps then or perhaps another time, "Why don't you believe me?" and then I hear the sound of someone sobbing on the other side of a door. I remember playing jacks with Nathan in the driveway and stopping suddenly to watch Win and Colt drag John, naked, howling, through mud and brush, and I hear Nathan's voice whispering to me, "Don't mind them, Jill, it's just a game," but I don't know how to play jacks, I have never seen a set of jacks in my life, and I know our father forbade us from playing any sort of games.

The first memory I have of my father is of him planting a sapling and then standing next to it, watching it. He was tall, and he towered above the little tree. I probably remember this because he seemed so powerful there, and perhaps I was scared, or awed. The memory is a still picture in my mind, and almost colorless: my father's tallness, his big hands and dark beard, and the tree with only a few small green leaves dangling from its grey branches.

§

In the days before everything that happened, my father gave me my own handgun. A Smith & Wesson revolver. I don't know what became of it. (In Maine, I briefly dated a guy who was fairly liberal and always voted for Democrats, but who was, as he described himself, a "firearms enthusiast", and he took me to a shooting range. I only stayed long enough to discover I couldn't shoot with any accuracy and had lost whatever ability I'd once had; every time I squeezed the trigger I closed my eyes and shot into the darkness.) My father handed the revolver to me as if it were a baby bird. "This is yours now," he said. "I don't ever want to hear of it not being with you. Sleep with it underneath your pillow. Loaded. Understand?"

That was the day John said to me, "He heard something on the radio last night. Got him all ready to raise hell. I don't think he slept, just kept cleaning every weapon we got, and loading them all."

Early in my childhood, I thought of my brothers as a team: indistinct, interchangeable, an entity that was not-mother, not-father, not-me. Soon after our mother left, though, I began to notice my brothers' differences, the delineations of their personalities. I paid attention. Nathan and John, the youngest, were playful, and sometimes included me in their games, generally as the Indian they were hunting. (Once, they threw rocks and our father saw them do it and whipped them with his belt) Win and Colt were always distant, always serious, but Colt would sometimes tuck me in at night and smile at me. Win spoke to me only when necessary, and usually to command: *Clear the table— Go inside— Be quiet.* Win taught Nathan and John how to shoot, and took them out to practice shooting at tin cans and logs (only our father would go out with me), and he took over most of our reading and arithmetic lessons after our mother left. John liked candy; Nathan daydreamed all the time; Colt often woke early and went outside to sketch birds; Win liked to climb trees.

Once, I was wandering through the woods, picking up pine cones and throwing them as far as I could, and when they landed I made a noise I thought sounded like an explosion, though I suppose it was closer to the sound of a toilet flushing. After I'd been doing this for a few minutes, throwing one pine cone after another, my hands sticky with pitch, I heard laughter. I looked around, then up. Win sat on the branch of a tree above me. He stopped laughing when I looked at him, and he turned away.

§

For three hours, we sat at the table. Our father stared at us, and we stared at him. In my memory, not one of us blinks. The shotgun doesn't move.

Finally, he said to Win and Colt, "You two take the others down to the storage cellar. Tie them up."

We didn't fight and we didn't speak. We all walked together down the stairs and into the cold, damp cellar, where John and Nathan and I sat against the cinderblock wall while Colt gently tied our hands and feet together with white cord. Win walked upstairs; Colt nodded at us, then followed.

Nathan began to weep. John hit him in the ribs with his elbow. Nathan whimpered, then was silent.

For two days, we sat down there. Colt brought us food and water when he could, and untied us long enough that we could go to the far opposite corner and release our bowels in the dark, the stench mixing with the thick scents of the concrete walls, dirt floor, wood ceiling.

"What's going on?" John asked.

Colt said, "We're waiting."

"Father?"

"Doing patrols."

Nathan said, "What about Win?"

"We're just waiting."

"Why do we have to be down here?"

Colt shook his head slightly, then looked away from us. "I've got to go back up."

"Take me—" John said, but Colt was gone.

At first, we talked to each other. John tried to tell us stories, but he could never put the pieces together, and so the old owl would fly off into the sky for no particular reason, and the deer would wander around the pond and talk to the fish about where there was a good, safe place to sleep, but the fish, of course, didn't know, and eventually John stopped trying to tell stories.

"We're going to be fine," John said.

"This is just a test," John said.

"You'll see," John said. "When this is all over, father will be proud of us."

We leaned against each other for warmth and to know another person was there. We stopped talking. Sounds sank into the cellar: the soft slap of footsteps in the house, the dim thrum of voices, the sudden flat crack of a door closing; thunder; a gunshot. Softer sounds, too: tiny movements in the dirt, shifts of the earth beneath us and beyond us. The noise hung in the darkness, and the darkness was material. Though I could not see a difference between when my eyes were open and when my eyes were closed (at both times I saw only blackness), I could feel a thick world beyond my sight, a depth that vanished into an endless, empty desert when I closed my eyes.

I slept, but did not know I slept until I awoke and blindness pierced my eyes and I felt my legs numb and cold against the ground and my back sore against the rough wall and my lips dry. I didn't dream.

I remember once waking in the darkness to hear John whispering, *I'm sorry, I'm sorry, I'm sorry.* I spoke his name, and then he was silent.

Colt brought us back upstairs during the evening of what I would discover had been Day Three. Time abandoned us in the cellar, and now and then during our stay down there I wondered if I'd grown old, and if my short hair had become long and reached below my waist. I wondered if I had wrinkles.

The only light on in the house was a small lamp with a soft red shade that had been set on the dining room table. Our father stood at the table, shotgun in hand. "Forgive me," he said, seeing our bewildered, shadow-sodden bodies rising out of the cellar. "It was for the good."

We said nothing. We washed and we ate dinner: chicken and potatoes that Colt had prepared and offered to us on blue porcelain plates.

I stepped outside and stared at a sky speckled with stars.

Our father told us not to leave his sight. He told us all to sleep in the living room. He never slept.

During the day, we wandered silently around each other in the house or a few steps outside. Win was the only one of us allowed to roam freely. If we strayed past the window our father watched us from, he would tap on it furiously, stopping only when we reappeared.

Win patrolled the woods and reported back every few hours. "Nothing yet," he would say. Our father would then breathe deeply and say, "We'll wait," or, "They're coming, don't worry, they're coming."

Rain on Day Five. I sat on the front steps in bare feet and let the water wash over my toes. The water made all the windows in the house shimmer. John would not go outside, because he said he hated being wet, he never wanted to be wet again, or cold. He whispered this to me, frightened, shamed. He sat inside all day, staring for hours at our father, who did not look at him, and who eventually walked away.

In the late afternoon, after the rain had stopped, as twilight shadows settled in the pine trees around the house, a car drove up the driveway. I do not know how it got through the front gate; Win must have forgotten to close it after returning from a trip to town for some item our father had decided was essential. Perhaps our father commanded for it to be opened as a lure, a way to suggest our guard was down, to lower their expectations and heighten the possibility of surprise. The car, a rusty blue Ford, drove slowly up the hill, clouds of dirt following, and stopped behind our truck. A tall man with a large belly and a bushy beard climbed out, wearing tattered jeans and a black t-shirt with its sleeves ripped off. He stretched his arms to the side, his head rolled back, his chest and stomach spread wide open to the world. He pulled up his jeans. He reached into the back of the car and lifted a rifle out.

The first shot went over the car's roof and hit the shoulder of the arm that held the rifle. I was kneeling on the floor of the living room, peering out the window. I wanted to watch and I didn't want to watch. I wanted to sink lower onto the floor and hide from the window, I wanted to climb between the cracks of the floorboards into the darkness, I wanted to run or fly away, I wanted to scream, but I did not move, I did not make any sound, I did not close my eyes. The man staggered backward. The second shot shattered the windows of the front doors and hit the man in the stomach. He collapsed. I watched our father approach, his favorite hunting rifle, a .32 Winchester Special, in his hand. I could not see anything of the man except a blob of darkness underneath his car. I saw our father stand near it, hold the rifle to his shoulder, and fire twice. He lowered the rifle and walked back to the house. I stared out the window until I heard his voice in another room calling us all together. We gathered in the kitchen. Our father, his green eyes cold and his voice calm, told Win and Colt to scout the perimeter. "What about the body?" Win said. Our father told John to take me and Nathan out to bury it. "We ought to leave it out for the crows," he said, "but we're civilized people."

We did what we were told.

I had seen dead animals throughout my life. I had watched deer get skinned, I had shot squirrels and chipmunks with a .22 and, later, out hunting with Nathan, I'd shot a partridge. I had buried the bodies of foxes and coyotes killed by my brothers, and once I'd even buried a massive porcupine our father had shot with a snub-nosed .38 revolver. Nothing prepares you for the sight of a dead person, though. It might have been easier if he had been shot in the head, if he were unrecognizable, if he were just a bunch of meat and bone, a carcass. But his face was the face of a man, an ordinary person, someone whose voice I could imagine (husky from cigarettes), whose eyes (open, brown) conveyed surprise and fear and suggested the loss of something like a soul, a remnant of a self now preserved only in the memories of people we didn't know. I didn't think about why he had come up the driveway until John said, "Poor bastard," his voice soft and sad, and I wondered if the man had really come here to destroy us or whether he'd simply had a gun he wanted our father to look at. I glanced at the rifle lying near him; it was an ancient and battered lever-action Savage. If he had come from the government, why didn't he have an M-16? Perhaps he was in disguise, pretending to be a collector, and we would discover that what looked like a Savage was actually the latest in sniper rifles, and that the car was filled with explosives and ammunition and high-tech communications gear, and that our father had saved our lives.

Nathan grabbed the side of the car and vomited onto the tire. John rubbed his hand through Nathan's hair. "I'm sorry," Nathan said. He wiped his mouth on a corner of his shirt.

"Nothing to be sorry for," John said. He kicked the rifle away as if it were a tin can. It tumbled down the embankment into the woods. "We just have to do this, and then..." I waited for him to say more, but he was silent.

We lifted the body out of the blood surrounding it. We carried it down into the woods. John went back to the house to get shovels. Nathan and I watched him, never letting our gazes drift toward the body. John returned with three shovels and we dug into the soggy ground, the dirt smelling, I thought, like worms. We pushed the body into the hole and covered it. We stood over the grave for a moment. "Should we say something?" I asked. No-one answered. We walked back up the embankment.

We didn't eat dinner that night. Our father paced through the house. He kept Win and Colt circling the perimeter all night. "Now you see," he said whenever I came near him. Sometimes he muttered it, sometimes he nearly screamed it, but always the same words: "Now you see."

I slipped in and out of sleep all night. The man's face filled my dreams. I walked through the house, trying to walk a different path from my father. Near midnight, John went into the kitchen and tried to make a peanut butter and jelly sandwich, but he seemed to have forgotten how to get the peanut butter and jelly onto the bread, and he held the butterknife in shaking hands over the open jars until finally he let the knife fall to the counter and covered his face with his hands. He sobbed and sobbed. Our father walked into the kitchen then, and for a moment did not seem to notice John, but then ran to him with a suddenness I'd never seen, a speed I could not comprehend, and flung John around, pushed him up against the refrigerator, held him by the throat. Tears washed over John's cheeks. Our father let go, pulled back, made a fist, and punched John across the face. John stumbled to the side and fell to his knees. Our father kicked him, then rested his foot on John's throat. "You shame me," our father said. He removed his foot and walked out of the kitchen.

I knelt beside John on the cold slate floor. At first, he pulled away from my touch, but then he let me hold his hand. After a long time, I helped him stand and led him up to his bedroom, and we slept beside each other on his narrow bed, our clothes still smelling like rain and dirt and blood.

§

In the morning, I cooked a pot of oatmeal, but no-one except our father seemed to have any appetite. Colt and Win were trading off perimeter duty now. We all seemed afraid to speak, as if words might be explosive. John remained in bed. As Colt, Nathan, and I finished our breakfast, our father came inside and placed his shotgun and revolver on the dining room table, amidst our bowls, then walked outside, unarmed for the first time in weeks. He sat on a boulder lodged in the hill at the edge of the woods. We could see him from the kitchen; he looked distant, small, indistinct. The grey rock of the boulder, barnacled with mint-green lichen, was clearer to my eyes than my father was. I could smell the dampness of the ground around the boulder, the orange pine needles rotting into the dirt.

Win came inside and talked with Colt for a moment. I cleared the table. Win picked up a crossbow and disappeared into the woods. Colt cleaned the dishes, scrubbing them, rinsing them, scrubbing again, endlessly. Nathan sat in the driveway and whittled a stick until nothing was left but the pile of shavings at his feet. John came downstairs around noon. I offered to make him some food, but he said he wasn't hungry. Half of his face was bruised. We stood in the kitchen and watched our father. "What do you think he's doing?" John asked me. I said I didn't know.

But I did know. Or I thought I did. In the afternoon, after our father had sat on the boulder for hours, hardly moving at all except to shift his weight, I went to him. "Are you praying?" I asked.

He looked at me, smiled, shook his head. "No," he said, "I don't know how to do that. I think I'm meditating. Maybe. Or trying to listen to the clouds. I've always thought that's what birds do when they fly on long journeys."

I stood beside him for a few minutes in silence, but he didn't seem to care if I was there or not, so I wandered into the woods to see if I could find Win. Instead, I found fresh deer scat in a clearing toward the edge of our property. I waited, hoping the deer might be nearby and might see me, might watch me, but I felt no eyes at all.

That night, Colt, Nathan, our father, and I played poker at the dining room table, where the guns still lay. John watched us from the other side of the room. Win had returned, and he sat in a chair at the front door, his shotgun held ready in his hands and the crossbow on the floor beside him. None of us were very good at card games, and we changed the rules constantly. In the last round, we decided all the cards were wild, and declared our hands by whim and impulse, allowing Nathan to win with six nines, his favorite number. "Why is nine your favorite?" Colt asked. Nathan shrugged and said he'd decided it when he was nine years old, and hadn't bothered to change his mind. Our father said he thought nine was a very nice number. Colt and I agreed.

Still our father didn't sleep. Nor did Win, who sat in the chair at the door all night and held his shotgun. Colt slept downstairs on the couch. John, Nathan, and I slept in John's bed. It was a small bed, but we huddled together in the darkness, listening to each other breathe.

I remember John lying beside me, his breath brushing my ear, saying, *Sleep now. Everything will be fine.* I remember cloudy moonlight, Nathan crying softly, John's arms around us, coyotes howling in the distance, and the echoes of our father's footsteps as he walked through the darkness of the house.

§

I was the last to wake in the morning. I slept deeply, dreamlessly, until the crack of gunshots shattered sleep, and I woke to bolts of sunlight in the room and the metallic smell of gunpowder.

I did not run downstairs. I pulled all the sheets and blankets on the bed over my body, and spread myself out underneath them so that, I hoped, anyone looking into the room would see only a jumble of covers and not the outline of my body. I had practiced this many times, hiding from my brothers, or from my father's rages. I lay there until I heard Nathan and Colt talking downstairs, and Nathan calling my name, saying, *Jill, it's all right. It's all right. Come down now, Jill, it's all right.*

I finally shed the covers, climbed carefully out of bed, and walked downstairs, aware of my bare feet on the stairs in a way I'd never been before, aware of their exact position, the skin against the wood, the bones against the muscle and skin, the blood streaming through it all.

Nathan and Colt waited at the bottom of the stairs. When I got close to them, they turned away.

Our father lay face-down on the floor in the living room, unmoving, his arms splayed out like wings, the wood of the floor around him glistening with his blood. For a moment I imagined he was melting, and then I envisioned the body spinning around on the floor until it disappeared in a sudden puff of smoke, and then I wondered when it would begin to smell of rot and decay and worms. I leaned against the wall, my legs shaking. Colt kept his back to me. Nathan stared at the beams of the ceiling and rubbed his hands together as if to warm them in winter, and I wished he would reach out, wished he would touch my shoulder or my arm and tell me what our father was doing in there on the floor where all he could do was melt and spin into smoke while light burned through the world around us.

"Where's John?" I said.

"Outside," Nathan said. Colt tried to grab me as I ran toward the door, but I slipped away from his hands.

The ground tilted and shuddered beneath my feet as I ran haphazardly from one side of the house to the other until I found John huddled against the wheel of the truck. His arms were wrapped around his knees and our father's Winchester sat at his feet.

"John?" I whispered.

He looked up. He didn't seem to recognize me.

I don't know how long I stood there. I thought I could will him to smile at me, and that once he smiled, everything would be fine. Our eyes stayed locked on each other, but he did not smile, and his face showed no glimmer of recognition.

A hand on my shoulder, hard, pushing. I fell to the ground. I turned and saw Win standing above me, aiming a crossbow at John.

"Look at me," Win said.

In my memory, John smiles.

I have no memory of the bolts from the crossbow hitting him in the chest and neck. I have no memory of him slumping down onto the ground, no memory of Win taking me by the arm and leading me inside. I have tried to remember running toward Win to push him out of the way, I have tried to remember standing between him and John, I have tried to remember the color of the sky, the sound of birds, the smell of dirt or trees, the taste of the air, but I cannot remember any of it, because I lay on the ground staring into John's eyes, the only sight in a blank and empty world.

Toward the end of the day, I realized I was lying in my bed. I thought I had woken from a nightmare. I walked downstairs, expecting our father to be making plans for the day and for John to give me a hug and tell me to cheer up, because everything would be better soon, because things always get better eventually.

Downstairs, Colt and Nathan sat together on the floor in a corner of the dining room. Nathan looked at me briefly, his eyes cold and tearless, almost black. He dug his fingernails into the wood of the floor.

Win was in the woods now, Nathan said, digging graves. "He's going to leave once he's finished. We'll call somebody when he's gone."

I sat down beside them, but I would not let them touch me.

Win didn't come inside. He knocked twice on the door to let us know he was leaving, and we opened the door and watched him walk down the driveway and disappear into the shadows of the woods.

The phone didn't work, because the line had been cut, probably by our father sometime during it all, or perhaps by Win. None of us could remember the last time the phone had rung, or the last time we'd used it. Nathan said we should go into town. Colt said we could take care of ourselves, we didn't need anyone's help. Nathan asked Colt why he wasn't going away with Win. Colt didn't answer.

We spent most of the evening cleaning up all the blood. We worked quietly and methodically, comforted by doing what we

knew we must do. We sat at the dining room table that night, but
no-one made dinner. I was certain I would never want to eat anything ever again.

Nathan said he would go to town for us in the morning. Colt
did not reply. Nathan spoke in a flat and certain voice, a voice I'd
never heard from him before. I have many memories of times when
Nathan was in tears, but after he left the house in the morning, I
doubt he ever cried again. I did not see him until much later, after
he had lived with foster families, after he had renounced us all. He
did what he had said he would do, though. He called our mother
from a pay phone at the drugstore, he told her something had happened, he told her to go to the house, he told her he was going off
to find Win and live with him and if she ever tried to catch him he
would shoot her just like John had shot our father and Win had
shot John, because, Nathan said (or so my mother told me), Win
was sad with love.

Our mother arrived toward the end of the day, walking up the
hill just the way she had walked down it years before. I watched her
from my bedroom window. I did not recognize her with her short
hair, long green coat, and determined steps. When I first caught
sight of her, a silhouette against the landscape, I thought she was an
animal, perhaps some sort of bird, and then I was certain she was
someone bringing something to us, and I wanted to warn her. Then
I remembered that Nathan had gone to town. What had become
of him? Had they destroyed him? I ran to my bed and pulled my
revolver out from underneath the pillow. I looked out the window
again, I saw her standing in front of the house, looking up, and I saw
her face, and I recognized for the first time that she was a woman.
I knew her face was one I should know, but for what felt like a long
time, though I'm sure it was not, the face was empty to me. She
noticed me and I thought for a moment she would smile, but she

did not. I heard, or imagined I heard, a gentle knock on the front door. I set the revolver on the windowsill and walked downstairs.

She stood in the open doorway. Colt held a shotgun in one hand, the barrel pointed toward the floor. I stepped up to him and touched his arm.

"The police are waiting down below," our mother said, her voice steady and cold.

"It's all right," our mother said. "You're safe now."

I could see she was waiting for us to come to her, to thank her and to embrace her, but we stood together, Colt and I, until our mother turned around and walked back down the hill.

Once she had disappeared, I followed.

Revelations

When I was a child, we lived inside the war. Our parents went away sometime during the last year, leaving me and my sister, Olly, to fend for ourselves amidst the rubble. Our house was old and solid, made of stone, and the shelling had mostly been to the other side of town, so all the walls of the house were still intact and there were only a few holes in the roof. Most of the windows had shattered, but we covered our bedroom's windows with trash bags taped to the frames, and that mostly kept the wind and rain out, except for the windiest, rainiest nights, but those were few and far between. It was awfully dry that year, in fact, which created its own problems—after the well ran out, we got our water from the river, but the river water was full of bacteria and we didn't always have enough fire to boil it. We were often sick.

The day J.C. died, we were healthy, though. There had been some rain recently, but not enough to bring out lots of mold and mildew, and that day itself was one of the sunniest of the spring. Because of the good weather, Olly and I decided to go into town and see if the war had ended. It hadn't, but we discovered Mrs. Carter had died in the night and we were able to take some of the onions and carrots she had stored up. We felt guilty about stealing food, and so we were always grateful to find people who had recently died. We took our snacks out to the town common and sat down for a picnic. Before the war, the common had had a bandstand and a grove of trees, but people had taken the bandstand apart for firewood and the trees had been shattered during a bombing raid, so there wasn't much to separate the common from the street except for occasional tufts of grass, but we remembered the bandstand and we remembered the trees and so it was still the common to us.

It's impossible to know if J.C. recognized it as the common, too, but it was the place where he came to die. He had arrived in town soon after our parents went away, and he lived in a little cottage less than a mile down the road from our house. The old man who had lived there (and whose name I have forgotten, if I ever knew it) left right after the war began. J.C. occasionally talked to us, but mostly he kept to himself. He was tall and skinny, with a head that was too big for his body. He wore clothes he seemed to have made himself, and he didn't have any skill as a tailor. He said his name was Jesu Cristo, but we could call him J.C. He said he was God incarnate. He said he was the savior. He said he would bring peace on Earth. He asked us if we believed in him, and Olly said he was standing right there in front of us so we didn't need to believe in him. This seemed to make him sad, and he went back to his cottage, and we didn't talk to him again for a little while, though now and then we would see him out staring at the sky and we would wave to him, but he didn't wave back. "Maybe," Olly said, "he doesn't believe in us." I told her not to be silly, but I didn't really think she was silly, it was just something to say.

Later, we saw J.C. carrying things into the cottage in big blue bags from the post office. "Is the mail working again?" I asked him.

"No," he said. "I'm building a temple."

"What for?"

"Contemplation," he said. "Prayer. Don't you know what a temple is?"

"Sure," I said. "But I thought they had to be old."

"No," J.C. said. "Anybody can make a temple. It takes a lot of work, though."

He went into his cottage and I heard the door lock. I went back to our house and found Olly working on the mud castle she was building on the dining room table. She spent a lot of time on this castle, bringing dirt in from a hole she had dug in the front yard. She devoted hours to trying to get the crenellations at the top of the walls perfectly even.

"That's not a castle," I said.

"Yes it is," Olly said.

"No," I said. "It's a temple."

"No, it's a castle. I don't want to build a temple. I'm building a castle."

"No you're not," I said.

Olly, her face streaming tears, threw a handful of mud at me, screamed, and ran out of the room.

We tended to fight when we got hungry, since we were most irritable when we were most hungry, but we didn't fight very often, because we always had plenty of space to wander around in alone when we wanted it, so we rarely felt like the other person got in our way. We had our own little worlds, really. Olly, for instance, never went up to the third floor of the house, but I spent a lot of time up there, in the places our mother had called "the servants' quarters", though we never had any servants. I brought our stuffed animals up there, because after our parents left, Olly had grown scared of all the teddy bears. (The only things she seemed attached to were a few little rocks she had given names to and carried around in her pockets.) I arranged the animals to sit in rows and pretended I was their teacher, telling them all the truths of the world. I told them about the giant man who held the Earth up in space so that we wouldn't all die, and I told them about the dinosaurs that ate the cavemen, and I told them that all the stars in the sky were lights from rocketships that were flying through the ten bazillion miles of space to come get us and bring us to Heaven, and I told them that humans are the only animals that can speak English and this is why we are the rulers of everything.

Olly and I spent much of our time together, though, because Olly liked to hear the stories I told her. At first, I told her stories about the things our parents were doing out in the world—fighting evil witches and dastardly kings, working as spies for the government, flying in warplanes and bombing remote regions of the Earth. Olly didn't seem to understand these stories, but she liked them. As she got older, though, she asked for stories about other people. I told her about Superman and Batman and Wonder Woman. She especially liked the story of how Wonder Woman discovered that Superman was insane and used her powers to tie him up and then smash his head in with a boulder. "She had to hit him again and again, didn't she?" Olly asked. "Yes," I said. "He was very strong, and she had to smash his head in over and over and over again to kill him." We laughed a lot at that, and then Olly began to sing, and soon I joined her:

> *She smashed his head in*
> *over and over and over again*
> *and over and over and over again*
> *and over and over and over again!*

Eventually, I began to tell Olly stories about J.C. In my stories, he was a wandering wizard who had lost his powers, but he didn't know why, and so he was making his way through the world to

find out what had turned him into a mortal man. I couldn't seem
to bring the story to a conclusion, I couldn't figure out why J.C. had
lost his powers or how he could get them back, and Olly asked me
to stop telling her stories about him because they made her sad,
so we went back to Wonder Woman and Batman. I even brought
Superman back from the dead so Wonder Woman could smash his
head in again.

As we had our picnic on the common, I heard movement behind
me and turned around and at first I didn't recognize J.C. He was
naked and purple. He had found some paint of some sort and covered every inch of his body with it. He stood on a big rock at the
other end of the common from us and held his arms out to his side.
He couldn't close his eyes because he had covered them with paint.
The paint had sunk deep into his pores and clogged them. His skin
couldn't breathe. He stood there for a long time—it felt like hours,
but I doubt it was much more than a minute or two—and then he
fell over, flat onto his face. I didn't do anything, just stared, but Olly
ran to him.

"Get up, J.C.," she said.

He didn't move.

"I like purple," she said. And then, more quietly: "Why won't
you get up?"

I went to him and stuck my ear down next to his mouth to see if
I could hear him breathing. I couldn't. I moved my head down to
his chest to listen for his heart, but I didn't hear that either. I took
Olly's hand. "Come on," I said. "Maybe he has some food and stuff
in his cottage."

"Why did he die?" Olly asked me as we walked down the road.

"I don't know," I said. "Or, I mean, I know the paint, the purple
stuff on his skin, that could have done it. Probably. But I don't know
why he painted himself purple or if he knew what would happen.

I guess he did know what would happen, though. At the end. It
seemed that way. Don't you think?"

"Sure," Olly said.

The cottage was built from cinderblocks and stones and mud.
It had a rusty tin roof. From outside it didn't look like much, but
inside it was cozy. It wasn't as small as it seemed from outside—
there was one main room, but it was at least as big as our dining
room, the largest room I've ever been in, and there was a little bedroom at the back, beside the kitchen nook. I immediately began
to think about moving in. The single fireplace would probably be
enough to keep the cottage warm through the winter, unlike our
house, where even if we had been able to light a fire in every fireplace, the house never would have gotten very warm, given the tall
ceilings and all the broken windows. Some of the windows in the
cottage were still whole, and the ones that were broken had been
carefully covered with thick boards.

We didn't find any food, though, or any evidence of food having
been eaten there. What had J.C. lived on? I imagined him foraging
in the woods, chewing on berries and grass, gobbling dirt.

Then Olly found a trap door in the bedroom that led down into
an apparently deep and very dark cellar.

"I don't want to go down there," Olly said.

"Me neither," I said. "But there could be food. It looks like a
good place for storage." I started to look for a candle in the kitchen
when Olly called me back to the bedroom—she'd found a flashlight
under the bed.

"It'll never work," I said, but I was wrong. "Those've got to be the
most powerful batteries in the history of batteries."

Olly handed me the flashlight and I pointed its beam into the
cellar. A wooden ladder led down at least ten feet to a stone floor. I
began the descent.

There was food—shelves of it, in cans and jars and bottles. The metal shelves ran from the floor to the ceiling on three sides of the ladder. The cellar was larger than the cottage, at least twice its size. I shined the light ahead—the shelves continued on and on, filled not only with food but with artifacts from the old world: books and newspapers, computers, dolls, tools, pens and pencils, cups, bowls, framed photographs, portable music players, sheets, towels, clothing of every imaginable sort…

I finally reached the end of the shelves and discovered there a little bed and desk. The chair at the desk was small, like Olly's chair in the bedroom at our house. The floor was sticky with something, and I shined the light down. At first I thought it was a pool of blood, but then I realized it was the purple paint. Cans of spray paint lay scattered in a corner, covered with purple fingerprints.

On the desk, I found a battery-powered lamp and turned it on. The desk was covered with bits of paper with strange drawings on them—stick figures, mostly, in abstract landscapes, or what I took to be landscapes. Only one of the pieces of paper had any writing on it, but I've kept it with me ever since. It took me days to decipher it all, the handwriting was so tiny, the letters so indistinct from each other. As far as I can tell, this is what was written on the paper:

THE REVALASHUNS OF JESU CRISTO

I have been alive 100000 years now LORD my GOD and you have in those 100000 years tormented me always with your ABSENSE! and I want to no only what I am sposed to no but you will not even let me have that. You are DEATH! That is all I no. I AM LIFE—I LORD AM LIFE! This is my revalashun. This is the only truth you have reveeled to me. This is the only thing I bleve and becuz I bleve it I no it is the TRUTH. This is the war this is the true war this. You are death. I am life. I am life. I AM I AM I AM I AM I AM I AM I AM!!!!!!

Looking at this now, typed, free of its yellowed paper and red ink and strange, minuscule handwriting, the words seem ridiculous. I am tempted to laugh. But when I first read them down in the darkness of the cellar, the shadows kept barely at bay by the low-powered lamp, the effect was a mix of absolute terror and profound sadness. I stared at the paper, puzzling out the words—LORD GOD ABSENSE DEATH I AM LIFE I LORD AM LIFE TRUTH I AM I AM I AM I AM I AM I AM I AM—and my hands shook and my legs felt like their bones had softened and my heart sped up so that I could feel every drop of blood shooting through my veins.

I AM I AM I AM I AM I AM I AM I AM!!!!!!

I grabbed the paper and ran past the shelves and back to the ladder and burst up into the afternoon sunlight.

Olly lay asleep on the blue and white quilt that covered the bed, but she woke when I looked at her.

"What did you find?"

"A lot," I said.

"A lot good or a lot bad?"

"I don't know," I said. "Food. Things. All sorts of things. I think J.C. was collecting them. Hoarding, collecting, I don't know. Something. The temple. I think he brought all this here from somewhere else. If this was all here when the old man was here, why would he have left?"

"That all sounds good."

"Yes," I said. I put the paper down on the quilt. Olly looked at it.

"I can't read it," she said. "Or not most of it. What is it?"

"Something J.C. wrote. I don't know what it is."

"That's okay," Olly said. "It's nice to have something from him. We can remember him this way and tell stories about him and tell people what he was like. Later. Don't you think?"

"Sure," I said.

The war lasted another two years. We moved into the cottage and lived there until the end. Our parents never came back, but we didn't expect them to. Nobody really came back, but new people arrived. Serious people, people with empty eyes. Some of them wanted our cottage, but we had found guns in the cellar and ammunition and we had used them to hunt squirrels and rabbits and deer, so we knew how to use them to protect ourselves. But we didn't have to protect ourselves for too long. People mostly left us alone once things got more settled. I began to be able to sleep through the nights again. Olly got her stories from the books she found in the cellar, and I read them too, though not as many and not as often.

And then Olly went away to get married, and I was alone in the cottage, and have been alone for some time now. I tried to tell people about J.C., but nobody wanted to hear stories about anything from before the war.

A few days ago, the food finally ran out. The last things I ate were some pickled beets. I'd never much liked beets. I should have saved something I liked for the end.

It didn't have to be the end, I suppose. I could have planted a garden, I could have even gone shopping at the new grocery store in town, but it felt somehow like a betrayal, and so I never did. I just ate what was in the cellar, until now there is nothing left to eat.

I wrote Olly a letter, telling her all about the changes, about how the common has been paved over so there will be, they say, fewer traffic jams. I told her the food was mostly gone. I told her she should come visit, and that I'd save some food for her. (But I didn't. I've lied about so many things, why not lie about that? She wouldn't expect anything else.) She'll laugh when she reads the letter, if she reads the letter. She's only written to me once, quite some time ago. "I used to love your stories," she said. "We lived on stories, didn't we? Stories aren't truth, though, and after everything that's happened, I just want some truth."

I should have written her another letter. I should have apologized for not coming up with a good ending for the stories about J.C. I wish I had thought of some way for the wizard to regain his powers. I hadn't meant to upset her, I just wanted to pass some time.

I know when she saw him all covered in purple, Olly thought J.C. had become a wizard again—and then, when he fell, that whatever forces had taken his powers had done something even worse.

I'm sorry, Olly. He was just a crazy man. There were a lot of them in those days, don't you remember? (There still are, I suppose, but they are more hidden now.) I shouldn't have given him meaning for you. That's the only thing I regret.

Her handwriting was remarkably neat and clear. That is what I remember thinking as I let the letter fall into the fire.

I wake up in the darkness every night. I reach for the flashlight, but the batteries have long since died.

I am hungry. If you were here now, Olly, that is what I would tell you. I am hungry.

A little German boy in town told me that in his language they do not say, "I am hungry," but rather, "I have hunger." It is not who you are. It is a possession that can be shed.

(She smashed his head in over and over and over again, and over and over and over again, and over and over and over again.)

The beets were a deep, rich shade of purple. Almost the deepest purple I have ever seen. They stained my hands and mouth, and when I saw my palms covered with the purple juice, I cried for the first time since we were children one hundred thousand years ago.

Getting a Date for Amelia

I felt bad about trying to sell Amelia, so I thought I could make it up to her by getting her a date. I figured, she may be a tard, but even a tard ought to be able to find somebody to love. So I told her, "Amelia, I'm sorry I took you out on the street the other day and tried to sell you for a dollar, but I'm going to make it up to you." She smiled, but I don't think she really understood.

Mom told me to stop picking on Amelia, it's not her fault she's mentally deficient. (Mom never calls her a tard, and she gets mad at me when I do. "At the least call her a *retard*," she says, but that sounds a lot worse to me, because I know *re-* is from the Greek and means "again", which would mean that in a former life Amelia was a tard and now she's a tard *again*, and I prefer to think that in a former life Amelia was smarter than any of us, though she might not have been as happy as she is now, because even though she's a tard and people can be insensitive, she's always seemed happy. Mom's pretty smart and Mom's never happy, at least when I'm around.) So I went out into the backyard and threw rocks at squirrels, which is my way of doing deep thinking. I was trying to figure out how I could get Amelia a date. It's not like we live in a town full of tards.

My friend Billy's an idiot, so I figured maybe I could get him to go on a date with her, take her to a movie or something. I told him people would think he was really sexy because he was dating a woman who was twenty-four. I told him all sorts of girls would want to date him after that. I told him he wouldn't even have to worry about coming up with something to talk about, because Amelia wasn't used to people talking to her about stuff. But he wouldn't have anything to do with it, even if I paid him my allowance for the week (only a dollar, but I figured it's better than nothing, and I'd take a tard out on a date for a dollar). "I'm not going anywhere near that tard sister of yours," he said. "She might drool on me and make me into a tard, too." Then he pushed me onto the ground and stole my allowance, which he hadn't done for a few months, so I realized we weren't friends anymore and maybe I should be more subtle about how I ask people to go on a date with Amelia.

I decided to try my friend Max next, because he'd helped me come up with the whole idea of selling Amelia in the first place. Max got angry when I told him I felt bad about trying to sell her, and said he thought I must be turning into a liberal, because they always feel sorry for people.

Max is probably my best friend, and he's certainly the smartest person I know. He skipped third grade and once Mrs. Klein couldn't help herself and told our whole class that Max's reading tests indicated he was reading at a college level, that his vocabulary score was the highest in the school, but that we should all be very sensitive in our interpersonal encounters with him because his emotional intelligence score was not as advanced as many of our own. (That afternoon, Billy beat Max up and tried to carve the word "nerd" in his forehead with a screwdriver, but Mrs. Klein stopped him just in time and sent him to the Time Out Corner because he'd had a negative impact on another student-citizen's self esteem.) Max told me he thought my attempt to sell Amelia had demonstrated a good entrepreneurial spirit, which is very American, but that like many liberals I was now feeling guilt for commodifying one of my family members. "You shouldn't let conscience impede your business sense," he said. "After all, your mother gets to take Amelia as a tax deduction, so why shouldn't you benefit from her status as well?"

I thought about this for a few days, but I still felt bad. After Billy stole my allowance, I went to Max and said, "Do you want to take Amelia out on a date? She likes to watch the numbers at the bottom of the screen during the financial news."

Max gave me a look like he'd just swallowed snot, and then his cell phone rang so he couldn't talk to me anymore. In any case, I didn't think Amelia would like Max, since he didn't seem like he'd be all that interesting on a date.

On the bus ride home, I asked Jenny Bixby if she would go on a date with Amelia, since I thought Amelia might be a lesbian, and people at school said Jenny was a lesbian. Jenny punched me in the nose. The bus driver saw her punch me, and he stopped the bus, walked down the aisle, grabbed Jenny's hair, and dragged her outside. "You can walk!" he said to her, then stomped back into the bus, and we drove off while Jenny sat on the side of the road and cried.

Getting a date for Amelia wasn't going to be easy, and I began to think that the only way she was going to get a date was if I took her out myself.

When I got home, Amelia was in the midst of water therapy, which meant she sat in the tub upstairs and blew bubbles in the water while her case worker talked to her boyfriend in Fiji on the phone in my parents' room, which was right next to the bathroom, so the case worker could hear if Amelia drowned.

I went upstairs and into the bathroom and said, "Come on, Amelia, get dressed. We're going out on a date." I don't mind seeing Amelia naked, because I don't think she looks much different from the big green Buddha sculpture Mom bought for the livingroom, but I've heard Mom and the case worker both talk about how much they hate having to see Amelia without clothes, as if she's some sort of freak or something out of *Jurassic Park* and not just a tard. (Mom's meatloaf's a whole lot grosser to look at than naked Amelia.) She spends most of her time sitting around the house looking out the window in her room, watching the birds in the woods behind the house, so her body's gotten flabby enough that she jiggles when she walks around, and Max told me one day that he thinks her legs may become vestigial, so they'll just flop all around like dead chickens. I told him all families have problems.

Amelia sputtered something in parrot-voice and began to get out of the tub. She's got two voices: parrot-voice and frog-voice. Parrot-voice is when she's excited; she coughs out the beginnings of a bunch of words and usually gets so worked up that her voice just keeps rising and rising till all the pieces of the words flow together in a single machinegun shriek. Frog-voice is what she uses when she's tired or sad (or drunk—before he drove off the bridge, Dad used to make Amelia drink with him), and it's kind of like the sound of a movie in slow-motion, like somebody trying to talk through their own throw-up after eating a bag of caramel candies.

I helped Amelia put her blue sweatpants and cranberry T-shirt on, and then we waved to the case worker, who was still on the phone. She waved back, and Amelia and I walked outside.

"I don't have any money, or I'd take you to the movies," I said. "I tried to get a few other people to take you out on a date, but they were all busy, so I thought maybe I should do it myself. I figure I've got to make up for trying to sell you somehow, so…" Amelia smiled and drooled a little bit, then said something halfway between parrot-voice and frog-voice, which is a rare thing, and it made me feel good about myself.

I took Amelia down to the woods out behind our house. Max told me once that our property is a fine approximation of the Arcadian ideal of pastoral America constructed within the confines of the post-modern suburban template, but he doesn't like mosquitoes and has been trying to convince his parents to move into Boston, so I don't really trust his judgment. We've got seven acres, which is more than most of the people around us, and it looks a lot like a rainforest now that Dad's dead, because he was always the one who would spend whole weekends carving the place up with his brushcutter and chainsaw. Mom said the woods are probably full of wildlife now, and we may have to move soon.

Amelia and I walked far enough into the woods so that we couldn't see the house, then sat down next to a little brook in the shade. It wasn't summer yet, but it sure was hot. Amelia splashed her feet in the brook and got her pink sneakers covered with mud and brown water. I laughed, and she did too.

"So, Amelia," I said, trying to be a good date, "what do you like to do in your spare time?"

She ignored me and continued to splash her feet, so that now the bottoms of her blue sweatpants were as wet and muddy as her sneakers. We both laughed.

"Do you have a favorite band or something?" I said.

She was still laughing. I realized it was useless to pretend to be a date for her. I was never going to make up for trying to sell her. To use one of Max's favorite expressions, I was on the negative side of the progress equation.

"Come on, Amelia," I said, "let's go back home. I'm a rotten date for you." I stood up, but she didn't. She was still laughing and splashing her feet.

I decided to leave her there. She'd know how to get home, and she seemed happy. Looking back now, with 20/20 hindsight, I can see that it was not a smart decision, in fact it's obviously the decision of somebody who shares genes with a tard, but she seemed so happy. The case worker had left by the time I got home, and I sat on the couch and watched reruns of *Gilligan's Island* until Mom came home. Some nights she stays in her office and sleeps under a desk, because she says if she ever wants to be anything other than a temp that's what she's got to do, but tonight she'd brought dinner from McDonald's and we'd finished the burgers and were almost done with the french fries when she said, "Have you seen Amelia today?"

"Yes," I said, "I took her on a date."

"What?"

"I wanted to make it up to her for trying to sell her for a dollar, so I asked people if they wanted to go out on a date with her, but nobody would, so I had to do it myself, so we went out back and she splashed her feet in the brook."

"Oh. Good. Well. Where is she now?"

"Probably still there. She hasn't come back. I kind of forgot about her."

"She's out back? Still? Alone?"

"Yes," I said, sensing that perhaps my decision to leave her out there had been less than satisfactory.

I won't report what Mom said next, but I will say that I had grabbed a flashlight and run out back into the woods before she could even finish her sentence. (Well, not that fast, but almost.)

I ran all through the woods, shining my flashlight everywhere, making shadows fly all through the trees so that everything around me danced—the trees and bushes and ground and sky all dancing as I ran.

Amelia wasn't there. Mom and I searched through the night, or at least for a couple hours, but we couldn't find her. Mom said she'd call the police in the morning if Amelia didn't show up. We watched reruns of *The A-Team* for an hour, then went to bed. I was excited, because I don't usually get to stay up so late on a school night. At the same time, I had trouble falling asleep, because I was worried about Amelia. I hoped she hadn't been eaten by wildlife.

In the morning, Mom called the police. They seemed awfully concerned, and spent a lot of time in the woods.

Two weeks later, the chief of police suggested we should send Amelia's picture to the company that puts the pictures of missing kids on milk cartons. "Nobody'd buy the milk," Mom said, so she didn't do it.

And then we forgot Amelia. Every time I asked Mom about her, Mom would say, "We've forgotten her, Joe. Remember that." Mom came home every night from the office and cooked dinner. "Life will be normal now," she said.

A year and a half after she disappeared, Amelia sent me an invitation to her wedding. It was just a postcard with a map of Wyoming on it, an X written with a green marker over the town where the wedding would be, and a note on the back: "Dear Joe— Getting married January 3 at 1pm. Please come. Love, Amelia."

Mom said it was a hoax. I begged her to buy me a plane ticket to Wyoming, but she wouldn't do it. "Amelia couldn't read or write. It's probably a trap to lure you out there so that they can kidnap you and sell you to some Mexican meatpacker."

I tried to save up my money and buy the plane ticket myself, but at the end of a month I only had enough to get a Coke and a pack of baseball cards at the drugstore near the bus stop. But in the bottom of a drawer in our kitchen I found a couple of postcards Dad had won in a poker game a few years ago, postcards with pictures of naked people chewing on each other, and I wrote Amelia a note: "I'm sorry I left you in the woods. I'll make it up to you. Hope you're okay. Love, Joe." I addressed it to Amelia in the town that was on the front of the postcard she'd sent us, and I asked Mom to mail it for me. "Sometimes I just don't understand you," she said to me, but she mailed it anyway.

I waited and waited, but I didn't get another postcard from Amelia. I thought about her a lot, and decided that she was probably pretty busy getting ready for the wedding. It would be a big wedding, I was sure, because Amelia would have lots of friends in Wyoming, and she'd be marrying a guy who owned his own helicopter and lived in a mansion with a swimming pool inside, and I was sure Amelia would have a pet dolphin that swam with her in the swimming pool. I never told Mom, though, because she'd just say I needed to cut down on my caffeine intake.

It snowed here on January 3, a whole lot more snow than I've ever seen. It stopped everything. Even the plowtrucks couldn't get through. We all just had to wait for the sun to melt the snow enough for us to come out of our houses and for the trucks to push the snow into piles and haul it away. It took an awful long time, and I didn't get to go back to school for two whole weeks, but eventually life was normal again.

Prague

"I have never been to Prague," my son says.

"I'm your mother," I say. "Don't lie to me."

He has lied to me ever since childhood, since infancy, in fact, when he crawled, bloody and blind, out from my womb six months late and said, "I love you. I never want to leave you."

Five years after that birth, he built a model of the Eiffel Tower with corn stalks and said, "I dream of other worlds, and I love you, mother."

The next year, he got his first car and his first girlfriend and he drove like lightning and made love like a rabbit—his terms, which he claimed to have thought of himself.

I am old now. He sits beside my bed. "Remember Prague?" I asked him. His father had called it the Sepia City, the land of all that is lost, the place where we went for our honeymoon and lived for the rest of our lives in dreams that resembled tattered street maps.

"You have never been to Prague, either," he says.

His father invented the Dream Machine and sallied forth on a tour of lands near the sky. He lived in the basement of the old farmhouse we'd bought together when we were young, and for the last twenty years he didn't come upstairs. I trekked down into the darkness a few times, but the journey wasn't worth it, because each time I saw him hooked up to his machine, his skin grown black where the wires dug into him, his eyes glassy with the onslaught of what he imagined, my stomach churned and my head ached. Each night I prayed to a God I'd forgotten to believe in, prayed for my husband to return to me, because the fields had grown wild and the animals were dead in the barn and our son had run off to Prague.

I've never been to Prague, myself, only looked at the postcard my husband sent me, a black and white picture of a young soldier embracing a beautiful lady, her arm cast behind her like a folded sail.

"Your father loved you," I whisper, the tube in my nose clenching my breath.

"Yes, of course," my son says, lying again. I watch him turn away to the shadow behind him, I see him speak but hear no words. He stands and says he has to go, he has things he must do, he has duties, life.

The Dream Machine waits for him in the basement, I know. It calls to him like an echo, like smoke. He'll be back to visit tomorrow, he says. But I know where he's going, and I know the fields will forever be ruined…the animals rotting…the sky a blister of memories…the city streets a lure for the young, who will wander and revel and dream, an occasional postcard the only memento of all that is lost.

The room is grey now, and the shadows wear white. They circle me and embrace me, they balm my skin and wash my hair, they feed me porridge and water, they refuse to read me bedtime stories, and they tell me I am not in Prague, but I know better. I've always been able to tell when people lie to me.

"I have never been to Prague," he said.

"Then what is this?" I held her postcard in my hand.

"It was all so long ago. A dream, that's all."

They come to me and tell me I have been crying in my sleep. They offer tea and more pills, they offer to call him for me, but I say there's no way to reach him now, it was all so long ago, and he's gone where the dreams build streets and castles, where my son should have been born, but was not.

Night stumbles across me. I hadn't recognized it at first. Tomorrow I will ask him to take me out of here, to get me some fresh air, to let me see the farm again and let me—

If I plead, he will forget me. He will say he will come back, but I know his ways. Instead, I will entrap him. I'll let him think I can forgive him, and I will hold the rusty butcher knife behind me. He will come closer. He will give me a farewell kiss. It will, indeed, be farewell.

They are knocking on my head now, tinkering with my teeth, moving my jaw across the room where I cannot reach it and where it sits on the cabinet calling to me, whispering smoke and drooling ash.

The city was so beautiful in spring.

My eyes roll down my cheeks and plant themselves in the shuddering blanket. Armies of priests plunge bayonets into my knees. My veins seek revenge, wrapping themselves around flagpoles and raining on parades.

Morning sighs and the man with the silver hole in his chest says, "Do you feel better now?"

I climb out of the cornfield and try to look him in the eye, but his eyes twist themselves into mirrors to blind me.

"Can you hear me?" he says, calling up from the basement.

"Your son is here," he says. I laugh.

"Mother," he says, and I reach toward him, but my arms have folded into themselves.

"Bring both flags to my funeral," I say.

Are those tears in his eyes? He has much to be sorry for. Triumph courses through me, but I scold myself: I don't wish to gloat.

He shivers in the sunlight and spreads himself across the room. The corn blows gently in the wind. The postcard lolls in my hand. I found it in the basement, where he keeps things from me.

Since he left, wind blows through the cracks in the house and coyotes howl at the horizon. I lie down in the dirt and let my tears summon mud. I lock the door and hope they never find him where I left him with the dreams.

"Bury me in Prague," I say. "Under the shadow of the castle, in a place where children come and go. I want to hear their voices."

I am grateful that he doesn't speak this time. When he doesn't speak, he doesn't lie. It's better now that we've learned to live in silence with each other.

The days have grown so short! I see the evening gathering itself, and I hear the coyotes in the distance, getting closer, moving with the moon on a moonless night.

He leans down and kisses me on the forehead.

"I love you," he says, closing my eyes.

It is not a lie.

In Exile

When Blin was born I dreamed of the sea, because so many of the stories my own mother told me in my young years described an endless sea, and the endless sea brought heroes home. I dreamed of depths and monsters, of fish the size of houses, of houses in the caves at the bottom of the blue of the sea. I imagined Lake Tenebro (where I swam each day in the warm winters of home) deeper and deeper than ever it had been: that was all I could imagine of the sea. Now that I can stand every morning with waves scattering themselves toward my feet, I wonder at how easily the truth overtook all that I imagined for so many years—overtook it with such force that I have trouble remembering what I once imagined, and to remember Lake Tenebro now I must think of the sea being captured, contained, hollowed out until it is a shallow, quiet place where children swim each morning during warm winters.

The wind picks up again, and I huddle into my coat. I can see the silhouettes of far-off villagers, and I know they will need me soon to help haul in the mermaids' catch, the bulging nets of seaweed and squid and drowned sailors, the treasure that we drag like a rippling whale over the beach and bring to the sorters, cutters, weighers, gutters, salters, traders, priests, and cooks.

It is a cold, damp life here, and I hate the sea.

§

Tell me, Lushan, is it because of you that I am here? Because you burned down Ursula's house in your rage at me? Because after years of war you did not like the peace you returned to? Because you wanted Blin to watch his mother run off through the forest at night?

Should I give you that power, Lushan? The power to determine for me why I fled? My melancholy makes me yearn to pass whatever choices I have made over to other forces; a pitiful, perhaps pitiable, condition. I write to you now on pressed mermaid scales with ink from a squid (common things here, though they still feel exotic to me). Are there travelers to take this letter for me? Will I let them take it?

It took me—assuming my count is correct—almost six months to cross to the coast, and then longer still to wander from one sad little settlement to another until I came to the village here, a place some people call a city, though it is smaller than the smallest borough of our smallest city. We do not do well, our people, near the sea.

I have wanted to tell you so much. I have seen so much, and I want to discover words for it all. I want you to think of me, and I want you to tell Blin stories about me, because I don't want him to forget that I—

(No, I will not send this letter to you.)

§

I reflect:

During the wars, I planted gardens. They surrounded our little house, the brightest flowers set to receive morning sun near the front door, the plants that provided most of our food set where the afternoon sun drifted through the tops of the forest's trees at the back of the house. The plants grew and grew until they were as tall as I, then taller, their stalks thick and green, each petal of the flowers larger than my hands. The house was hidden by the garden, and the neighbors laughed when they passed by. "Does Amimone hide in her garden?" they said between their chuckles. "Have the flowers devoured her?"

One time, a child came to the garden, one of the children from the far end of town, the son of a family I did not know. At first I thought he was a girl, but he was not. He tried to climb a fireflower, and seemed surprised when it bent under his weight. He screamed as he drifted to the ground. "Make it go faster!" he said when I came running. He climbed up again, and this time the stalk broke and he fell to the soft dirt, the yellow flowers scattering around him. "Was that better?" I asked. "Yes!" he said. "Please don't do it again," I said, adding: "I like the flowers and don't want them all to fall to the ground." He cackled and ran off into the forest.

I wish I had asked his name, because I'm sure that within a year or two he was called to the wars. All the men were, and even some of the stronger women or the ones without children, and the children themselves once they were ten years old, and I'm sure the boy who visited my garden was nearly ten. Every morning the old crier would wander through the streets, hollering the names of the next to go. At night, sometimes, she would go through the streets more slowly and call out more quietly the names of the known dead, and the names would whisper down the streets and through the cracks in doors and windows and walls.

Until the day when the crier ran through the city, calling out the end of the wars. The news removed decades from her, and when she stopped running, she stood tall, her eyes bright, her grey hair glistening as if it were gold. The evil one had been destroyed, she yelled out toward the houses and the sky. His lands were ruined, his armies slaughtered, his slaves freed, the awful darkness of the past eons lifted. A week later, our soldiers returned, battered and battle-scarred but emboldened, radiating victorious fury. They tromped through the streets, cracking the paving stones with their heavy boots, they trampled the commons with revelry, they emptied the pubs of every last bit of ale, they ravaged wives and daughters and husbands and sons in desperate lust. I saw Lushan when his brigade tumbled through the city gates, but though his face was familiar the inferno in his eyes frightened me, and I turned away and ran home and locked the door, holding Blin in my arms as if he were still the infant he had been when his father went away. We stayed huddled together until Lushan and a gang of fellow soldiers stumbled toward the house, screaming and calling to every god and demon whose name they could remember. They slashed my flowers with their swords, dug in the dirt with their boots, splattered fruits and veg-etables over their heads and under their feet, laughing the whole time, hollering, pounding on the walls and the locked door. "Come out, wife!" Lushan called through the window. "Come and see your husband's victory!" He stood back so I could watch as he lowered his pants and held himself, engorged, and then the widow of his old friend Mot, drunk and half-naked, her breasts drooping from her tattered blouse, knelt down beside him and brought him to a climax as the other men cheered her on.

In the morning, they all lay like puppies in the yard, their clothes dampened by dew and piss and vomit. I unlocked the door and brought them water one-by-one, saving Lushan for last. "I dreamed you had a beautiful garden," he said. Tears dripped down his face as he embraced me. I wrapped my arms around him, but I did not hold him tight.

§

After the harvest and the feast and the apportioning, I brought the scraps that were given to me (the newcomer, the stranger, the alien) back to the hut I call my house, and I inventoried my belongings. I developed this habit soon after I left the city, because who can tell what disappears in the night unless they know exactly what they have before sleep?

Tonight I have my cloak, one dress that is frayed but still elegant, a heavy shirt and heavy pants for working, two sets of underwear, a sweater, two pairs of socks, leather boots with their soles recently repaired by an old and raving cordwainer I met along the shore, a red blanket, a bone knife, a canvas satchel, a whale-oil lantern, some bits of flint, a wooden mug, a metal plate, a fork I whittled from a tree branch, Blin's favorite doll, four quills I made from the feathers of a gull, a pile of pressed scales, and a bladder of ink. I add tonight's acquisitions: a batch of seaweed, a belt from a drowned man, a rusty telescope from a sunken ship, and a new bladder of ink.

My eyes and skin sting from the salt blown in off the sea. I sit on a bit of driftwood beside the little fire that warms the hut, my house, and wish I knew where to find a tea kettle and some tea. Tonight that is what I miss the most: a hot cup of tea held in my hands, the steam warming my face as my lips touch the edge of the cup.

§

I reflect:

At the time my friendship with Ursula deepened, I was living a happy life, raising Blin by myself, tending my garden, walking to the center of the city once a week to buy or sell or gossip. I worried about Lushan, who had been at the wars for more than a year by that time, but I no longer dreamed of him, my body no longer ached for his, my thoughts were not all prefaced by *What would Lushan do— What would Lushan think— What would Lushan say...*

I had known Ursula my entire life, of course. We were born a month and three houses apart. But she spent most of her time farming the commons, while I was part of a family of woodworkers.

After Lushan went to the wars, though, I began to rely on Ursula, who had become a healer and who sold better herbs and remedies than the dealers in the center of the city. I was scared of her at first, this tall, hawk-faced woman with long grey hair and a voice that sang bawdy songs at night, loud and lovely, shimmering through the trees. I bought my herbs and thanked her quietly every time until one day she said, "I might as well be a golem, it seems."

"What?" I said, shocked that she had said anything to me other than the price of what I wanted to buy.

"Have I done something to offend you?"

"Offend? No," I said.

"Then why don't you talk to me?"

"What should we—would you—do you want to talk about?"

"Tell me your favorite song."

"'Lorelei of the Springs,'" I said. It was not my favorite song, but it was the only title that came to me.

"I don't know that one very well," Ursula said. "Do you?"

"I know a bit of it."

"Then hum it for me."

"Hum?"

"Unless you want to sing it?" Ursula said.

"No no. I don't think I remember. Much of it. The song."

"Try humming it."

"I don't think—"

"Try."

And so I did. And not too badly, if I do say so. Only a few wrong notes here and there.

"Ahhh, yes yes yes!" Ursula said. And then she sang:

> *Bright Lorelei,*
> *Drowning in the spring,*
> *Couldn't someone bother to save her?*

Dear Lorelei,
This song that we sing,
The only thing history gave her!

"Those aren't the words, are they?" Ursula said.

"No, I don't think so."

"Well, they should be." Indeed, I have remembered them ever since that day.

§

I have thought recently of Pin and Pem, the youngsters who, shortly after the wars ended, decided everything needed to be stirred up again, and so they went to the village of men over on the borders of the Rathgeel mountains and dropped as many insults and insinuations as they could think of. They had been good children, twin brother and sister, and their parents were hardworking masons, their father one of the few who had not gone off to the war, his skills determined by the city council to be too valuable at home—his primary job in those years was to maintain the city's walls—and I remember seeing Pin and Pem out helping their parents many days, cutting stones or slathering mortar or pushing a wheelbarrow. But after the wars ended and the soldiers returned home, life became more chaotic. The pubs were busy at all hours, thieves and vagabonds haunted the night, the whores returned to Bethelsgate Bridge, and one night a group of revelers tried to set off fireworks and managed only to blow off somebody's arm and blast a head-sized hole in the city's south wall. Two days later, Pin and Pem set out.

We don't know, of course, what they said in the village of men, only what they said they said. Ursula heard the tale from one of her customers, who worked for the city council and overheard the interrogation. Again and again, Pin and Pem said, "We told them terrible things, the worst we could think of." The interrogators asked, "What did you say?" Pin and Pem said, "Terrible things." "Such as?" "Terrible things."

The result? "They laughed at us and told us to go home to our mummies and daddies, or they'd send us off to the desert lands. We told them terrible things, threatened them something awful, and they just laughed and said there's nothing we could do or say to make them do anything but laugh. And then they told us to stop wasting their time."

Wasting their time, indeed. The wars had been good to those men. They traded in every item imaginable, and taxed the major roads through the Rathgeels, the only roads that led to the rich lands, the last battles of the wars having ravaged everything to the west.

Many people did not believe Pin and Pem's story. They said the twins had run away because their father did awful things to them at night, or their mother was a madwoman, but, these gossips and gobblers said, the world beyond our city was too terrible, too frightening and lonely and ruined, the village of men too ghastly even to speak of, and so the twins returned, because an awful father or a mad mother is easier to bear than the plains where dead voices sing from empty cisterns and exhausted wells, grass grows black around informal graves, and smoldering dirt sends strands of smoke to the violet sky.

§

I still think of you, Lushan, as I write this. It is not a letter, no, because I will not send it. You will not ever see it. I will destroy these words as soon as I am done with them. But they must live for a moment, and the thought of you gives them life for me.

You did not think I was sympathetic to all you had seen. Day after day you sat in the house, drinking ale until you collapsed. I cleaned up the vomit and the spilled and broken bottles, I washed the piss from your clothes, I carried you to bed, I let you grope and fondle, I bore the puke-stained kisses and the fumbling thrusts as you tried to enter me before you collapsed into yet another oblivion. You had been noble—I knew because you told me so yourself, and on the days when your friends came to call, before they all gave up on you, they told me too about your gallant deeds and courage, while I covered my bruises and limped to get them all more food, more drinks. By the end of the year your belly hung like a sack from your shirt and you wheezed when you hauled yourself up from the chair.

I began to look forward to the nights when Mot's widow, Elaine, showed up in the shadows at the edge of our yard. I listened at the window to your grunts and sighs, to her moans. I heard her ask you to live with her and love her, I heard your cruelty to her, your silence. "Bring her inside," I told you one night, and you did. I watched as you pushed her to the floor and tore her clothes off as she shrieked and screamed, horrified, and you smothered her with yourself. That is what it is to love him, I thought. Now you know, I thought. Should I have been more kind? Should I have shown sympathy, should I have pled with you and begged you and torn you from her? Perhaps. Instead, I watched, and then, as you seemed to be finishing, as blood from her mouth stained the floor, I went to Blin's room and picked him up—he, who had learned not to sob for fear of your slap—and carried him through the dark streets until, finally, we reached Ursula's house.

§

Later:

As I ran through the dancing shadows cast by the flames of the burning house, Lushan's tormented face hovered in my eyes, a silent raging ghost my memory was powerless to kill. As I ran, the shadows dissipated into darkness and the meadow I ran through rose into forest, a dungeon of trees and undergrowth and impenetrable black night. My eyes stung with smoke, my lungs were tight, aching, and my legs shivered terribly, forcing me finally to fall to my knees on the damp forest floor like a resting marionette.

The ghostly image of Lushan's anger gave way to the darkness, but a voice took its place, a voice that mixed my own with his, saying: *What have you done? You left your child and your lover in the flames, you ran from it all, from your child and your lover and your husband, you ran into the forest to hide in the shadows and die in the damp darkness, you will be remembered as the woman who destroyed everything she touched, you will be a legend for children to curse with rhymes and jeers, you cannot return, you cannot turn back, you cannot correct what you have done, you you you—*

My eyes adjusted to the darkness and though my head was heavy, I looked up and saw in between the far-off tops of trees a shard of an orange moon, smoky clouds brushing across it. I stood, and began to walk through the forest and toward the sea.

§

There was time, though, between the night I fled to Ursula's house and the night I fled to the forest. There were entire days of anxious happiness.

§

ne something to offend you?"

No."

vhy don't you talk to me?"

I could have fled then. I could have chuckled and smiled and said my thank yous and walked out into the misty rain that fell that day, walked out and not turned back, perhaps not ever returned—there are, after all, other healers, other sources of herbs. I could have hid in the house and tended my garden and raised my son and waited for my husband to return from the wars.

Instead, I stayed, I spoke, I hummed. *Those aren't the words, are they? No, I don't think so. Well, they should be.* When I walked out into the grey day, I was smiling. I returned the next day, even though I didn't need any herbs. I needed conversation, incidental chatter, nothing to be remembered, nothing to take seriously, nothing but a light tune to decorate the emotions rising toward the words. Distraction, amusement, company. Ursula helped me with the garden, and she helped me with Blin, and she helped me with the house—until one day we found ourselves spending the nights together as well as the days, and our lives entwined, and we were our own sort of family.

None of that is anything I should blame myself for. No, I do not have anything to answer for until the night Lushan kicked through the door of Ursula's house and threw her against the wall, then grabbed the little shovel beside the fireplace and spread hot coals throughout the house. As the flames crawled up the walls, up the curtains, toward the thatched roof, Blin screamed, Ursula picked him up and carried him outside, and Lushan faced me, the fire-filled shovel in his hand.

§

An old woman who says her name is Faith comes to visit me. She brings whale meat and cooks it over the fire for me.

I tell her she does not need to cook my food.

She asks if I am offended. I tell her no. She says she is well known for her cooking, and she is pleased to cook for someone. She saw me during the apportioning, and she was shamed by the behavior of the villagers. They don't understand, she says. Understand what? I ask her. That if we do not take care of each other, we will all die alone, she says. Faith says she does not want to die alone.

We eat together and tell stories. When we begin, the stories I tell are not true ones—I tell her my husband and son were killed in the wars, that the city I lived in was destroyed in a battle, that I was the only survivor. Her eyes fill with tears as my story becomes more and more vivid, as I lose not only my son and my husband but my parents and my siblings and my aunts and uncles and everyone I ever knew. I describe the dragon fires that consumed the city, melting the immense stone buildings that were so large they nearly touched the sky. The air filled with the smell of death, I say. The smell of burning. I tell her that I wandered for weeks and months, and here my story begins to resemble the truth, because my imagination is tired and I am ashamed of myself for lying to an old woman. I tell her about the kindness of the people who brought me food or gave me a blanket or clothes, about the fear that filled me when I slept outside at night and heard bandits in the forest, heard people screaming as they were robbed and tortured and killed. I don't tell her that there were many days when I tried to return home, but discovered I had lost my way, that the only sure direction was the direction leading to the sea.

She says she once lived in a place far from here. She was a young woman, and her husband was injured in a duel—he fought for her honor, she said. But he died within a year of being wounded. She was afraid of the other man, the man who fought her husband, and so she joined a band of players and journeyed from town to town as the cook to the players, who staged comical, bawdy tales in brightly-colored costumes. With time, though, the costumes' colors faded and the players drifted away one by one until there was only Faith and the old man who had brought the players together. He was a sad man, and she watched him die, but she would tell me no more about him than that. Eventually, she found her way to the sea.

After Faith leaves, promising to return soon with more meat and perhaps some stew, I wonder if it is such a bad thing, after all, to die alone.

§

Spring reveals the sea to be a sheet of gold at dawn. I am beginning to forget you, Lushan. I am now writing a letter to Ursula, one I might send, if I can discover words that explain things, or, lacking explanation, offer apology. The image that shadows my eyes now is not of Lushan's face, but of Ursula's back as she carried Blin in her arms to safety outside the house. It is the last image I have of her, because after I escaped Lushan, after flames fell from the roof and covered Lushan—after I dashed outside as he burned—I did not see Ursula anywhere. She had escaped and carried my son with her deep into the center of the city. She did not see me run out of the house, she did not hear my cries to her, she did not know I hid in the shadows and the smoke. I am sure she thinks I stayed behind to watch what had been wrought, and in my dreams I do stay behind—I stand on the edge of the fire, my skin searing, and I stare at Lushan's screaming face as the flames devour him.

I have burned you in my mind, Lushan, and I have watched the son and the woman I loved disappear into safety. That is the story I will cling to, the story I will remember, the story I am not afraid to tell.

§

Faith knocks gently on the door. I open it and she steps in, breathing hard, but smiling. She says she has brought wonders to cook today. We will feast on wonders. I tell her to rest while I unpack what she has brought, but she brushes me away and excitedly opens the sack to show me whale meat and bright, plump sea vegetables. She says that once upon a time the mermaids fought ravenous warriors away from the treasures of the sea, but one day, after the sea turned bright red at sunset with the blood of men and mermaids, the fighting stopped and the mermaids and men ate together in happiness.

A good story, I say.

Faith shrugs. The details of the story were better once, but she has forgotten them.

§

The sun rises. Faith walks up the long beach toward my hut, a heavy sack carried on her curved, ancient back. We will tell each other stories, and perhaps I will tell her about my husband who burned to death and the woman who saved my son from the fire, and we will smile sadly at the vagaries of chance and life. Perhaps I will burn these mermaid scales before Faith arrives, and all our stories henceforth will remain unwritten, will live and die quickly in the air, will depend entirely on our memories and the ink of our dreaming.

Or perhaps you fled the fire, Lushan, and chased me into the forest, then, defeated by the darkness, you stopped and returned to the city and to Blin and even, perhaps, to Ursula, who still, perhaps, sings a song of Lorelei, who drowned in the spring, because no-one could bother to save her.

The Lake

They wouldn't allow us near the lake when they hauled the bodies out. We stood, huddled against each other, at the edge of the road, looking down the grey embankment at the police trucks and the rescue equipment, the boats, the divers, the men in uniform standing between us and a last view of all we had lost.

I insisted on going to the morgue and making the identification myself, though Gabe told me someone else could do it, my brother or his, someone.

—It shouldn't have to be our last memory of her, he said.

—I want to go, I said. I want to see her face.

When he said again *someone else, someone else,* I screamed at him, I pounded his chest with my fists, and, in the end, he agreed, and went with me, and it was done.

§

For a few weeks, ours became a community of loss. Other parents, ones I'd never liked before, became my friends, their stupidities and thoughtless comments over the years swept away by what we shared in grief. We cooked for each other, we talked for long and empty hours, we exchanged memories, hoping that words might bring some life to the death we lived. Gabe and I had never been religious, but we began going to church because other parents would be there, and because any rituals were comforting.

The lake became a sacred place. Even as the water froze in winter and the shores grew thick with snow, there wasn't a day when I didn't find other parents there, standing on the bank, looking out at the calm water, our faces placid, our eyes incapable of tears. We stood like beacons or totems or guards, at dusk or dawn, morning and afternoon, not waiting so much as bearing witness to the peace that seemed so unjust.

§

There was an investigation, of course. They said it was a mechanical failure, that the brakes on the schoolbus gave out as it came around the corner, the speed at which it moved was not excessive, the driver was not at fault. The lake gets deep very quickly, they said, and the water was cold, the force of the impact enough to stun, wound, even kill the passengers.

The passengers.

No fault. An accident. A very unfortunate accident. A tragedy, the newspapers said and the television reporters said and the condolence cards said, and we, too, said: a tragedy.

We were left to live inside the shadow of that tragedy, and we carried on as best we could after the funerals, after the burials, after the cards and flowers were packed away, after we got so we could walk past the closed door of her bedroom without pressing an ear to the wood to listen for what we knew was not there. It was months before Gabe or I could open that door, and when we did it was a bright day, motes of light drifting through the room, and we sat on the bed, hands together, and assured each other it was all right to cry.

§

By summer, the lake had dried up. The muddy crater that remained quickly filled with sand that no amount of rain made wet.

We had lived eight months without Julia, and I went to the lake every day. I and the others who stood faithfully on the banks watched the water drift farther and farther from the shore, but no-one ever ventured out to where the lake had been until the water was gone and the mud turned to dry white sand. When the sun shone down, the sand was too hot to touch, and so we waited until evening to walk, always barefooted, into the crater where the lake had been. All of the parents were there every day, kneeling down, fingers pressed into the sand, digging. Soon, there was a breeze that never died. It blew soft clouds of dust around us.

Gabe stopped going after a week.

—What do you think you're going to find there? he said.

—I don't know, I said.

He stood in front of me, blocking the door.

—Why do you want to be there, then?

—I don't know, I said. Where else should I be?

He sighed, and I knew what he thought. He had returned to work, had won every case he'd tried, tripled his income, bought us a new car and talked about moving somewhere else, a place where every inch of everything could not summon memories. He never told me to go back to work, but every day he suggested something I could do, something that would distract me: volunteering at the hospital or library, joining the board of the conservation society, learning golf.

—I already have something to do, I said.

—You spend your whole life at that goddamned lake.

—It's where I should be.

Now, standing in front of the door, he said quietly:
—Please don't go.
—I have to, I said.

§

No-one brought children to the lake, though of course there were brothers and sisters, cousins, friends. The survivors, the living. I rarely saw children in town, even. Once, though, I saw a boy running down the street, his face glistening with tears as he screamed for his mother. Every car stopped in the street and every person stopped moving to watch him. He ran between people and between cars, he flailed, he fell to the ground and stood and fell again. His screams grew louder, more piercing, and the crowd shivered as people took tiny steps away from him, until finally one woman, older than most of us, approached the boy and touched his head gently and smiled and embraced him, kissed him, held him until the rest of us began to move again and continued with our days.

I returned to the lake. Holes dotted the sand. A father and mother had dug so many feet into the lakebed that all I could see of them were hands rising out of the hole to drop a few more grains from their fingertips. For a moment, I thought the pair had found water, but when I looked again I saw that the sand at the side of their hole had been moistened by blood from raw hands.

My own hole remained more broad than deep.

I'd forgotten all the names of the children, and, what made me more sad, the names of the parents—my true companions, the only people who understood the language I uttered when I chose to speak, the only people who didn't look at me with sympathy or pity, because who among us had enough to spare? I remembered knowing their names, but I did not know them now. Now they were strangers again, and I feared them, feared they would find what I was looking for and would destroy it, feared they knew what I was looking for when I did not.

I watched the other people around me and hoped my hole would not engulf theirs, but I feared it would, because though I tried to force myself to move closer and closer to the center I had dug, all I could do was pull back the sand from the sides. I knew the others were watching me. More and more each day, I could feel their eyes staring, I could hear the whispers caught by the ever-present breeze.

The other people had begun to push their piles of sand into my hole to keep me away. I did not blame them. I would have done the same.

§

—I'm buying a house in Colorado, Gabe said one night late in the summer. You can come with me or . . . not . . .

My hands ached from swollen joints, broken fingernails, and cracked skin. I covered them with lotion every morning before I left and every night when I returned, but the sand was stronger, it was wiping my flesh away.

—How can you leave here? I said.

—I can't stay.

—Who do you know in Colorado? You don't know anybody. How will you get a job, how will . . .

—I already have an offer from a firm. It's very good money. In Boulder. Everybody I know says Boulder is a wonderful place to live, it's heaven.

I ran out of the house and drove in the old car to the lake. The sky was full of clouds, but bits of moonlight shone through and drifted over the white sand. I sat near the road, my back against the front wheel of the car, and stared down at the place where our daughter had died.

Only a few parents remained, digging, and their shadows spread across the sand like chasms. As I watched them, I realized words had formed on my lips, and the words became whispers: *Eliza, Tommy, Maria, Lily, Jack, Tizzie, Eveline, George, Lucia*... I whispered them all through the night, again and again and again until the dawn, giving words to memory and to the wind.

Sometimes in the middle of the night I would go into Julia's room and turn her little radio on very low so that it whispered to me while I sat on the floor, my fingers drawing patterns across the carpet. I imagined the radio told me stories—stories dreamed up by young people who had grown old, the sentences left as remnants of a writer's youthful self, some part of that self preserved in each word, alive now in the whispers weaving their long-ago life into my own.

§

Two days before Gabe was to leave, water returned to the lake. It bubbled up through the sand into puddles, filling all the holes. One of the diggers screamed, *Water!* and seconds later I felt cool liquid against my own hands. Murmurs and cries echoed through the breeze. The puddles spread and joined until the entire lake was one thin sheet of water, and the water rose. Not until the water had reached our knees did any of us move to the shore of the lake. The last to leave was a small woman with short red hair. She swam from the far side, and when she climbed out of the water to join us, the light blue dress she had worn every day had shed all the dust and dirt that had encrusted it, and it clung to her body like seaweed.

Within only a few hours, the lake was as deep as it had ever been.

—The water has returned, I said when I stepped into the living room where Gabe was looking at a TV show about politics.

—Shhhhh, he said. I'm watching this.

—Did you hear me? The water's returned.

—Will you *shut up*! I'm *watching* this.

I went to the kitchen and poured myself a glass of milk. I sat at the table, looking out the double windows at the back yard, where shards of starlight sprinkled over the garden I had neglected all summer.

Eventually, Gabe trudged upstairs to bed, but I waited in the kitchen with all the lights turned out until I couldn't keep my eyes open anymore. I lay my head down on the table and slept.

§

A week after Gabe left, people began to say they saw faces in the water, the faces of the children. I still went to the lake each day and stayed long into the night, but though all the other parents around me knelt down on the bank and looked into the lake, I could not force myself to look. Their squeals of joy, their sudden outbursts of love and happiness, disgusted me.

I had begun to remember their names now, too, though I could not remember which names went with which children. (Were Richard and Beatrice the parents of Lucia or Tommy or Eveline? Were May and John the parents of Eliza, Jack, George?)

For the first time, children visited the lake. In the beginning, they came alone and stood far away, but soon enough a few children—siblings, I'm sure—walked down to the water, where the family knelt together and stared into the gentle ripples. Some of the children shed tears into the water, and some yelped or wailed, but most were silent.

I began to spend more time at the house, packing up Gabe's things and hauling them to the post office in town. I enjoyed filling boxes with his collection of Matchbox cars, his racks of neckties, the many books he'd bought and never read. He had taken with him only what he could fit in his car.

—What do you want me to do with the rest of your stuff? I asked.

—Doesn't matter, he said, getting into the car. He drove off without looking at me, without waving goodbye.

I could have destroyed it all, the books and neckties and Matchbox cars, the NFL mugs full of pens that didn't work, the portable television set, the camping gear we'd never used. Destroying Gabe's things didn't occur to me, though; all I could do was pack them up, put labels on the boxes, and bring the boxes into town day after day. Most of the clerks at the post office weighed my boxes and charged my credit card without comment, but one clerk, Marsha, talked to me, first about the weather and the heaviness of the boxes, then the Red Sox and the absurdities of postal bureaucracy. I enjoyed seeing her, but as I brought more and more boxes to the post office, I became self-conscious, wondering what people thought of me, and I tried to go at different times each day so I might get a different clerk, but there were only three, and one day Marsha said,

—Are you sending all her things away?

She covered her mouth with her hand suddenly, as if to put the words back in.

—I'm sorry, she said, her voice so soft I could barely make out the words.

—It's okay, I said. These are Gabe's things. He needs them more than me.

§

As the house became barer, the bookshelves empty, Gabe's closet left with nothing but bits of lint and dust, the walls freed of all decoration, I found it easier to sleep at night and easier to breathe during the day. I called a moving company and had them take away all of the furniture except for the kitchen table.

Some days I never went to the lake at all.

Finally, the house contained nothing of Gabe's. The only room I hadn't touched was Julia's.

§

When I brought the last of the boxes into town, one of the other parents, Stephen, followed me to my car.

—Haven't seen you out at the lake recently, he said.

—No, I said, I haven't been there.

—Don't you want to see the children?

—I don't think so. I don't know.

—They smile at us. We saw Tommy. Our son, Tommy. We saw him. He smiled at us. He's happy now.

—I'm glad, I said, and closed the door of the car.

Driving home, I slowed as I passed the lake. Cars clogged the sides of the street. I was sure what the parents said was true, that they saw their children's faces floating like reflections in the water and the faces were smiling, joyful. If I had thought it was some sort of mass delusion, I would have been more tempted to park my car with the others and walk down to the lake, to kneel on the shore and wait for Julia's face to slip across the water. I yearned for the comfort of fantasy, of relief from the grey life I lived, but the only fantasy that appealed to me was one I could control, one I could turn off, a world I could escape from when I wanted and return to at will.

§

After two months away, Gabe called.

—I miss you, he said.

—Do you?

—Yes. Of course I do. I just… needed some time on my own.

—And now?

Silence for a moment.

—I'm taking care of a child, he said. A friend of mine's daughter. She's eleven. Her parents are in Switzerland, skiing. They're professionals. She usually goes, but she has to be in school right now. She's always seemed fond of me, and I told them if they didn't want to have to hire somebody to take care of her, I'd be happy to. They told her to call me Uncle Gabe. Isn't that great? Uncle Gabe. They're coming back next week and…

—Did the furniture arrive? I asked.

Silence.

—Yes, he said.

—Good, I said.

—Will you come out here?

—No, I said.

—Why?

—Because I don't want to move.

—Will you?

—Will I what? I said.

—With time, will you want to move, do you think?

—I don't know. I can't predict the future.

I told him I was tired and I wanted to sleep. He thanked me for sending out the furniture, the paintings and prints, the clothes, the neckties, the Matchbox cars, the mugs and pens. He said his house was a dream, it was big and had a breathtaking view of the plains, it had walk-in closets and ceiling fans, it had a fireplace and a cathedral ceiling in the living room and skylights in the bedroom and outside a garage plenty big enough to turn into a pottery studio, which is something I'd always wanted, wasn't it, a studio right at home?

He said he would never come back east.

He didn't ask where I slept now, even though the movers had brought him our bed. Perhaps he thought it was a sign that soon I would join him and we would start our life again. Perhaps.

I climbed the stairs and walked into Julia's room. I undressed and pulled the sheets back on her bed, then lay down in it. I closed my eyes and slept more deeply than I had in years, a dreamless, restful sleep.

Night after night I slept in Julia's bed, wrapping myself tightly in the blankets, her teddy bear clenched to my chest, the radio quietly playing old folk songs that weaved their sad, hoarse tones into my dreams.

§

A knock on the door one night.

I was just about to go upstairs to sleep. I stood at the door and listened to my breathing. Another knock. Another. I did not look out the peephole. I knew who was there.

Another knock.

I opened the door.

One of the children, the brother of Lily, stood on the front step. Behind him, arrayed in the flickering glow of the single orange streetlight at the end of our driveway, stood other brothers and sisters, and behind them, in the darkness, their parents.

—Will you come with us to the lake? the boy said.

I could not remember his name.

—No, I said. Please, I said. Please go away.

—The water is getting colder. The faces are fading. Soon the lake will freeze and snow will cover it.

—No, I said.

—This could be the last chance.

He took my hand in his. It was small and warm. He led me out into the cold night. The other children gathered around us, and then the other parents. We walked together down the dark street and to the lake.

—What is your name? I asked him as we approached the shore, but he did not reply.

Looking out at the dark water, I hesitated.

The brothers and sisters, mothers and fathers pushed me gently forward. I felt their hands against me, their shoulders and arms, hips, thighs. As we moved closer to the edge of the shore, I pushed against them.

—No, I said.

I staggered and nearly fell. I lunged out of the crowd and back toward the street. They stopped, but did not turn. I scampered up the embankment to the pavement, the hard surface somehow comforting.

I watched a little girl bend down and touch the skin of ice at the edge of the lake.

§

Tonight, as I lie here in Julia's bed, silver flakes of snow fall through moonbeams and tap lightly against the window. The whispers on the radio had not predicted snow, but it is falling nonetheless, falling on the houses and the town, the church, the forests to the west, falling softly on the lake, where parents kneel over the water. I imagine the water unfrozen, and I imagine the snow falling on the faces in the water, and I imagine the faces open their mouths in joy and laughter so that, for a moment at least, the parents see the children catch the snow in their mouths as it softly falls. But I know the water is ice, and the snow has covered the ice, and the faces are not there, I'm sure of it. In the morning, the snow will lie in thick drifts in the yards and on the roofs of houses, on the sides of the roads and the banks of the lake. It will cover the gravestones in the cemetery where Julia and so many others were buried last year, it will hang like cotton in the trees around the cemetery and on the iron posts of the gate.

Tears streaming down the sides of my face, whispers in my ears, I listen to the snow falling gently through the night air, gently falling over all the living and the dead.

Lonesome Road

When her son Harry was killed in the war, Shelly didn't get out of bed for a few months. Jack tried to sympathize, but he didn't have it in him. After Shelly's boss at the factory finally called and told her not to come in anymore, Jack swore a blue streak and phoned Shelly's mother and told her to come get the stupid wreck of a cow lying in his bed. Harry had been just like a son to him, Jack said, but he needed to get on with his own life. If Shelly wanted to rot away, that was her choice; he'd be damned if he'd go down the same path.

Shelly's mother lived in a little house at the far end of a dirt road. The house had been built as somebody's summer place forty years ago, but something happened along the way, and Shelly's mother got it at auction for next to nothing. It had once been painted red, but the paint had faded to the color of rust.

Over the years, Shelly's mother had gotten pretty good at living off what she made as a receptionist at Dr. Martin's office, and it wasn't a burden for her to take care of her daughter for a while. She'd seen plenty of people come in to the office with illnesses that had more to do with their minds than their bodies. She'd learned not to judge. After work one day she'd even asked the doctor about Shelly, and he said he'd be happy to see her. Shelly didn't want anything to do with him, though. "Nobody's gonna make me feel good about my dead son," Shelly said. "There's something wrong about feeling good when your son is dead." Her mother agreed that this made some sense, but, she said, Harry would have been disappointed in her. That made Shelly cry worse than she'd cried even when she was eight and fell out of a tree and broke both her arms. That's what it reminded Shelly's mother of—her inconsolable, broken child.

Things got better after that, though. Slowly, as the winter melted into mud season and mud season gave way to a particularly dry spring, Shelly started doing little chores around the house, and then she made sure to have dinner ready every night when her mother got home from work, and eventually she even went out and got a job at the new Wal-Mart that had just opened in town.

The same week she got the new job, Rick Jasper came back from California to spend some time in his house across the street. Everybody in town had heard about him—the famous record producer who had decided to buy a place in the middle of nowhere (but a straight shot up the highway from Boston) so he could relax now and then. He purchased the Galipeau farmhouse, fixed it up, hired a caretaker, and visited when the urge hit him. He seemed like a nice enough man, Shelly's mother said, though he mostly kept to himself. He'd come to a yard sale she held; he bought some old Burl Ives albums, and she respected that.

They knew he was back when suddenly one night all the lights in his house were on after months of darkness. "Looks like a UFO or something," Shelly said, staring out the picture window in the living room, a cigarette in her hand.

"I told you about smoking in the house," her mother said.

"A bunch of cars drove up there just before you got home. Nice cars. Lexuses. I don't think I've ever seen anybody drive a Lexus down this road before."

"You're gonna make me want a cigarette if you keep smoking in here."

"It's like the house is glowing. How many lights do you think he's got in there? I bet we could live for a year on just a month of his electricity bill."

"You wouldn't like it if I got cancer," Shelly's mother said.

"No," Shelly said, "I wouldn't."

§

At the end of the driveway, like a scarecrow beside a marble statue, Shelly's mother's mailbox stood next to the mailbox for the Galipeau farmhouse.

"You're Lola's daughter, right?"

She hadn't even heard him come up behind her. "Yeah," she said. She'd been flipping through the bills, making sure there wasn't anything she needed to hide from her mother.

"I'm Rick."

"Hi."

"I'm sorry about your son."

"Oh."

"I get the *Record* when I'm in California. To keep up with what's going on back here. I can only imagine what it must be like for you."

"Yeah."

"I'm…" She thought he looked a bit like a shy kid at a dance, the kind of kid who wore a suit that didn't quite fit. "Well, I'm having a party. Tomorrow. Nothing formal or anything. Just some friends, some fun. If you'd like to come…well, I'd really like it. If you came by."

"Oh. I…"

"Bring your mother. You're my neighbors. I want to be more neighborly."

"I don't think my mother would…"

"It's not even really a party. A get-together more like. Please?"

Shelly bit her lip. Eighth grade dance, that's what it felt like, yes indeed. She hadn't danced with anybody then, not even Fat Dave, the only person who asked her.

Rick Jasper said, "Eight o'clock. Or whenever. Just come over."

§

Of course, he hadn't meant it. She knew that. That's why she didn't tell her mother about the party. And why she was surprised to see him at her register the next day to buy a Snickers bar.

"We had a nice time last night," he said. "I wish you could have been there."

Later, she would come up with lies she could have told him—that she'd had to work a late shift, that her mother had been sick, that she forgot it was bingo night and her mother always had to go to bingo night. "I'm sorry," she said.

"No problem. Come by sometime, though."

"I saw the lights. You turn on all the lights when people come. And then last night you turned a lot of them off. It was dark for a little while."

"You've been spying on me." He smiled.

Behind Rick Jasper, a woman with a cart full of dog food coughed loudly and shuffled her feet.

"I turn all the lights on so people can find the house. Like a beacon. But you're my neighbor. You don't need a beacon."

As he walked away, she asked why the house got so dark for a little while last night, and he said something in reply, but Shelly didn't hear it because Rick Jasper was too far away and the woman with the dog food was telling her exactly which of the coupons she'd brought went with which bag of dog food.

§

"Why didn't you get the mail?" her mother asked.

"I forgot."

"You forgot yesterday, too."

"I'm tired when I get home."

"Me, too, but I remember the mail."

§

Rick Jasper's house hadn't been all lit up as a beacon for nearly a month. Shelly watched it every night. Just a few lights on, and sometimes only one.

"Where are you off to?" her mother asked.

"Across the street."

"What?"

"Rick Jasper. He asked me to come by."

"Where in god's name did you meet Rick Jasper?"

"His house looks lonely."

"Are you feeling all right?"

"I'll be back later."

"Shelly—"

§

Shelly stood in the middle of the road and smoked a cigarette. It was summer, but a cold night. No wind, just cold, with a grey and starless sky.

She walked slowly down Rick Jasper's smooth, paved driveway. It must be strange driving on it, Shelly thought, after driving on the dirt road, like suddenly dropping into a new world. She imagined the sound, the roaring rumble of rocks and sand beneath a car's wheels turning to a soft, steady hum.

Standing in front of the immense porch, Shelly thought the house seemed much smaller than it did from a distance. It had the small windows of most New England farmhouses, windows designed to keep the cold out during winter. Its doors, too, seemed small.

"I was wondering when you'd come by," Rick Jasper said, opening the door seconds before her knuckles knocked on it.

"I've been busy," she said.

"Come in."

It was just a farmhouse. Small rooms, lots of doors. The sort of place that makes everything feel cozy. Even now, the smell of hay and livestock lingered in its wood.

"Can I get you something to drink? Coffee, tea, wine, beer, juice, water…"

"No, I'm fine, thanks."

He led her into what seemed to be the central room in the house, a room she would be tempted to call a living room, but it was so sparsely furnished that she wasn't sure the name fit. There was a long couch against one wall, a few chairs against another wall, and a wooden table in the center. On the table sat a record player more ancient than any record player she'd ever seen before.

"Like it?" Rick Jasper said.

"Sure."

"It's a Victrola. The kind you crank. I got it at a yard sale a year ago."

"Do you have records for it?"

"I do. Want to hear one?"

"Sure."

He went into another room and came back a moment later with a large black disk in his hand.

"Just some old blues," he said as he turned the crank. Soon, music came from the giant flower-shaped speaker. A high voice, guitar. Scratchy and distant.

"Sam Collins," he said. "'Lonesome Road Blues.' Nights like this, I think it's the most beautiful song ever recorded. And the saddest." She wanted to say something, but Rick Jasper stood so still, one arm folded across his chest and the other pressed against it, his hand reaching up to cover his mouth, that she didn't dare speak.

I cried last night and the night before
And I swore not to cry no more

The song ended and the record continued to spin, a soft hiss drifting out of the speaker, until Rick Jasper came alive again and lifted the needle.

"Old voices," he said. "They always get me. It's like hearing something from outside of life."

"I've never heard anything like that," she said. She wasn't sure if she meant it as praise.

"No, I'm sure you haven't."

"I guess there's a lot I don't know."

He cocked his head. "There's a lot none of us know, isn't there?"

"Sure."

He sat down on one of the chairs. "I mean," he said, "have you ever thought about how little we know about anything that's..." He ran his hands through his hair. "Do you want to sit down? Are you sure there's nothing I can get you?"

"I guess a glass of water would be good. It's pretty dry in here."

She sat on the couch while he went to kitchen. "I put in an artesian well," he called back to her. "The water's great. I could drink it all day. Straight from the core of the Earth, I think. The core made of ice."

He brought her water in a heavy ceramic tumbler. The glaze was dark and strange, like a universe splashed across rock.

"A friend of mine made that cup. He was a potter. Brilliant man. Died last year, a heart attack, out of the blue. Awful. He was my best friend. Thirty-nine years old and he has a heart attack. Amazing, isn't it? Healthy guy, but a bad heart. We'd been lovers once, but we were better as friends. I miss him terribly." Shelly stared at the cup, afraid to touch her lips to it. "It got me thinking about all this stuff. About all we don't know. Surprises and ignorance both. I mean, even when you look up at the sky, at all the stars—don't you ever get a sense that there's far more that we don't know than we do—that we're like mosquitoes trying to contemplate quantum mechanics or something?"

"My son Harry, he was, I think he was like you."

"I'm sorry. I mean—I mean, I'm sorry for rambling on. Like me?"

"He was always sensitive."

"Ah."

"But his father, Rex, before he left us, he was always talking about faggots and queeries and all that. Not talking about them good or anything."

"I see. Rex?"

"Yeah. Harry's father. I don't know where he is now."

"I've never actually known anybody named Rex."

"Me neither. Just him. And a couple dogs."

She sipped from the cup. It tasted like ordinary water to her.

"Do you ever try…"

"What?" she said.

"Say late at night, do you ever try to…talk to your son?"

She sipped water.

"I'm sorry," he said. "It's just this has become very important to me recently."

"I stopped trying."

"To talk to him? Why?"

"Because how else could I get on with my life?"

Rick Jasper nodded, but Shelly didn't think he had heard her.

"I should be getting back," she said. He didn't say anything. He didn't move.

"I'm going to go now," she said.

"Goodbye," she said.

The sky was clear and black and full of stars when she stepped outside, but the air had grown even colder, and she was shivering so much by the time she crossed the street and climbed the front steps of her mother's house that she could barely grip the doorknob enough to turn it and let herself in.

§

She hadn't intended to go back. She had told herself she didn't want anything to do with a weird rich gay guy from California. But it wasn't true. While her mother did the dishes, Shelly stared out the picture window at the single light on in Rick Jasper's house.

"Are you sleeping with him?" her mother asked as Shelly walked toward the door.

"No," Shelly said. "I'm forty-four years old, a hundred pounds overweight, and a woman. Not the sort of thing he likes, as far as I can tell." The door swung shut behind her.

She stood in the road and smoked a cigarette.

He opened the door just before her knuckles hit it.

"Thanks for coming back," he said.

He put the record on the Victrola.

> *You did cause me to weep,*
> *you did cause me to moan*
> *You did cause me to leave my home*

"Do you believe in ghosts?" he asked.

Shelly smiled. She almost laughed.

"I don't know."

"It's an important question."

"Okay."

"Belief is everything. Openness. A willingness to..."

"You said you have beer?"

"Sure. What do you like?"

"Anything."

He brought her a beer she'd never heard of, one they didn't have at Wal-Mart. He must have gotten it from the hippie market in town. Its taste was sharp, but she liked it.

"Did you ever think, when you talked to your son, to Harry, afterward, did you ever think that he said anything back to you?"

"No," she said. "I'm not crazy."

"I know, I wasn't suggesting that—"

"Do you know a lot of famous people?"

"What? Sure. I guess. Yeah."

"Did you know Johnny Cash?"

"I met him a few times."

"I like him a lot. I was sad when he died."

"He's great."

"Do a lot of famous people believe in that stuff, like ghosts and stuff?"

"Some do. Sure."

"And past lives and stuff, right?"

"I guess so."

"And crystals and all that?"

"I guess."

She finished her beer. "Is that what people do when they come up here for your parties? Do you have, like, séances?"

"No, not... No."

"Do you have orgies?"

"No."

She laughed. "I was kidding."

"Oh. I tried to tell them about... but..."

"About what?"

He stared at her. His blue eyes seemed to glow in the soft light. After what felt like hours, he walked into another room. Shelly thought perhaps she should go home, but just as she was about to stand up, Rick Jasper came back. He put a different record onto the Victrola.

At first, the only sound was a steady hiss and occasional scratches. But then a voice, far away, a whisper, not singing but speaking:

...in the cold of it all I thought I could hear you but you're not there anymore are you do you hear me you're not there but I'm trying to say that the cold here is thick like muddy clay and I can't see out through the darkness but I hear you breathing and I don't think it's a dream—

Rick Jasper pulled the needle off the record quickly, violently, making it scream.

"I'm sorry," he said. "Maybe another time. I'm still getting used to this. I'm sorry."

She stood beside him and rubbed his back and stared at the pitch-black, unlabeled record as it spun silently on the turntable and finally came to a slow, slow stop.

Outside, the stars were as bright as she had ever seen, and the smoke from her cigarette drifted toward the sky in ribbons.

§

"Don't you have to go to work?" her mother said.

"I don't know," Shelly said.

"You don't know?" her mother said.

"Are you sick?" her mother said.

"What's wrong?" her mother said.

"I don't know."

§

They threatened to fire her because she disappeared for three days, but her manager knew she'd had a tough time of it and he took pity, telling her this was the first and only break he'd give her, next time she was out for good, no joke.

Once Shelly seemed better, her mother pretended nothing had happened.

"You're forgetting the mail again."

"I'm sorry," Shelly said.

"Would you rather cook or do the dishes tonight?"

"I don't know," Shelly said.

"Well, I've done the cooking the last few days, so why don't you do that?"

"Okay."

She made spaghetti, because that was about all they had in the house. It was time to go shopping again. No matter how much food she bought, there was never enough.

After supper, she looked across the street at the Galipeau house for the first time since she had last visited it. Just one light. She imagined Rick Jasper sitting near the Victrola, listening to the voice. What had unsettled them both so much that night? She didn't know. She couldn't describe what it was she had heard, but she knew what she had heard was something horrible. She had never felt so cold and empty as when she had listened to that voice.

"Please don't smoke inside," her mother said.

§

"I didn't know if you'd come back," he said.

The room was surprisingly sunny during the day. The Victrola looked battered, dusty. A miracle it worked at all.

"I need to know what that record was."

"A voice. A lost voice."

"I keep thinking about it."

"What do you keep thinking?"

"There's something wrong about it."

"Maybe."

"It bothered you," she said.

"Sure. I'm getting used to it, though."

"Did you make it?"

"Not exactly. The record is much older than I am."

"Who's the voice?"

"Bruce. My friend, the potter."

"Your lover."

"For a while."

"When did you record it?"

"I didn't."

"When did he record it?"

"It's not a recording."

"Then what is it?"

"A pathway...a conduit..."

"I don't understand."

"I don't either, really. I just know it's Bruce's voice. And not only his. It changes. Some other friends. My father, once. Sometimes voices I don't recognize. But Bruce is the one that comes back most frequently."

"This is some sort of trick. Why are you doing this?"

"It's not a trick."

"Goodbye."

"Shelly—wait! You could—you could hear him if you wanted—"

She knew what he meant, and she believed he believed it. The room had grown smaller and darker around her, and she had to get out.

The sun was warm outside, comforting. She lit a cigarette. Rick Jasper stood in the doorway.

"It's nice out," Shelly said.

"Come back, please," he said.

"Come on outside."

"No, I ... I have work to do." He closed the door.

§

They told her they had to let her go because she was making too many mistakes at the register. She asked if they could give her work stocking the shelves and they said no, they already had people to stock the shelves. They were sorry to let her go, they said. They all wished her the best.

"What are you going to do now?" her mother said.

"I don't know," Shelly said.

"Well…"

"Yeah."

"We'll figure it out," her mother said.

Shelly made supper and did the dishes. At least she could do that. She watched TV for a few minutes with her mother, a crime show, but it was too bloody.

She looked out the window. At first, she thought Rick Jasper didn't have any lights on, but then she saw a dim glow in one of the windows.

In the morning, she saw that all the windows in the house had been covered from the inside. She walked across the street to get a better look. It was brown butcher paper. She knocked on the door. Again.

"You look like hell," she said when he finally opened the door.

"Long night," he said.

The room was as it had always been, but now there was a scattered mess in a corner of the floor: dirty plates, empty Coke cans, discarded bottles of Budweiser, bags from potato chips and cookies.

"This place is becoming a bachelor pad," Shelly said.

"I've been working," Rick Jasper said. "Recording the voices."

Beside the Victrola on the table sat a squat black box that Shelly assumed was some sort of tape recorder.

"What's with the windows?" Shelly asked.

"It has to be dark. A lot more comes through when it's dark."

He pressed a button on the tape recorder. A different voice than the one before, less distant but just as scratchy:

...Hello? Hello? I can hear you out there. Do you hear me? Ricky, is that you? I can hear you, son. It's cold here. Where are you? Do you want me to sing to you, Ricky?

He pressed another button and the voice stopped.

"My mother died ten years ago," he said. "Cancer. Discovered it in the last stages. Three months later she was gone. I'd just produced my first record. At least she got to see that."

"Did she used to sing to you?"

"Sure, when I was a little kid."

"And that's what her voice sounded like?"

"That was her voice."

"Okay."

"I recorded it last night."

"Okay."

"You still don't believe me."

"I don't know."

"Then why are you here?"

"I wanted to know why you had covered up the windows."

"Well, now you know."

"Yeah."

His fingers roamed over the Victrola. "You should go," he said.

"I'm sorry," Shelly said.

"I just need some sleep. I'm very tired."

"Okay."

"Come back tonight. If you want."

"Okay."

"If you want to hear him."

She cleared her throat. "I don't know what I'd think of that."

He smiled gently. As he closed the door behind her, she thought she heard him whisper, "Be careful," but a strong breeze had begun to blow and she wasn't sure if it was his voice or a random sound in the wind, something her imagination had turned into those words, that voice.

§

A few weeks later, Rick Jarvis came to say goodbye. It was a Saturday morning, bright and humid. Shelly's mother answered the door and told Mr. Jarvis he should come inside for a cup of coffee.

"Thank you," he said, "but I can't. I've got to go. I'm heading back to California. But I just wanted to say goodbye to Shelly."

Shelly stepped outside and her mother closed the door.

"Sorry I didn't come back," Shelly said.

"It's for the best," Rick Jarvis said quietly.

"I saw you took down the paper on the windows."

"Didn't need it anymore."

"Did you get your recordings?"

"No, I stopped."

"Yeah? Why?"

"I couldn't figure out... anything. Sometimes a mystery just seems better being a mystery, you know?"

Shelly nodded as if she understood what he was talking about. He handed her a CD. "Sam Collins," he said.

"'Lonesome Road Blues,'" she said.

"Good memory."

"For some things, yeah."

"My memory's all shot to hell these days." He stared up at the blue sky as if wondering where the clouds had sneaked off to.

"When will you be back?" Shelly asked.

"Well," he said, "actually, I won't. I'm selling the house."

"Oh."

"Not the right place for me, really. Or maybe too right. I don't know."

"So I guess I won't see you again."

"You could come visit L.A."

"No, I hate cities."

"Me, too," he said. "So maybe I'll be back one day."

"Maybe."

He stuck his hands in his pockets as if he were cold, and Shelly thought he might say something more, might even give her a friendly hug or a little peck on the cheek, but he just looked at his feet and turned around and walked down the driveway.

Shelly played the CD on the little boombox she'd given to her mother for Christmas one year.

"What's the noise?" her mother said.

"An old song."

"She's no Loretta Lynn."

"It's a man. Sam Collins."

"That's a man?"

"Yeah."

"Crazy."

Shelly stood at the window and watched until she saw Rick Jarvis drive down the road, dusty dirt clouding the air behind his Mercedes.

The sun sat low in the sky, its white light wiping out everything in her vision: the car, the road, the house. She turned around to shield her eyes, but the light didn't lessen. The whole world was a single plane of blinding white.

The hot summer air faded quickly.

She was cold now, shivering.

She knelt down, trying to get away from the light, but she couldn't escape it. She closed her eyes, but the white light still filled her vision.

In the far distance she saw a sliver of darkness. She reached toward it, but it was beyond her. She tried to crawl forward, but she could not tell which direction she moved in, and the little spot of darkness, the tiny promise of respite or reprieve, always lay distant from her. She heard breathing and reached out, hoping to find her mother, but her mother was not there. Shelly called out for her. She barely recognized her own voice in the vast silence engulfing her. Hunger filled her, and her shivering grew more ferocious, more violent. Her mouth was dry, her eyes stung, she coughed out dust. She heard breathing again and voices somewhere, they were familiar but she didn't know why, didn't know who they belonged to, didn't know why they were so far away from her. She tried to speak to them, but her throat was filled with dust and her words were scratchy whispers. Then silence.

§

The only sound that came from the Victrola's speaker was the soft hiss of the needle on the record.

"How long do you want to wait?" Bruce asked.

"A few more minutes," Harry said.

"So you believe now?"

"I don't know what I believe."

"It was her voice, wasn't it?"

"I don't know. Let's just wait."

The silence continued. "All right," Harry said.

Bruce lifted the needle and together they watched the record slow down until it was still. Bruce held Harry's hand, leaned in, rested his forehead against Harry's.

"Would it be better," Bruce said, "to believe it's real... or not?"

"Good question," Harry said.

Bruce wrapped his arms around Harry, kissed him gently, and hummed an old tune he hadn't known he knew. Together, they danced a slow, slow dance and let the twilight turn to darkness around them.

How Far to Englishman's Bay

Max had made the decision that April morning to close up the bookshop and go away for once and for all, but he hadn't told anyone yet, and he needed somebody to take the cat, so it was a good thing Jeffrey showed up an hour before closing.

"I think Carmilla wants to go home with you," Max said, watching Jeffrey roam, as always, through the military books. Jeffrey didn't reply. He took a tattered *Shooter's Bible* off the top shelf and held it up.

"Do you really think this is worth ten bucks?"

"Yes," Max said. "But you can have it for free. And the cat."

"The cat?"

"Carmilla."

"For free?"

"Book and cat. Hell, take anything else you want, too."

"Are you feeling okay?"

"Just fine."

"I hate cats."

"It would do you good to have something to care for, something to be responsible for. And she needs a home."

"But she lives here."

"Well…" Max sighed. If he had to tell somebody, it might as well be crazy old Jeffrey. They'd known each other since high school—thirty-five years now. Off and on, of course, as their lives took them in different directions, until they both ended up back here in the center of New Hampshire, the middle of nowhere, back where it all began. In school, Jeffrey had been an avowed socialist, class valedictorian, and a pretty good football player, but a knee injury his first year at Duke had ended everything, and he left school and wandered through the Midwest for a while, doing occasional work so he'd have enough money for pot, and then somehow or other he ended up back in New Hampshire, landing a job at a machine shop in Rochester, a job he still had. He'd stopped smoking pot a long time ago, and for twenty years now he'd spent every spare cent he had on guns and ammunition and knives and body armor. Once Max opened the bookstore, he kept his eyes out for books Jeffrey might like, just to make sure he'd come by now and then, just to make sure he'd have someone to talk to.

"I'm going away," Max said.

"A vacation?" His strolled an index finger across some bindings.

"No. Permanent."

Now Jeffrey was listening.

Max said, "I need somebody to take the cat. I can't take her with me."

"What do you mean *permanent?*"

"Today's my birthday," Max said.

"Happy birthday. But—"

"I'm fifty years old."

"No."

"I am."

"No, I mean, you can't. Happy fucking birthday, buddy, but you're not going to do it."

"I am," Max said. "I don't honestly feel like I have any choice. It's hard to explain. I feel awful leaving you behind, though. I do."

"No."

"Please take the cat."

Jeffrey threw the *Shooter's Bible* to the ground and ran out the front door.

§

Max's apartment sat above the bookstore, a rambling series of small rooms that had been built sometime around the end of the 19th century. He'd bought the whole building with the inheritance he got after his parents died on Christmas Eve twenty-two years ago when a drunk drove a pick-up truck straight into their little Volkswagen Golf as they were on their way home from church. "They're in a better place now," the priest told Max at the funeral. Max somehow resisted the overwhelming urge to punch the sanctimonious ass in the face. He clenched his fists, but didn't raise them; instead, he replied, "They're not anywhere. They're dead," and turned and walked into the cold night and never set foot in a church again.

When he first bought the building, he'd been excited to do work on it, to fix up the fixtures and paint the walls and design the bookstore, which he named The Dusty Cover because he thought any used bookstore worth visiting ought not to set people's expectations of cleanliness too high. He took great care with the few rare and valuable books that came through, but they didn't interest him as much as the ordinary volumes did, the stray paperbacks and battered Book Club Edition hardcovers, the books that had truly been used. Loved, even. Within a few years, the store and his apartment both had a sagging, lived-in feel to them, and he had never quite finished painting or retrofitting very much of it, so now the ceilings were cracked and in some places crumbling, the walls looked like a coffee stain, the floors were scratched and soiled, and the air itself seemed to hail from another era. It was all he could have hoped for, a temple of entropy, a bell jar, a tomb.

The fluorescent light in the kitchen ceiling had long ago lost its globe. When he turned it on, the light buzzed and flickered. Max opened the refrigerator. A bottle of ketchup, a jar of Dijon mustard, two different bottles of salad dressing, a few slices of turkey, a gallon of milk, a lemon. He closed the refrigerator and opened a cupboard. A box of Ritz crackers, a bag of chocolate chip cookies, a granola bar. He put them on the counter, found a plastic bag from a stash under the sink, and packed the crackers, cookies, and granola bar into the bag. A few cans of Coke sat on top of the refrigerator, and he grabbed those, too. He liked Coke warm. It hurt his teeth less.

Much as he wanted to leave right away, he hated driving at night, so it would be best to wait till morning. In the square little living room, he turned on the TV and sat on the couch. The cushions were thin and desperately needed to be reupholstered, or, better yet, sent to the dump. The couch had been in the house he grew up in. It was one of the few things he salvaged from there. It had been a good, solid piece of furniture. He'd gotten a cover for it at Wal-Mart a couple years ago because he finally couldn't stand to look at its pattern of brown and yellow lines. It was better with the drab grey cover.

On the TV, the President was giving a speech. Max turned it off. From the battered coffee table, he picked up an issue of *The New Yorker*. His subscription had run out months ago, but he was so far behind in reading them that it didn't matter.

The phone rang. He walked to the kitchen and looked at the caller ID.

He answered: "Hello, Jeffrey."

"You can't go. I won't let you."

"You'll be fine," Max said. "I'll leave the front door of the shop open. Do whatever you want with the place. There's a little bit of money in the cash register. And please look after the cat. I really can't take her with me."

"This is the stupidest fucking thing you've ever done."

"That may be true. But I'm still going."

"Bring me with you."

"I can't do that."

"What've I got here?"

"You've got your job, you've got...your guns. What about all the things you've wanted to do?"

"But I don't. I don't want anything. I just want it all to stay the same."

"No, I don't believe that." Max hesitated, but then said what he'd long been thinking: "You want somebody to break into your apartment and you want to shoot them. This is what you dream about, isn't it? Or maybe that's not what you dream about—"

"It's not—you fuck—I don't dream about—"

"Maybe what you dream about is being somewhere in public and somebody, some criminal, starts threatening people, and you whip out that pistol you always have on your belt, and you blow them away and save everybody's life. That's what you dream about, don't you? Being big and strong, saving the day? The hero of violence and power?"

"Fuck you."

"No shame in it," Max said. "We all want to be a hero. Somehow."

"Fuck you. Fuck you. Fuck you!"

"Good night, Jeffrey." Max hung up. He picked up *The New Yorker*, but none of the words made any sense, so he tossed it back on the coffee table. He stared at the TV and thought about turning it on. No point in that. He got up and opened the door to a walk-in closet where he kept boxes of LPs. He flipped through a bunch he didn't care much about, albums that had seemed interesting when he was young but which he hadn't listened to for ages and would never listen to again. (Had he really once spent money on an Air

Supply record?) A few guitar chords had been haunting him all day, and he'd only just remembered what they were from. There it was. One of the first albums he ever bought: Pink Floyd's *Animals*. He hadn't listened to it for a long time, but he'd played it so many times in the last years of high school and beginning of college that it was permanently seared in his memory. He'd bought it because he liked the cover, the picture of a pig floating between smokestacks. When he first listened to it, he didn't know what to make of it. The sounds were nothing he'd heard before, and his ears didn't know how to shape sense from them, but he knew there was something there, and as he kept listening it drew him back and back until certain strains wrapped around the world, and late at night, alone in his room, headphones on, he would fall asleep thinking he was somewhere, anywhere other than in his bed in his parents' house in the middle of nowhere.

He put the record on the turntable, then lay down on the couch. He closed his eyes. The cat startled him when she jumped up on his chest. He hadn't heard her come upstairs. He should probably feed her. Later.

§

Carmilla's whining yowls pierced his sleep. For the first time in months, he didn't remember a dream of ocean waves falling against a rocky shore. He didn't remember dreaming of anything.

Max's back, shoulders, and neck ached from spending the night on the couch. "I can't feed you or you'll puke in the car," he said to the cat as he walked to the bathroom.

Later, after a shower and a change of clothes, he let Carmilla lap the milk left in the bowl from his Cheerios. While she was distracted, he grabbed the cat carrier from the storage room at the far end of the apartment. He closed the door in the living room so she wouldn't be able to run off and disappear, scooped her up, and dropped her down into the plastic box. She moaned deeply as he carried her downstairs and out to his car, a ten-year-old Subaru parked in the narrow driveway next to the building. She yowled during the entire three-mile drive to Jeffrey's apartment.

As he carried the cat up the front steps, Max noticed the police officer standing in the entranceway.

"Do you live here, sir?" the police officer asked when Max stepped inside.

"I'm bringing a cat to a friend who lives here. Why?"

"The building's closed except to residents right now."

"What happened? I need to bring the cat in."

"Who are you visiting, sir?"

"Why? What's happened?"

"Which apartment did you want to go to?"

"Apartment four. Jeffrey James. Can't I just drop the cat—"

"How do you know Mr. James, sir?"

"We're friends. What's happened? Can I please just—"

"I'm sorry, sir. There's been an incident."

"Incident? What do you mean incident?" But he knew. Visions filled Max's mind: Jeffrey with his Sig Sauer and his AK-47. Jeffrey with his shooter's vest packed with ammo and extra magazines, hundreds and hundreds of rounds, enough for a war, enough for apocalypse. Going from apartment to apartment, kicking in doors as if he were a Ranger in Iraq, firing at any movement. Bang, bang, bang. You're dead.

"Jeffrey James, sir. I'm afraid it looks like suicide."

"Oh," Max said, setting the cat carrier down on the floor. Carmilla had stopped moaning, apparently reconciled to her current reality. "How many other people? Did he...?"

"Himself only. I'm afraid I can't say anymore. Can I have your phone number, sir, so we can contact you? We're still sorting things out."

"What time did he...?"

"Last night. A neighbor heard the gunshot and called it in."

"Yesterday was my birthday."

"I'm truly sorry, sir. If I could have your name and phone number..."

"Of course," he said, and spoke the words and numbers automatically, numbers that would ring a phone in the bookstore, a phone Max would never answer again. He thanked the officer, picked up Carmilla in her carrier, and walked back to his car.

After nearly two hours of driving, his mind blank, Carmilla silent in the carrier on the passenger seat, Max realized he'd forgotten his snacks and his Coke at home. He needed gas anyway, so he stopped at a gas station and convenience store just over the Maine border, filled up, and bought some oatmeal raisin cookies, a Snickers bar, a couple of twelve-ounce bottles of Coke, a gallon of water, a bag of cat food, and a package of red plastic bowls. In the car, he let Carmilla out of the carrier and poured water into one bowl and food into another. He was sure he could find somebody who liked cats along the way. He wasn't on any timetable. He just needed to get to the farthest shore and let whatever peace was there wash over him.

He opened a bottle of Coke for himself and quickly ate two cookies. Cookies, Karen had said, would be the death of him. In childhood and even up through his mid-twenties he'd been trim and almost scrawny, but now he had the figure of a person who'd been pregnant for a while. He'd tried to stay healthy when he'd been with Karen, but even she had said more than once that he was getting a good gut. That was a long time ago. After she left, he stopped caring. He'd last been to the doctor eight or nine years ago, and the doctor had told him he should exercise and pay attention to his blood pressure and his cholesterol, and Max nodded and did his best to look like he took it all seriously, much as he did during those last months and weeks with Karen, when she said that she worried about him, when she cried and screamed and pounded his chest and said nobody could not care about losing a child, when she told him she'd been sleeping with one of the waiters at the Thai restaurant on the corner of Main Street, when she said she was leaving, finally, for real this time.

It didn't matter.

Carmilla, contented, curled up on the back seat. When Max started the car, she perked her head up, but she seemed to have grown used to the movement, and now she let herself fall asleep as Max drove them toward the edge of the world.

§

Most of the winter snow had melted, trees and lawns were beginning to green, the last vestiges of mud season giving way to spring. Maine seemed somehow more alive than New Hampshire had, more vibrant in its shedding of the cold months, its skies more blue than grey. Perhaps this was just a particularly sunny afternoon, Max thought.

He hadn't ever driven a lot in Maine, just some trips to estate auctions and big library sales, and he always lost his way. But there was no great pressure of time right now, so it didn't matter if he meandered off of Route 1, a road he hated purely because he'd gotten trapped in summer traffic a few times. There wasn't much traffic today, but nonetheless, he didn't want to drive Route 1, and so he sought out the smaller roads, ones bumpy with cracks and potholes after the frost-heaves had retreated.

He stopped at some woods near Sebago Lake and let the cat out so she could relieve herself. He demonstrated for her by peeing on a tree. She was mostly terrified of this new place, its strange sounds and scents, but eventually she did what she needed to do. Max half hoped she'd dash away and he would then have a reason to be rid of her, but she didn't stray far from him. After half an hour or so, they got back in the car and headed off, traveling back roads until, by late afternoon, Max saw signs to Brunswick and turned in that direction, hoping to find a place where he might get a good sandwich. There were open parking spaces in front of a little diner in town, so he parked the car, told Carmilla he'd only be a little while, and went inside.

He found a booth and squeezed himself into it. A waitress, probably of high school age, with black hair and radiant blue eyes, handed him a menu, said her name was Melissa, and asked him if he'd like something to drink. "Coffee," he said. When she brought it, he ordered a club sandwich with turkey, not toasted because though he very much liked toasted club sandwiches, inevitably they cut his gums all to hell. She brought the sandwich quickly. It was divine.

He handed Melissa a $20 bill and told her to keep the change. She smiled, apparently at a loss for words, not at all used to a 100% tip. He asked if she liked cats.

"Sure," she said. "But I don't have one."

"I have a cat in my car that needs a home. She's eight years old and very friendly, used to being around people in the bookstore that I once owned. If you'd like to take her, she's yours."

Melissa followed him to the car and peered through the window at Carmilla. "Are you sure?" Melissa said.

"I can't take her where I'm going," Max said. He opened the door, careful not to let Carmilla slip away. He took her in his hands, but she hissed and scratched and howled. He'd never seen her so enraged, even at the vet's office. She fought with her claws and teeth as he forced her into the carrier. "She hates the box," Max said, meekly, as he brought it out and handed it to Melissa.

"I'm sure she'll be fine," Melissa said.

"Once she gets settled," Max said. "She's a good cat."

"Thank you," Melissa said, "for everything."

"My pleasure." Max went to the driver's side, opened the door, and climbed in.

"Just keep going north," Melissa said as Max closed the door. He couldn't quite hear what she said next, but it sounded like, "Go to Englishman's Bay." He rolled down the passenger's-side window to ask her what she was talking about, but she was gone.

§

The woods grew deeper, darker, wilder as Max drove on and twilight fell. He put a CD into the player, a recent Bonnie Raitt album, to try to keep himself from thinking about Jeffrey, but it didn't work for long. He stopped hearing the music, his mind straying to speculations about where in the little apartment Jeffrey had killed himself—had he slumped on the futon in the main room, had he sat on the twin bed in the tiny bedroom, had he stood in the kitchen area or the bathroom? Which gun had he used? One of the pistols? The utterly illegal sawed-off pump-action shotgun he was so proud of having made? Probably that, yes. Max then thought of all the mess, the blood and brains scattered everywhere. Who would clean it up? The police? Probably not. The landlord would have to call in some sort of cleaners. He'd have to bring in painters and even perhaps carpenters, people to fix whatever the shot had ruined. It would take time. People would have to wonder what this Jeffrey James had been like, what had driven him to this point, this decision. Who had loved him? Who had cared?

Max shook his head and grit his teeth. Beyond the car's headlights, the world was dark now. The trees loomed among shadows.

Soon, though, he found his way to the shore road, where the trees were few, and the smell of the ocean filled the car, and now and then the sound of a particularly large wave crashing against the rocks made its way in between the music and the noise of the engine.

Fifty years old. What a meaningless concept, he thought. He didn't feel any different today than he had a week ago. A pointless number, fifty. Not even old, really, not these days, when plenty of people lived to be 90 or 100. He didn't feel any better about it, though. He feared nothing so much as age. Or, rather, he didn't fear it; it disgusted him. The slow failures of the body. The creeping feebleness and dementia. He remembered his grandparents, their homes and bodies giving off a thick scent he forever afterward associated with growing old—a scent redolent of rotting fruit. In the store, he struggled to remain civil with elderly customers. Their eyes and minds were failing, what did they want with books? How could they possibly get any enjoyment from them? In his last year with Karen, some weeks after Melody died from only one day of life, Karen's parents came to visit and help with things, and Max got blind drunk on Jim Beam. He cursed her parents for their age, for their doddering around his house, for their oh-so-loving concern that seemed, he said, to be nothing more than senility, and swore he wouldn't pay for them when they ended up in a nursing home, shitting their beds, mewling and puking. Karen's parents left, and implored her to come with them, to escape Max, but she stayed a while longer. "I didn't mean it," Max said in the morning, once he remembered a bit of what he'd said. Karen nodded. She believed him.

"You never really mean anything, do you?" she said. He shrugged. It was often true, but not that time.

Gas stations had become rare up here, and so Max stopped at the first one he saw when he was down to a quarter tank. He went inside the store, used the bathroom, bought a bottle of Coke, a bottle of iced tea, a bag of chocolate chip cookies, and a Snickers. A blond young man stood behind the counter.

"How far to Englishman's Bay?" Max asked, after getting his change.

"Another hour or so. Stay on Route 1 toward Machias, then head down to Roque Bluffs. Someone will find you there."

"Someone will what?"

"Someone will find you there."

"What are you talking about?"

"Don't worry about it, old man."

"Hey," Max said, "who do you think—"

"You should go. It's very dark tonight, and you could have trouble finding your way."

Max stared at the boy's cold blue eyes and decided not to press the point. He'd always thought people in Maine were strange, and the farther north you went, the stranger they got. They were isolated, suspicious, stubborn, as if their lives were carved from rock.

The boy was right, though. It was very dark tonight.

§

Max stayed on Route 1 until somewhere near Machias, but must have missed a turn, because the road became narrower, bumpier, then turned to dirt for a while. He didn't think he was anywhere near what might be a town. He had always had a pretty good sense of direction, though, and his hunch that he was driving toward the ocean paid off soon enough when he reached the shore road again. He followed it down until it ended at a spot of rough grass and gravel, the driveway of a stone cabin with a few small, square windows, a roof of wooden beams, and a hand-painted sign above the door: La Maison Ravissante.

The heavy wooden front door was open, and Max stepped into a warm, softly-lit room that smelled of woodsmoke and baked apples. A small girl, maybe ten years old, with auburn hair and bright blue eyes, stood with her back to a fireplace at the opposite end of the room.

"Excuse me," Max said. "Are your parents here?"

"No," the girl said, smiling to reveal a missing front tooth.

"I mean the people who own this place."

From behind him, a soft voice said, "Hello." Max turned to see a tall, rugged young man, black-haired and bearded, dressed in jeans and a grey flannel shirt.

"I'm just trying to find Roque Bluffs. Am I anywhere near there?"

"Near enough."

"Well, that's a relief. If I go back to the road, where do I need to turn?"

"The night is dark."

"Yes, I know, believe me. But I need to get to Roque Bluffs."

"No you don't," the young man said. "Come in. Sit down. Warm up by the fire. You're where you need to be."

The little girl pulled a leather easy-chair up near the fireplace and gestured for Max to sit down.

"I think I'm supposed to go to Roque Bluffs."

"No," the young man said, placing his strong hand on Max's shoulder. "Tonight, you need to be with us." Gently, the young man pushed Max toward the chair. "We'll take care of you. Let me bring you some dinner. You must be starving."

Max wanted to say something, wanted to ask them who they were and what this place was, wanted to say that no, he wasn't hungry, he wasn't thirsty, he wasn't cold—but he was very tired, and he didn't have the stamina to say any of that. He found his way to the chair and sat down, and the warm fire was, indeed, comforting, and suddenly he was, yes, quite hungry, and ravishingly thirsty. The man brought him a tray with a large glass of water and a wooden bowl filled with thick beef stew. Max ate. It was the most flavorful stew he'd ever tasted. The meat was so tender it seemed to melt on his tongue.

"My name's Melanie," the little girl said.

"Hello," Max said between slurping bites of stew.

"You're old," Melanie said.

"Older than you, yes," Max said. He gulped water.

"You smell old," Melanie said.

Just as Max thought of something to say to that, he forgot what it was. The little girl laughed at him, then ran around a corner and disappeared. Max lifted the glass of water, but it fell out of his hands and spilled all over him. He reached for the bowl of stew, pulling it closer, but it slipped in his fingers and poured across his chest.

"Come along," the young man said from behind Max. "I'll clean you up and put you to bed."

The man lifted Max in his arms like a firefighter come to rescue him. He carried Max up stairs and to a pool of warm water and soap, then to a bed in a dark room.

When Max woke in the middle of the night, a bright moon shining onto his face through a window above the bed, he vaguely remembered his arms and legs fitting into manacles on iron chains. He laughed at the strange memory, then turned onto his side.

The chains reached from his wrists and ankles to heavy bolts in the floor.

He screamed through the night, until his voice was dust and he couldn't help falling back to sleep again.

§

He woke to music. Bright morning sunlight stung his eyes. Somewhere outside, a chorus sang. The voices were high, ethereal. Max sat up. He was naked, with no sheet or blanket on the bed. He was not cold, though—indeed, the room's heat was almost choking. He lifted one arm. His flesh was bruised and red where the chains bound him. The chain on his left leg was not quite long enough for him to swing himself into a sitting position on the bed.

"Hello ... ?" he called, his voice rasping.

Some moments later, the door opened and Melanie, dressed all in white, walked in.

"Good morning," she said.

"What are they doing to me?" Max said.

"Cleaning you up," she said. She hopped from foot to foot and chanted, "You're a mess, you're a mess, you're a mess." She giggled.

"Please help me," Max said.

Melanie ran to him and planted a kiss on his lips. "Help me help me help me help me help!" she screamed, then fell down on the floor laughing.

A figure appeared outside the door. "Melanie, leave the old man alone."

Melanie walked out of the room. A woman—perhaps twenty years old—stepped inside and closed the door behind herself. Her hair was long and a very light brown, almost blond. Her breasts were large, the nipples vaguely visible through the soft white fabric of her dress. She knelt down beside Max. Her hand rubbed his stomach, then her fingers slowly, gently moved lower.

Without even knowing what he was doing, Max swung his arm and hit her across the face, the iron manacle on his wrist slicing her lip open. The force knocked her to the floor. She held a hand to her mouth.

"I'm sorry," Max said. "But—you can't—I don't know why I'm here and you—"

The woman stood up. Blood had fallen onto her dress. She opened the door and walked outside.

A few minutes later, the bearded young man came into the room. His clothes were made of fur and the skins of animals.

"Why did you hurt Merissa?" he said. "She wanted to give you pleasure. She pities you."

"What are you doing to me?" Max said.

"You came to us."

"But why are these chains—why am I—what am I doing here?"

"It sometimes happens."

"I had dreams of the ocean. I knew I had to get away. I knew I was..."

"Yes?"

What were the words? He couldn't remember. Other words came to him: "Getting old."

"Yes."

"Is that why I'm here?"

"Perhaps," the man said. "It sometimes happens." He walked out of the room and closed the door behind.

Later, a pale young man with sharp, uneven features and matted yellow hair brought a bowl of fish chowder to Max and fed him with a wooden spoon. Max didn't speak, merely let the young man feed him, and said nothing when the young man's lips touched his, the tongue wiping away some last bits of chowder. For the first time in many years, and against whatever remained of his will, Max found himself aroused. There was, in his nakedness, no hiding it. The young man seemed not to notice. He set a large porcelain chamber pot under Max and waited until he could take away the wastes.

Days passed, and every few hours (judging by the sun), the young man came in and fed Max the most delicious food he had ever eaten—stews and chowders and soups at first, then hardboiled eggs and cheese, then larger and larger pieces of beef and pork. Now and then Melanie peeked in the door and giggled, but no-one else visited him. The young man washed him with hot water, soap, and a plump yellow sponge. He provided a porcelain chamber pot and waited while Max shat and pissed. The young man was attentive, always ready for Max to release his wastes, always careful to clean every bit of his body.

And then, on what seemed to Max to be perhaps the eighth or ninth morning, Melanie woke him by running into the room and jumping up onto the bed while screaming, "It's the big day! It's the big day!"

The tall young man who wore the furs and animal skins quickly entered, swept Melanie into his arms as she bounced, and stole her out of the room. The silent young man with matted yellow hair then came in, carrying a wooden pail from which he fed Max a particularly large meal of pork, ham, mashed potato, carrots, turnips, and rice. "Please stop," Max said as the young man pushed more food into Max's mouth with the wooden spoon, but the boy did not seem to hear him, or did not care, and the feeding went on and on until Max was certain he would vomit. But he did not. From a stone pitcher, the young man poured thick buttermilk into Max's mouth. Max coughed and nearly choked on it. The buttermilk splashed all over his face, even into his eyes. The young man carried the pail and pitcher out, then returned a few minutes later with a bucket of hot water, soap, cloths, and a sponge. He spent even more time than usual cleaning Max, wiping away the remnants of the meal with the cloths, and then, with the sponge, attending to every inch of his skin. The cleaning was slow and sensuous, once again arousing Max, and this time the young man noticed, letting his hand and the sponge provide pleasure, forcing Max to close his eyes, to try to think of something else, but the food had relaxed him, and the washing had calmed him, and he could not distract himself from the gentle, rhythmic pleasure. Afterward, the boy continued to clean him, then, finally satisfied with his work, he kissed Max gently on the lips and departed.

The tall young man came in and unlocked the manacles around Max's wrists and ankles. "Try standing up," the man said. "Use me for support."

Max slung his arm around the man's shoulders and together they tried to heave him up. His muscles were weak, making his legs feel like liquid. His stomach was larger than ever before, and as he tried to stand he realized he didn't quite know what to do with such a belly—its weight was unfamiliar to him, skewing his perception of his own center of gravity. If the young man hadn't been holding him, Max would have fallen forward onto his face. He chuckled as the image entered his mind: himself, tipping over, rolling onto the now-massive cushion of his front.

"Hans!" the young man called, and the pale boy (*He has a name!* Max thought) entered. "Take the other side," the man said.

Together, they helped Max out into the hall, where Merissa waited with a white sheet that she carefully wrapped Max in. He felt some shame in his nudity, his immense stomach, his weakness, but more shame when he saw Merissa's bruised face and thick, slit lip. He had done that. "I'm sorry," he whispered as she wrapped him in the sheet. She did not look into his eyes.

Everyone, even Melanie, helped get him down the stairs, with a few people below and few people behind, shuttling him like a large piece of furniture. He tried to distract himself from the pain in his hands and feet, tried to remember a song or two, something, anything to get his mind off of where he was now. (How had his stomach grown so immense and his muscles so useless in such a short time? It had only been eleven or twelve, maybe thirteen days, he was certain.) He couldn't remember any songs. He couldn't remember even quite how he'd gotten here, or where exactly this *here* was.

At the bottom of the stairs, they helped him back onto his feet, and he did his best to balance and to walk. The front door of La Maison Ravissante opened, revealing a warm and sunny world. He squeezed through the door.

A few feet from the front of the building stood a large chair, a rustic throne made from heavy, dark, knotted wood. Hands jostled Max, spinning him around until he was placed just right, then pushed him down into the chair. Someone put a crown of evergreen branches on his head. It shed needles onto his forehead and down the back of his neck.

People had gathered around him—new people, all young, mostly blond, mostly blue-eyed, dressed either in the simple white clothes he'd seen so often or some sort of animal skins. They took hold of the bottom of the chair and hoisted him above their shoulders. They carried him around to a staircase leading down to the sea.

"Where are we going?" Max said, his voice sounding odd to him, small and willowy. "What's going on?"

Melanie skipped along beside. He called out to her. "What is going to happen?"

She giggled and bounced and stuck her tongue out at him.

More people waited down on the rocky beach. Men and women, all, it seemed to Max, in their early twenties or so, all wearing animal skins and carrying tools of some sort: knives, gaffs, axes.

Little fires set in cairns dotted the beach.

The chair lowered to the ground. Water tickled Max's toes. Ocean spray scratched his eyes. Sand and salt flared his wounds.

"The old man has arrived!" someone said.

"He's better than the last one," someone said. "This one was all bloody when he got here."

"We cleaned him up, though."

"He needs to be here."

"We need him," someone said.

A knife flashed, cutting below Max's eye. Instinctively, he raised his hand to defend himself. Another knife sliced his palm.

"What are you doing to me!" he screamed, but his voice was little more than a whisper, a flash of air in the wind.

Laughter all around. Hans stepped forward, pulled down his white pants, and sprayed a stream of warm piss into Max's face. Melanie bounced around behind everyone, singing out, "The old man is here, the old man is here, the old, old, old, old man is here!"

Merissa pressed herself against Max's left side. She unbuttoned her shirt, bared a breast, pressed the nipple to his lips. The crowd cheered her on, voices calling out: "Is that what you want, old man?" and "Is that what you miss?"

He closed his eyes. He could not feel the fingers in his injured hand.

His brain exploded in light. Someone had hit him in the back of the head with something hard, a piece of wood or stone. He tried to turn to see, but his skull didn't want to do what his mind commanded.

Everyone stood back. Clouds writhed across the sky. Larger and larger waves smashed onto the beach.

Melanie waded forward and climbed onto the chair with Max. She wrapped her arms around his neck, then whispered in his ear: "Remember, forever and ever and ever. You are our savior. We love you. I love you."

Her tongue tickled his ear. Her teeth tore at the lobe. He tried to raise his arms to get her off of himself, but he didn't have the strength. She bit deeper. The pain was hot. Her breath in his ear turned to a splash, then a high-pitched ringing that spread misery across his forehead and through his eyes and throat and heart.

Melanie knelt in the water beside him and smiled, half his ear displayed between her teeth.

The other people ran in, their tools raised high, their laughter and screams louder than the growing noise of the waves. For a moment, Max feared Melanie might be trampled, but she easily got out of the way, bounding back toward the stairs leading up to the house. His skin was slashed, his bones battered. Hans took a carving knife to Max's genitals. It was all pain and all nothing. The world turned red and then black when they thumbed out his eyes. They left him his tongue, a fact that, somewhere in the far recess of his consciousness, provoked surprise.

He could not see the care they took when cutting open his stomach, the reverence with which they held his viscera, the gentleness with which they placed these parts of him in each flaming cairn along the shore.

He did not know that a wave knocked him from his chair and splayed him on the beach. He did not hear the people leave him, nor feel the tongues of the cats that licked his wounds. He did not know where he was, did not perceive the cold or night. For longer than anyone expected, nearly into morning, the wind carried the sound of his singing.

The Voice

He used to hear voices at night—not so much multiple voices as one voice, though its inflections and accent varied from time to time, depending on the thickness of the clouds and the brightness of the moon.

When he first heard the voice, he had been uncertain, thinking perhaps he was dreaming, because it was night; thinking perhaps he had had too much to drink, because he had been drinking too much then; thinking perhaps this is what happens to a man who cultivates solitude and claims it is not loneliness, a man who cannot remember the touch of another's hand. The voice sounded like a man's voice, but a young man, the sort of man he himself had been not too long ago, a softly lilting voice imbued with innocence, though the more it talked, the more the innocence took on an added weight, a burden of experience, and the voice hardened slightly, and occasionally cracked.

The voice began by telling him stories. It told of being a child, of flying a kite late in the summer in a corn field empty of corn, of getting older and going to far-off cities wrapped in shadows that shed broken glass, of stumbling in cobblestone alleyways and knocking on unfamiliar doors, of fleeing to a lost island of sunlight and misty rain where the wind blew melodies instead of screams and the unfamiliar language spoken by the crowds turned words into sculptures and balloon animals and jewels.

He listened.

After the stories, the voice questioned him. It asked him who he was and why he was listening and why he was alone. He said *I don't know, I don't know, I don't know.* The voice chuckled and then said it would tell him a joke because that might cheer him up, and it told him a joke, something about a cow and a milkmaid and a man from the city, and though he didn't understand the joke, he laughed anyway, and the voice told him more stories, tales of everyday life with the people whose words turned into things (pudding, fountains, coins, nooses), and then, after months of stories and questions, after he had begun to say who he was, perhaps, and perhaps why he was listening and perhaps why he was alone, he said he looked forward to the nights now when the voice would be there, when he could listen and talk, and he feared one night the voice would not be there, and this fear consumed him, filling his days with nervous twitches and frantic glances toward windows and the sky, causing him to make mistakes at the button factory where he managed the money, causing him to rush home and lie down in his bed and wait for the day to recede and the moon to rise and the voice to return. He talked to himself while he lay there, telling stories of his past adventures, the people he had spoken to and argued with and been hurt by, the few kisses he had collected, the few favors he had won, until he talked so much one night that by the time the sun rose he had heard only his own words, and so he lay in bed in silence and let the day pass over him, and then the night returned, the sky clear of all clouds, the moon burning bright as the sun, but no voice spoke to him, and he did not speak, and he waited in the silence of every day and every night, certain he was not listening hard enough, afraid to speak, because once again his words had crowded out the world, and so alone he lay in bed day after day and night after night, hardly moving, always listening, until only his body remained, still and silent and untouched.

Thin

Charles had always been thin—as a child he'd been compared to a scarecrow, as an adult he was often suspected of alcoholism or heroin addiction—but he got thinner when his tooth began to hurt. He lived in a one-room apartment above a bakery in a town that had once been home to the world's largest popsicle-stick factory, a town that now offered visitors little more than empty storefronts and pizza parlors bestrewn with flickering, half-dead neon signs. He picked up his breakfast every morning in the bakery, where his landlord, Miriam Stewart, gave him a cup of coffee and a blueberry muffin, and he walked half a mile down the street to the high school where he had been a janitor for almost fifteen years now, the same high school where he had been a student twenty-two years ago, the building in which he'd spent more hours of his life than any other.

Except for in the winter, he always ate his muffin and drank his coffee when he arrived at work; in the winter, he ate and drank as he walked, because otherwise by the time he got to school on most days, the coffee would be cold and the muffin would be frozen, and though it was painful to hold them in his bare hands as he trudged through the frigid air (or snow or freezing rain), he preferred numb fingers and stinging skin to cold coffee and an icy muffin.

It was not winter now, though; it was spring, and Charles received his coffee and muffin as usual, but when Miriam said goodmorning to him, he did not smile and say goodmorning in reply as he usually did, because this morning one of the teeth in the back of the left side of his mouth pounded with aching pain, and as he was about to smile at Miriam, the pain shot through the muscles on the left side of his face as if he'd sneezed broken glass. He turned away so that she would not see the sudden tears in his eyes. He dashed out of the bakery as if he were late to an important appointment, nearly spilling his coffee and dropping the waxy bag with the muffin in it. Now Miriam would think he was strange—or, rather, since she already thought he was strange (what sort of man works at the high school as a janitor for so long, what sort of man lives in that tiny old attic of an apartment year after year, and what sort of man—he'd heard her whisper to friends as they bent over the counter to request a particular cake or pastry—is so *thin*?), she would now think he was truly disturbed, perhaps even dangerous. Miriam had been three years ahead of him in school, she had been popular, a cheerleader and a class president (though not of her senior class), she went to community college for a couple of semesters before she married Herb Stewart and had three children and bought the bakery and became the pleasantly plump, red-faced, blond-going-to-grey-haired woman that everybody in town knew was not only likely to become chair of the schoolboard, but was also spending an awful lot of time with that twenty-year-old Morelli boy who had started working at the bakery after he'd been fired from his father's auto garage.

By the time he arrived at the high school, Charles had imagined a number of different scenarios involving Miriam and her suspicions about his erratic behavior, and he was certain that if she did not confront him the moment he came back from work and ask him why he'd been so rude to her, then perhaps she would call up the principal of the high school and warn him that Charles was not the best person to be spending time around impressionable children, and that he might even be a security risk, because clearly he was not entirely right in the head, and why would the school district have been so careless to employ such a person anyway, to which Charles hoped the principal would reply that the school district not only conducted semi-annual background checks, but also exceeded the state standards for drug testing of its employees, and hadn't Charles, after all, been for many years not only a valued employee of the high school but also a tenant of Mrs. Stewart herself, and hadn't she praised him many times for the punctuality of his rent payments, but Charles knew the principal would not think of these things, if he even knew about them, and that he would probably have to stop and wonder exactly who Charles Knott was, because the principal had only been at the school for three or four years now and there were quite a few janitors, after all, and of course they all looked rather similar in their grey uniforms, though if Miriam thought to tell the principal that Charles was the thin one, then of course he would know who she meant, because the principal had probably passed Charles many times and wondered if there wasn't something wrong with him. It was unlikely that Miriam would call the police, but just because something was unlikely did not mean it was impossible.

Charles opened his locker in the staff room and stuck his coffee and muffin inside. He seldom used his locker, because he seldom brought anything with him that needed to be stashed away, but the school provided all employees, from the principal on down, with lockers, and the union insisted the lockers were an essential part of their contracts, so Charles always opened his locker each morning when he arrived and each afternoon when he left, and today, despite the throbbing in his jaw, he paused for a moment to be grateful for the benefit of the locker, because otherwise he would have had to throw his muffin and coffee out.

When he returned to his locker at the end of the day, the muffin and coffee were still there, and Charles tossed them into the trashcan he had emptied only a few minutes before. He had eaten nothing all day. He had spoken as little as possible, doing his best to nod and, when absolutely necessary, to offer what bit of a smile he could. His job was routine enough that there was really very little need for him to talk to anyone, and most of the students and teachers hardly noticed him even when he was at his most gregarious (those times when he uttered a quiet hello to people whose names he did not know). Sam, one of the other janitors, always talked to him, but Sam talked even when nobody was listening, and as long as Charles kept nodding as Sam told him about the red Ford Mustang he was going to buy once he won the lottery and the house he'd build on the lake and all the women who would visit him and how he wouldn't have to be working at this stupid shit-ass job anymore, not that he wanted to offend Charles, he said, because he knew Charles had been working there an awful long time and of course it's not as bad a job as some, but, Sam said, he himself wasn't the sort of guy who could really be *contented* with this kind of work, because he had big plans and big dreams, which wasn't to say Charles didn't, and he really admired how Charles had settled into his life so well, and he hoped someday he could settle into his own life, and winning the lottery, which he planned to do, was certainly going to help that a lot. Charles nodded.

On the way home, Charles walked slowly. He always got back to the apartment after the bakery had closed, but Miriam stayed for at least an hour after closing to clean up and get ready for the morning. If he walked slowly enough, he could avoid having to see her. Each step brought pain to Charles's mouth. The roots of the bad tooth would throb, and then his foot would hit the sidewalk and the left side of his face would ache, then the tooth would throb more and his face would ache more, and Charles found himself walking so slowly, trying to keep the throbbing and aching from overwhelming each other, that he was hardly walking at all, and when he realized this his hands began to sweat and his knees shuddered a bit, because he was certain he looked like a fool and that the people in the cars driving by were all wondering what that fool was doing standing there on the sidewalk, his head bent at an odd angle, his legs shuffling forward a little bit at a time, and then he wondered what would happen if a police car drove by, because perhaps he could be arrested for loitering or causing some sort of public nuisance, and he began to walk faster, doing his best to ignore the fact that it felt like the bones in his face were cracking apart and that his bad tooth might suddenly explode and blow a hole in his cheek, which would really cause a terrible scene, and then he remembered Miriam and he started walking more slowly again.

It was dusk by the time he got back to his apartment, and Miriam was nowhere to be seen. He unlocked the green door at the side of the bakery, stepped into the still and silent shadows of the main floor, and walked up the stairs to his apartment. When he had first moved in, he had put an extra lock on the apartment door, and then a few years later, after a string of robberies in a neighboring town, he added another deadbolt lock as well as a chain, because though he had repeatedly asked Miriam to install an alarm system, she said it was unnecessary and expensive, but she didn't mind if he continued adding locks to the door of the apartment if that made him feel better. He kept the keys on different key rings and in different pockets of his pants, which meant it took him two or three minutes to unlock the apartment, because first he had to gather all the keys from all his pockets (he wore pants with many pockets), then he had to unlock everything, and then he had to return the keys to his pockets, a different pocket for each key. This process did not make him feel much better when his entire head screamed with the pain of his bad tooth, but the locks were on there now and he'd lived with them for many years, so he was used to the routine, and he'd never had anything stolen from the apartment (not that there was anything much worth stealing other than his *G.I. Joe* comic books), and the thought of leaving some of the locks unlocked when he was gone was far more disturbing to him than the time it took to lock and unlock them.

Not having eaten anything all day, Charles was hungry. Once he entered the little apartment, he opened the battered warhorse of a refrigerator and looked for anything that was soft and yet still edible. He wondered how old the eggs were, sitting there in their grey cardboard carton. He picked the carton up and looked for a date, but there was no date, and so he tried to think about when he had bought the eggs, but he couldn't remember exactly which trip to the grocery store it had been, and he certainly hadn't been to the store in the last week, and eggs probably weren't good after more than a week, they probably developed various diseases, and perhaps grew mold inside them, or perhaps something happened to cause a baby chicken to begin forming, and if he cracked the egg open he might find a gooey, half-formed baby chicken inside, and the thought of that made him bring the carton of eggs over to the plastic blue trashcan under the sink and toss the whole carton of twelve eggs into it without even looking at them, and he swore he would only buy eggs at the store if he knew that he was going to eat them, because he was certain the image of the proto-chicken would haunt him for hours and perhaps even days.

His tooth still hurt.

He should have bought yogurt. That would be a good thing to eat. Or pudding. Except pudding tended to be a bit too floppy, too much like cold rubber, and the first bite of pudding always made him gag, though he didn't mind it so much once he'd made it past the first bite. The only vegetables he had were hard ones beginning with the letter C: carrots and cucumber and celery. Even if he had been able to eat such vegetables, they were probably not in very good shape now, having sat in the refrigerator for at least a week. The cucumbers usually rotted first, and he remembered picking up a cucumber that had been sitting in the refrigerator for many weeks, he remembered thinking it didn't look too bad for how long it had sat there, and when he touched it his fingers went right through the skin and into the gelatinous guts. He'd nearly vomited. Why had he bought more cucumber? He often had a fantasy of having some cucumber in balsamic vinegar, a treat his mother used to make him when he was a kid, but he always forgot to buy the vinegar. He wanted to throw the cucumber out before it rotted, but he was afraid to touch it after his previous experience.

His mouth ached.

He closed the refrigerator. Perhaps he should take a nap. That would do him good.

The phone rang.

He knew it must be Jim, because who else, other than pollsters and telemarketers, ever called him? And usually just about at this time of night, to ask if Charles was doing anything, to see if he would put up with a visitor, because Jim wanted to get away from his wife for an hour or so to smoke cigarettes, which for some reason Charles had let him do in the apartment, and he had not figured out a way to tell Jim that he didn't much care for the smell of the cigarettes lingering in his furniture and clothes, that he didn't appreciate having to tell Miriam again and again that no he did not smoke but sometimes his friend Jim did and that was why the apartment smelled the way it did, and more than once he had had to explain to co-workers that no he had not taken to smoking and that his clothes only smelled that way because he had been around his friend Jim, and now at work sometimes one of the guys would say something about how Charles must have been around *his friend Jim* recently, and Charles would nod and blush and walk away.

Charles answered the phone and Jim asked what he was doing. Charles said he was trying to figure out something to eat, because he had a toothache and wasn't sure what sort of food he could eat without causing himself pain. Jim asked if he wanted a visitor. Charles said sure.

Jim lived less than a mile up the road with his wife, Kate, who was morbidly obese, which amused Jim tremendously because he said it would be wonderful if Charles had married her instead, because then they could be like Jack Sprat and his wife-who-could-eat-no-lean. Jim was plump, but not, Charles thought, exactly fat. During the summer, he worked at a nearby amusement park, playing the role of a crazy man with a wild beard who ran after a train that was the primary attraction at the park, a steam train that drove at an excruciatingly slow speed from one end of a two-mile-long track to another, and half-way through the ride Jim would run out wearing his tattered brown costume, carrying a fake shotgun in his hand, screaming at the train and scaring the tourists. For this he got paid just a bit more than minimum wage, which he said was a good supplement to his income, the majority of which came from managing an adult bookstore.

By the time Jim arrived, Charles had made himself a bowl of linguine and covered it with olive oil. He'd had pasta with tomato sauce the night before, and he didn't feel like having it again. He sucked the linguine into his mouth, but nearly choked to death when he tried to chew it, because the pain was excruciating and the unchewed linguine wriggled down his throat like a tapeworm. He scowled with frustration, coughed, and decided he had had enough to eat, that he didn't need to risk his life for the sake of dinner. He emptied the bowl of linguine in the garbage and washed it in the sink, scrubbing it carefully with a sponge covered with soap to get all the oil out.

Jim knocked on the door and Charles unlocked it and let him in. Jim said, "Hey, how're you feeling?" and slapped him on the shoulder, sending lightning bolts of agony through the entire left side of Charles's body. Charles moaned, the room drifted into a soft haze around him, like the transition to a flashback in a movie or the effect of a particularly long night at a particularly dull bar, and he was worried that he would fall over and hit his head and get a concussion or, worse, be knocked out and locked in a coma, a vegetable brain in a human body, kept alive at a hospital by machines and tubes until eventually even the nurses forgot him and dust settled over his emaciated form and the hospital was sold to a developer who would demolish it to build a shopping mall, and for one brief and terrifying moment Charles imagined himself comatose and forgotten in a dark corner of the hospital that turned suddenly bright and airy when the wrecking ball crashed through the ceiling.

"You okay?" Jim said, and Charles blinked a few times, bringing the room back into focus, and said, "Yeah, yeah. It's just my tooth, it hurts." He tried to smile, but only one side of his face wanted to respond, and a bit of drool slipped out the other side. His tongue felt swollen and numb.

"I had to have my wisdom teeth out a couple years ago," Jim said. "All four of 'em. They wanted four thousand bucks for the whole thing, a thousand bucks a tooth. I said no way. But they were really hurting, so I had to do something. I got a pair of pliers and stuck 'em in my mouth and just dug in and pulled until the fuckers came out."

"You pulled out your own teeth?"

"Sure," Jim said. "Hurt like hell, but I washed my mouth out with a lot of whiskey and went to bed for a couple days. My head swelled up to the size of a basketball and I had these weird fucking dreams, all about hungry dogs, but after a couple weeks I was fine, and it saved me four thousand bucks, so I figure I did the right thing."

Jim lit a cigarette and sat down on a couch that had been in the apartment when Charles moved in, a couch that had only the thinnest skin of upholstery left on it, but Charles couldn't bring himself to replace either the upholstery or the couch, and so he covered it with a couple of red sheets he'd had in his closet and never put on his bed. A large McDonald's cup half-filled with water and cigarette butts sat on the floor beside the couch, where Jim had left it a few days ago. He sucked on his cigarette, let the smoke settle in his lungs, then exhaled through his nose. He watched the white stem of the cigarette turn to ash, then, in a minor miracle of muscle memory, flicked the ash into the McDonald's cup without even glancing at the sludge lurking there.

"So how was work today?" Jim asked.

"Fine," Charles said. He sat in a recliner positioned with a good view out the window. Jim had told him that a recliner as comfortable as his should be in front of a big-screen TV, but Charles's TV had broken a few years ago, and he never had it fixed or bought a replacement, first because he didn't have the money, then, later, after he had saved for a while, because he didn't mind living without a TV, since it provided him with more time to look after his plants, to read comic books, and to play a complex board game replicating Napoleon's invasion of Russia, a game that he played against himself, taking one side one day, another side the next, carefully moving the intricate figures of each army until he could find ways to outwit his own best moves while remaining as historically accurate as possible.

"You always say work is fine."

"My tooth hurt."

"So work wasn't fine, was it? It fucking sucked, because you had to go around cleaning up those little assholes' messes, wiping their shit off the toilets and all, and the whole time your tooth was fucking killing you, right? Right?"

"Sure," Charles said, the *s* sound coming out more like *th*.

"Why do you lie to me?"

"Lie?"

"You said work was fine. It wasn't fine. It fucking sucked."

"Okay."

"Christ, you're impossible! Come on, Charles, wake up and smell the cat food! Don't just say *fine* when things are not *fine*, when things are fucked up, when life is one big goddamn dumpster full of rat shit! Look—ask me how my day at work was."

"How was your day at work?"

"It was full of fucking morons and perverts! I had a guy come in—a big bald guy with cauliflower ears and hands as big as my foot—and he wanted to know where the kiddie porn was, where the magazines with the little girls were hid, and I was like, 'Man you are a fucking goddamn pervert, get the hell out of this place!' and he was like, 'I got my rights,' and I said to him, these were my exact words, I said, 'Sick fucks like you have no fucking rights, asshole,' and he—he actually threatened to call a lawyer and have me charged with infringing his goddamn civil fucking liberties, can you believe that shit? Then I had some asshole try to sell me insurance. Fuckheads."

Jim dropped the smoldering filter of his cigarette into the McDonald's cup and lit another. "You haven't asked me how Kate is," Jim said. "You always ask me how Kate is."

"Ith hard to say."

"Huh?"

"Howth Kafe?"

"What? Oh. Man, you're in bad shape. You ought to see a dentist."

"I'll be fine," Charles said. Despite having worked for the school district for as long as he had, he was still hourly, and had no health insurance.

"I'll bring over my pliers if you want."

"No, ith okay."

"Anyway, Kate's doing well. Today she was watching some TV show about soldiers in Iraq and she saw some guy she went to beauty school with, he was over there with the Marines or the National Guard or somebody, and she was all flusterated, said she couldn't believe they would let somebody like him in, because, well, you know what guys in beauty school are like, a total faggot, you know, probably even wears, like, I dunno, panties and shit. I don't know why she got all carried away and everything, 'cuz I'm like, well better him than me, I mean, I'm *glad* we've got fags that want to go over there and get blown to shit by the rockets and IUDs and all, because you gotta be fucking nuts to be in the military these days, you know, so I got lots of respect for those guys, but Kate, fuck man, she was all ready to write letters to the newspaper and call the Pope and shit. I think it's because she thinks I'm a fag, so she's bitter." He dropped his cigarette into the McDonald's cup. "Why are you looking at me like that? I told you Kate thinks I come over here and give you head."

"What?"

"Yeah, she thinks the only reason I come visit you is because I feel sorry for you and we're like fuckbuddies or something, like you've got a cute little ass and all I want to do is stick my big ol' cock up inside it, because I sure as hell don't get much out of sticking it in her anymore. She's got goddamn idiotic ideas sometimes. Watches too much TV, you know, that fucking Oprah shit and everything. I go out tonight and she's screaming at me, 'Yeah, Jimmy, go see your *boyfriend!*' Can you believe the shit I got to put up with? Be glad you're not married. Be fucking glad." Jim looked at his watch. "Well, I should get back," he said, and stood up. "That firefighter TV show's on in half an hour, and you still don't have a goddamn fucking TV." He slapped Charles on the knee. "Take care of yourself, man," he said, and walked out, leaving, as always, the door wide open behind him.

§

Charles had fallen asleep in the recliner, and he woke at dawn, his entire jaw throbbing, and he remembered dreaming of Celia Annie. He sat up, thinking perhaps she was in the room with him, even though he hadn't seen her since he was twenty, when he told her he loved her, and she cried and said she didn't think he could love her, not in the way he meant, and even if he did, she didn't think of him like that, her best friend, no, he was too pure, like a spirit, and after that he said he would never talk to her again, and he did not, though even now he felt some pinch in the back of his mind, some tug in his heart, some yearning to know where she was, some hope that she would find him, and the last image he remembered of her, with her long blond hair tossed by the breeze whispering off a lake, her blue eyes filled with tears—that last image did not feel like a dream, but instead had the substance of memory, even though he knew he'd seen her last at the Dairy Queen where they'd worked together that summer, the summer he decided never to go back to college and she fell in love with Arty Kober and moved with him to Montana. Now and then Jim reminded him about Celia, because he'd told Jim all about her, had fled crying and screaming to Jim that summer, the only friend he dared tell, and so every few months Jim would say he thought Charles needed to get out more and meet people, needed to find himself a girlfriend or a boyfriend or just get a cat or something, and Charles said no no no, he was happy as he was, he didn't want to have to adjust to another person, he couldn't imagine a person who would find anything interesting about him, which was not entirely true, particularly late at night when he couldn't sleep and the apartment and the bakery were so still and quiet that it felt like being unstuck in time, each second lasting days and hours, but he would never tell Jim that yes there were people he saw here and there, in passing, that made him wish for a hand to hold in his own, for a warm body beside his in the darkness, for lips to touch his lips. But if he thought about more, a dull nausea grew in his stomach and groin, because Celia had been right, he didn't want to know a person that way, and he didn't want them to know him that way, despite moments of sudden desire, despite the eyes of kind women and gentle men that haunted him, sometimes for weeks, but yes, Celia had been right, he did not want to know them that way, he could not know them that way, and people were just images, just ghosts passing by, and he could not love an image, no, he could not love a ghost.

A beam of sunlight shot across his face. Even closing his eyes was painful. The tooth no longer merely ached and throbbed, it pulsed and pricked and stung and rattled, as if a jittery, microscopic porcupine had taken up residence between the root and the bone.

Without quite knowing that he was doing it, Charles made a fist and punched the side of his head. He felt nothing. The pain from his tooth was so overwhelming that no other pain could squeeze attention from his busy nerves. He was certain someone had buried an icepick in his mouth, and the only solution was to pull it out. He reached in, surprised that there was room for his hand, because he'd been sure his teeth had expanded and filled most of the empty space between his tongue and his throat, but he had no trouble extending his thumb and forefinger in, and he knew the moment he touched the wretched tooth, for in that moment the tooth let out another shrill shot of pain, overwhelming his entire nervous system so that he could feel each hair on his bony arms stand up and prepare to eject from his skin. He grasped the tooth in his fingers, and with one simple, determined pull he wrenched it from his jaw and out of his mouth.

He stared at the yellow-black remnant of tooth in his hand. This was the monster, this was the culprit, the malicious, malignant sediment of torment, captured and extracted at last. A wave of peace washed over him, and he decided it was going to be a beautiful day.

Then he realized his mouth was full of blood. He ran to the bathroom and spat into the toilet. Blood dribbled down his jaw and gushed over his lips. He gasped and choked. He ransacked the toilet paper, pulling hunks off the roll and sticking them into his mouth until it had filled with sodden, bloody pulp and he feared he might not be able to breathe. He blew the blood and fiber into the toilet. Blood continued to fill his mouth.

He had forgotten to lock the door after Jim left. This proved to be a lucky failure, because he knew he needed help, knew that if he remained with a mouth spewing blood that he would drown or suffocate or gag himself to death, and so he raced out of the apartment and down the stairs, trying to let the blood pool in his mouth and then release discreetly from pursed lips in a little trickle, but the trickle became a sticky river that flowed over his chin, down his neck, and across his body, finally finding exit in his shoes, so that he sloshed and slopped down the stairs, splattering footprints as memorials of his steps.

Miriam screamed when she saw him and untangled herself from the twenty-year-old Morelli boy's naked lower half. The scream sounded to Charles like a song he had heard as a child, something his father had tried to play on an electric guitar, his father the mail-man who yearned to be a rock star, but ended up dead at forty with a ruined liver and a pile of undelivered mail. Charles remembered that pile of mail as he collapsed to his knees and the familiar sights and morning smells of the bakery drifted away, and then even his memory melted into a smoky realm of darkness.

§

After a ride in an ambulance and a day at the hospital, Charles emerged with a sewn-up hole in his mouth and a bill for nearly as much money as he made in a year. He decided that with a bill like that, he could afford to take a taxi home. The driver was an old man with a grey fedora hat that sank down over his ears and thick glasses that made his eyes seem as small as a mole's. He did not speak dur-ing the entire fifteen-mile drive, and asked for his fee by pointing to a chart posted on the ceiling. Charles took his wallet from his blood-encrusted pants and paid with two pristine twenty-dollar bills, the only money he had.

Miriam tried to speak to him when he stepped into the bakery, but he ignored her and walked up to his apartment. Out of habit, he pulled the first key from his pants and tried to unlock the door, but it had not been locked, and the sensation of the key refusing to turn was at first jarring, but then he replayed the events of the morning in his mind and realized he had had no chance to lock the door, that he had, instead, run for his life. Nonetheless, he felt a pang of regret and fear.

He closed the door behind himself, but did not lock it, because if it had been unlocked all day, there was no reason to lock it again. He took off his clothes and left them in a pile on the floor, then put on new underpants and a T-shirt, because if he died in his sleep, he did not want to be discovered naked, particularly if Miriam was the person to discover him.

Seconds after he lay down in bed, Miriam knocked on the door. She opened it slightly and peered in. "Charles?" she said softly. "How are you?"

Charles wanted to pretend he was asleep, but he knew he should be polite, because she had, after all, saved his life by calling 911 and making sure he didn't choke before the ambulance arrived. "I'm fine," he said. "A little tired. They gave me a lot of painkillers."

Miriam stepped into the apartment and stood holding the handle of the door. "Do you need anything?" she said.

"No," he said. "I just need to sleep."

"Are you hungry?"

"No, thank you."

He closed his eyes and waited. He opened his eyes, and Miriam was standing closer to his bed. "I just wanted to talk a little bit, to say, well…" She forced a cough. "About Nick. And what you saw. That was, it doesn't, it…"

"I didn't see anything at all," Charles said. "All I could see was blood."

"Oh good," Miriam said quickly, then, "No, I don't mean—what I mean is—well, I just hope you feel a lot better." She smiled and touched him gently on the arm. He closed his eyes and heard her walk away and close the door quietly behind her.

§

Though Miriam brought Charles food every morning, and Jim convinced Kate to cook him food for dinner at night (which gave Jim an excuse to visit every evening and smoke), Charles found it difficult to eat. The hole in his mouth only occasionally hurt; a mild hurt, barely qualifying as an ache. He rarely felt hungry, though, and he could not convince himself that any sort of food would fit into his mouth. Miriam sat with him during the mornings, and she had begun to tell him about her life, about how she was certain her husband Herb had been seeing prostitutes, and eventually she said she missed Nick Morelli, who had just joined the Navy, because he had made her feel special and beautiful, which Herb had never really done, and Nick had told her stories about stupid girlfriends he'd had, none of whom could bake anything, none of whom got his jokes, and she said she missed hearing his jokes, even the ones she only laughed at because she knew she was supposed to, and she knew Nick had never had any girlfriends, because he wasn't the best looking boy around and he certainly wasn't the smartest, but she loved him, she did, and Charles could tell she was waiting for him to try to cheer her up, but he couldn't think of any words to speak.

Jim brought food from Kate each night and told Charles about things he'd seen on TV or arguments he'd gotten into, but it was clear he found Charles, who mostly lay in bed, to be less interesting than he had been before, and some nights now Jim did not show up, and when he did he yelled at Charles for ignoring the food, for wasting away, for not appreciating his friends. Charles never responded, because what was there to say? He was ashamed that people were trying to help him and he could not be helped. Every time he saw the food Miriam or Jim brought, his stomach churned with guilt, and he could not look them in the eye, and he wondered why he didn't say anything, why he didn't tell them that he appreciated their attention. For some reason he could not quite grasp, their attention weighed on him, it filled him, and he was certain that if they would leave him alone he would be fine, and he would recover and be healthy, he would get up each morning and walk down and pick up his muffin and coffee and go to work and listen to Sam and clean the bathrooms and empty the trash and then walk home, satisfied at having completed another day, but not now, no, he did not want to get out of bed, he did not want to open the door and walk down the stairs, not now while everyone was watching him and waiting for him, not now.

Now Celia visited him in the night, and he realized that he had been waiting for her. She did not bring him food, but she sat beside his bed as a shadow in the moonlight, a shadow covered by a spider's web, and after a long while she took his hand in hers, and she smiled. "I'm sorry," she whispered, her voice warm and close. He smiled and tried to speak to her, but no words would form, no sound would issue from his throat or mouth. He imagined they were characters in a comic book, superheroes wearing capes, and that they had adventures in places called Poisonville and Foxrock, where they battled shadows together and solved elaborate puzzles left in the corners of vast and mossy labyrinths created by dashing devils, men from hell who sought, always, to lure them away from each other. They went to parties and smoked cigarettes in long black holders and drank gallons of gin, but never too much, because around every corner was a new threat, a thief to be beguiled or a murderer to be caught. At the end of their story they sat together on the edge of a lake and laughed and laughed through the darkness.

His mouth had begun again to bleed. He sat up. Celia did not hold his hand. The chair beside him was empty. He was alone, of course, and who was he to think he would ever be the hero of a story, what sort of person would want to read tales of him, after all? He clenched his fists. Celia had been kinder to him than she should have been. He had hoped for too much and dreamed for too long, and her kindness was the greatest wound she had inflicted, he saw now, the wound that had cut across all his narrow days since then, and it was his own fault for not noticing, his own fault for believing that eventually things would heal themselves.

He lay back down and closed his eyes.

When Miriam found him in the morning, she knew she should call the ambulance or the police, but instead she set the muffin and coffee onto the table beside the bed and sat in the chair she had come to think of as her own, a simple wooden chair, and she stared out the window at nothing in particular, watching the day slowly move toward its end, the sky seeming to fall into the hills of the horizon, until just before the last light disappeared, Jim stepped quietly into the room, set the food Kate had cooked beside the cold muffin and coffee, and placed his hand gently on Miriam's shoulder. At that moment, a neon sign across the street flickered on, a splash of light that etched their silhouettes onto the glass, until Miriam stood and led Jim downstairs to make the necessary calls and leave the room to its silence or its ghosts.

New Practical Physics

I. Introduction: Weights And Measures

He goes to the library to study, but he becomes distracted. He is a master of procrastination, and so despite having two large papers due for classes, he spends his time roaming the stacks. He thinks about writing a story about a graduate student, but it would have to be a particular kind of story, not some vaguely-autobiographical chronicle of ordinary existence. The stories he wants to write are fanciful, filled with strange locales and bizarre events. Much more interesting than stories about students.

He goes to a computer terminal to search the catalogue and decides to see what will happen if he types into the search field the first two words that occur to him. This is a large university, and the library is excellent. *Magnificent nonchalance* nonetheless returns no results. Nor does *unscrupulous financiers. Heathen schools*, however, brings three results, though two are for the same book: *A discourse concerning the conversion of the heathen Americans, and the final propagation of Christianity and the sciences to the ends of the earth* by William Smith, 1727-1803. The other result is a twenty-four page illustrated collection of stories for children, *Juvenile Casket,* including the stories "The Country School" and "Heathen Worshippers", printed in Concord, New Hampshire sometime between 1840 and 1861.

None of this particularly interests him. He is writing a paper about modernity and Nicaragua and a paper about a handful of science fiction stories from the 1960s. He doesn't know what to say about either subject. His cell phone vibrates in his pocket. He takes it out and looks at the screen. Miguel. He could slip into the stairway and answer, but decides he doesn't need to deal with all the drama right now. It can wait till he gets home.

II. Simple Machines: Levers And Pulleys

He finds a few books in the stacks and brings them back to a table where two other students are studying quietly. He hates sitting at tables with undergraduates, because so often they seem to look at him as if he is some sort of alien, a slightly grotesque figure, at best an anomaly. But final exams begin in ten days, and people are cramming, trying to learn everything they didn't learn during all the weeks they avoided coming to the library. Even two days ago, Ben would have had no trouble finding a table of his own on this floor.

He puts his books onto the table and pulls a notebook from his backpack. A red-haired girl to his left glances at him. "What?" he says.

"Nothing," she says.

III. Work, Power, Friction

Driving home, he realizes his frustration with the car in front of him is irrational. He should not be getting angry, because the car in front of him is following the speed limit, and there's nothing wrong with following the speed limit. It is probably a good habit to get into. He wonders why he is in such a rush to get home. He'll only have to face Miguel.

He stops tailgating the car in front of him.

The closer he gets to home, the slower he travels. He wonders if he could keep slowing down enough to never quite stop moving, but never arrive, either. Didn't Zeno's paradox have something to do with that? Miguel would know. Perhaps as they sink into their inevitable argument tonight, he can ask Miguel how to travel without getting anywhere.

IV. Pressure In Liquids

Miguel is waiting, of course. He's been drinking. He sits in the living room, a bottle of Jack Daniels at his feet, the TV on. "Where've you been?" he asks.

"The library," Ben says. "Studying."

"I called you," Miguel says.

V. Pressure Of Air

"I know. But I was in the library. I couldn't answer the phone," Ben says.

"You knew it was me?" Miguel says.

"Yes."

VI. Liquids And Gases In Motion

"So you knew it was me and you deliberately ignored my phone call."

"I knew it was you. I was in the library. I couldn't answer the phone."

Miguel picks the bottle of Jack Daniels up, lifts it to his lips, drinks, then flings the bottle at the wall. It bounces off without breaking.

VII. Elasticity And Strength Of Materials

"If you're going to fucking be like this I can leave," Ben says.

"Is that what you want?" Miguel stands up unsteadily. He crosses the room and picks up the bottle.

"We're going to have to talk at some point," Ben says.

VIII. Forces Acting Through A Point

"Fine," Miguel says. "Let's talk."

"In the morning. When you're not drunk."

"I'm not drunk."

IX. Accelerated Motion

"You are piss drunk and I'm not going to try to have a conversation with you," Ben says. He walks to the kitchen and pours himself a glass of cranberry juice.

Miguel walks toward him. He holds out his hand and touches Ben's shoulder gently. "Don't leave me," he says.

"We'll talk in the morning," Ben says.

X. Three Laws Of Motion

Ben considers locking the bedroom door, but he isn't angry enough to be that cruel. Miguel comes in eventually. "Are you asleep?" he asks.

"Yes," Ben says.

Miguel stands beside the bed for a moment and stares at Ben, then takes his shirt off, his pants, his socks, his underwear. He climbs into bed and wraps his arm around Ben. He unbuttons the fly on Ben's boxers and strokes him for a moment, but Miguel seems to realize his drunken clumsiness isn't achieving anything, and stops. Soon, he is snoring.

XI. Potential And Kinetic Energy

Miguel is still asleep when Ben gets up in the morning. Ben takes a shower, gets dressed, and decides to buy breakfast at Dunkin' Donuts rather than make something at home. The less time he spends at home, the better. He can eat his breakfast in his office while he looks at the first drafts of papers for the freshman composition class he's teaching. He should have returned the drafts by now, but he hasn't been able to concentrate very well, and every time he sits down with one, he doesn't know where to begin to make comments. Yesterday, he caught himself before he wrote, "Learn English," on one paper.

The line at the Dunkin' Donuts drive-in is long. He doesn't mind waiting. He listens to news on the radio, but soon it disappears in static, so he turns it off and sits staring at the brake lights of the car in front of him and listening to the humming engines all around.

When the driver of the car in front of him finishes placing an order and moves forward, Ben lifts his foot off the clutch too quickly, and his car stalls.

XII. Heat And Expansion

Ben stares at one of the papers and nibbles on a bagel, then notices he's being watched. Neill Blythe, a freshman in his comp class, stands in the door of the office. "Hi," he says. Ben smiles. He doesn't know any other openly gay undergrads, though supposedly there are many. Neill's doing the typical I'll-rebel-against-the-entire-world-by-dying-my-hair-pink-and-wearing-make-up-and-lots-of-political-buttons schtick that so many gay kids seem compelled to do before they settle down into a boring middle class life like everybody else. Ben never really went through that phase, and he enjoys seeing other people do it.

"I haven't read your paper yet," Ben says.

"That's okay," Neill says. "I had another class in this building, so I just thought I'd say hi."

XIII. Transmission Of Heat

Ben stares at Neill for a moment. "Do you want to sit down?"

"Sure," Neill says. He looks around the office. "Pretty spartan."

"I've only got it for a term, so I haven't bothered to decorate."

XIV. Ice, Water, And Steam

If this were a movie, there would be two possible resolutions, Ben thinks. If it were a Hollywood movie, he would have feelings for Neill but not act on them. Well, no. If it were a Hollywood movie, he would be the Bad Gay Guy, and therefore he *would* act on his feelings. Because in a Hollywood movie, the Good Gay Guy is witty and full of catty conversation. Ben has never considered himself witty or catty. Nor does he have any fashion sense. Thus, he must be the Bad Gay Guy.

The other type of movie he was thinking of was an independent film, an art film. In a movie like that, he would be the Tortured, Complicated Gay Guy, and he would probably act on his feelings for Neill (he would certainly have feelings for Neill if he were the Tortured, Complicated Gay Guy), but then feel guilty about it, and either kill himself or kill Neill. Or both. Or just look Tortured and Complicated. In soft focus and probably black & white.

There is no movie for what actually happens. He talks with Neill for a few minutes about school and Neill's bad relationship with his mother, who is convinced that he's going through a phase ("Maybe you are," Ben says. "Or maybe she is. So what?"), and then Neill says he has to go meet some friends at the library, and Ben says goodbye to him, and that's that. He has feelings, but they are not feelings of lust for Neill, whom he doesn't find at all attractive. His feelings are of regret and nostalgia, because his own life as an undergraduate had been so comparatively dull, so grey and monotonous: tortured, but uncomplicated. That was him, the Tortured, Shallow Gay Guy, and not really tortured enough to be interesting. Not the sort of story anybody ever bothers to film.

XV. Steam And Gas Engines

He reads three papers that morning, but finally he gives up and decides to go to the library to do some more research. As he walks across campus, he thinks he should probably get something to eat, but he's not particularly hungry. He never eats enough, and doesn't like interrupting his day to get food. Inevitably, he's embarrassed by whatever he eats. Why do people always seem to be judging him when he eats? They probably aren't, but nonetheless, it feels like they are. So he tries to eat in secret, when people aren't around. He isn't supposed to eat in the library anyway, though sometimes he does—some crackers or a granola bar, usually. He feels like a criminal whenever he unwraps them, because the wrappers are always loud, like gunshots or particularly vociferous flatulence.

Ben climbs to the sixth floor of the library, his favorite place, a place where the shelves are set tightly together and there are no computers or particularly good areas to study, so when people come up to get a book they don't usually linger. He sets his jacket and bookbag on a stiff metal chair at a desk in a corner, then begins to roam the stacks. There are no books about Nicaragua up here, but there are some about science fiction. He's not interested in them, though. He wants to find a book he's never seen before, something that will be new, exciting, unexpected. He wants the book to open some new world to him, but he fears that he knows all the worlds books can offer, and none of them will be enough.

After walking through various shelves, he decides to try a remote corner of the floor, a spot that has always scared him, because it is dark and he's not sure where the light switch is. He walks toward the corner, and as he gets closer, he notices someone sitting on the floor between some shelves. He pauses for a moment, but then continues walking. He sees the light switch. He flips the lights on. Neill sits on the floor there, tears streaming down his bruised face.

XVI. Magnetism

Ben knows what he should do. He should be compassionate. He should get down on the floor and hold Neill's hands, because the boy is clearly horrified, clearly shaken, clearly in need of comfort—but he can't bring himself to do this. He remains standing. "What—Neill—what happened?" he says.

Neill shakes his head.

"Are you hurt?" He realizes it's a stupid question.

XVII. Electricity At Rest

Neill says, "I'm okay. Just got hit, that's all." He wipes tears from his face.

"I can take you to the infirmary," Ben says. "I can help."

"I'll be fine," Neill says. He pulls himself up and pushes past Ben. "I'll be fine."

XVIII. Electric Currents

Ben knows he should follow Neill and make sure he gets home safely, or gets somewhere safely. But Ben doesn't move. He thinks about Miguel, remembers stories Miguel told him of being at home, of being beaten as a kid for not being macho enough.

Or maybe Neill wasn't hurt because of his hair, or a slogan on one of his buttons, or because he made a pass at somebody he shouldn't have. Maybe it was entirely unrelated. It could have had nothing to do with Neill being gay. Maybe somebody thought he had money and tried to rob him. Or maybe Neill was in the wrong. Maybe he had tried to hurt somebody. It was entirely possible.

Ben goes back to his seat and takes out the folder of his students' papers. He finds Neill's. The assignment was to write a personal essay about a childhood experience. Neill's essay is titled "The Key".

XIX. Electric Circuits

The essay doesn't prove to be very illuminating. Or very well written. Five pages (all one paragraph) about losing a key his grandfather gave him when Neill was five years old. His grandfather said he'd known pirates, and the key opened a treasure chest, but he never told Neill where the treasure chest was. Apparently, the grandfather was now dead. Apparently, Neill never found the treasure chest. Ben takes out his favorite red pen and writes at the end of the essay, "I think you can probably be more specific about some of the details. There's no need to leave your reader in the dark about everything. What is the significance of this story?"

He is surprised Neill didn't write about coming to terms with his sexual orientation. Ben had written such essays in college, even though he'd been far less outgoing and confident than Neill. Did Neill not trust him as a teacher? That seemed unlikely.

His cell phone vibrates. He looks at the screen. Miguel. He glances around the floor, but he seems to be the only one there. He answers the phone with a whispered, "Hello?"

XX. Magnetic And Chemical Effects Of Electric Current

"I'm sorry," Miguel says.

"About what?" Ben whispers.

"Everything," Miguel says.

XXI. Electric Power, Heating, And Lighting

Something about his tone is terrifying. His voice is thick, the words slow and heavy. Miguel had told him stories of trying to kill himself when he was younger, of being convinced he was an abomination. He had been happy with Ben for these past two years now, and had never spoken of wanting to kill himself, but Ben knew the impulse was there, that it could always reappear.

"I'm coming home," Ben says. "I love you."

Miguel is silent, but just as Ben hangs up, he hears Miguel ask, "How much?"

XXII. Electric Generators And Motors

He runs into the apartment. On the drive home, he had built up images in his mind of Miguel lying with his arms slit open in the bathtub, or hanging by his neck from the hot water pipe that crossed the living room ceiling, or drenched in his own vomit on the kitchen floor after swallowing a bottle of pills.

Miguel lies on the couch, hugging his knees to his chest. Ben kneels down beside him. Miguel's eyes are full of tears. "What's wrong?" Ben says. He kisses Miguel on the forehead. He wipes tears off his cheeks. He leans in to kiss Miguel's lips, but Miguel turns away.

"What's wrong?" Ben says. "You can tell me. I love you."

XXIII. Induction Coils And Transformers

It isn't until Ben sees Miguel's hands that he begins to understand. The knuckles are swollen, the fingers bloody.

"I'm sorry," Miguel says.

"Tell me what happened," Ben says.

XXIV. Alternating Currents

He makes tea. Earl Grey, their mutual favorite. "Earl Grey for the gay," Miguel always says. Ben brings him the cup and Miguel sips it slowly.

"You followed me to campus this morning?" Ben says.

"No. I came in later. I was going to apologize for being an asshole last night. And then…"

XXV. Sound Waves

"And then?" Ben says.

"I saw him. The boy. In your office. And you both seemed happy. You seemed like you were having a real conversation. He knew how to talk to you. He didn't just know about diffraction and fermions, all that shit you hate."

"I don't hate it," Ben says.

XXVI. Musical Sounds

"You don't understand it," Miguel says. "So we can't talk about it. What I spend my day doing. We can't talk."

"We have a lot to talk about. We've always done just fine. It's not like we speak different languages at each other."

"Isn't it?" Miguel says.

XXVII. Illumination: Lamps And Reflectors

"So what did you do?" Ben says.

"I wasn't going to do anything. But then when he walked out of your office, he seemed happy. Can you imagine being happy at his age? I didn't hate him, I just—I don't know. I followed him. I didn't try to hide myself. He stopped and asked me if he knew me. I said no. He asked me if I wanted to fuck him, because he said I was following close enough behind him I could fuck him while we walked. I didn't say anything, because I couldn't believe what he'd said. He turned around and kept walking. I followed him into the library. He kept going up these stairs. I'd never been up there before. Finally, we got to a corner, and he unzipped his pants and pulled out his dick. He asked me if that's what I wanted. I said no. He said it was. I said no. He said he wouldn't give it to me anyway, because he wasn't a whore. He said obviously the only man I could get was a whore. He said nobody would fuck somebody as ugly as me. He said I was probably some illegal, and he was going to call INS. I was angry, but I laughed at that one. I mean, come on. He started swearing at me. I think he didn't like it that I laughed. But then he said I smelled like shit. He sounded like my brothers at home. He pushed me. And I just lost it. I lost it. I slammed him against the wall. I kicked him in the balls, I punched him, I kept punching him, I couldn't stop. He fell to the floor. I looked at him. I didn't know what to do. I put my hands in my pockets and walked away. I just walked away. He could be dead. I could have killed him. Stupid little kid, I could've killed him. He's dead now."

Ben holds him as he sobs. "He's not dead," Ben says. "He'll be okay."

XXVII. Lenses And Optical Instruments

Ben listens to Miguel breathe. He imagines that he is watching himself, that he is staring down from a distance at these two bodies entwined and trembling, that the words they whisper are indistinct and strange. Perhaps he is getting ready to land on Earth and is observing human behavior. Perhaps he has landed already, even though nothing is familiar here.

He tells Miguel about finding Neill. "He's going to be fine. Some bruises, that's all. You're a physicist, not a boxer."

They take a shower together. They haven't done that for a long time. The water pours down their bodies, but never quite enough, because the water pressure in the apartment isn't very good, and so to stay warm they have to keep switching from one side of the shower to the other in a gently awkward dance punctuated by giggles and shrieks when cold air meets their wet skins.

XXIX. Spectra And Color

After the shower, they go to bed for a nap. Ben holds Miguel to him tightly, resting his head on Miguel's chest.

"Did you tell him who you were?" Ben asks.

"No," Miguel says.

XXX. Radio Telegraphy And Telephony

"I have to face him in class, that's all," Ben says. "If he knew I knew you, he might try to press charges or something."

"I'm so sorry."

"Don't be," Ben says. "It's going to be fine."

XXXI. Cathode And X Rays, Radioactivity

Ben wakes at night. Miguel is not beside him. He smells food cooking—something spicy. He walks out of the bedroom. Miguel stands, fully dressed and even wearing an apron, at the stove. Ben didn't know they owned an apron.

"Are you going to eat dinner naked?" Miguel asks.

Ben says, "I think I'll stay naked for as long as I possibly can." He smiles. Miguel shrugs and returns to the food sizzling on the stove.

Appendix

Physics is a science. The sort of physics that will be found in this book differs from the kind that everyone unconsciously studies all his life, chiefly in that it seeks to answer not only the questions "why" and "how," but also the question "how much."

—Newton Henry Black and Harvey Nathaniel Davis,

New Practical Physics: Fundamental Principles and Applications to Daily Life

The MacMillan Company, New York, 1930

The Last Elegy

I received a letter from Grete. I hadn't heard from her in at least a decade, since before the war. After Andrea's death, I didn't want to stay in contact with anyone who knew her, or anyone who had known Anders, because I didn't know any other way to escape my sadness than to erase all the memories of what had happened, the memories of the cabarets and theatres, the cafés and galleries, the late nights that became early mornings as we talked about politics and poetry and philosophy, the hopes we had. Hope has always been a source of sadness, because it makes me vulnerable to fantasies and delusions, and it took me many years to see that time with Anders and Grete as anything other than the most awful delusion of my life.

In her letter, Grete tells me she is ill, and she would like to see me again before she dies. She asks if I ever finished the elegy for Anders. She still lives in the apartment she shared with him, though it is different now, having been damaged in the war. She says she got married again, but her husband is no longer alive, and now she is alone, but she has wonderful friends. She still paints occasionally, though she says materials are sometimes hard to come by. She says she has missed me all these years.

I lie awake and stare at the rusted tin ceiling of my little bedroom. Perhaps I, too, am ill; perhaps I am dying. Perhaps the elegy I should write is for myself. Self-pity is my strongest talent. But I am not to blame for what happened. I may have been a fool, but I was a brave fool to risk so much, to feel so much, to lose so much. (I tell myself this, just as I have for many years now, even though after all this time, the sadness remains.)

§

Afterward, everything reminded me of him. For weeks, it seemed every item in my apartment, every object in the city had some memory attached to it. A pen he had given me sat on the desk. Above the desk I had hung a postcard he'd sent from Venice. I threw them both away. We'd talked about nearly every book I owned, and so I covered the bookcase with a sheet. One night, drunk and maudlin, tears streaming down my face, I carried all the books out to the street and threw them one by one into the river, saving his favorites, Baudelaire and Rimbaud, for last. (He read to me in French. I knew no French.) I had stuck a scrap of paper with the date of his birthday on it to the wall so I could not forget it. I took the paper in my hand and tore it into the tiniest shreds I could and threw them all out the window. I covered my ears when I heard familiar songs echoing through the streets at night. I avoided the parks where we had wandered so aimlessly so many times. There did not seem to be a café anywhere in the city that we had not been to at least once, and so I stopped going to cafés.

"Anders is dead," she told me. "Don't talk to me about Anders anymore."

§

This is the first time I have been on an airplane. It is noisier than I would have expected. For some reason, I thought once we got up off the ground, everything would be silent. When I first came to the city, I came by boat. Now, looking down at it all, it is not familiar. It could be any city in the world.

The plane descends.

It could be any city in the world.

§

I met Anders because of Grete. A newspaper had asked me to write about new artists, and, not knowing of anything better to do with my time, I accepted and began going to gallery openings, even though I knew nothing about art. Grete's opening was the liveliest I'd ever attended, a hot and crowded room full of laughing people and abstract paintings in pastel colors, badly lit with small lamps set on tables every few feet throughout the room. Now and then someone jostled a table, a lamp fell, an explosion, laughter.

"This is my husband, Anders," Grete said, leading me to him by the arm. "He hates parties," she said. "He's an actor. You might have seen him in *Werther* at the State Theatre. He's a genius," she said. "You'll love him."

I didn't like parties any more than he did, and so, after dutifully taking notes about a couple of paintings, I stepped outside with him. He gave me a cigarette and we walked down the street, stopping eventually at a café where a man on the balcony above played an oboe, its soft notes bobbing away on the breeze.

Anders spoke to me in clear, formal English. He said he had spent some years touring the British Isles, but had not yet had the chance to see the United States, a place that, in his mind, contained two types of territories: The West, a wild frontier enthralled and terrorized by the ghost of Jesse James, and New York City, which he talked of as if it were the size of Texas and filled with nothing but cigar-chomping capitalists and ladies bedecked in the furs of white leopards. I told him his impressions were entirely correct.

As Anders talked, I paid close attention to his face for the first time, his soft skin and eyes of such a light blue they seemed nearly translucent. His thin nose bent slightly to one side and his lips were narrow and somehow childlike. High, prominent cheekbones gave him a regal air, and he showed no trace at all of a beard. His dark blond hair was unfashionably long, and now and then he brushed strands back over his little ears. In the shadows and smoke of the café he had, I thought, the face of a nymph.

§

Grete meets me at the airport. The skin of her face is sallow and slack, her eyes sunken deep into shadows, her hair thin and grey. She was a tall woman once, but she is not now.

We ride to the apartment in a black taxi. "My English got better during the war," Grete says.

"Your English was never bad."

"Still, it got better. Anders made me read Shakespeare, thus I always sounded like Shakespeare. I don't sound like Shakespeare anymore." She laughs, and I force a smile.

The city is full of rubble. I don't want to look at Grete, so I stare out the window of the taxi. Shops with bright new signs stand beside shops with shattered windows. Women and men in expensive clothes climb into big American cars. An old man pushes a wooden cart filled with cabbages down the street.

"Do you still write poetry?" Grete asks.

"Not in a long time," I say.

The old man pushing the cart stops to rest. When he sets the end of the cart down, cabbages roll off onto the cobblestones. He leans over, picks them up, and puts them back in the cart, but for every cabbage he puts back, two or three more fall. We drive on.

§

As a young man, I quite inadvertently made a name for myself in certain parts of the world as an elegist. My first book was a slim volume of poems memorializing a lost love at a time when, because of war and illness, such a subject could find favor with a large audience. Intoxicated by the sudden attention, and even more so by the sudden wealth, I gave in to the pleas of my publisher for more and more poems, a seemingly endless series of elegies published in memory of every imaginable occasion, until newspaper cartoonists repeatedly turned me into a caricature (portraying such things as a man who writes verses for each grave in a graveyard stretching off to infinity), and my name appeared often in books and magazines, as well as some of the lesser motion pictures of the day. Each week I received hundreds of appeals for more elegies, poems to memorialize not only particular people, but also pets and objects and lost elections. Each week, I wrote fewer and fewer, as my poems felt even to me as if they had become parodies of their own parodies. Finally, unable to write a single word on a piece of paper without succumbing to utter nausea, I fled.

"Fame is so nice when you don't have it," Anders said to me once. We were sitting on a bench in a park at twilight.

"I'd rather have love than fame," I said, though I wasn't sure why.

"And what have you had for love?" He said it casually, not looking at me, watching people walk through the darkening shadows around us.

"That's how I started writing elegies," I said. "A lost love."

"Lost?" He turned to me. "How do you mean?"

"I wrote poem after poem to her. As if she had died."

"But she had not died?"

"No. We were great friends, and I had thought, I had hoped, that we might be something more than friends, eventually, but...no."

"I'm sorry," he said.

"And you? What have you had for love?"

"I love Grete," he said. "I have loved others. Three or four people, I think. When I was younger. But Grete was the first who could accept me for all that I am. And I realize how rare that is, how lucky."

Anders stood up, and a flock of birds that had gathered around our bench took flight, rising toward the grey sky, startling me, and for one tiny moment I thought he had shattered.

§

The apartment is not as I remember it, because most of the building has been rebuilt. The walls are clean and white, illuminated by light from many windows and from fixtures overhead. The air is fresh, and immediately I miss the old, comforting odor of cigarettes and incense and wine and people, the rich scent that used to relax me the moment I stepped inside. The furniture is much the same, the couch familiar in its hardness, but the doorknobs are all different, and as I wander through the apartment I find myself opening doors, feeling the knobs in my hand, each one smooth and smoothly-turning. I am fascinated by how new the doorknobs feel, free of any past or history, so typically American and out of place here. I laugh at myself, a previously intelligent and cultured man reduced to ruminating on doorknobs.

Grete makes me a cup of tea, and we sit across from each other in the little living room, me on the couch and her in a large chair with worn, red upholstery. I look around the apartment, noticing the framed posters from cabarets and galleries.

"I lost all my pictures in the war," she says. "I have no photographs of anyone. The posters were sent to me by friends in Sweden. They found them in their attic. They forgot they'd put them there."

We sip our tea. She smiles and looks out the window. "There is so much to say. I don't have enough words."

I nod.

"You're the poet," she says. "Words are your business. I make pictures, that's all."

"I haven't written a poem in a very long time," I say.

"Why?"

"Because I couldn't finish the poem for Anders. It's the only one that feels worth writing, but I cannot write it."

I expect her to question me, to prod me, to praise my talent and remind me of something or other that Anders, or even Andrea, might have said on the subject. But she does not.

"It's funny," I say, my voice sounding strangely hollow in my ears. "I've spent every day since he asked me to write it feeling... well, feeling elegiacal. But I could not, I cannot, write..."

I am not a man who cries easily, except at chamber concerts and the conclusions of sentimental motion pictures, but suddenly, surprisingly, tears fill my eyes, and when Grete sits beside me, placing her hand gently on my back, I bow my head and weep.

§

During many evenings, before we would go out for dinner or to see a show, Anders and I spent an hour or two in my apartment, looking through books, reading poems and stories to each other.

He had a lovely voice, high for a man, but his years on the stage had taught him fine articulation, and he had a perfect sense of cadence, so that his readings were the most emotionally affecting, and most natural, I have ever heard. Some of the purest moments of bliss I have experienced were those times when I listened to him and closed my eyes and let the sound of the words wash over me.

"What do you think makes a poem great?" he asked me one night. (We both had a weakness for grand questions.)

"Truth and feeling," I said.

"Doesn't one destroy the other?"

I told him I would need many more days to ponder the topic, and that really the only way to know a good poem was to read one, and so I read him the end of Spenser's "Epithalamion":

> *So when I have with sorrow satisfide*
> *Th' importune fates, which vengeance on me seeke,*
> *And th' heavens with long languor pacifide,*
> *She, for pure pitie of my sufference meeke,*
> *Will send for me; for which I daylie long:*
> *And will till then my painful penance eeke.*
> *Weep, Shepheard! weep, to make my undersong!*

I remember that moment well, because it was the only time Anders seemed truly moved, moved to the point of being unable to speak, by anything that I read to him. Finally, after long silence, he said, "I think we should go out and have a terrible amount of fun."

§

"I always thought you were in love with Anders," Grete says to me. "Fond enough of Andrea, but in love with Anders. Why do you think that was?"

"I don't know," I say. "It's not something that can be understood with logic."

"No," Grete says, "I suppose not. Maybe poetry."

"I'm not sure any words help explain such things."

"Perhaps you should try painting," she says. "For me, the world makes more sense when I can shape it with colors."

"What color would you make me?"

"I'd begin with bright red, and then paint over that with a deep purple, and then cover it all with grey."

§

I first met Andrea at a dinner party at the apartment. She answered the door, handed me a glass of champagne, and led me inside. I noticed her eyes first, because they were as blue as Anders's eyes. "I'm Andrea," she said. She wore a light red dress, and amidst the curls of her blond hair rested a lily.

"Are you a relative of Anders?" I asked.

"Oh yes," she said. "Very much so. But he will not be here tonight."

"Does he have a performance?"

"Of a certain type, yes."

Waiting at the table was Gilbert Barton, a British playwright I'd seen at various parties and gallery openings, a friend of Anders whom I found repulsive. Anders accused me of disliking Barton because he suffered the same disease as Oscar Wilde, but I assured him that I did not much care about that, unfortunate as it was, and that it was Barton's pathetic qualities, as well as his need to dominate a conversation, that made me dislike being in his presence. Grete felt sorry for him, though, because his plays were not popular and his life seemed to be perpetually crumbling into ruins, and Anders told me he liked Barton because he always felt sane and successful when the wretched man was around.

As I stepped into the room, I noticed that Barton's doughy face was red from, I assumed, already having had quite a few glasses of champagne, and he looked like some sort of waterlogged elf. He was regaling Grete with his latest tale of woe. "And then he tells me that because *he's* the director he can change any line he likes, and I tell him no no no *no*, that's not how it works, and he says he's just trying to make the play actually into a comedy, and I tell him that it was a comedy before he got his hands on it but now it is most certainly a tragedy, and a dull one at that—Oh, hello Edward, what are you doing here?"

"I was invited," I said.

He chuckled. "Well, how nice."

We ate salad and steak and drank more champagne. Barton talked about actors and directors, how awful they all were. Andrea and Grete hardly spoke. I made little grunting noises of surprise and approval whenever it seemed necessary, but mostly I focused on drinking champagne. My gaze kept drifting to Andrea while Barton talked, because there was something familiar in the angle of her nose and in the shape of her lips hiding beneath the mask of lipstick and in her eyes.

Later, sitting on the couch with Barton while Grete cleared the table and Andrea slipped off somewhere to get some bottles of wine, I learned the secret that had been kept from me, and that had I been more observant I would have easily discovered on my own.

Barton ran his hand up and down my leg, and when I pushed him away, he said, his voice a vicious whisper, "What do you want then? *Him*?"

I stood up without quite hearing what he had said. Andrea walked into the room then, a bottle of red wine in either hand.

"He's the one you want, isn't he?" Barton said. Andrea stopped. She set the bottles down on the coffee table in front of the couch.

"What are you talking about?" I said.

Andrea said, "Gilbert's being boorish. Just ignore him."

"Gilbert's always boorish," I said.

Barton stood up, unsteadily but successfully, and grabbed Andrea in an embrace. He thrust his hand beneath her dress. "It's still there," he said. Andrea pushed him away and he fell backward, tripping over the side of the couch and banging his head on the coffee table. He lay on the floor, blood from a gash in his forehead pouring over the wooden floor. Andrea ran to the bedroom and closed the door. Grete stood behind me. "I'm sorry," she said, and together we lifted Barton up onto the couch and covered his head with a towel.

"Just go," Grete said to me. "He'll be fine. We'll all be fine."

§

I didn't see Grete and Anders for another week. Nor did I see Andrea. I forced myself to go out during the days, even during early mornings, because the thought of walking the streets at night nauseated me, and often I went to sleep just as the sun slipped low enough in the sky to drench the city in shadows. The bustle of the market at morning comforted me, the noise of voices and the air filled with clashing, mingling scents of meat and fruit and flowers and people. I ate bread and cheese and apples, I drank beer, I avoided the cafés. I sat at a window in my apartment and watched people walking outside. I wrote notes about them on scraps of paper, imaginary portraits—a man with a tattered top hat became a secret agent seeking codes in long-forgotten books hidden in the dust of little shops; a woman with a child wrapped in a shawl in her arms became a mother widowed in the war and still in mourning; a man with a vague face and brown clothes became a movie star from another country. In the little stories I wrote about them, every person on the street was somehow lost and somehow lonely.

I was drinking one last bottle of beer when I heard a gentle knock on the door. I ignored it at first, but then there was another knock, gentle still but more insistent. I heard Anders's voice call my name. I finished the beer. He opened the door.

"Hello?" he said. "Haven't heard from you for a while."

I made some sort of meaningless movement, a nod or a shrug.

"I've wondered how you are," he said. "I'm sorry about what happened with Gilbert. I know you don't like him, and I'm sorry we invited him, but we thought, I don't know…"

"You thought it would be fun to play a joke on me."

"No," Anders said. "There was no joke at all."

"Gilbert getting drunk and insulting me was not a joke? Andrea was not a joke?"

"Andrea is not a joke."

"A little performance, then?"

"No," Anders said. "Not a performance. I wanted to talk to you about that, and I meant to tell you earlier, but it didn't feel right yet, and then… I don't know. I don't always have the best judgment."

"I don't understand anything that you're saying."

"Andrea is me, Edward. Andrea is more me than Anders is."

I am ashamed to admit it now, but I laughed. I was exhausted, a bit drunk, confused, and I laughed. Anders pursed his lips and looked away from me. After a moment of stillness and silence, he walked out of the room without closing the door.

§

Grete and I go to dinner at a basement restaurant where a year ago she helped the owner choose the colors of paint for the walls. Everything is bright: bright reds and yellows, bright green trim along the floor and ceiling and windows. The owner is a young man with a limp and a missing eye and blond hair cut so short he looks bald when he is not standing directly in front of us.

We eat a salad and drink water and white wine.

Before our dessert arrives, Grete says, "I am ill. I have cancer."

"Yes," I say.

"I'm told I have about a month to live, perhaps less. My husband died in the war. We had a daughter, but she was with him. I don't have any possessions to speak of, most of my paintings will be taken care of by the galleries, and the owner of the main gallery will serve as my estate agent. But I would like you to arrange my funeral. If you are willing."

I cannot speak. I want to say, *Yes, of course.* I want to say, *I will do whatever you need.* These are things I should have said to people in the past, and I know I will not get many chances to say them to anyone else during what's left of my life. But I cannot speak.

"I know it is a terrible thing to ask," Grete says. "I do not ask because I want you to write a poem. I do not want a poem. At the funeral, I want to be remembered not merely as myself, but as the woman who loved Anders. I want him to be remembered. And Andrea, too. By someone who can remember them both, and with joy."

My fingers slide across the edge of the table, feeling the sharp angle.

"Can you remember us all? With joy?"

I weave my hands together and hold them in my lap. I whisper my answer: "Yes."

§

"Wait—Anders!" I stood at the top of the stairs and called down to him. He stopped and turned. "I'm sorry," I said, as loudly as I could, the words like cinders in my mouth.

We sat in my room and drank gin. I turned on a small lamp, and in the shadows I could see both Anders and Andrea in his face.

"I am performing tomorrow night," he said after we had talked about Grete and Barton and the time when Andrea had first walked down the street in daylight, terrified of being laughed at, but instead gaining friendly smiles and responses from merchants and shopkeepers of, "Can I help you, miss?" and "Miss, would you like..." A slowly rising comfort with the self that had been so long hidden, so long hurt.

"Performing?"

"At a nightclub. I will be Andrea. Singing." He smiled sweetly, then covered his smile with his hand.

"Are you embarrassed?" I asked.

"No," he said. "Happy. Because you'll be there, won't you?"

"Yes," I said. "Of course I will."

He leaned forward and gave me a soft kiss.

§

Back at the apartment, Grete shows me some of her new paintings. They are small, because she still has trouble finding large canvasses that she can afford, but she says she has enjoyed painting in miniature, it suits her personality now. The paintings are not much larger than postcards. They are more figurative than the paintings of hers I knew from before, the paintings that brought her some fame in certain circles. These are gentle paintings of women in long, flowing dresses, women with hats that cover their eyes, women dancing in the rain.

It is a cold night in the city, a night with a sky of slate. Grete lights candles throughout the apartment instead of turning on the lights. We sit together on the couch.

"Who introduced him to Hirschfeld?" I ask.

"Barton, actually," Grete says. "Gilbert had been to the Institute, had met Hirschfeld a few times. He always said there was more to it, tried to play up their friendship, but the one time I talked to them together, Hirschfeld barely seemed to know him."

"I was not horrified when Anders told me."

"I know."

"He thought I was. He thought I was angry because of the procedure. But that wasn't it."

"I know," Grete says, and rests her head on my shoulder. Soon, she is asleep. The little flames of all the candles flicker and the room shimmers with shadows.

§

In the nightclub, everything was either bright or dark, and most of the brightness huddled near the stage, where Andrea stood in a sparkling blue dress and sang soft songs in a breathy voice, popular tunes of the day, songs that began with innuendo and finished with melancholy, their last notes trailing off as the little pianist bent low and held the keys down until long after the melody had drifted away and the light on Andrea had faded into smoke.

She performed there many times, and I went to every performance. Barton went to some, as did Grete, but both soon grew tired of it, and Barton, thankfully, returned to England.

During the third or fourth week she had been performing, Andrea said to me after the show one night, "Wasn't the audience wonderful? I'm afraid I'll never get to sleep. Let's go for a drink!" And so we ended up at a little bar a few blocks away, a place where actors went after finishing their work, and we drank gin and laughed about the hunger in the eyes of the audience each night, and we tried to forget all that was going on around us.

"Let me take *you* home for once, Edward," she said as we found our way out of the bar.

"You shouldn't walk back alone," I said.

"I'll be fine. It's not far at all."

"I don't think—"

"Oh shush," she said, and we strolled toward my apartment.

"Won't you offer a lady a nightcap?" she said, and I ushered her inside and poured her a bit of whiskey, which was all that I had.

I had recently bought an old phonograph, a beastly large thing that amused me as much for its unwieldiness as for its music. Andrea put a record on and began to dance to it. She pulled me off of the chair where I was sitting and I danced with her. "Isn't this marvelous?" she said, and kissed me.

"Don't walk home alone tonight," I said as the song came to an end.

"What are you so afraid of?" she said.

"It's not safe at night now."

"It's not safe at all anymore." She sat on my bed and I sat beside her. "When you look at me, do you see a man pretending to be a woman, or do you see…something more?"

"Don't worry about what I see," I said. I tried to kiss her, but she stood up. She pulled hairpins out of her hair and let it fall down below her shoulders. She grabbed an old shirt of mine that was sitting on the floor by the bed and wiped her face with it as if she were trying to wipe off her skin as well as the rouge and mascara and eyeshadow. She unzipped her dress and stepped out of it. She removed her underwear.

I sighed and stood up. I touched her arm and let a finger wander up her chest to her neck, her chin, her cheek. "You have," I said, "the most beautiful eyes I've ever seen." She looked away.

I gave her some of my clothes, and she put them on. Anders stood there with tears in his eyes. "Will I be safe now?" he said.

"You can stay here if you'd like."

"No," he said. "I'm sorry. I'm exhausted, I don't know what I'm...I'm sorry—" He picked up Andrea's clothes and walked out into the night.

§

Grete asks me to call her doctor. She is not feeling well. She has no strength or appetite. The doctor arrives and talks with her in a light and cheery voice. He is a small man with a giant mustache. He takes me into the kitchen and tells me she should be in the hospital. I tell him she does not want to be in the hospital, that she wants to die here. He says she will die soon.

While Grete sleeps, I look through the papers she has given me. Mostly they are contracts and old bills and various legal documents, but among them is a letter from Anders, probably the last he wrote:

> *My dearest Grete,*
>
> *Never doubt that I loved you. A complicated love, yes, but the greatest love of my life. I owe you my life. The one regret I have is that I could not be the husband you deserved. The one good thing about being born into the wrong body was that you became my wife. We have a new world ahead of us, and as excited as I am by it, as much as I have wanted it for years and years and years, there is a tinge of sadness, too, because I know that, in some way or another, I am leaving you behind. Never forget me, as I will never forget you.*
>
> *Pleurant, je voyais de l'or—et ne pus boire—*
>
> > *All my love,*
> > *Anders*

§

I stopped going to the performances, and I avoided Anders. He left a note under my door asking me to meet him in our favorite park at noon the next day.

I arrived late, but he was still waiting. He stood beneath a tall tree and smoked a cigarette.

"If this were a melodrama," he said, "I would ask you if you hate me."

"Why should I hate you?" I said.

"I don't know. But suddenly you disappeared. I thought you must be angry."

He offered me a cigarette, and I took it. He lit it with a silver lighter.

"Tell me about you and Grete," I said.

"What do you want to know?"

"Do you love her?"

"Yes. Very much."

"Do you have the regular relations of a husband and wife?"

"Sexual relations, you mean?"

"Yes."

"Sometimes," he said.

"What about Barton? Did you have relations with him?"

"No, of course not." He laughed contemptuously.

"Why of course not?"

"I'm not a homosexual," he said.

"Neither am I."

"Then why are you angry at me?"

I began to walk away, but he grabbed my arm. "Edward, I wanted to talk to you because I want to tell you about a doctor I have met, and what he has told me."

"A doctor?"

"Yes. Who can help me."

"How?"

"There is a procedure. It will give me the body that is natural to me. Andrea's body."

I pulled away from him. I ran away from him.

I stopped. I covered my face with my hands. People probably walked past, but I did not notice them. Eventually, I recovered myself. Anders remained where I had left him. He leaned back against the tree, his face covered with tears. I went to him and embraced him. "I don't want you to be Andrea," I said, even then horrified by how selfish I sounded, how much like a child.

§

Grete lies in her bed, swaddled in blankets, her eyes open, but foggy. She no longer speaks.

"Do you remember going to Venice with Anders?" I say to her. "He said it was to celebrate what was going to happen, to celebrate Andrea, but you also knew it was to say goodbye to him. I was angry when you went. I wanted to go with you, I wanted to share that moment, all those moments you got to have with him. I was so distraught that I didn't understand how awful I was being. I thought I could convince him to save himself. I didn't think about you at all, Grete. I didn't think about you as it was happening. I hurt so much. I wrote him letters. Long letters, sometimes more than one a day. All he sent back were a couple of postcards. You both seemed so happy when you returned, so refreshed and healthy. I hated you then. I thought if you didn't exist, perhaps something different would happen. I blamed you for what I thought he was doing to himself. Killing himself. During the whole time you were in Venice, I imagined one thing after another, fantasies of the life he and I could have together. I thought he would make me strong. I thought we could explore the world together, go hunting in deserts, sleep on the sidewalks of strange cities, without cares and without sorrow. I lived the life of a sleepwalker. I wandered the streets and talked to him, whole conversations I wanted to have with him, all the while everyone looking at me like I was a madman. I wanted to show him America. I wanted to bring him to New York and introduce him to all of my friends, the friends I had abandoned. I could get him work on Broadway and in the movies. I knew I could. I wanted to. I wanted nothing so much as to help him and to make him happy. I wanted him to look at me and smile and laugh, I wanted him to be grateful, because then I would know I had done something worthwhile in this life, I had helped someone, and they loved me, they could love me, and me alone. I was so desperate for someone to love me and only me that I couldn't see what effect this was having, I was blind to how much I wished for, how much I hoped for. I imagined moments when we could sit together, just the two of us, on beaches or in beautiful hotels, sharing moments no-one else would know about. That's all I wanted, Grete. Moments only he and I would know about."

She closes her eyes. All the while I am talking, I think to myself: You mustn't talk, you mustn't remember, you must stop talking, stop remembering, you must stop...

§

After he returned from Venice, Anders came to see me. I asked him if he had gotten my letters, and he said he had.

"I'm worried about you, Edward."

"About me? How can you worry about me?"

"You have built up some idea of me that I don't understand," he said. "You have imagined me as something, someone...I don't know."

I took his hand. "Please," I said, "don't say anything."

"I don't want to hurt you, but I have to speak. You are trying to box me into being someone I'm not. You are pushing our friendship toward something unnatural, something beyond what it would be if you would relax and let things happen as they will happen. I begin the procedure next week, Edward, and that will change everything."

I let go of his hand. I turned away from him. "Please don't do it," I said.

"I have to do it. It is all I want in the world."

"Anders—"

"Anders is dead. Don't talk to me about Anders anymore."

My bones ached as I struggled to keep from screaming. I stood with my fists clenched and every muscle in my body taut. He put his hand on my shoulder, but I pulled away.

"I'm sorry," he said. "I never wanted to hurt you."

As he walked away, I whispered, "Please don't forget me."

§

We only met one more time. At a café, of course. I had ignored the notes he sent and I locked the door when he came to my apartment. It was not because I hated him, though I'm sure he thought that. It was to preserve myself. A thousand thoughts and ideas flashed through my mind in those days, all the shards of shattered fantasies that I barely understood. My intellect and my emotions had been severed from each other. Waves of sorrow filled me, raising questions in my mind: What had I wanted from him? Why had I behaved as I had? If I had gotten all that I wanted, what then? What was the all that I wanted?

I made plans to return to America. I contacted friends, I reserved a berth on a ship.

I don't know why I answered the door that day when I had not answered it any of the days before. Any of the other knocks could have been the last, but somehow I knew this one was.

He asked if we could talk. He said he had a request. He invited me to a café. I did not speak, but I followed him out.

He said he would begin the first surgery the next day. We ordered coffee and ate sugary pastries. He laughed as I got sugar all over my fingers and chin.

"Will you write me a poem?" he said.

I finished the pastry and did not look at him.

"A poem for Anders," he said. "An elegy."

I brushed the sugar off my fingers and stood up. I did not look at him. "Yes," I said.

As I walked into my apartment, my legs were shuddering so violently that I fell to the floor. I rolled onto my side and hugged my knees to my chest and squeezed my eyes closed as tightly as I could, trying to obliterate the world.

§

I did not return to America then. I cancelled the reservation on the ship, I told my friends I needed more time. In truth, I was embarrassed, and I did not want anyone who had known me before—who had known me as the famous poet and the delight of all the best parties—to see me as I was now, devastated and confused, ashamed of all that I had felt and thought. Also, I'm sure that somewhere within the snarled knot of my emotions was curiosity about and even concern for Anders and Andrea. I would not have admitted it to anyone, including myself, but I wanted to see the results of the doctor's magic procedure.

I received a letter:

Dear Edward,

It is Andrea who writes to you now. Forever
Andrea. I wanted you to know that the first operation

*went well, and that though I am tired and in some
pain, I am also excited and full of joy. I am sitting
here right now wearing a silk nightdress and a pearl
necklace (of all things!). They were both presents from
Grete, who is here with me. I will soon be moved to
the women's hospital for the major part of the procedure. I hope you are well. Please remember the poem
that Anders asked you to write. I know you cared
about him deeply, and that you care about me, and
I do not have the words to tell you how much such a
poem would mean to us, or how much you, my dear
Edward, meant to Anders and mean to me. Please
take care of yourself. I look forward to seeing you on
my return.*

Your Andrea

Six months later, Andrea returned to the city from the clinic
where she had been convalescing. For a month, I avoided seeing
her, making one excuse after another, despite phone calls and letters
from her and from Grete. I wanted to be sure I would respond in
only the best way, and that I would not foist my disappointments
onto her, because there was nothing either of us could do about it
now. Finally, I called Grete and asked her and Andrea to meet me
at our favorite park.

She looked vaguely different from how she had looked before,
like meeting a woman who you've only seen in magazine pictures.
We embraced and kissed and cried together for a moment and then
laughed at ourselves. Grete stood on one side of me and Andrea on
the other, and we all held hands as we walked through the park.

Andrea continued singing at the cabaret, and I went to see her
whenever I could, but I had decided definitely to return to America,
and there were people to say goodbye to and dinners to attend and

arrangements to make, so I did not see her or Grete as often as I wished, and then one day we were all standing at the docks together, and I was walking up onto the ship and waving goodbye and watching the city drift away over the dark horizon.

Andrea rented a small room in the city, and Grete began to put a new life together for herself. They both sent me postcards and letters. Andrea did her best to keep her tone light and optimistic. She said she felt younger, that it seemed her entire brain had been changed as well as her body, that the last remnants of Anders had died and a new emotional life had arisen within her. But sometimes I perceived a sadness beneath her words. She hinted that many of Anders's friends spurned her, and she suggested that she was having trouble finding work other than singing at the cabaret, a job that no longer paid well. She said she worried about the political situation, but more for Grete than herself, because Grete was better known and might be targeted by the government. She said her health was not always good. She said she missed me and hoped I would be able to visit again soon. She did not mention the poem.

Grete told me the story of Anders's change had begun to circulate in the newspapers. So far, very few good photographs of Andrea had been taken, so she was able to walk down the streets without being recognized. The cabaret tried to publicize her, but she quit, saying she wanted to be known for her singing, nothing else. She had not found another job, but at least she was not hiding away in her little room every day. Thanks to Dr. Hirschfeld's advocacy, Andrea's legitimation papers had come through, and she was now officially allowed to use her name and sex on legal documents. Grete said that Andrea seemed to have a new group of friends, and even a man who paid some attention to her, a man who knew her history. Grete said that Andrea had talked to a doctor about what sort of operation might allow her to become a mother.

And then I received a short note from Andrea telling me that she was very sick, and that she was in a hospital. She said that she thought death was near, but that she did not have any regrets. She said she had dreamed of her mother, who had died long ago, and that in the dream her mother came to her and embraced her and told her that she loved her.

The next week, Grete sent a short note to let me know that Andrea had died of paralysis of the heart.

§

It is a gloriously bright and sunny day. We stand in the cemetery, Grete's few friends and I and the minister, and they wait for me to speak. We stand near where we believe Andrea's grave was; we will never know for sure, because this area was destroyed during the war.

I brought a stanza of Edmund Spenser to read in case I could not think of any words of my own, but I do not have the will to read it.

I step back, silent.

The coffin is lowered into the grave.

I look out over the city and hold in my hand the yellowed piece of hospital stationary on which Andrea, too weak to speak, had written her final words. I found the paper lying on the table beside the bed where Grete died. The handwriting is uneven and the ink is faded almost to nothing, but I can make out the words well enough, and as I stand here and read them again and again above a city of ruins saturated with the past, I know now what Anders and Andrea wanted from me, and why they thought it required a poem, because only a poem can begin to answer the question Andrea wrote on that paper, the question I know will haunt me until I am able to leave this horrible world: *What did I do to deserve so much love?*

Mrs. Kafka

When I escaped Prague in 1939, I brought with me a sheaf of notes from my time as a doctor at the Prague Asylum—notes primarily concerned with a single patient, a woman whose name has been lost to time, but whom we at the Asylum referred to as Mrs. Kafka. I don't remember what impelled me to stuff those notes into my valise. They were not complete. I grabbed what I could in my last moments at the Asylum, and again in my last moments before escaping across one border and then another and another. I'm not even sure of the notes' exact order, for I was careless with dates in those days, though it is clear from the internal evidence that some come before or after the others.

I had not sat down to read through the notes with any care until recently, as I was putting my papers in order for a cadre of graduate students who insist that their research depends on knowing the details of my biography. I expect it would be best to classify these notes as fiction—narratives where metaphor must stand for a reality that cannot be recovered. Tell the world that, like many naïve young men of privilege, I dreamed of creating literature. Or tell them something else. I don't care. It's too late to matter to me.

With the knowledge that at one time I thought these notes were as meaningful as my life, I present them here for you. I have numbered them merely to show their separations and to allow convenient reference should it be needed. They are, as so much else in my memory of that time, without inherent order until the end.

1.

Mrs. Kafka attacked a patient today. She said the other patient insisted on impersonating Archduke Ferdinand. She said if I would give her a gun, she would make him a better impersonator. When I reminded her that she cannot have weapons of any sort, that none of the patients can, she said she admired my will to change history, that it was an endearing quality, like the laughter of a little child, and that it would doom me.

2.

An extended session of analysis with Mrs. Kafka. Highlights from much circular discussion:

Q: How are you?

A: In spite of insomnia, headaches, worries? Better, perhaps, than before.

Q: What do you worry about?

A: Easier to say what I don't.

Q: All right. What *don't* you worry about?

A: Nothing.

Q: Really?

A: Why would I worry about nothing? By definition, it doesn't exist.

Q: You're clever.

A: Now you're being patronizing.

Q: Not intentionally.

A: People think intentions are important.

Q: Aren't they?

A: I fart on intentions. And my farts are intentional.

Q: What do you prefer to intentions?

A: Fruity wine. Lots of fruity wine. Nobody accuses you of intentions if you have enough fruity wine.

Q: Intentions are something to be accused of?

A: Of course.

Q: Can you explain?

A: Were you dropped on your head at birth? Anybody with half a brain can tell you intentions lead to misery, misery, misery. Stop intending. Look at all the people here, the ones you've locked me up with. They're full of intentions. A lot of good it does them. Look at the stupid Austrian. What is he but an intention machine? There's the problem. There's every problem.

3.

Mrs. Kafka: I may be a Jew, but—

Q: Are you a Jew?

Mrs. Kafka: I may be. One day. Depends who's taking notes. You distracted me. What are you writing there? What was I saying? Oh yes. I am glad I will never be an Indian.

Q: A Red Indian?

Mrs. Kafka: Red, green, blue Indian. Any Indian. Once they call you an Indian, they try to destroy you. That's how you know they're after you. Look at America. Where are the Indians? The ones in Buffalo Bill's show, they're not Indians, they're Spanish Mexicans. Nobody would pay money to see an Indian perform, especially not with guns, even toy guns, even guns that just smoke and couldn't harm a fly. Nobody gives Indians guns. They'd shoot you, the Indians would. Who could blame them? So if you have a gun, you're not an Indian, because they won't give Indians guns. And then look at the Indians in India. Do you know how many Indians will have starved to death under British rule? Guess. You can't guess. You'll never guess high enough. You'll think I'm exaggerating, but check the numbers later, twenty-five years from now, and you'll find out. Thirty million. Thirty million dead Indians in India. Another how many dead Indians in America—North America, South America, all America. Everywhere you look, dead Indians. Don't ever let anybody call you an Indian, no matter what.

4.

Mrs. Kafka has resisted talking about her husband. Even the most casual question receives silence and a scowl. Today, though, she stood on a chair in the dining room and announced that she was ready to give a speech. None of us had notebooks or recording equipment ready, thus we were not able to record most of what she said verbatim, but it was quite repetitive, so I can write here a general summary.

Marriage, Mrs. Kafka said, is a bourgeois institution designed first of all to determine the lineage of property and then to allow people to control each other and to be controlled, whether husband controlling wife or wife controlling husband or the state or the church controlling the married couple. No human being, she said, would choose marriage in a free and open society. The extent to which someone desires marriage demonstrates the extent to which they have succumbed to the oppression of the state and the church. Marriage is an institution that channels our fear of freedom and allows us to indulge our desire for slavery in a socially acceptable way.

5.

Despite her antipathy to marriage and her determination not to talk about her husband, Mrs. Kafka demonstrates no repression with regard to sexual topics. The opposite, in fact. She has scandalized more than one nurse with her jokes and stories.

Yesterday, Mrs. Kafka told me: "When I was a child, I brought my mother's porcelain penis to school and told everyone on the playground that it was a lollipop. Half of them had licked it before the teacher caught me."

6.

"You wouldn't know," Mrs. Kafka said, "because you were a physician out in the middle of nowhere, but Prague used to be a city of bears. It's because of the circuses. There were circuses in all the outlying areas. For a while, it seemed, everyone you knew was in a circus. But it was the bears who especially loved Prague. You would see them every morning, riding their unicycles to work. They were majestic. You would wave at them, or tell them how beautiful they were, and they would nod sagely, but never more. The children were sad that the bears would not wave back at them. The bears were gregarious with each other, especially after dusk, when they returned to the city and filled the bars that nobody else ever went to at night. Often, we stared through the windows. The bears knew we were watching them, but I don't think they were performing for us. I think they genuinely loved each other, loved being in each other's company in the soft light of the gas lamps of the seedier bars in the city. We wanted them to love us, but we were fools."

7.

A breakthrough in analysis this afternoon: For the first time since I have been her consulting physician, Mrs. Kafka wept.

8.

Q: Would you like to be a wolf?

A: That's stupid. You can't be *one* wolf.

Q: How many wolves can you be?

A: Eight or nine, at least. Maybe six or seven. But not all yourself. Together. The pack. One wolf among others.

Q: Do you dream of wolves?

A: No, I dream of a desert.

Q: Are you in the desert?

A: No, I see the desert. But it is not a desert as we imagine an uninhabited, empty desert, desolate or sad or anything like that. It's a desert because it is the color of desert. In a dream, if something is the color of something, then it is that thing, at least partially. That's how you know you're dreaming, because the colors are so rich, because of all the somethings that the color includes.

Q: I'm not sure I follow.

A: I didn't ask you to follow. It's a desert because it is the color of a desert. And there's a sun, a very hot sun. (Not all deserts have a hot sun, of course, but this one does.) There's a crowd of people, a huge mass of them, rippling and undulating. And bees. A swarm of bees across the desert. Also, a team of athletes, a horde of them, ball players and wrestlers. I am on the very edge of every swarm and horde and crowd, but I am part of it because of one small appendage, a hand, a finger, a foot or a toe, something like that. I can only be there, outside the crowd, the swarm. It's very difficult not to be engulfed. All of my energy goes to that. The swarm moves, the crowd presses forward and then back and then sideways, the horde is chaos. I keep a molecule of myself in each, but it takes all my effort, all my concentration, because they do not move in any pattern, their movements cannot be predicted. North, east, west, south. They swirl. None of the pieces of the crowd, the swarm, none of them remain in the same relation to each other, that is what causes all the movement and what makes it so unpredictable. It's perpetual motion, endless tension, endless effort to stay there on the periphery. But I have never felt more happiness than in this dream.

A violent, vertiginous, eternal joy. When I awoke, I could not stop crying. I am still crying now, but I have no tears.

9.

Mrs. Kafka tells me I should let her travel to Zürau, where she says she always got the best postcards. I asked her why she needs postcards, and she said everybody needs postcards, and that I was the stupidest person she had ever met, and whatever college of charlatans gave me a degree ought to be burned to the ground and laughed at. I told her I could get her postcards from the city. She said Prague hadn't had any good postcards in twenty years and therefore she must go to Zürau. I said that was out of the question. I said I would see if I knew somebody in Zürau or near it and if they would send some postcards for her. She said that would never work because Zürau is full of mice, and the people there don't understand about mice, and so they let them do whatever they want, the mice, which ruins most of the postcards. You can't be from Zürau if you want to find the best postcards, because if you're from Zürau you think postcards covered in mouse droppings are no different from other postcards.

10.

Remarks by Mrs. Kafka this week:

—Cut flowers are terribly thirsty. You must water them. Without water, your pills stick in my mouth like splintered glass. Once upon a time, I was able to drink a large gulp of water. Now, I'd just choke. You need to pay particular attention to the peonies, because they are the most fragile. Please spray them lightly.

—Do you like wines, Doctor? Have you ever tried Heurigen?

—Bismark also had his own doctor, and he was just as annoying as you.

—A lake doesn't flow into anything. That's what makes it a lake.

—You need to buy a little book about these matters. You need to know these things.

—We get three copies of each newspaper twice a week. There's not enough time.

—Every limb is as tired as a person.

11.

Q: What did you say?

A: Wrestling-matches.

Q: You said something after that.

A: With the late ancestors.

Q: I don't understand.

A: [silence]

12.

A terrible smell came from Mrs. Kafka's sleeping area. One of the nurses told me she had found dried feces hidden beneath Mrs. Kafka's bed. When the nurse tried to clean up the feces, Mrs. Kafka attacked her.

Mrs. Kafka was in restraints when I talked with her.

Q: Why did you want to save those?

A: My children.

Q: I don't understand.

A: They are my children. I made them. They came out of me. I am their mother. Their names are Ludwig, Bella, Sergei, Thomas, Anastasia, Emily, Sasha, Ludwig the Second, Otla, Catherine, Ramses, Matthew, Mark, and Luke. Where are they now?

Q: I'm afraid we had to dispose of them. We need to be hygienic.

She screamed for over an hour, until her voice was no more, and then she chewed her tongue and the insides of her mouth and spat blood at us until we filled her mouth with bandages.

13.

Mrs. Kafka has no family that visits her. I have sent letters to the names and addresses in the records, seeking more information and encouraging the addressees to get in touch with me. The letters have been returned as undeliverable. I have ventured out to the addresses myself. All the buildings are empty.

14.

A: You only like women with sad, dark eyes.

Q: Why do you say that?

A: They leave their necks uncovered. They call out to you. They press themselves against you. They take your hand, caress you, they kiss you. They mark you with their teeth. They violate you. They suffocate you. Sometimes, they beat you. They are tyrants for a time, but then they let you go, and you go away, or they make you go, they chase you off like you're some sort of animal. A pathetic animal. A rodent, vermin.

Q: We're done for today.

15.

Mrs. Kafka smiled at me this morning when I arrived on the floor. I asked her how she was feeling. She said I would be fine. I asked her again how she felt. She said the next decade would be a difficult one for me, certainly, but I have the sort of selfishness one needs for self-preservation. I was tired, for I hadn't slept well (I haven't slept well for quite some time), and I did not have a good reply or another question, and she seemed to know this, for she walked away, off to the other side of the building where there is a window she particularly likes, and she didn't say another word to me all day.

16.

We have given Mrs. Kafka a pencil and some paper. She has been calm for a few weeks now, and so it seems safe for her to have access to such things. I'm not sure she has had writing utensils before—certainly, not during my time treating her, because of the fear that she would stab someone with the pencil or draw obscene pictures or write terrible words. But I thought it could be useful for her progress. So far, she has shown no interest.

17.

Mrs. Kafka wrote me a poem in English:

> *The turkeys have escaped the farms!*
> *The farmers are all up in arms!*
> *Call the rollers of big cigars!*
> *Call the drivers of fancy cars!*
> *Call the soldiers and gendarmes!*
> *Sound the sirens and alarms!*
> *Close the restaurants and bars!*
> *Go to Venus, go to Mars!*
> *Escape from animalistic charms!*
> *The turkeys have escaped the farms!*

(I cannot read more than the most basic English. One of the other doctors is translating the poem into German for me.)

"Where did you learn English?" I asked Mrs. Kafka.

"Is it English?" she said.

"Yes," I said.

"I never knew," she said.

"But you wrote it, yes?"

"Of course. That's my handwriting. Those are my words. I'm hardly illiterate, you arrogant country bumpkin. Are you drunk? Do you just sit around drinking vodka all day, like some lazy Communist, spewing drivel about the working classes while profiting from their labor? You goddamn fucking Bolshevik! I remember Kronstadt, you fucker! Trotsky will die with an ice pick through the frozen sea of his brain! *Arriba, arriba!* Trotsky will die and no-one will cry, and no-one will cry, and no-one will cry! *Dónde están los Trotskistas?*"

I held the poem out in front of her to stop her rant. "You didn't know you wrote it in English? Was it something you had memorized?"

She took a moment to catch her breath. "You caught me, doc. I wrote it. It just happened to be in English. I never gave it any thought. I wanted to give you a poem. I thought maybe then you'd show me your penis. You're not circumcised, are you? That will save you in the end."

I pointed to the poem. "This is in English, but you don't speak English?"

"Who said that? Do you know one of the words for *rooster* in English?"

"You seemed surprised when I told you the poem is in English."

"English, English, English. You really were dropped on your head at birth, weren't you?" Her face filled with contempt, and she walked away.

An hour later, she found me in my office. She spoke in English. I turned on the recording machine and my colleague later translated what she said: "Build bombs. That's what we need to do, us Indians. We need lots and lots of bombs. If we can put them on storks, we can send the bombs to England, and we'll wipe them all out. It's the least we owe them. Wipe out England, then get more bombs and more storks and head to America. Warn the Japs about wooden buildings. We learned, and they can benefit from our learning. Don't build cities from wood. They all go up in flames. Indians never learn that. Indians think lumber is magic. This is how I know

I'm an Indian. Indians can only speak English, because we bombed England and saved the words, and we all believe lumber is magic."

My colleague handed me his translation and said, "I don't think she understands English very well."

18.

Mrs. Kafka gave me a note this morning in English:

> *I'm sorry for what I said. When I am angry, my words*
> *are wrong. Thank you for giving me something to write*
> *with. I have found a language north of the future. It*
> *can never be translated. English is a bloody language,*
> *but German tastes like ash. Do not try to translate.*
> *I would be grateful if you could find someone to*
> *teach me a few words in a much older language, a*
> *more forgotten one. Czech is terribly stupid. I have*
> *forgotten all the Hebrew I learned as a child. It seemed*
> *like a good thing to do at the time. Do you know any*
> *Sumerian? Can you find someone to help me? I need a*
> *minor language. These other words will kill me.*

My colleague translated it, again protesting that Mrs. Kafka's knowledge of English seemed to him irregular, though he could not say how, because it has been many years since he had heard a native speaker.

I showed the translation to Mrs. Kafka at our session in the afternoon:

A: I didn't write that.

Q: I know. You wrote in English. But is this a valid translation?

A: Of course not.

Q: Why of course not?

A: I would rather talk to you about Oedipus.

Q: Let's stay on track.

A: Oedipus is everything.

Q: What does Oedipus have to do with the note you gave me?

A: Are you, a doctor, in this place and time, here, now, seriously asking me that?

Q: I'm beginning to suspect you change the subject whenever we get close to anything that has meaning for you.

A: Then talk about Oedipus.

Q: What does Oedipus mean to you?

A: Mommy, daddy, me.

Q: Could you explain?

A: That is the explanation.

Q: How so?

A: You're the doctor. You're the one who is supposed to believe it as the truth, the explanation. Not me. I'm the patient, the victim of your—your—your [in English:] *words, your metaphors.* [German:] Why am I doing your work for you? Oedipus! Oedipus, Oedipus, Oedipus!

Q: You don't believe in Dr. Freud's ideas, is that what you're saying?

A: Freud knows nothing about wolves. Or anuses, for that matter. Someone will write that one day in French, I'm sure of it.

Q: What is the relationship? Wolves and anuses, I mean.

A: Clever, doctor. You want me to say that because I shat out my children, I am not able to be a wolf-mother. You forget the pack, the horde, the crowd, the swarm. It's always moving. In English they can say, "Still moving," which is a perfect paradox, and exactly the nature of the swarm. There is not one wolf. Give me back my children. Dr. Freud is dead now.

Q: As far as I know, actually, he's still alive.

A: It doesn't matter. September, that's what matters. September is the end.

Q: The end of what?
A: Oedipus. Everything.

19.

Mrs. Kafka has told every nurse she's seen today that she thinks the Asylum needs to show motion pictures. I visited her this evening and asked if there is a reason why the movies have become, suddenly, so important to her.

"They were always important," she said. "Especially their French titles. They drew me in. I knew the weekly programs of all the cinematographs by heart, even the weeks when I didn't go because I was too busy. But I went often. I would always seek out a picture with a French title. I could never resist."

"Do you remember any of the titles?" I asked.

"Of course," she said. "I cannot pronounce them. I remember their letters, so lovely and alien and graceful, but I never knew their sounds." She wrote me a list:

> *La Leçon du gouffre*
> *L'Enfant de Paris*
> *Le galant de la Garde française*
> *Un intrigue à la cour de Henri VII*
> *Pêche au hareng en mer du nord*
> *La Tournée du docteur*
> *La Broyeuse de coeurs*

"I don't know that we can get any French pictures right now," I said.

"It doesn't matter," she said.

"But I thought you wanted to see movies."

"They're ghosts. Dust and ashes, a nitrate memory. Except the last. You might be able to find that one somewhere. You'd like it. The woman is a dancer. She's beguiling. She entrances a man named Pierre. He tries to resist, but he cannot escape the maelstrom of her seduction. *Maelstrom* is the word the advertisements used, and I always remembered it. He puts off a visit to his fiancé because of the dancer. He goes to a café with her, and then, suddenly, right there in front of them in the café stands the fiancé and her mother. Pierre is destroyed. The fiancé will never speak to him again. The dancer laughs and flirts with another man, a *torero*, who then proclaims his love and tries to send her a letter, saying he will let the bull kill him if she does not respond to his love. Pierre intercepts the letter. He does not pass it on. The *torero* throws himself onto the horns of the bull. The dancer and Pierre are horrified, and they realize how brittle—how shallow— is their love. They part, and Pierre's fiancé forgives him and kisses him on the forehead. What becomes of the dancer, we'll never know."

"It sounds wonderful," I said. "I'll see if there are any theatres that are showing it."

"There aren't," she said. "There won't be. It doesn't matter."

20.

Mrs. Kafka asked if she can borrow a typewriter. I offered that she could use the typewriter in my office in the afternoon, if she desired. She did, and visited me just before 4pm. She said nothing. I gestured to the typewriter and paper. She walked to the desk, rolled a piece of paper into the machine, and typed very slowly, deliberately, as if she were terrified to hit the wrong key. This is what she typed (in German):

If I am not the typist, I am the paper the keys strike.

She smiled, thanked me, and walked back to whatever she had been doing before.

21.

She handed me a slip of paper on which she had written, in pencil:

> *These are the last German words I will write. Writing makes me more and more fearful. (This is what you want to know, isn't it, Doctor? My emotions?) Writing in German is the worst. Every word is twisted by the hands of spirits—their characteristic gesture—and the words twist against me, the one who writes. Most especially when I write like this. Et cetera et cetera. Ad infinitum. (My father died in a madhouse.) The only consolation: It happens whether I like it or not. What I "like" is of no help to me. Better than consolation: I, too, have weapons.*

Her eyes were full of tears. I asked her gently if she would like to talk about this, but she shook her head vehemently and held her hand out, seemingly without volition, to keep me away.

22.

I continue to try to raise the subject of Mrs. Kafka's husband. She refuses to talk to me at all.

I always ask gently, but the more time I spend with her, the more I think the key to so much of what she has become is her husband and, especially, what happened that night. The police report is frustratingly vague. I must get her to tell me in her own words. I must be stubborn, persistent, vigilant.

23.

If I do not bring up the subject of her husband, she will talk to me.

If I mention her husband and she is in a good mood, or feels she has something important to communicate to me, she will continue to talk, but without acknowledging the question.

More often than not, she simply stops talking.

I have found the key, but I do not know how to insert it into the lock.

24.

A: There will be pictures of the Austrian as a child. You should study these. Put them beside the other pictures, the terrible ones. You have no idea how many terrible, frightful pictures are coming. You will all look at them, but you won't see them. You must try, though. Even if you can't see and you know you can't see, you must try. Promise me? Look into the child's eyes. Could those eyes see the other pictures? Could Dr. Freud's eyes see through the child's eyes?

Q: I don't understand.

A: I know. That is your best quality. It's why I talk to you.

Q: Did your husband understand you?

A: At the end of winter, everything will be terrible.

25.

The police report describes an altercation, reports by neighbors of overheard screams, but the reports differ about whether the screams were those of a man or a woman. The witnesses all insist that their own testimony is true.

What the police found: A man dead, a woman covered in blood, no murder weapon.

That is all that is known.

26.

They are here.

After the Sudetenland, we of course knew this was an eventuality. But I cannot reconcile myself to the words as I write them—

They are here.

27.

The asylum is abandoned now. I knew to stay away, I had received all the warnings, the official notices. My services were no longer needed. A single official piece of paper cast me into another world.

Within this world, though, there are gaps, and I fit through them as best I could in the middle of the night and made my way back to collect a few last things at the office, a place which, officially, did not exist for me.

The entire building was infested with insects, more insects than I knew were in Prague, endless lines of insects on the walls and floors and ceilings, making the building seem alive, its solid masses shimmering. I lit my pipe and blew smoke to clear the way, a pathetic gesture, but not nothing. I found papers and books and set them alight to scatter the creatures. I made my way slowly, up and up the endless steps to my office.

Mrs. Kafka remained. I found her in the kitchen, frying cockroaches. She held a wooden mallet in her hand and slammed it onto the counter, crushing the bugs. She peeled the carcasses off the counter and dropped them into a pan on the stove. She looked older than she ever had.

"Come with me," I said. "I can save you."

"No," she said, "you can't. It's kind of you, though."

"Come with me. You must come with me."

She smashed the mallet down again.

"You think these are cockroaches, don't you?" she said. She held a carcass to her tongue. "You are no entomologist. These are dung beetles." She bit it in half.

"We must go now," I said. I took her arm, but with far more strength than I would ever have imagined she could summon, she pushed me back, and I stumbled and fell to the floor—roaches and beetles and spiders and earwigs crawled through my clothes, over my skin, and the only thing that kept me from screaming was the knowledge that if I opened my mouth, it would fill with vermin.

I stood quickly, frantically brushing the creatures from my body. "Let me help you," Mrs. Kafka said. She picked the insects off of me and flung them into the darkness, where it seemed, though it could not possibly be true, that they transformed into moths and butterflies. My mind rattled, though, and I did not trust my senses.

My clothes were shredded, my skin covered in scratches and welts, but the insects had retreated.

"You must go," Mrs. Kafka said.

Somehow, I made my way through the flames and the smoke. Somehow, I drifted into the night, past the guards and the police, home. Sirens screamed behind me as the Prague Asylum burned.

I am writing this in a café in Paris. Across the street stands a cinema where two films play: *La règle du jeu* and *La Broyeuse de coeurs*. I wish I had time to see them, but I don't. I must be gone before September.

I will get my things together, I will pay some bribes and collect some documents, and I will board a ship and sail across the ocean to the harbor of Boston, and then I will travel south by rail across a high range of mountains, watching the narrow, somber valleys, rough and ragged, open out on either side of me, and I will see mountain streams rise among the rocks, crashing down in waves

to the foothills, plunging under bridges as our train rushes over—
and a chilly wind will howl from the darkness, and all of us who
are passengers will shiver, and we will cling to each other, living
by each other's breaths, but then dawn will vanquish the darkness
and the train will rise from the valley and in that morning of our
future I will see sunlight fall on the Statue of Liberty as she holds
her sword aloft.

Where's the Rest of Me?

Cowboy From Brooklyn

It was the end of May, 1937, and Ron Reagan was up against a deadline. He'd promised a yarn to the editor at *Astounding Stories*, and he was out of ideas. People knew him as the guy who wrote about alien invasions, but he didn't feel much like writing about alien invasions right now, and anyway, he thought it would be a good idea to avoid getting too typecast. He should write a western. Enough with these space stories. Why did he keep writing space stories, anyway? He'd always liked reading the westerns, and just because he'd grown up in Brooklyn and never ridden a horse in his life didn't mean he couldn't come up with five or ten thousand words of something. But first he had to write this space story.

Love Is On The Air

"He was a good-looking guy, and nice, and a bit naïve, and so I fell for him," Jane Wyman told their son later. "We all make mistakes. Hindsight being twenty-twenty and all that. But what could I do? I was a bit player in unpopular radio shows. He was a failed writer trying to get work as an entertainment reporter. We had lunch and talked about our dreams. We were just kids, really. I'd never even seen a man naked before. How was I to know…anything?"

Accidents Will Happen

Ron didn't often go to the sorts of bars where he'd meet men like Alejandro, but at least a few nights a week he could get away from the apartment and Jane and the kids. He always told her he was going out to wander around and try to come up with ideas for something to write. That was true most of the time, but he never told her the sorts of places he wandered to. Friday night he'd found his way beneath Brooklyn Bridge; Sunday he strolled over to a parking lot on West Street; tonight it was this basement bar a few blocks off Washington Square. He told himself this was research, that he'd be able to write an article for one of the slicks and maybe then turn it into a book, something about the difficulties of doughboys home from the war, the trauma of returning to ordinary life, the temptations offered by months and years among men. He told himself he was attracted to this bar because it was quiet, because the men inside seemed respectable, because he needed a stiff drink after all of Jane's complaints about him being aloof and there being bills to pay and why didn't he get a real job and stop writing one-cent-a-word crap. He told himself it would just be for a few minutes, a quick drink, nothing serious.

The Fight For The Sky

He'd made the June 1 deadline for the story by working through the night, but he hadn't heard anything from Tremaine for a few months, so Ron stopped by the Street & Smith offices on 7th Avenue (a few blocks from the women's prison) one hot, humid afternoon. F. Orlin Tremaine, editor of *Astounding Stories,* sat in a dusty office amidst piles of paper of all sorts—manuscripts, newspapers, magazines, stray pages from books. The office smelled of tobacco and wood pulp, making the already-oppressive air nearly gelatinous. "Reagan, right?" Tremaine said. "You sent us a story?" Ron said he'd published three stories with *Astounding* over the previous eighteen months, and that Mr. Tremaine himself had requested a story of 5,000 words to fill a hole he had in an upcoming issue, and he wondered if the story that he'd brought down to the office on June 1 was acceptable or if there was something perhaps wrong with it. "Story?" Tremaine said. "I asked for a story? Really. Don't remember that, sorry. Sure it was me? I don't really do that, son. You've probably got me confused with somebody over at *Amazing* or *Wonder Stories*." Ron said he was sure it was him; he would never forget a request from *Astounding*, as their pay was better than the others. The title of the story was "The Fight for the Sky", and it came in at almost exactly 5,000 words. "Sent in June?" Tremaine said. "June, June, June…" He riffled through piles of papers and envelopes. "Ah! June! Yes. Okay. Right. Your story. Sorry, it fell into the Big Middle." Ron was not familiar with the term. "I'm filling magazines here," Tremaine said. "I've got *Astounding*, I've got *Clues*, I've got *Top-Notch*. So each month when I need to fill 'em, I sit down with a pile of stories and go through 'em until I've got all the puzzle pieces put together. But I need to be fair to my writers, don't I? So I turn the stacks over and the next month I start from the bottom. It's an excellent system, I must say, and eminently fair, except that it has one side-effect, as all excellent systems do, and that side-effect is that it creates a Big Middle, and I'm afraid sometimes, unfortunately, stories get stuck in the Big Middle. As yours did. I'm very sorry for that. I'll move it to the top and get back to you soon. Have a good day, Mr. Reagan."

Prisoner Of War

"At some point," Jane said after yet another night broken not by the screams of the baby but of her husband, "don't you think it would be a good idea to maybe try to talk about what happened over there?"

Storm Warning

Ron didn't dare stay all night at Alejandro's grimy apartment very often, but Jane was getting more and more work out in Los Angeles, and the children, now seven and five years old, were perfectly happy with her parents in Cleveland. Jane told her mother that she and Ron hoped to buy a house in Ohio soon because it was such a better place to bring up children than New York or California, a statement which Jane's mother assumed meant that Ron's drinking had become a problem again. Though he missed his children, Ron had no other complaints about the arrangement, because it meant he and Alejandro were able to spend real time together, and nobody bothered him about his smoking or his drinking or how he spent his days. Alejandro's apartment was a single room at 45 Grove Street, relatively big for what he paid in rent, with huge windows, good light, and plenty of space for an easel and canvases.

An Angel From Texas

After Jane found his collection of Alejandro's postcards from Cuernavaca, she insisted Ron see a shrink. He said it was all just for work, that he had a big article he was doing that had a good shot at the *Saturday Evening Post* or *Collier's*, a real exposé, and he'd needed to get to know some of these freaks, these perverts, he needed them to trust him so that he could write about them and their world, that's what writers do, as she ought to goddamn well understand by now. "You can see a psychoanalyst or a divorce lawyer," Jane said. "One or the other. Make your choice." He threatened divorce for days. She packed a suitcase for him. "Fine," he said, "I'll find a shrink. I ought to get a professional's point of view on this stuff anyway. For my article." He looked through the phone book and went to a few different appointments but every one made him feel like a criminal. Jane wouldn't let him quit. She went to each appointment with him and waited outside. Dr. Mac McClure was the fourth. He was six feet tall, three hundred pounds, wore cowboy boots that he rested on his desk, and spoke with an accent he swore was west Texan. A steer's skull hung above his massive desk. There was no couch in his office, only a couple of big leather chairs in front of the desk. "I know your name from somewhere, don't I, Mr. Reagan?" he said. "You didn't happen to write a story called 'The Battle of San Francisco Bay' a few years back, did you? That was a right good story, I must say, and I said to myself when I read it, I said, Mac, wouldn't it be good to meet this man, this man who wrote this story, because this man is an interesting man, a complicated man, a man of many contradictions, and I do believe we could do some excellent work together, I do indeed. And Lord above, here you are. Trust in Providence, I always say, trust in Providence."

The Big Truth

When in November 1937 he still hadn't heard anything from Tremaine about "The Fight for the Sky", Ron stopped by the Street & Smith offices again. He'd sold a few westerns and even a Doc Savage story recently, but it was nearing Christmastime and he could use some extra cash. Tremaine, he discovered, had gotten a promotion and wasn't editing *Astounding* anymore. "I'm John Campbell," said a crewcut man sitting in front of a rolltop desk and fitting a cigarette into a holder. Ron said, "I've read your stories, Mr. Campbell." Campbell didn't seem impressed. Ron asked about "The Fight for the Sky". Campbell sighed. "Tremaine liked it, but I'm not going to buy it, and I'll tell you why. Sit down, Mr. Reagan." Ron moved a battered typewriter off of a chair and sat. "The problem with your stories, and I've read a few others—the problem," Campbell said, "is that at their heart they're fairy stories. I mean they're stories a queer would write. And I'm looking at you right now, Mr. Reagan, and I know you're not a queer, so I have to ask myself, as any reasonable man would: If you don't look like a queer, why do you write like one? This is perplexing to me. Sure, I know a lot of queers don't look the part, but they're passing. They're covering up. It's sad, really. The point is, you can spot them by their mannerisms, by how they walk, their body posture, all that. And their words, the way they tell stories. There's something ineluctably effeminate about it. And normal people have an inherent aversion. Take an extreme case, for example a full eunochoid—now, if you have some training in endocrinology, you know what a eunochoid is, you can understand the biological processes, and it may even present an interesting case, but to the average man, Bill Blow, I.Q. 95, ask him why he doesn't like Cecil Jones and he won't be able to tell you, but he'll *know* he doesn't like him. And your stories, they're like eunochoids. You might as well submit them on perfumed paper in purple ink. What I'm saying, man, is put your *balls* into the story. Not somebody else's, your *own*. Nice to meet you, Mr. Reagan."

Heritage Of Splendor

Ron sold a few stories to John Campbell in the 1940s ("You found your balls!" Campbell wrote in his first acceptance letter), but by the end of the decade he was moving away from fiction, having met at a cocktail party the agent George Ward, who specialized in getting his authors jobs writing feature articles for the slicks and books of nonfiction for, as he called it, "the vast audience of intrepid laymen and the occasional bored housewife with a college degree." One Friday in 1949, Ron happened upon Campbell at a Hoboken diner where both by chance had stopped for lunch, and Campbell asked him what he was working on, leading Ron to tell him about the new breed of what he was going to label "mystical psychologists" in an article George hoped would sell for big money and lead to a book project. Campbell liked the idea. "If a man were cynical enough," he said, "he could make a fortune taking some of the basic ideas of psychoanalysis, adding a bit of science fiction, and then selling it as a religion, don't you think?" Ron must have looked puzzled, because Campbell continued without waiting for a response: "I like your term, that *mystical psychologists* label, it's catchy. But let's remember that the non-mystic facts are that every human being has an innate *something* that is convinced of personal immortality. A conviction so general must have something on which it's based, don't you think? But what could it be? Well, here's a proposition: Right now, you are two billion years old. An essential life-force in you has existed as an unbroken line of development for the full length of the existence of life on Earth. Now, if you could ever integrate the most powerful analytical tool in the known universe—the human mind—with the immense data-pool of our collective two-billion-year experience . . . well, then you'd be on your way to levitation, teleportation, telepathy, mental-powered transmutation of the elements, you name it." Campbell smashed his cigarette into the brass ashtray on the table. "You know, if somebody was *really* cynical, what he'd do is take all that and then say it's the true revelation of Jesus Christ. Spread that gospel around, and by the end of a decade he'd have more money than God."

The Rear Gunner

Ron asked Alejandro if he'd ever thought of doing illustrations for magazines. "I'm not sure I'd know how," Alejandro said. Ron convinced him to let him show some drawings and paintings to editors he knew. Only John Campbell liked them. "There's talent here, real style, but if I didn't know you, Ron, I'd be sure you were a fairy. This is fairy art. Look at this. Okay, it's called *Prometheus*, but jesus, man, *look* at it." Ron reached out for the painting, but

Campbell pulled it back. "And you know what? I'm putting it on the cover. Yes, I'm putting a naked man—and a naked man's *ass*—on the cover of *Astounding*. Why, you ask? Because dammit, that's a nice ass, and the boys over in the goddamn advertising office keep telling me our covers aren't attracting a broad enough audience, so what the hell. I'm not about to put big-titty women and bug-eyed monsters on the cover of my magazine, but goddammit, even I'm enough of a fairy to know a beautiful, mythic male ass when I see one." He was still laughing as Ron walked out of the office.

The Hasty Heart

The last morning they woke up together in Alejandro's apartment was a cold Tuesday in December 1947. Ron woke first and stood up, naked and feeling naughty. He yawned exaggeratedly and Alejandro opened his eyes and enjoyed the view of Ron's penis lifting, full of morning spunk, and he chuckled and saluted it and welcomed it to his mouth. Soon, they were back in bed, Ron's fingers curled around Alejandro's rigid haft, while Alejandro, gentle and teasing, stroked the back of Ron's spongy scrotum, until eventually they needed to change the sheets and take a shower, and while soaping each other slowly, Alejandro said, "I'm going to have to go away for a bit," and as they rinsed he said, "I need to go back to Mexico. My mother is sick," and as they dried each other with threadbare towels that Ron was certain must date to the previous century, Alejandro said, "I don't really know when I'll be back, but I'll write you all the time, mi amor." It was then, for the first time since they'd known each other, that Ron collapsed into Alejandro's arms in tears.

Bedtime For Bonzo

"The first time," Ron said to Dr. Mac after nearly a year of sessions, "was when I was a kid, high school, just playing around, you know, as boys do, everybody does that, it's perfectly normal, and then we got girlfriends and wives and we gave it up. But then there was the Army, which I don't think really qualifies either, because what else were we supposed to do? I mean, we all thought we'd be dead at any moment, and some of us did die, a lot of us, we lost our friends, we lost everything, so why not mess around, right? I don't see anything wrong with that, but I also know that somehow it was the war that made me into this. Don't you think? Because after I got back, I just couldn't really do anything with Jane anymore. Well no, that's not true. I could do what we did, it was fine, it wasn't torture or anything, but it was quick and mechanical. So I looked for other ways. That's when I started going to the places where there were guys who were after the same thing. It was still pretty quick, but there was a pleasure to it, it was like it had been when we were all bunking with each other before we headed over to Berlin. There was a danger, definitely, because I didn't know these men, and yet we were, well…there was a danger. Obviously. Of course. And that was part of the fun, the attraction. The first guy I went home with was named Franklin, and he had a nice place over on the East Side, not expensive but tasteful, and that was the first time in my entire life, I think, when I'd felt like I understood what the fuss was about, you know, the excitement, the passion of…of passion. Of sex. And beauty. That's what it was. He was beautiful. Tall, blond, fit. He worked as a gardener for a very rich man, and so his skin was tanned and there wasn't a bit of fat anywhere on him. Like Doc Savage, you know? *The Man of Bronze.* Piercing blue eyes. We met over in the meatpacking district, just one of those anonymous encounters at night, but there was something about him that made me want to stay with him, and something about me—" *"Something?"* Dr. Mac said. "Didn't he tell you what it was? That something?" Ron nodded slowly. "Yes, he said…he said my penis—" "He didn't say 'penis,'" Dr. Mac said. Ron said that was true.

"He said my cock was a *thumper*." Ron chuckled at the memory. "I loved his arms and his lips and his hair, so short and blond, and we just couldn't stop touching each other—" "Touching?" Dr. Mac said, and Ron said, "Yes, touching, and…and…" "Fucking?" Dr. Mac said. "Yes," Ron said, "I suppose that's the word. If you want to be crude about it." Dr. Mac said nothing. "So anyway, we decided to go back to his place, because though Jane was away, I promised myself that I would never bring a man back to our apartment, and I never have. Franklin lived alone, so we went to his apartment, and we just went straight to his bed, and honestly we stayed in bed until at least noon the next day, just learning each other's bodies, just…" "Just what?" Dr. Mac said. "Fucking," Ron said. "But not only that, we would talk and then we'd play around some more and—" "Play?" Dr. Mac said. "Yes," Ron said, "we played. It was play. It was as innocent as two little boys—" "Fucking," Dr. Mac said. "No," Ron said. "Playing. It was joyful. It wasn't love, I don't think, because we didn't really have a lot to talk about or any real deep interest in each other as people, you know, out in the world, the real world, but we had this connection, this bodily connection, and it was glorious, we just lived in bed together, and it was in his bed that I felt—for the first time in so long—that I felt alive."

The Winning Team

It took half a bottle of rye whiskey, but Alejandro convinced Ron to model for a nude portrait. Ron stood in a corner of the apartment, his left hand supporting him against the wall, his right arm reaching up to touch the top of one of the windows. "If the wind blows this curtain open," Ron said, "the whole street will get a nice view of my cock." Alejandro told him he'd heard half the Village had already had more than a nice view of his cock, so what was he worried about. "Touché," Ron said. "And not true. Only maybe a quarter of the Village." The curtain was blue silk, soft and light, almost translucent, and a breeze from the open window brushed it against Ron, tickling and exciting him. "It's a good thing this portrait is from the back," Alejandro said, "because otherwise your horn would get me arrested for being a pornographer." Once Alejandro had the form sketched out, Ron rested on the bed, drank the rest of the bottle of rye, and fell asleep. A few days later, he returned to the apartment to see that Alejandro had been working on the painting almost continuously, and Ron had become a Titan reaching through a ring of fire toward the stars.

Code Of The Secret Service
Ron kept his postcards from Alejandro in a cigar box in the bottom left drawer of his desk. "Why not hide them better?" Dr. Mac asked. "Jane never went into my desk much," Ron said. "But once you started having problems," Dr. Mac said, "she suspected an affair, and you knew she did, she didn't hide her suspicions, so why not put the evidence somewhere where she wouldn't look?" Ron shrugged. "I don't know," he said.

Recognition Of The Japanese Zero Fighter
Jane found him at his desk, drunk and weeping over the postcards from Alejandro, scattered like a failed poker hand. He'd received a letter in response to his own, the one Dr. Mac and Jane had made him write, the one in which he said no, he couldn't see Alejandro now that Alejandro was back from Cuernavaca, and he didn't want to see him again, at least not for a long time, because their relationship had been unhealthy and he was now trying to get better, and he hoped that Alejandro would himself get help and become clean and pure and good again. Alejandro's reply was written on a torn-off cover from *Astounding*, a naked man rising to the stars, just a few

words: *Goodbye. Love. A.* Jane put her arm around Ron's shoulders.
He pushed her away. She tumbled backward, hitting her head on the
wall. He screamed at her, terrible things, and she turned away and
shielded her eyes from him, telling herself that it was the booze talking, he didn't really hate her, no he couldn't really hate her this much,
no-one could hate someone this much, and she tried to pull away
from him as he groped for her, but he tore her blouse and he spat on
her, and he ripped her dress away and it was only then that she could
get into a position to push him back as he struggled to unbutton his
pants. She stood over him as he wept on the floor, the pathetic man,
kissing a postcard and holding his limp and silly penis, and she forced
herself to think about the sunlight in Los Angeles and the wonderful
house she had bought without telling him, and the blue, blue pool the
children swam in so freely, so happily.

The Angels Wash Their Faces

Dr. Mac asked him if he was a religious man. "No, not really," Ron
said. "I went to Sunday school, but I stopped when I was about
fifteen. I suppose I believe in God. I'm just not very good at it." Dr.
Mac leaned forward, eyes ablaze. "How long have we been meeting,
Ron? Eight, ten weeks now? Well, I've learned a lot about you in that
time, and I believe I have a real good sense of you, and I believe you
know I have a real good sense of you, isn't that correct?" Ron said
that was correct. "Now, it is against my professional practice to offer
everyday advice, as you know, but the advice I am about to give you
is much more than everyday—it is, indeed, advice for all of your
existence and even, yes, for your immortal soul. You do believe in
an immortal soul do you not?" Ron said he believed in an immortal
soul. "Therefore, my boy, I must say that in my professional opinion
the best thing you could do for yourself, for the health of your body
and your mind and your immortal soul, I believe the best thing you

could do is to get to know and to love and to worship our savior, Jesus Christ. Now, you do not need to say amen, and you do not need to go join an evangelical congregation or become a holy roller like some gesticulating negro, but you need to find some way to allow the truth of Jesus Christ our savior into your heart. Do you not agree?" Ron said that he agreed.

Law And Order
There are no depths, Alejandro once said, only surfaces. Surfaces upon surfaces.

Brother Rat
"No no no," Dr. Mac said, "I don't want shared credit. I don't want any credit. I have a good thing going here, no need to muddle it up with a new approach. But I've had my lawyers draw up a good, solid, and I think eminently fair agreement by which I will receive 40% of the royalties due to the author, given that at least that much of the book itself is based on your interviews with me." Ron looked over the papers Dr. Mac had handed him, then said, "That's fine. But I'm having my lawyers add a clause releasing me from having to credit you or compensate you for future volumes that I am sole author of." Dr. Mac put the papers into a black folder. "That's fine," he said. "Though I do hope we can continue to collaborate. It's been such a fruitful relationship for us both." Three months later, Dr. Mac fell asleep while watching his new television, and never woke up, his heart having stopped beating.

Million Dollar Baby
Ronald Reagan's first book, *The Revelations of Jesus: Good News for Mind and Soul*, was released in December 1951. After a few weeks, it began to sell steadily, and entered the *New York Times* hardcover

bestseller list on January 20, 1952 at number 14. Over the next month, sales continued to increase, and on March 9 it knocked Rachel Carson's *The Sea Around Us* to second place and stayed in first until October 26, when Tallulah Bankhead's autobiography sent it to second place, followed by the Revised Standard Version of the Bible in third. *The Revelations of Jesus* remained among the hardcover top ten until August 1955, by which time the sequel, *Further Revelations of Jesus*, released in April 1953, was holding steady in second place and Ronald Reagan's third book, *Sharing the Mind of the Christ*, released in June 1955, was number one.

Going Places

Nancy Davis was the host of an interview show on DuMont Television Network, *Morning Light*, and at first she and Ron didn't get along. Her opening question during his initial appearance on her show was, "Why don't you consider your book sacrilegious?" Ron gave her his now nationally-famous chuckling smile and said, "Well, Nancy, don't jump to conclusions. Some people might say, particularly if they couldn't get out of the Old Testament, that the words and ideas of Jesus Christ are, in fact, sacrilegious. Now, I don't happen to believe that, myself. But it might be said." Ron thought then that if he were writing a science fiction story about Nancy Davis, he would say that death rays shot from her eyes. After the show was over, she came to his dressing room and said she was beginning to think he believed all the things he'd written in his book. "Of course I believe them," he said. "The words in that book, which I do believe are the real lessons of Jesus Christ, updated with today's mental science—those words have saved my life." She said she hoped that they might talk again, and she gave him a slip of paper with her home telephone number written on it.

Swing Your Lady

Before she could agree to marry him, Nancy said she would need to know everything about his life before the book and the seminars made him famous. His life as a pulp writer, his time in the Army, his life with Jane, the divorce, and, most importantly, all the various struggles he referred to so vaguely in the book and in his speeches. She and Ron were sitting in the large and eminently tasteful living room of her apartment, a room with an expensive view of Central Park, a bookcase of leather-bound books she'd never read, and no furniture less than fifty years old. Ron was silent for longer than she'd ever seen him stay silent in a conversation, a moment that felt weighty, almost crushing, as if time itself was the only bulwark against a colossal threat. "Like my father before me," Ron said finally, "I was an alcoholic. Not too bad before the war, but it got bad after, because the war was bad. I saw dear friends killed right in front of me, I saw towns and cities destroyed, I did some terrible things that I don't need to dwell on, the terrible things a man does in war. I had trouble getting back to work afterward, and I blamed Jane, and I drank too much because it helped me stop feeling my fears and my failures. Jane convinced me to get help, and I got help, and eventually I got better. But I'd been a terrible husband to her, and a terrible father. A terrible, weak man." Nancy said there were rumors of other things, of left-wing politics, maybe even a flirtation with Communism, and there were, too, whispers of sex perversion. "I was drinking an awful lot in those days," Ron said. "I hardly knew who I was. There's honestly not a lot I remember. It wasn't really me. This is me. Here, now. This is me." He kissed her delicately on the lips.

Hell's Kitchen

Ron's second appearance on *Morning Light* was less tense and awkward than the first. He and Nancy had kept their engagement secret, and would continue to do so for the next year, until she could get free of her contract and better position herself as an upstanding housewife and potential mother, but interest in Ron's ideas had spread widely, and he had refused many other interview opportunities, instead encouraging reporters and publicists to spend $20 to attend one of his seminars. "Tell me about your view of sin," Nancy said after the initial pleasantries at the beginning of the show. "Well, Nancy, I'm glad you're interested in that, because it's one of the central ideas not only in *The Revelations of Jesus*, but really in my entire approach to life. Sin is, in my view, and certainly the view of Jesus in the gospels, anything that is unhealthy to us as an individual or to a society. Usually both, because a healthy society needs healthy individuals. Take for instance something we don't necessarily see as sinful, even if we do condemn it—*Communism*. I believe that Communism is sinful. It is sinful because it seeks to destroy the healthy passions of our free enterprise system, and it is a disease that spreads in a society. If our body is a temple, and God instructs us to treat it as such, we must resist disease. Not to resist disease is to commit sin. Whether we're talking about our own body or our family body or our national body, we must do whatever we can to protect it, to nourish it, to keep it healthy and strong. When I was a young man, I made my living by writing stories about alien invaders, and as I grew older I realized that what I was writing about was, in fact, the threat of sin. This is what Nazism was, and it is why our triumph over Hitler was a great triumph for God. And it is what Communism is. An alien invasion. The ideas invade the individual first, and then the individual spreads them, not knowing he is being controlled by a kind of virus or demon, and what was a disease of an individual becomes a disease of a group and then a whole culture and nation, eventually of the whole species. I've given over my life to finding ways to combat this invasion. I've given my life to Jesus."

For God And Country

On June 2, 1953, Ronald Reagan appeared before the House Committee on Un-American Activities and testified about the relationship between Communism and other types of personal and social
failure that undermined the health of the national body. Frank S.
Tavenner, Jr., Chief Counsel for the Committee, questioned him
for nearly an hour about his techniques for diagnosing and treating such mental diseases or, as Mr. Reagan preferred to call them,
sins. Mr. Tavenner asked Mr. Reagan how such sins were related to
each other, and if one might, in his opinion, lead to another. "Certainly," Mr. Reagan said. When asked to elaborate, he replied, "If
we talk about sin, we talk about weakness and desire—about the
desire produced by weakness, and the weakness that furthers that
desire." Mr. Tavenner asked Mr. Reagan if he was asserting that a
person tempted to Communism might also suffer other perverse
desires. "I think that is incontrovertible," Mr. Reagan replied. "And
I would urge all of our legislators to pay particular attention to the
ways that individual weakness of desire can undermine the health
and strength of our nation. Recent hearings have shown the per-
vasive power of sin in the industry that creates our entertainment,
and only the most callous or disconnected man would suggest that
our entertainments are not at least partly a reflection of ourselves,
of something inside us, and so we should guard against sinfulness within them just as we guard against sinfulness in ourselves.
It is the same with our government, which should be a reflection
of our nation and its ideals. For instance, for our government to
employ someone of weak moral character, someone with perverse
desires—for our government to do that would be to weaken the
national body itself."

King's Row

Nancy Reagan gave birth to her first child, Peter, nine months after she married Ron. A year later, she gave birth to Andrew, and the next year James. Her husband spent much of the time of her pregnancies on the road, often leading two or even three seminars a day. Reporters who attended the seminars wrote that Reagan would talk for much of the time, telling stories of his heroic experiences in the war, of the many celebrities he spent time with in New York (and, more recently, Hollywood), and of the important work he did for the government in combating Communism. The particular benefit of any individual story was hard to identify, but after about an hour and a half of storytelling, the audience would break up into small groups where members of the Revelation Society would then help them find the moral, intellectual, and, especially, psychological benefits in what they called "the teachings". Each seminar ended with the audience reconvening in the auditorium for the climax of the seminar: a few individuals would be chosen to go onto the stage and participate in a preliminary analysis by Ronald Reagan. More than one researcher comparing reports of the seminars at this time has remarked on the frequency with which blond, blue-eyed men in their early twenties were chosen for the preliminary analysis, with at least one researcher suggesting that the same person was used at each event. Photographs prove, however, that despite superficial resemblances, numerous men participated.

Beyond The Line Of Duty

"Some may call it unorthodox, even quackery," Vance Britten, Vice President of the Revelation Society, told a reporter for the New York *Herald Tribune* in 1954. "But there's one thing to remember. Really, the only thing that matters. Ronald Reagan has cured every sinner he worked with. He has cured ulcers, arthritis, asthma. He has brought happiness and optimism to millions. He has shown his followers a new, scientific—indeed revolutionary—path toward the enlightenment that Jesus Christ stood for so many centuries ago. He has shown how that enlightenment fits into a continuum of human history, our biological inheritance, the rock-solid reality of our two billion years of existence. He has shown us what immortality truly means."

Smashing The Money Ring

"The sudden fame, the wealth, it all wore him down," Nancy Davis told a reporter for a BBC radio documentary in 1983. "He was a good man at heart, a kind man. But it was too much for him. That's all. It was too much for him. He went to pieces. There was nothing any of us could do for him."

Night Unto Night

Despite the tax problems, despite continually hostile press coverage, despite the FBI inquiry, despite moving from New York to Hollywood to Montana to England to Switzerland and then, finally, to a giant yacht in the Pacific Ocean—despite it all, the family was happy and business was good for many years. "We're a big organization now," Ron said to anyone who asked about the obstacles, "so of course we've had growing pains. But look how much we've grown! I sincerely believe the good that we've done outweighs whatever challenges we have faced. The challenges only make us stronger." The books continued to sell, the seminars continued to be popular, the individual analysis sessions continued to fill, despite their ever-rising price tag. Every day, Ron received letters from people who said he had changed their lives. He had given them hope, cured them of pessimism, made them proud to be who they were, helped them understand their individuality, helped them fight the invasion of sin, helped them embrace human immortality, brought them into an understanding of the truth of Jesus. He read these letters each night during his alone time. Nancy had been the one to insist on alone time for him, and she protected it zealously. "I don't care if you drink," Nancy said. "Maybe you have to. Maybe that's who you are. But we've built something here, and if you ruin it, Ron, I swear to you I will make every day of the rest of your life a living hell. If I ever smell alcohol on your breath again in public, if I ever see you unsteady before an audience again—I swear." She went to his study every midnight, let herself in with the only copy of the master key, and helped Ron to bed. Usually, he had passed out with his head on the desk, though sometimes he collapsed on the floor. Often, he reeked of urine and vomit. Sometimes he was awake, occasionally he was coherent, now and then he was sober and working and proud of himself. Every morning, she poured coffee and Dexedrine into him, and he said he loved her, and she sent him on his way.

Hellcats Of The Navy

In October 1968, Ron was eating breakfast in the main cabin of the yacht that now served as his home and headquarters. Nancy was nearby, talking with the captain, when she heard her husband scream. Immediately, she assumed an assassin had found a way to get on board. That was one of the main reasons, aside from the endless tax troubles, they had moved to the yacht: Ron was convinced that people wanted to kill him. Nancy thought this was a bit paranoid, but not entirely unrealistic, and now she was certain it was more than realistic, it was a fact. She ran to the cabin and found Ron sobbing over a four-day-old *Los Angeles Times* that had come in with the mail at dawn. "What is it, Ron? What is it?" she said, again and again, but he pushed her away. He crumpled the first pages of the newspaper, then threw them across the room. Nancy went to retrieve them, but he screamed at her to get away, to leave him alone. She did. An hour later she found him with a nearly-empty bottle of tequila in hand, leaning over the starboard railing, trying to position his uncooperative body to jump into the ocean below. She pulled him back and helped him to their cabin, then went to retrieve the newspaper. There were reports on the progress of the war in Vietnam, reports on the election campaigns, and reports on a massacre outside Mexico City. Most of the pictures were of Mexico, including pictures of corpses—pictures that were, she thought, tasteless and shocking. (What purpose could there be to putting pictures of dead Mexicans in an American paper?) None of that should have so upset Ron, though. His behavior had been a bit more erratic recently, his generally excellent memory less and less reliable, and it was possible, indeed likely, that the alcohol and amphetamines had reached a toxic level in his brain, and she should begin to implement the detoxification plan she had had Dr. Winter draw up for just such a situation.

She's Working Her Way Through College

Vance shared a recent article from a psychological journal with Nancy. He said that it was the funniest thing he'd read in ages. "'Reagan's success,'" he read aloud in the high-pitched voice of a cartoon egghead, "'indicates society's periodic need to re-conceptualize its leaders. Reagan thus appears as a series of posture concepts, basic equations which re-formulate the roles of aggression and anality.' Can you believe people get published with this shit? Listen to this: 'Motion picture studies of Ronald Reagan reveal characteristic patterns of facial tonus and musculature associated with homo-erotic behavior.'" Vance was laughing so hard he couldn't keep reading. Nancy took the journal from him and looked at it. Ron stepped into the cabin then and genially asked what they were

doing. Vance grabbed the journal from Nancy, who tried to pro-
test, and he read, returning to egghead-voice: "'Vaginal intercourse
after watching films of Reagan proved uniformly unsuccessful, pro-
ducing orgasm in 2% of subjects. Homosexual behaviors, however,
increased, and Reagan films repeatedly produced proximal erec-
tions in at least 88% of subjects.'" Ron snatched the journal from
Vance's hands, opened a porthole, and tossed the Winter 1967/1968
Proceedings of the American Academy of Psychological Sciences into
the ocean.

The Bad Man

By the spring of 1969, Ron's drinking was mostly under control
and he'd given up Dexedrine, but memberships in the Revelation
Society were dropping and interest in individual analysis had nearly
disappeared. Nancy and Vance had carefully diversified Ron's
assets, allowing him an impressive income despite the Society's
troubles, but the Society was within months of needing to declare
bankruptcy. When a local CBS news affiliate in San Francisco asked
for an interview, they all agreed it could be a useful way to remind
the world of Reagan's charismatic genius. What they did not know
was that the interviewer, Johnny Barrett, had investigated some of
the rumors around the young men Reagan frequently singled out
in his seminars, and he had also heard that Reagan's fondness for
whiskey had never truly left him. Barrett carefully positioned two
glasses and a bottle of Old Overholt on the little table between their
chairs on the studio set, filling his own glass and offering Reagan a
drink just as the show's opening credits rolled. "Oh no," Ron said,
"I've been on the wagon for many years now." Barrett smiled, took a
sip himself, and then asked innocuous questions about the Society,
Ron's family, the huge yacht he lived on, his days as a pulp writer,
and the many medals he said that he won in the war. A few min-

utes before the mid-show commercial break, Barrett said, "Now, you know, as with all celebrities, many rumors have sprung up around you. One that's been especially persistent recently is that you have a particular interest in certain young men who attend your seminars. Only one has ever come forward with any accusations, and he says the others were well paid to keep their silence about your activities with them. What do you have to say about that?" Ron smile-chuckled and said, "Well, you know, whenever a man achieves a certain amount of fame or success, people will line up to lie about him, to try to bring failure to him and some sort of spotlight to themselves." Barrett sipped his whiskey, then said, "So you're denying the accusations?" and Ron said that of course he was denying them. "We were able to track down a few of the others," Barrett said, "and they allowed us to tape record them as long as we wouldn't use their names. Let's play the recording—" The studio filled with the sound of a tentative voice, a man saying yes he'd been at the seminar and he had, at the end, gone up onto the stage and participated in preliminary analysis with Mr. Reagan, and that after the seminar he was invited to Mr. Reagan's dressing room, where Mr. Reagan propositioned him in a very vulgar way. Another voice said he, too, was summoned to Mr. Reagan's dressing room, and he thought what Mr. Reagan wanted him to do was funny, kind of a lark, so he went along with it, though now he had regrets. A third voice said that he went to numerous seminars, and at each one he was called onto the stage, and after each one he spent time with Mr. Reagan, performing perverse actions with him, and once he even stayed with him through the night. Barrett turned to the camera. "Response from Ronald Reagan when we return!" The show cut to commercial. Ron had already poured himself a drink, apparently without realizing it. By the time the commercial break ended, he had had three. He continued drinking throughout the program whenever the camera seemed to be on Barrett, but this was an illusion, as the two cameras were always running, and the show's director quickly decided it was best to stay on Reagan. "These are all lies," Ron said. "They are greedy, greedy people trying to take me down." Barrett noted that Reagan seemed to be struggling still to overcome temptations. "It is an eternal struggle," Ron said, "and that is the nature of the life that is, the billions of years we have in our souls, the life flows through us and so there is temptation that, of course, is what Jesus warned us against and which I help people to, their sins, overcoming sins, I help people—I help people. That is all you bastards should care about, but you don't, you just want to tear me down like a sheet on a two-dollar whore." He stood unsteadily, supporting himself with the chair. "How do I get out of this goddam viper pit?" he muttered. By this time, Nancy and Vance had pushed their way into the studio and, though five minutes remained of the show, they helped lead Ron off. Johnny Barrett watched them go. "Ronald Reagan, ladies and gentlemen, in his full glory." Later that night, the Revelation Society issued a press release saying that on account of extreme exhaustion, Mr. Reagan would be taking a break from his duties and spending a well-earned vacation at sea. In truth, though they could hardly know it at the time, he would never be seen by the public again.

Nine Lives Are Not Enough

Reagan's yacht, the *Santa Fe Trail,* became his Xanadu in the early 1970s after the Society went bankrupt and Nancy and the kids left. He hardly talked to the small crew, and most thought he didn't know their names. Now and then he would ask the captain to travel in a particular direction, but it was rare. "We need to dock somewhere, Mr. Reagan," the captain said one afternoon in April 1973. "We need supplies, we need repairs. We're not in good shape." The mail and supply boats hadn't found them in weeks. Ron only knew this because he was down to his last case of whiskey. "Head to Mexico," he said. "Get me to Mexico." The captain said he would do his best.

The Last Outpost

Johnny Barrett spent a week in Ayutla de los Libres in October 1975, talking with people about the man they knew as Jack Browning, a gringo who spent most of his time in Vargas's bar a few blocks from the centro. Jack Browning told people he was looking for Alejandro, but every time somebody named Alejandro went to him, he said no, no, not you, you're the wrong one, you're not my Alejandro. Señor Browning always had plenty of money, and he always paid well. He said he was going to Cuernavaca, but he never got very far down the road before somebody had to bring him back. "He would have died out there," Vargas said. "He'd pass out on the side of the road. Sometimes, he'd just throw himself in front of cars or trucks. He didn't know where he was or where he was going. So we always brought him back." Johnny Barrett asked to see Señor Browning's possessions. Doña Ana kept them at her house, where he had spent most nights. She was an old woman and had cared for him like she was his own abuela. Everything he owned had been in an Army-issue duffel bag. Some clothes, two bottles of tequila, a Swiss Army knife, a wedding ring, a big leather wallet stuffed with cash from various countries, and the tattered cover an old science fiction magazine. Some words had been written on it with a pen, but the paper was so faded and worn that Barrett couldn't make out what they said. When Barrett got back to San Francisco, he told his producer, who hadn't wanted him to go on this wild goose chase in the first place, that yes, this Jack Browning fellow could have been Reagan, but he just as easily could have not. "Who knows what became of the old guy," Barrett said wistfully, and his producer shrugged and said, "Who cares?"

The Killers

It was a cool, perfect night in Manhattan. As they sat together on a bench in Washington Square Park, Alejandro asked, "How do you want to die?" Ron scowled. "What kind of question is that?" he said. Alejandro said, "It's an important question. We have to envision our death, don't you think? To appreciate our life. So for me, I want to die surrounded by flowers. All sorts of colors, all sorts of fragrances. To die in beauty. That's what I want." Alejandro entwined his fingers with Ron's. "Now your turn." Ron shook his head. "I dunno," he said. "Of course you do," Alejandro said. "Just use your imagination." Ron pulled his hand away. "People could see us," he whispered. Alejandro stared at him and raised his eyebrows expectantly. "Fine," Ron said. "Okay. How do I want to die? Somewhere seedy. In a boarding house, maybe. The kind of place where they're not surprised if you die. Or get shot. That's what I want. I want to be lying on a bed in a boarding house, waiting for some hired guns to come in and shoot me, and then they do. That's all. Just a kind of fate. You know they're coming, you wait for them, and then they do what they always said they'd do, what they were always going to do from the beginning of time." Alejandro ran his hand through Ron's hair. "Sometimes," Alejandro said, "I feel like I don't know you." Ron took Alejandro's hand in his again. "I'm just joking with you," Ron said, resting his head on Alejandro's shoulder. "I don't want to think about dying." Quickly, surreptitiously, gently he kissed Alejandro's cheek. "I think you're the only one who really does know me," Ron said. "As much of me as there is to know, anyway." They sat on the bench for a while without talking, then went back to Alejandro's apartment, which now seemed strange to Ron, as if he'd never seen it before, with all its mess of canvasses and brushes and paints, objects that now seemed to him to have been here for millennia—he and Alejandro were additions, new life, and as Alejandro took him in his arms, Ron was certain they would stay here, just the two of them, complete, forever.

Expositions

This dream... is itself action, reality,
and an effective menace to all established order;
it renders possible what it dreams about.
                —Gilles Deleuze,
                  The Logic of Sense
                  (trans. by Mark Lester)

Anne calls to tell him she's got a job. He should be pleased, he knows, but envy stifles pleasure. If he'd stayed married, at least some of her income would be his. If he had fought the divorce, maybe she'd have to pay him money.

"I'm happy for you," he says. "What's the job?"

"Code cleaning, simple stuff, minimum wage to start, but I'm not complaining. It's something."

"Yeah," he says, pitching his voice high, reaching for enthusiasm. "And you?"

"What?"

"Any prospects?"

"Possibilities, sure." He hadn't seen anything posted in days. He hadn't looked hard. Why bother? Not much difference between official postings and spam. At least the spam sought him out.

"I found this job because one of Talia's friends works here, and they've had a couple people leave to go on the wire. It's not a bad option," she says. "They've worked the bugs out."

"Right. Only a few people fry each month."

"It's not that bad. It's safer than walking down the street."

"I'm not in a city. Moose walk down the street here."

"Well, watch out. Moose are ferocious."

"Yeah," he says, "but at least they're alive and interacting with the world."

"You're not interacting with the world. At least on the wire, you'd get paid to be a vegetable. Anyway, what else is there?"

"Fast food," he says. A joke, of course. Her father had been a McDonald's manager, back when McDonald's needed managers.

She doesn't laugh.

"Are you doing okay, George?"

"Sure," he says. "I've seen worse."

"I miss you," she says.

"It's okay," he says. "You'll get over it." He hangs up and hardly realizes it. Her face is frozen on the screen in his hand. He wipes it away.

§

When they had lived together, George and Anne had been able to afford an apartment, pooling their income from her job at a biotech lab at UNH and his various construction jobs. They'd talked about having kids someday, once they could save up enough so that kids wouldn't bankrupt them. Then wire tech spread, the housing market for anything other than luxury estates went from bad to nonexistent, and Anne got laid off. She did some freelance work, but even that dried up, and eventually there wasn't any money for rent.

They lived in their car for a while, then Hampton Beach for a summer, and finally Anne's parents took them in, but George drank a lot and was always an angry drunk. He didn't blame them for kicking him out; he'd have kicked him out, too, if he'd had any choice about living with himself. Anne stayed with her parents, and George headed north with a backpack of booze to keep him drunk enough that hitchhiking felt like an adventure. He'd trade sex for rides if he could; the smaller bottles of booze if he had to. It was only a hundred fifty miles to the ghost towns where he'd heard people could squat without any trouble (so long as they didn't require electricity or running water). You had to be pretty desperate to head in that direction.

For the first time in his life, George's luck was good. He found a farmhouse that wasn't completely ruined just outside Colebrook in Lemington, and when he told the three guys there that he was a carpenter, they agreed to let him stay. The guys had all been in college together in Connecticut until they hit their loan limits and were expelled. They stole a car and headed north, figuring they ought to be able to find someplace to hide in the rubble of the Northeast Kingdom Autonomous Zone.

"I'd forgot the name," George said.

"We studied it in a class I had," said Tod, a scrawny white guy with blond hair that kept falling in his eyes. "I was a political science major. It was an extraordinary case study, really, because nobody had ever seriously considered that the economically conservative, socially liberal libertarian groups in New Hampshire would find common cause with the anarcho-communists in Vermont, but—"

"Uh huh," George said. "So are you guys all, like, fucking each other?"

"Tod and I sometimes do," said Femi, a black guy with, George thought, a soccer player's body. "He's queer, and I'm sort of like, whatever. There's not a lot of girls up here. Will's not much into it, but if you get him drunk enough, he'll give you head."

Will laughed. He couldn't have been more than 25, but he was already almost completely bald. "I love you guys," he said, "but I need pussy."

"Or your hand," Femi said.

"I've got a nice hand," Will said.

George said, "What do you eat?"

Will said, "Aside from pussy?" The three guys laughed.

"Look," George said, "it took me forever to get up here, and I've had a fucking rotten time of it, so just quit it with the stupid fucking frat boy shit and tell me how it works up here."

Suddenly Tod wrapped one arm around George's neck and, with the other arm, held a pistol to George's temple. "It works like this," Tod said. "This is our house. We do what we want and how we want to. You might be helpful to us, you might not. If not, you go away or we kill you. We've got crops, we've got fresh water, and we figured out how to survive in the winter. Oh yeah, and I've got a thousand rounds of .45 ACP ammo, Femi's got at least a hundred shells for his 12-gauge, and you wouldn't believe what Will can sculpt with his hunting knife."

"If you're gonna shoot me," George said, "then just shoot me. If you're gonna fuck me, fuck me. I don't care. If you're gonna rob me, then please shoot me as well, because all I've got's a last bottle of vodka, and I don't really want to have to get through a day up here without that."

Femi gently pulled Tod away from George. "Don't mind him," Femi said. "He's seen too many gangster movies."

Will, meanwhile, had opened George's backpack. He pulled out the vodka bottle and handed it to him. "We've got plenty to drink," Will said. "We used to have an old van, and we robbed a couple liquor stores. The van's dead, but we've got enough alcohol to poison an army."

George smiled. "I could kiss you right now," he said.

Will pointed at Tod. "He'd like that more than I would. Why don't you two kiss and make up?"

And so they did.

§

Eight months later, Will and Femi were dead and Tod had disappeared. Will had gotten fed up with the threesomes between Femi, Tod, and George, and so he headed off one night after drinking most of a bottle of rum. It was his bad luck to stumble onto a house where the first thing he saw was a teenage girl playing with a doll outside. He began to feel her up, she resisted, he pushed her to the ground and tore at her clothes, and then her father, a man the size of a bulldozer, picked him up and threw him across the yard. Somehow, Will managed to get to his feet and run back toward the farmhouse. The girl's father was preoccupied for a moment with comforting his daughter, but their house turned out to be full of people, and they didn't have a hard time tracking Will down. Unfortunately, they didn't find him till he got back to his house and started screaming for Tod and Femi and George. "You fucking faggots, get out here and help me!" were his last words before an arrow lodged into his right shoulder. He screamed, another arrow came, landing in his throat, and his scream cut to a cough and then a gurgle and then nothing.

Tod, Femi, and George should have stayed in the house. Femi had always liked Will, though, and he grabbed the shotgun from his bedroom and started firing through a window. That stopped things for about an hour. Then they saw the fire in the field beside the farmhouse. There hadn't been any rain in three weeks. The fire grew larger and larger on every side of the house. George and Tod didn't think fighting would do much good, but Femi was determined, so he charged toward the fire with his shotgun. Flaming arrows fell all around him, then one punctured his leg. He tripped and was soon consumed by flames. His shotgun shells exploded all around him.

Tod had filled a bucket with water and was throwing it at the walls of the living room. "It's no good!" George yelled, then grabbed Tod's arm to haul him out, but Tod pulled away and ran to get more water from the barrel in the kitchen. "We've got to go!" George screamed.

He ran toward a small, open area behind the house, the only area he could see that wasn't blocked by flames. There had been a marsh there a few months ago, and it was still just wet enough not to burn quickly. George ran without looking, instead feeling his way away from the flames and the wall of heat they pushed toward him. His skin stung, his eyes screamed, his nostrils burned, his tongue tasted of ash. He looked back once and saw Tod behind him, and he was glad, but he knew if he looked back again something terrible could happen, and he needed not to look back, and so he stared ahead at the darkness as he ran.

By the time his legs gave out and he fell to the ground in a forest, he was sure he must have run for days.

§

George has an apartment building all to himself now. A few months before everything went to hell in Lemington, Congress passed a law to let the wire tech companies go from being marginally profitable experimental ventures to the most powerful corporations on Earth. They'd proved they could hook people into what they called a digital energy processing network without causing permanent damage or death (at least not at a rate greater than that of the airlines or pharmaceutical corporations or any other major industry), and so all of a sudden the country's unemployment and energy problems were solved in a nicely capitalistic way, with an added bonus of potentially infinite growth in computer processing capabilities. The public didn't care about the complex science, not when unemployment was pushing 30%, the southwestern states had been consumed by drought and wildfires for a decade, and Miami had built a twenty-foot-high seawall around its entire coast. Some pundit said this digital energy processing stuff was like putting a wire into a person and plugging them in. "Plug me in!" became the slogan of the year.

At first, only about 10,000 people were allowed to go on the wire commercially. They were people who'd been out of work for ages, people who were destitute, a small sample of the surplus population. The mayor of New York pulled some strings to get 2,000 homeless men from his city shipped off to the clean and climate-controlled wirehouses that had been built in the droughtbelt (where land was cheap and plentiful). The energy harvested from one person could power a wirehouse the size of five football fields, and most of them were only as big as three. The first wirehouses only held about 100 people, but engineers soon enough figured out how to stack the processors, and six months after the first commercial wirehouse went online, ground was broken for a wirehouse that would itself be able to accommodate 10,000 processors. Quotas rose, and within three years almost ten million people were on the wire with contracts for various lengths of time up to five years. For the use of their bodies, pluggers were generally paid about $5,000 a year, and considering that they had no expenses for clothing, food, travel, or everyday existence during their time on the wire, for most it was at least marginally profitable. Some wirehouses offered profit sharing deals, which, though not guaranteed, were sometimes immensely lucrative.

And so George has seen the world change as fast as one scene in a movie dissolving into another.

However, George is not optimistic for the future. The drought-belt is not getting smaller. Sea levels are not receding. Recent hurricanes have wiped out entire island nations. Optimism is a mental illness.

George thinks perhaps now would be the time to take up smoking. But cigarettes cost money, especially ones with real tobacco. He doesn't envision himself as the kind of guy who would smoke the faux cigarettes, the ones made from ground up airliners and pulverized cockroaches. He still has some dignity, after all.

Then he sees someone who looks a bit like Tod drive into town in a new Subaru, one of the expensive ones with the turbo engine that can run on seventy-seven different types of biomass if the solar nanos in the self-regulating paintjob aren't enough. A car for the apocalypse, they say. Just in time.

The car stops at the coffee shop down the street from George's apartment building. George walks down to the coffee shop, and there, indeed, stands Tod, with a burly Asian guy holding his hand. Tod looks good, not so scrawny, not so pale, his hair stylishly cut, and wearing clothes that fit so well George assumes they're partly intelligent.

"Well, look at you," George says.

Tod's so surprised he nearly spills the latté the kiosk just handed him. He gives George a hug. "You look great," Tod says.

"No I don't," George says. "But you do. So does he." He points at the guy beside Tod.

"This is Karl," Tod says. "We could go back to your place if you want. It might be fun."

"No," George says. "I didn't mean it that way. I meant, you know, you look like you've done well for yourself."

"I went on the wire for a year," Tod says. "Took a stock option and compounding interest rather than a flat fee. It was early on, and turned out to be a good bet. What about you? What are you up to?"

"No good," George says.

"You should go on the wire," Tod says. "I bought in to some of the confiscation of the Northeast Kingdom Autonomous Zone—our old haunts, you know—and we're opening a wirehouse in Colebrook to zap up the area. We've still got some plugs available, and once we're fully operational, we'll infuse a two-hundred mile radius with airwire. Could get exciting."

Karl says, "We don't live in the world anymore. The world lives in us."

Tod smiles. "Isn't he cute? I'm going to make him a guru and put him on the air. He'll be more famous than God. He'll be his own God. Aren't you happy you've met him? Aren't you glad you know me?"

"Sure," George says, and chuckles. He's missed Tod, the pure innocence of his arrogance, the stupid joy he finds in life: always, for him, a life filled with possibility and hope. It feels like centuries since they escaped the fire. He leans in and kisses Tod's cheek. "On second thought, let's go back to my place," George says. He looks at Karl. "I've always wanted to fuck God."

§

And so he goes on the wire.

Just for fun, before leaving, George and Tod and Karl did a black-market deal for some old hand grenades, and they threw them through the windows of George's apartment building. "Death to property!" Tod screamed. "Cleanse your rebirth!" Karl screamed.

"Fuck God!" George screamed, and as fire flooded the collapsing building, Karl and Tod and George jumped into the Subaru and drove north at 100 miles an hour to the wirehouse Tod named Phoenix 1. It was a simple white rectangular building, unmarked and unremarkable.

Tod and Karl lead George inside to a small office overlooking a massive room that makes George think of an airplane hangar or a nuclear power plant or a spaceship from a sci-fi movie.

Tod takes a screen from a drawer in an old grey desk and calls up a contract. "Just got to decide the terms," Tod says. "A month, six months, a year, two years, five years. Two years offers a three percent hazard bonus, five years has a seven percent hazard bonus. The bonus is applied to the final amount at the moment you wake."

"Five years," George says.

"And do you want the flat-fee payment of $25,000, or a quarterly investment of half percent profit, with interest?"

"Profit."

"Smart choice. Okay, just handprint here."

George sticks his hand on the screen.

"Ready?" Tod says.

"Sure," George says. "Wait, just one thing. The hazard bonus. That's because I could die?"

"It's comprehensive. Brain death, physical death, but also any wire-induced psychosis or schizophrenia that the brainscan shows occurred during your time with us."

"Sounds great."

"It's all very rare," Tod says. "For most people, it's just dreamless sleep. Feels like nothing."

"Nothing," Karl says, "is the future of everything."

§

He will forget everything.

It will feel like nothing when he wakes.

He will wake.

§

He wakes in flashes. No light at first, just cold air tasting of cold metal.

Swirls of color and light. Like a busy carnival at midnight. (I've never been to a carnival, he tells himself, but he doesn't believe it.) Hands touch him, arms lift him to his legs, his legs won't hold weight, hands hold him, arms carry him.

Underwater voices surround him, speaking languages he's never learned.

Bright light. The world is white and it scratches his eyes.

Gloved hands hold mechanized syringes that prick the skin on his arms and legs. (These are my arms and legs, he tells himself, but he doesn't believe it.)

The room smells like thunder.

No, that's not it. The room smells like torn paper.

No. The room smells like yesterday, which was not yesterday, because yesterday he was asleep.

The room smells like nothing.

The room smells like everything.

He screams.

(These are my screams, he tells himself, and he believes it.)

A kid (kid? 20 years old maybe, maybe 30, but a kid, yes) with short blond hair and blue eyes sits naked across from him and holds a half-erect penis in his hand. "There's no need for that," the kid says.

George realizes he's naked, too. At least he's not holding his cock in his hand. Where is his hand? It seems to have gone away with the people who had arms and syringes. (The nurses, yes, that's the word, nurses, a perfectly good word, nurses.)

"You made it through just fine," Tod says from behind the grey desk. "Everything's in perfectly good order, and—are you listening? George?"

"I just, for a moment, I was—there are gaps," he says.

"Perfectly normal," Tod says. "Like blackouts when you drink too much. Nothing to worry about. Should be gone after a couple days. If they persist for more than a week, let us know, but it never happens."

"Nothing ever happens," George says. "Everything happens."

"What? You're muttering."

"Nothing," George says.

"Okay, then. Your accounts have been credited, and I've taken the liberty of getting you a house in Portsmouth. It's furnished, everything you need should be there. Any questions?"

"Where's Karl?"

"Karl?"

"From before. The guru. The god."

"Karl..." Tod laughs. "Oh, Karl! Yes, of course. Karl. Sad sad case. Too many drugs. We were at the mayor's orgy in Manhattan and he jumped off a balcony from the forty-seventh floor. He thought he was God. Hell of a delusion." Tod laughs again.

George stands in a mansion, not a house. How did he get here? He can't remember, but here he is, standing in a room that's nearly as large as his old apartment building, a room with floor-to-ceiling windows framed with gold, massive crystal chandeliers hanging from a distant ceiling painted with clouds and cherubs against a pale blue background, and antique furniture splayed across a marble floor. In the center of the room stands a mahogany desk, its surface covered with a pyramid of white powder. Tod peaks out from behind it.

"Isn't it great? Nobody cares about cocaine anymore, it's cheap as dirt, but I knew you'd get it."

"Get it?"

"*Scarface!*"

"I…"

"1983? Al Pacino, directed by Brian DePalma, written by Oliver Stone, loosely based on the 1932 Howard Hawks movie?" Tod steps closer and slaps George gently on the temple. "Did we totally fuck up your head?"

"No, I get it, I'm just…overwhelmed."

"Of course you are. Five years ago, things were different, right? I was just a punk with some spare cash, and one day I saw a sign, it said, 'THE WORLD IS YOURS', and well, now, yes, indeed, she is mine. Oh, you don't even know!"

"Know?"

"We forgot to tell you! I bought out my partners, consolidated my power, raised an army, and seceded from the U.S. It's a good thing you were in my wirehouse, because I pretty much wiped out most of the others with a…well, *surgical strike* would be too precise a term. Sabotage sounds so tawdry, though. I, let's say, exploited known weaknesses in the security and energy systems of twelve wirehouse networks throughout North America and made it so that most of what used to be known as New England is now pretty much, well…mine."

"Wait, I don't understand what you're telling me. There's no more United States?"

"Oh, there's a United States," Tod says. "It's just smaller. In every way. Think of it as The Confederate Flyover States of America, because the Western states became territories of Canada, so that pretty much just left the U.S. to be the old South, the Midwest, and the droughtbelt. And Mexico didn't want them, so…"

"But the people," George says, "in the other wirehouses. The ones you did whatever to. What about them?"

"Well, they're dead, of course."

"How many?"

"Who knows. Why bother counting? Ten million, thirty million, what does it matter? They were absolutely unnecessary to the economy, and I can produce enough energy with just my own wirehouses to power everything for centuries, so what's the loss?"

"So you're President now?"

"President? That's a silly title. I'm Emperor, I'm King, I'm whatever I decide to be. I am the Power. I renamed everybody else named Tod into something different, so I am just Tod. Come here—" He runs to one of the windows, dragging George along with him. "Look out there—" The window overlooks a small, quaint city with the steeple of a white church rising from its center. "What do you see?"

"I don't know."

"It's Portsmouth."

"That's Portsmouth?"

"I had it remade into a much more picturesque place than it was before. But don't pay attention to that. What do you see—the people, I mean. What sorts of people do you see?"

"I don't know. They're very small."

"Well, of course, we're half a mile away. Don't be so obtuse. Look."

"I don't know, Tod. This is all too much to take in—"

"*They're all white!*" he screamed. "Isn't it great?"

The room's walls and floor and ceiling all undulate and ripple for a moment as George's knees tremble and his stomach tries to crawl up his esophagus. He leans against the wall. "They're all white," he says, without knowing why he says it, but it seems like he should say something.

"What we figured out," Tod says, "is that the energy in the airwire can be used for more than just transmitting power or for transmitting digital information—it can also be used to alter molecular structures. It's damn difficult and requires a phenomenal amount of both basic wire energy and processor energy—I mean, we're talking orders of magnitude upon orders of magnitude here—but it can be done, as I have proved by turning everybody white and thus eliminating racial differences within the borders of my country. Welcome to utopia."

"Nazi utopia," George says.

"Oh please! Nazi schmazi! There are no death camps, no jackboots and uniforms, no painfully unsubtle propaganda, no *Triumph of the Will.*"

"What else have you done?" George says.

"Where to begin! I was just born to be emperor of the world. You live in the most peaceful, most prosperous country the planet has ever known. We have effectively unlimited energy, we have so much computer processing power that there are very few problems that can't be solved, the basic structures of the universe are now at our command—frankly, you and I are now standing in the best of all possible worlds."

§

George lies in bed and remembers that it is the bed in the mansion Tod gave him and he remembers the conversation they had and then wanting to run away but not having the strength and he remembers saying he needed to take a nap and he remembers Tod showing him the bedroom and telling him the house is fully aired and so anything he needs he just has to speak and it would all be great and wasn't it wonderful to be in the best of all possible worlds.

The house is aired, so he can just speak what he needs.

"I need to know if I am dreaming."

All the lights in the house flash on, the bed shakes, the air pricks every centimeter of his skin with microscopic needles.

"I know I'm awake," he says, "but that doesn't tell me if I'm dreaming. I could be dreaming that I am awake. Please just tell me."

"You are not dreaming," a voice says. It's a soft voice with a generic American accent, a voice he can't identify as either male or female. Just a voice.

"I could be dreaming that you said that," George says.

The lights go out. The bed is comfortable. The room is quiet. The voice says, "You should get some rest."

"You're probably right," George says. "Goodnight."

"Goodnight," the voice says.

§

Thin light abrades the darkness. He is lying down and there is a bed underneath him, but it is not the bed his body remembers; it is rougher, tighter, and somehow he knows it is narrow, with a thin mattress. A hand holds his hand. He turns and sees a body sitting on the bed with him. He squeezes the hand, the body turns, he looks up at the face, and the face is Anne.

"Where are we?" he says.

"One of the sub-basements of the wirehouse. I made them wake you. Wife's privileges in a time of war."

"We got divorced," George says.

"What are you talking about?"

"After we lived with your parents."

"We never lived with my parents."

"Of course we did," George says. "I was intolerable. I'm sorry about that, but—"

"You've only been awake a little while. You're going to be confused. Just rest."

"Where's Tod?" George says.

"Who's Tod?"

"He brought me here."

"Brought you here? When?"

"I don't know. When I plugged in. When was that?"

"You tried to kill yourself, George. I brought you to the hospital. They thought going on the wire would be the best thing to help you heal. That was nine months ago. But there's a war now, and—"

"I don't understand," George says.

"It's okay," Anne says. "Just sleep. You're confused. We're safe here, I think, for now. Just sleep. You'll remember everything later."

§

He dreams he is writing a movie. He knows it's a dream because he has no idea how to write a movie. Tod sits behind a mahogany desk in an office in Hollywood. Rectangular windows behind the desk let so much sunlight through that Tod is little more than a silhouette. George types out the script on a sheet he holds in his hand.

"I'm having trouble with the exposition," George says. "My characters talk too much. They explain things to each other. I don't know what to do."

"Have them take out guns and shoot each other," Tod says. "Every movie needs a gunfight. There's never been a good movie without a gunfight."

"Okay," George says. "I'll just have them shoot each other."

"But we need to care about them," Tod says.

"Right."

"Before they shoot each other, we have to care, or else why bother?"

"Right."

"So tell me what you've got so far."

"There's a giant room," George says, "and Al's in the room sitting at a desk, and on the desk is a pile of cocaine, a giant pile, a whole pyramid of cocaine. That's what I've got so far."

"It's a good image," Tod says, "but nobody would believe it. Who puts a pile of cocaine on their desk?"

"He's selling it," George says.

"Why would anybody sell cocaine?" Tod says.

"It's worth a lot of money," George says. "People kill each other for it. It's illegal, and addicts want it, so it costs a lot of money, and Al has killed all his rivals, so now he is the biggest seller of cocaine in the Yukon. He's got a dog named White Fang."

"What is this, a children's story? I don't want a fucking children's story about some sort of magic powder and a wizard with a dog."

"No, it's not a children's story. He swears a lot. And there are naked women."

"Good, I like that. But ditch the cocaine. Nobody cares about cocaine."

"Okay," George says. "What should I replace it with?"

"I don't know," Tod says. "It's your story. You figure it out. Put in everything, put in nothing, see if I care. I just want there to be a gunfight."

"Okay," George says. "I'll put in a gunfight."

§

He wakes again, and again Anne is beside him on the narrow, thin bed.

"If I dream about you twice," George says, "are you real?"

"Definitely," Anne says. "Two dreams equal one reality." She has a British accent, very cockney, like Audrey Hepburn at the beginning of *My Fair Lady*.

"You look great," George says.

"No I don't," she says. "But I love it when you lie."

An explosion rocks the world above them. Smoke, dust, and bits of brick and stone tumble down. Red emergency lights flicker on. At the far side of the room there is a metal staircase rattling against the wall. Tod comes down it, nearly tripping over his feet as he runs. He's wearing a fur cap and a military uniform of some sort. "Come along!" he screams at them. "Keep calm, and we'll carry on up above!"

Anne leads George toward the stairs, and they follow Tod up and up until finally the stairs twist into a spiral and the spiral leads to a far-off light and the light grows larger until it is a hole in the darkness of the sky. They climb through the hole into a blizzard of snow in a frozen city. Big Ben and the Empire State Building stand encased in ice against the horizon.

Tod calls out, "For the empire!" and takes a green plastic gun out of a pocket in his uniform pants. George thinks it must be a water pistol, but Anne apparently needs to know for sure, because she asks, "What is that?"

"It's a typewriter," Tod says. "I'm gonna write my name all over this town with it, in big letters!"

"Stop him!" George screams, but he doesn't know why.

Tod pushes Anne aside. She falls into the snow. Tod stares at George.

"This is a dream," George says. "I know that. This one. This is a dream."

Tod points the typewriter at him. "Get out of my way Georgie," he says. "I'm gonna spit!" He pulls the trigger, and a few drops of water squirt from the barrel. They fall to the snowy ground and don't quite form a letter, at least in any alphabet George knows.

Anne stands up and brushes herself off. "Don't mind him," she says. "He's seen too many gangster movies."

CUT TO: A cluttered apartment in a small brick building during an air raid. A wife tells her husband he needs to put the typewriter away and they need to turn the lights off and they should probably just go to bed. Close-up on the husband's face. A tear slips from his eye, but we can't tell if it is because of what he is writing or what his wife is saying or something else; all we know is that there is a tear.

CUT TO: The face of a young man, blond and blue-eyed, stereotypically Aryan. A tear slips from his eye, then the tear turns to blood. Pull back to reveal him standing in a line of soldiers at attention, their arms raised and pointing straight out in salute.

CUT TO: Oscar Wilde, old and ailing, sitting at a wooden table in a farmhouse. A few sheets of paper lie on the table, and Wilde takes one and, after a pause, writes on it with a pencil. We slowly zoom in to see the words of a poem:

> *with a flattering word.*
> *The coward does it with a kiss,*
> *The brave man with a sword!*

Suddenly, his hand crumples the paper, but we are so close now that it seems to be crumpling the screen itself.

CUT TO: George, alone on the sagging porch of a rotting farmhouse in northern New Hampshire. He holds a snub-nosed .38 revolver to his head. A tear slips from his eye. Pull back to reveal the overgrown lawn of the farmhouse. On the lawn sprawls the body of a young man, blond, shot through the heart. Pull back more to reveal a line of police cars on the road, their lights flashing, police officers with rifles and pistols drawn and pointed at George. Slowly, George lowers the gun. The police rush in.

CUT TO: A narrow prison cell. George sits on the single cot in the cell. A hand touches the bars of the cell. Pull back to reveal Anne.

CUT TO: Outside the prison gates. A grey, cold day. George walks out of the prison wearing a coat that is too thin for this weather. Anne approaches him. She covers him with a warmer coat. He smiles. They embrace and kiss.

FADE OUT.

§

"He will wake," Tod says to Anne. "There's no doubt of that, all his vital signs are great. It'll be slow, but he'll wake."

"But won't he feel—"

"It will feel like nothing when he wakes," Tod says.

"Won't there be memories of what happened?"

"He will forget everything," Tod says. "Not just the war, unfortunately. Wire tech is pretty primitive, compared to what we'd like it to be, and what I firmly believe it will be. Right now, though, to use an unfortunate metaphor, it's like carpet-bombing the brain. Better than electroshock by far, and not nearly as bad as a leucotomy, but we only use it for the tough cases. And George was a tough case. You know that better than anybody, Bob."

"My name's not Bob," Anne says.

"Sorry," Tod says. "A tic I picked up in the war."

§

George brings Tod a new draft of the first twenty pages of the script.

"The problem you're having," Tod says, "is that you haven't established a foundation of reality. If anything could happen, and any situation at any time could be a dream, then why should the audience care?"

"Do you care about your life?" George says.

"What's that supposed to mean?"

"At any moment, we could wake up. So why do you care about right now?"

"Because this isn't a dream."

"How do you know?" George says.

"Because this is life, this is now, it's what we are, we live in the present tense. Look, quit it with the drunk frat boy metaphysics, okay? Just establish a basic level of reality, put in some gunfights, and I'll get you financing."

"The reality is in the patterns," George says.

"The what?"

"Repetitions. Echoes. Reality is what doesn't go away."

"I don't want philosophy, George. I want entertainment. Pure, simple, brainless entertainment."

"With a few gunfights," George says.

"With a few gunfights," Tod says.

"Okay." George tosses a Luger pistol onto Tod's desk, then draws an M1911 Colt .45 from the holster on his belt. "Pick it up, you Kraut bastard," George says. "I don't kill unarmed men."

Tod grabs the Luger.

The pistols fire.

§

A writer friend once told me that the secret to a happy ending is stopping before the end.

§

Anne says, "I could kiss you right now."

And then she does.

Fade to black. The end.

§

I'm sorry. This was supposed to be a weird little science fiction story about harvesting people for energy in a society suffering from an advanced case of capitalism, a society where a good chunk of the population is irrelevant to the economy's health. That was all I wanted to write. But I can't forget what I keep trying to forget.

I've been divorced now for, what, two years? Twenty months, actually. Legally. It would be nice if I could stop writing about Anne. It would be nice if I could stop turning Michael into a Nazi. It would be nice if I could manage to get a book written in the next couple months so I don't have to pay back the advance and so people will stop emailing me about the third book in the trilogy.

Usually I ignore the emails. I responded to one today, though: "READ SOMEBODY ELSE FOR FUCK'S SAKE AND LEAVE ME ALONE." I thought it would make me feel better. It didn't.

(I already gave back the money I got to write a screenplay. Why anybody ever thought I could write a $100 million movie, I don't know. Sometimes having a great agent is a liability.)

Just before he said he'd never speak to me again, Michael said, "If you write a story about me, I'll kill you."

"If you kill me," I said, "then I'll know you read my story."

Then he called me a pathetic, self-loathing closet case, and he said he would never read a word I wrote and he hoped he'd never see me again because if he did all he'd want to do is spit in my face.

But there's really no reason you should care about that. In the grand scheme of the universe, it doesn't matter in the least.

In the grand scheme of the universe, I don't matter in the least. (Frankly, nor do you.)

Just before the divorce became final, Anne said, "You only tried to kill yourself to get attention. You didn't actually want to die."

She was right. I didn't want to die, and I don't want to now, either. I just wanted to go to sleep.

And then I just wanted to write a story, but the story became too much like a dream, and now it's too much like life. You didn't come here to hear about my life or my dreams. You came for some excitement, some fantasy, a bit of escape.

I'm sorry. I'd give you your money back if I could.

I don't think this is the foundation of reality that I was seeking for my story.

I can still hear bombs in the distance.

§

They managed to make their way down into the city. They huddled around a burning trash can with a few other people. They helped collect pieces of paper, cardboard, and wood scraps to add to the fire. They waited through the night and slept fitfully, without dreaming. Morning brought warmth and quiet.

Within a few weeks, the war had ended and the snows had melted. George and Anne and Tod found an apartment building that wasn't too burnt out, and they stayed there for a while. Eventually, the electricity came back on. Eventually, the government sent emergency crews to clean things up. Eventually, Anne got a job working in a biotech lab at UNH. Tod was hired as a political consultant for a mayoral candidate in Manchester, then became the New Hampshire chair for a gubernatorial candidate's campaign, and when the candidate won, Tod went to work in his administration. George quit drinking and pieced together work as a reporter, then as a movie critic, then Tod got him a job as a writer of political ads for Democratic candidates throughout the country. Anne and George will eventually get divorced, but they'll stay on speaking terms. George will have a few flings with Tod for old time's sake, but they'll both know it's not anything they should count on. Tod will move to Washington, D.C. Anne will move to Boston. George will move to Los Angeles. They'll be happy enough.

A lot of that is in the future. Some of it may not even come true.

For now, let's stick with this: Anne and Tod and George have just got the electricity to work in the apartment building they're squatting in. George uncorks a bottle of red wine he found at a liquor store, one of the only bottles in the whole place that hadn't been shattered in the bombing. They don't have any glasses, so they pass the bottle around until it's empty. They smile a lot, and giggle, and look into each other's eyes.

"We're still alive," George says.

"And right now," Anne says, "that's something."

"Here's to something," Tod says, and they laugh.

Knowing now is the right time to end the story, George hopes he never wakes up from this dream.

The Art of Comedy

We had all failed by then—failed as husbands, failed as lovers, failed as humanitarians, failed as despots, failed ourselves, failed the people we cared about, failed to remember what we should have remembered, failed to learn what we were expected to learn, failed to be all we could be, failed to understand—and somehow we met one night, the group of us, a failed congregation, under a bridge on the outskirts of Pittsburgh. We burned some trash to keep warm. We huddled together in silence until dawn threatened us with light, and someone said we should create a traveling show, and someone else chuckled, and someone else nodded, and we all agreed that yes we should create a traveling show together, a way to join our failures, a way to celebrate and to get out of Pittsburgh.

There were five of us, including me. My failure was a failure of nerve: I had once been in love, but I had been silent, I had suffered and enjoyed my suffering, had thought it somehow ennobling and artistic, and I had lost not only the object of my love, but the capacity for love itself, as if it were a bit of skin shed in a wound. I had wandered, I had rambled, I had learned to stop dreaming. I had stopped beneath the bridge, because I liked the shadows there, and I liked the smell of burning trash, the sharp sting in the nostrils, the grit on the tongue.

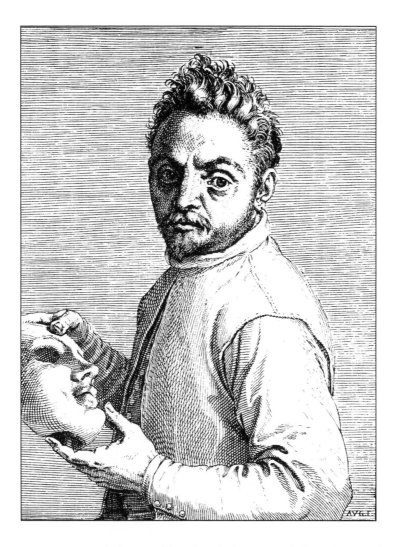

A woman with fierce red hair handed me a mask. "You lost this," she said, and pressed it against my face. I feared for a moment that the mask would never be removed, but she pulled it away and smiled at me and I took the mask in my hand. She told me it had been mine long ago. "I'm young," I said, and she laughed. "You are always young," she said, "that's your role." I must have looked perplexed, because she asked me if I remembered meeting the Emperor of the Moon, and I said, "No, of course not, who is he?" and she said he is the Emperor of the Moon, and she said that I visited him quite some time ago when I went out to get geese for my master and I flung a blanket over the geese and the geese flew high into the air, carrying me along with them, up through the top of the sky and to the moon, which caused me so much excitement I forgot to hold on to the blanket and the geese flew free and I fell down, down, down and landed in a lake on the moon, where three fishermen captured me in their net and declared I was the best fish they had ever caught, so they brought me to the Emperor of the Moon, who said I was a strange fish, probably some sort of pelican, and I protested that I was not a pelican, but that I was a man, and he laughed and declared that nothing so strange as I could be a man, but I said, "Of course I'm a man!" and he asked if I ever loved a woman, and I said I once loved Isabella, and he said that did not prove I was a man because after all everyone alive loved Isabella, and he stared in my eyes for a long time, seeing something no-one else could see, and then he tore off my mask and threw it toward the sky and I ran away, evading guards and jesters and courtesans, and I have been looking for my mask ever since.

The story of my encounter with the Emperor of the Moon became our first play. We scavenged for props and set pieces in junkyards throughout the purlieus of Pittsburgh, and we cobbled a wagon together from cast-off remnants of sunken boats that had washed to shore and jalopies that had jumped the bridge. The wagon was heavy even when it wasn't laden with boards and planks and beams and tattered costumes and battered puppets. Because it was so heavy we all had to pull it along, yoked together like emaciated oxen, and by the end of a day of traveling we were always exhausted, and we collapsed to the ground with burning muscles and shredded lungs. The difficulties of travel prevented us from performing on the days when we had pulled the wagon any distance, an unfortunate situation, because once we began performing we found it painful to stop. Sometimes we stayed in a town for weeks at a time, performing continuously except for short breaks to empty our bowels or scrounge for food. By the third or fourth day, we had no audience, but we continued our performance, because to stop would have been, we all seemed to agree, to die.

It was in a small town in Ohio that exhaustion finally took its toll. We had been performing for two months at that point, making our slow way across the land, and the nights and days of endless performing interrupted only by tedious, undifferentiated hours of dragging the wagon had made us wan and hollow and listless. Sometimes ours was a play about a man who only got halfway to the moon before he fell out of the sky. Sometimes the songs we sang, which, when we had begun, had had many choruses and marvelous moments for solo kazoo, got chopped down to just a few notes, a quiet word or two, then silence. Audiences booed and hissed and spat at us and demanded their money back.

The only person who seemed to be anything other than a ghost of himself was Captain Manducus, whose real name really was Captain, because his father had been a sailor in the navy and hoped the same for his son. ("Shouldn't he have named you Admiral?" I asked once. He said, "My father was a pragmatic man. He didn't want to get his hopes too high.") Captain had failed to live up to his father's most basic expectations, and had developed a severe fear of the sea. He went to business school, and, after graduating, became an expert in bankruptcy, plunging six different companies into it with great

aplomb. He was born for the stage. He dressed in our most elaborate costume, one made of garbage bags elegantly rendered into a flowing cape and baggy pants, with a doublet of origamied cardboard and a hat carved from a greasy pizza box. He terrified audiences by vowing to devour their babies whole. Every time we threatened to take a day off, to wander through a town or lie out in the grass of a field, Captain told us we were becoming sorry specimens of humanity, we were letting down our audiences, we were failing once again. He climbed onto the back of the wagon and shouted at the moon: "Tonight we will come to you, tonight, tonight, tonight!"

That was the night Camerani died. We had not found food in nearly a week, and everywhere we traveled, audiences thought our show pathetic, and none of them would pay us money. A few threw rotten vegetables, and we ate them greedily. While we were performing a particularly slow version of our play, trying to conserve our energy without stepping off the stage, Camerani suddenly came to life and ran away as if struck by lightning. None of us followed him immediately, but after a few hours, I wandered in the direction he had run off, and found him lying in a pile of chicken excrement not far from where our play continued in its leisurely way. He had scared the chickens off, and in his hunger had devoured what they left behind. "I'm dying," he said when I approached. He smiled, then issued the loudest, most horrible fart I've ever heard, and expired.

"We could eat him," Captain said when I told the troupe what had happened.

"No," said Rosalba. "Whatever killed him is still in his body. It would kill us, too."

And so we let time and the weather wash him away, though we did not stay around to see how it did so, instead choosing to continue on, hoping we might find some place where we could eat, some audience willing to pay for what we could offer, while Camerani's decomposition progressed in our imaginations.

"Perhaps we need a new play," I suggested.

"We don't know any other stories," Captain said.

"I know many stories," said Rosalba.

She told us the story of a man who begged for his life because he had seduced a young girl—just as the man was about to proclaim his love and devotion to the girl, the seduction was interrupted by

her father, who wanted to talk to the man about a business proposal. Seeing what the young man was about to do to the girl, the father quickly tore his daughter's clothes off and proceeded to make love to her. The young man, who was honest and honorable despite his attempt at seduction, pulled the father off of the daughter, whereupon the father gathered his clothes, dressed, pulled out his sword, and threatened to kill the young man. The young man pleaded with the father to be kind to the daughter and also to spare his life. The father enjoyed listening to the young man plead, but he was afraid of the sight of blood, and so, much to his own shame, had no intention of killing him. Instead, he handed the young man a mask that he himself had once worn, and he insisted the young man wear it for the rest of his life. It was a dark mask with sharp eyes and it frightened the young man, but he put it on. When he felt it on his face, he knew it was a terrible mask, one that would make his every glance evil, but he did not want to die, and so he kept the mask on and fled the house. Within a few days, he was captured by police officers who had found him standing atop a pile of dead bodies, all of them men near his own age, all of them with their faces torn off. The police shot the young man, and just before he died, he removed the mask and thanked the police for their kindness. A servant of the father, a maskmaker, had watched the young man go mad, and he reported to the father and daughter what had happened, and the father celebrated while the daughter screamed and screamed and screamed until her voice disappeared and she coughed up blood.

"That's a very sad story," I said.

"Yes," said Rosalba, "but if Captain plays the daughter, it will be very funny."

Captain did not want to play the daughter, and so we continued to travel, continued to starve, and continued to hope another story would find us while again and again we told the tale of the man who visits the Emperor of the Moon.

Luckily, right around this time, Pulcino fell in love with me. He was the oldest of our troupe, and quite ugly, with bad posture, a big belly, pockmarked skin, and spindly chicken legs. Over the course of our starvation, though, he had become more and more beautiful. His stomach had shrunk down to a normal size, which allowed him to stand up straight, and his legs, we discovered, were muscular, though slightly feminine. His skin became smooth, its duskiness now alluring rather than seeming to be some mark of impending death. He could smile now gently and generously.

I had gone to find some water at the edge of a reservoir, and I had wanted to get away from the other members of our troupe, because Rosalba's story still hung in my head, making me sad and wistful. The scars of my failure throbbed with each beat of my heart. Pulcino found me sitting on the grass beside the reservoir, and he sat beside me, his arm over my shoulders. He said nothing. We stayed like that for an hour or more, until finally he touched my face, turn-

ing my head toward him, and stared into my eyes. I turned away. "Why won't you look at me?" he said. I told him I knew where this would lead. "Where?" he said. I told him it would lead to failure. "That's what we know best, isn't it?" he said. He held me in his arms and rested his head on the back of my neck. The sun settled behind the reservoir, tossing splinters of itself across the water. I turned back to Pulcino. He removed my mask and kissed me.

Two days later, the troupe had created a new play, a love story. We traveled to another town after our first rehearsal. The wagon felt lighter to me, and Pulcino stood beside me while we pulled it. The first audience was small, but after we had performed our love story twice, the audience grew larger, until by the second day of our continuous performances (we did not stop to eat or drink, and we were all afraid to empty our bowels after what had happened to Camerani) it seemed the entire town had come to see our play. Each person had paid five dollars for a ticket, and many people brought food and even grills so they could have a barbecue while watching us. They brought us burgers and wine and beer. They told us that they laughed and cried. Wives said they appreciated their husbands more now, husbands said they would stop hitting their wives, children promised to marry only for love, and the mayor vowed to make it illegal for anyone to kill a man who kissed a man or a woman who kissed a woman, because, he said, love is so rare in this world that we must celebrate it, whatever form it takes, and the audience stood and applauded the mayor, and all the men in the audience kissed each other, and all the women kissed each other, and all the children shouted with joy.

We were perplexed by our sudden success. The audience came back again and again. Of course, we were pleased to be able to afford hotel rooms for ourselves and to be able to replace the wagon with a pickup truck. But we all knew our story was too simple, that it hid the truth of the characters we portrayed, that it reinforced too many prejudices while seeming to be open and affirming. Rosalba played a maiden whose true love had died in a war, Captain played an evil soldier who wanted to take advantage of Rosalba's mourning to make her marry him, I played a young artist Rosalba hired to paint a portrait of her lost love, and Pulcino played a man who bore a strange resemblance to that lost love and who served as the model for the portrait, then fell in love with my character. Captain, the evil soldier, schemed to make sure Rosalba saw Pulcino kiss me, because, being evil, he was certain it would cure her of her nostalgia and her grief, and that she would be angry with me and destroy the portrait. Instead, Rosalba was furious with Captain, because she saw through his scheming, but it was too late—Pulcino, consumed with shame, jumped off a bridge and drowned. Rosalba felt she had lost her love a second time, and she and I wandered the world together in mourning.

We played this story in town after town. With our pickup truck, we were able to travel across the country much more quickly, and soon we were in Maine, where even the hardiest fishermen broke down in tears at the end, and kissed their wives and kissed their friends. Soon enough, we replaced the pickup truck with a tractor trailer, hired a driver, and bought a bus to carry the actors and crew across the country as if we were rock stars or politicians on campaign.

It was in Boston that we first discovered other troupes trying to play our story. None of them had the success we did, the large audiences and (now) $50 tickets, but some were doing quite well, mostly by rearranging the story so that Rosalba and Pulcino fell in love. As we had become more successful and as the stages we played on had become larger, the set pieces more elaborate, we discovered that we were perfectly comfortable not performing for hours and even days at a time. We could now afford to live well, and we also had time to see some of the troupes that imitated our success.

A troupe in Texas offered something we had heard about, but never seen ourselves before. They told a similar story to all the other troupes, a variation on our story, but they did so more lewdly. Because of local strictures and statutes, none of the performers could remove all their clothes, but they found creative ways around this prohibition, and their performance was tremendously arousing. The play ended happily, with all of the lovers loving each other and the evil Captain now converted to Christianity, but the most remarkable element of the production had just begun, because the audience found the resolution so inspiring that, amidst ecstatic shouts of "Praise the Lord!" and "Hallelujah!", nearly every member of the audience began groping the people sitting around them. They tore each other's clothes off, they swooned, suckled, sucked

and sang; they blushed, they blew, they bleated, they blubbered all over each other until the entire theatre was a roiling mass of bliss.

We did not participate. It was too depressing, because we knew what it meant for us. Sitting in our hotel bar, drinking scotch and beer and vodka and wine, we reminisced about the good old days of starvation and want, the days when we feared life off of the stage, feared the death it would bring. Everything had changed, and the changes would, we knew, continue. The new sorts of plays would become vastly more popular than our play was, and though we would surely be given a theatre of our own in Las Vegas, the joy would soon be gone, and the need, as well. We had been performing once a day, and planned to reduce our performances to three per week, and we all knew we would be happiest with even fewer.

In the morning, Pulcino and I were the only members of the troupe still in the hotel. Everyone else had signed out and walked away, disappearing into the dawn. "We should go, too," Pulcino said, "before it gets too late and people notice."

We dressed and each packed one bag. We left the hotel through a back door and walked to a bus station, where we bought tickets to Boston. "We can head north from there," Pulcino said. "We've got enough money that we can buy a house on a lake or on the ocean. It will be beautiful." He kissed me. "Maybe we can write a book together, our memoirs. We started it all, you know."

The closer we got to Boston, the slower the bus seemed to travel. Pulcino had gotten fat again, and he found the seats uncomfortable. His skin was thick and baggy, his face jowled, and his posture seemed to get more bent each day. I still enjoyed his jokes, but not much else, and his obsession with checking his bank accounts every few hours wore on me. By the time we got to Boston, simply sitting beside him made me grit my teeth, and the night before, as we had rested in a cheap motel room and got drunk on peach schnapps, I found myself recoiling from his touch, and he told me I didn't love him anymore, that he was repulsive to me, and I said that was true, but not because he was fat and jowly, not because he wheezed when awake and snored when asleep, all of which I found somehow endearing, but because being loved made me sad (which was true, but just a story, and, like every story, incomplete). He held me tightly; his tears burned like acid on the skin of my back. We fell asleep together, and as I held him I knew I loved him, but only while we were in each other's arms, and he was too much for me to hold now, and I was too little for him.

In the bus terminal, I told Pulcino I needed to find a bathroom. I walked outside and hailed a taxi and asked the driver to take me to where I could fly away, which he interpreted as the airport, and that was good enough for me. Six hours later, having landed in Pittsburgh, I got in another taxi, and eventually, after a few wrong turns, we found the bridge I was looking for, and I paid the driver and he drove away, leaving me to stand in the twilight shadows shimmering beneath the bridge. Garbage littered the ground, and I gathered pieces of it in my hands and stuffed them into the metal basket that still stood there, apparently untouched since we had burned trash in it so long ago. I took a match from a book of matches I'd picked up at the airport bar, and I lit the trash on fire and watched it burn. I opened my suitcase, removed my mask, and placed it over my face.

Eventually, other people stood beside me at the fire. They gathered more garbage to keep the flames going, they shared cigarettes and whiskey, they muttered stories to each other, but none of them looked at me for long, and none of them wanted to remove my mask. My failure was complete.

Walk in the Light
While There Is Light

Baskerville decided to become a monster because he had chewed his way far into the Earth, and he lived now in the space he had chewed for himself, a musty cavern beneath a knoll in an unnamed wilderness in northern Maine. He had been on vacation, alone, hiking and camping, trying to forget his latest failed encounter with something resembling love, when he was seized with the desire to devour some soil. His friend Cal the Freudian would have said this desire was fueled by a need to consume and obliterate his mother—the Earth, of course, being the biggest mother of them all—but Baskerville thought this was bullshit, because Freud was bullshit, and if Cal had been there with him, Baskerville would have accused him of being a coprophiliac for all the bullshit he ate, and that would have set Cal a-thinking for so long that he might have shut up for a while.

Baskerville hadn't seen Cal in many years, though. Not since becoming a monster. Not since eating his way into the knoll and sealing the passage behind him with saliva-saturated mud.

He hadn't seen anyone in ages. His hair and his fingernails were unruly, and in the darkness of his cavern, a few of his teeth had grown and grown until now they jutted between his lips down a few inches below his chin. No light came into the cavern, and Baskerville didn't know if his eyes worked anymore, but his other senses were stronger than ever, and he spent much of his time listening to worms and bugs crawl around him. Sometimes he thought he heard distant voices, but he was convinced these were illusions, like an amputee's memory of a leg.

Needs were few in the cavern. When he got hungry, Baskerville ate more dirt, adding a new room to the cavern every couple of months. A spring provided a brook of water for him to drink. To empty his bladder and bowels, Baskerville went to the farthest wall and released his wastes into an apparently-bottomless pit that had opened there. He always listened to hear if his wastes had hit the bottom of the pit, but they disappeared into silence. This frightened him at first—for whatever reason, he found it more comforting to think of his urine and excrement settling somewhere instead of plunging toward the center of the Earth for all eternity—but now he took it in stride. Monsters, he decided, shouldn't think too much.

His biggest problem was time. There was a lot of it. Living alone in darkness, Baskerville had removed himself from history and progress and anything else that required days to be distinguishable from each other. To pass the time, he sang old songs to himself.

> *You've been talking about your brickhouse*
> *but you oughta see mine.*
> *It ain't so pretty but it still looks fine.*
> *I am gone, I'm long gone,*
> *My road is rough and rocky all my way.*

Baskerville had forgotten why he remembered the songs, and why he seemed to be able to sing a different one each day, and why his fingers strummed an imaginary guitar.

Sometimes, when he didn't feel like singing and when the darkness seemed particularly thick and when his teeth hurt and he feared he might finally need to chew his way up to the world he had so happily left behind so long ago—sometimes, he screamed out to the echoing emptiness:

"Hateful day when I received life!"

Or, if he were particularly filled with bile and eloquence:

"Accursed creator! Why did you form a monster so hideous that even you turned from me in disgust? God, in pity, made man beautiful and alluring, after his own image; but my form is a filthy type of yours, more horrid even from the very resemblance. Satan had his companions, fellow devils, to admire and encourage him, but I am solitary and abhorred!"

Yelling for so long hurt his throat and numbed his ears and made all the worms and bugs in the walls scurry around and cause little bits of dirt to rain on him for hours. The exclamations always had a good effect overall, however, letting him chuckle and guffaw at himself for quite some time. "'God, in pity, made man beautiful' [chuckle] 'and alluring,' [chuckle] after his own image' [chuckle, guffaw]. Hey grubs, you hear that? That was a good one, eh, that sure was good, wasn't it?" And then he inevitably fell over onto his ever-growing stomach and laughed until he fell asleep.

§

Sometimes Baskerville wakes up in the middle of the night and screams.

The only way he knows it is night is because he screams.

Even as a child, when he woke up in the middle of the night, he screamed.

§

He woke screaming and knew it was night. He knew it was time. How he knew, he did not know, but he knew: It was time to leave.

He began chewing. He told himself a story of what would happen when he emerged:

And so he quitted his retreat and wandered into the wood; and now, no longer restrained by the fear of discovery, he gave vent to his anguish in fearful howlings. He was like a wild beast that had broken the toils, destroying the objects that obstructed him and ranging through the wood with a staglike swiftness. Oh! What a miserable night he passed! The cold stars shone in mockery, and the bare trees waved their branches above him; now and then the sweet voice of a bird burst forth amidst the universal stillness. All, save he, were at rest or in enjoyment; he, like the arch-fiend, bore a hell within him, and finding himself unsympathized with, wished to tear up the trees, spread havoc and destruction around him, and then to have sat down and enjoyed the ruin.

This story scared him. Previously, when he had thought of escape, he had imagined himself celebrated. He had imagined that people would be amazed at his experience and his transformation, that they would contact newspapers and television stations, that scholars and scientists would vie for the opportunity to study him and Hollywood producers would clamor to outbid each other for the rights to his tale. He imagined going on a lecture tour around the world and speaking to learned societies—he had even prepared his lecture in his mind, daring to imagine how his life might explain a particular philosophical point:

When I was a child, before my time underground, I loved circuses, and for some time as an adolescent I traveled with a circus. I often watched a pair of artists busy on trapezes high up above the crowd. They swung, they swayed back and forth, they leaped, they floated in each other's arms. One hung by his hair held in the other's teeth. "That is human freedom," I thought. "Self-controlled movement."

But no. No! I didn't want freedom. Only a way out—right or left or any direction at all, it didn't matter. I made no other demands, even if the way out also proved to be a mere illusion. A small desire—the disappointment would not be any greater—to get out—to move on! Simply not to stand still with arms raised and pressed against a wall of mud.

Oh, it would be wonderful to be celebrated! Some nights, while his screams echoed through the dirt beneath the world, he savored the wisdom he would share with the crowds that surely awaited his emergence.

Now, though, he was not so sure. His new vision gave him pause. He bore a hell within him. He found himself unsympathized with. He wished to tear up the trees, to spread havoc and destruction around him. He sat down and enjoyed the ruin.

He held dirt in his mouth so long it nearly evaporated.

§

Baskerville discovered that if he kept chewing his way back to the surface of the Earth, he did not wake up screaming. He also discovered that the more dirt he ate and the closer he got to the surface, the more he remembered from his life there.

He remembered his mother asking him a question: "What's in your mouth?"

He remembered his answer: "I don't know. I found it behind the refrigerator. In a little can."

He remembered a dog named Moonpie and a dog named Mooncalf and a man named Moonbelly in a story called "City Life" that he read in a class at a land-grant college where the smell of manure and silage from the fields often wafted into the classrooms.

He remembered law school. He remembered tort reform. He remembered glorious debris under auditorium seats. He remembered the bar exam and the job offer and the partnership yearned for, never achieved. He remembered dinner parties and cocktail parties all full of laughing aristocrats. He remembered toilet bowls and vomit.

"The price of food is going up."

"A rat bit little Nell."

"The streets were scary, but home was just as perilous."

He remembered all that. But most of all he remembered words threaded and shuffled in between all the others:

"This is an unhealthy relationship."

§

He knew he was close. He could almost smell the fresh air. He could almost see the sun and moon. He could almost hear the howling wolves and the tittering birds.

He rested because his stomach ached. He belched. He farted. He smacked his lips. He sang a bit of a song:

> *Bo weevil meet his wife:*
> *"We can sit down on the hill", Lordy*
> *Bo weevil told his wife:*
> *"Let's trade this forty in", Lordy*
> *Bo weevil told his wife, says:*
> *"I believe I may go North", Lordy*

The song was supposed to be fast, but he sang it slowly. He did not remember the exact tune. Long ago, he had heard the song on a scratchy record at his grandfather's house. He had listened to it over and over through a rainy afternoon, trying to learn the words. Finally, he gave up trying to learn the words and instead learned the pattern of clicks and spits the record issued as it played. He couldn't remember the clicks and spits now, though; all he could remember were the words. He sang them slowly, mournfully.

§

Upon his emergence from the underground, the first impression produced by Baskerville's appearance and behavior was that he was a schizophrenic escaped from confinement; it remained only to be shown whence he had escaped. He was brought into state custody and subjected to a series of tests and studies conducted by awkward, excitable medical students. He showed no consciousness of what was going on around him; his look was a dull, brutish stare; nor did he give any indication of intelligence, until pen and paper were placed in his hand, when he wrote clearly and repeatedly, "Kaspar Hauser."

§

From *The Atlantic Monthly*, January 1861, page 63:

"When it became evident that the first conjectures concerning him were wrong, strenuous efforts were made by the police to sound the mystery, but without the slightest success. He himself could give no clue; for he neither understood what others said nor could make himself understood. With the exception of some six words, the sounds Caspar uttered were entirely meaningless. He recognized none of the places where he had been, no trace could be obtained of him elsewhere, and the most vigilant search brought nothing to light. The surprise which his first appearance produced increased as he became better known. It then became more and more evident that he was neither an idiot nor a lunatic; at the same time his manners were so peculiar and his ignorance of civilized life and his dislike for its customs so great, that all sorts of conjectures were resorted to in order to explain the mystery."

§

Baskerville explained to the medical students that Kaspar Hauser had only had six words when he entered human society, and so wasn't able to explain himself well at first; Baskerville, though, had plenty of words. He had certainly lost some of his vocabulary during his time in the dark—for instance, he identified an umbrella as a "floppy disk"— but he was nonetheless certain he could be of considerable help in their scientific inquiries into his condition. The students nodded and smiled, nodded and smiled, nodded and smiled, then fed him pills. A week later, he was released, free on his own recognizance, no longer subject to medical discourse.

The city swarmed and spumed about him. The students had given him a tourist map and pointed out their favorite coffee shops and brothels. He followed the map as best he could, weaving through alleys and avoiding dangerous thoroughfares, hoping some purpose might suggest itself, but none did, so as night replaced the grey day, Baskerville sat in the shadows beneath a bridge just beyond the territory the map suggested was of any interest. Hoping to alleviate his hunger, he stuck a handful of dirt in his mouth, but it made him cough and retch and it hurt his teeth. Exhausted and dispirited, he curled up against the bridge's concrete pillar and fell asleep.

§

He dreamed of voices:

...don't you think that is an admirable sentiment?...

...it might very well come from someone who was convinced that the business is supernatural...

...I fear that even he has not quite grasped the significance of this sentence...

...I confess that I see no connection...

...this exceeds anything which I could have imagined...

...we are coming now rather into the region of guesswork...

...how in the world can you say that?...

...it is the scientific use of the imagination...

...but we have always some material basis on which to start our speculation...

...I think anything out of the ordinary routine of life well worth reporting...

...there seems to be danger...

...well, that is what we have to find out...

...your request is a very reasonable one...

...well?...

...nothing...

...au revoir, and good-morning...

He woke to discover two women, both wearing white, standing over his hospital bed.

"How did I get here?" he asked.

"You have many questions, of course," one of the women said.

"And we have many questions for you," the other woman said.

"How are you feeling today?"

"How long have you been feeling?"

"What is normality for you?"

"What is the problem now?"

"Do you feel?"

"Have you actually been?"

"Have you had any serious feeling in the past?"

Sharp fluorescent light coming down from the ceiling pushed the room back and forth. Baskerville said, "What is wrong with me?"

"The disease cannot be cured, but we can try our best to control it," one of the women said.

"There is no problem. You'll be well," the other woman said.

He slept.

He woke.

It was not a hospital. Maybe it had been a hospital before, but now it was not. It was a very white room, and he was lying on a bed in it, but it was not a hospital room or a hospital bed. Slowly, he sat up. The room was not as white as it had seemed—that was an effect of the sun pouring through the window opposite the bed. His face had been wrapped in sunbeams. He blinked and squinted.

It was a bedroom. Yes, he remembered now. He had been here before. This was his bedroom. He had lived here as a child. The house had been in the family for generations. His grandfather and his great-grandfather and his great-great-grandfather and his great-great-great-grandfather had all been farmers here. (His great- and great-great- and great-great-great-grandmothers had all been burned at the stake.) His father had become a lawyer and had had the house retrofitted, refurbished, structurally adjusted. Baskerville himself had inherited the house when his father died and his mother took off to live with a landscape architect in a yurt. Yes, he remembered now.

He climbed out of bed. He was wearing his favorite pajamas, the ones covered with cartoon pictures of Leo Tolstoy burping out a balloon filled with the words, "What is art?"

Baskerville stood at the top of the stairs. "Cal?" he said quietly, not certain why he had said it. But Cal should be here. "Cal?"

Art begins when one person, with the object of joining another or others to himself in one and the same feeling, expresses that feeling by certain external indications.

The house was silent.

"This is an unhealthy relationship."

And it is upon this capacity of man to receive another man's expression of feeling and experience those feelings himself, that the activity of art is based.

He walked slowly down the stairs. The downstairs rooms seemed barren, despite their furniture. There wasn't enough. Things were missing. He could not remember what.

If people lacked the capacity to receive the thoughts conceived by the men who preceded them and to pass on to others their own thoughts, men would be like wild beasts, or like Kaspar Hauser.

He opened the screen door and stepped onto the porch. The morning was cool, dry, sunny. The grass needed to be mowed. The barn was sagging and full of bats and swallows. He had never known this house when it was surrounded by livestock, but he could imagine his grandparents working with the animals, and he could imagine roosters crowing in the morning and cattle making their cattle sounds and ducks and geese and sheep and all the other animals waking up, admiring the day, wondering what awaited them and how it might be different from their dreams.

Baskerville climbed into his car, a little hybrid that got excellent gas mileage, and drove into town. It was a college town, and so had a coffee shop, the Sunday Café, which he visited at least once a week. He knew all the people who worked there by sight, but he didn't know any of their names and they didn't know his. (This was typical for him; he was amazed by people who easily became friendly with strangers.) The clerk at the Sunday today was the one Baskerville had once pointed out to Cal and said, "He's kind of cute," and Cal had said, "He has a wife and a dog," and Baskerville had said, "How do you know that?" and Cal said, "I heard him talking about them," and Baskerville said, "He's still cute."

Baskerville said to the clerk, "There's a guy I usually come in here with, a little bit taller than me, a little bit heavier, sort of, well he's got big shoulders, his name's Cal, he comes in here with me a lot, you might have seen him, have you seen him?"

The clerk thought for a moment, shrugged, thought, said, "Nope. Don't think so. Can I help you?"

Baskerville ordered a latté and while he waited, he talked to other customers. The customers were wary, more so than usual. A gigantic monster, they said, had arrived the night before, armed with a gun and many pistols, putting to flight the inhabitants of a solitary cottage through fear of his terrific appearance. He had carried off their store of winter food, and placing it in a sledge, to draw which he had seized on a numerous drove of trained dogs, he had harnessed them, and the same night, to the joy of the horror-struck villagers, had pursued his journey across the sea in a direction that led to no land; and they conjectured that he must be speedily destroyed in the breaking of the ice or frozen by the eternal frost.

"No," Baskerville said to the customers. "You've got the wrong story."

His latté was ready. He paid the clerk and went back outside.

As he walked down the sidewalk on Main Street, sipping his latté, Baskerville thought about regret. He was able to remember more of his life every minute, and with each added fragment, his regret deepened. When was the last time you were happy? he asked himself. It's not that I'm *un*happy, he said to himself. I'm content, more content than I've been in a long time. But happy, no,

I wouldn't say that. I was happy when Cal and I were—yes yes, now I remember—when we both quit our jobs and decided to be utterly irresponsible and spent the little bits of savings we'd accrued, spent it on a flat in London—it was March of the year of the Iraq invasion, I remember, because we stayed up till one in the morning to watch the U.S. president on TV and we drank wine and we screamed and swore at the president on TV—and the moment I remember being most happy was a morning where the light was just like this, and the air was just like this, bright and clear, and we sat together in the tiny kitchen of that tiny flat with the windows open and the door open and we drank coffee and read the *Guardian* and yes, he said to himself, that was happiness.

He began to whisper a song.

> *I am gone, I'm long gone,*
> *My road is rough and rocky all my way.*

Suddenly Baskerville dropped his latté and dropped to his knees and began to tear at the asphalt of the sidewalk with his fingers. He needed to dig, he needed to find sustenance. His fingernails cracked, splintered, broke. The skin at the ends of his fingers disintegrated. Blood poured from his hands. The asphalt would not crack; it was new and strong. He could not pull it up. He had no effect on it at all. Starvation consumed him. Sunlight burned his skin.

"Hey mister, you okay?"

He looked up into the little boy's face.

"Don't talk to strangers," the boy's mother said.

"I'm okay," Baskerville said, standing up, brushing himself off. "I just dropped my drink."

"When I dropped my ice cream," the little boy said, "I cried."

Baskerville smiled at the boy, but the boy did not see because his mother had pulled him away. "What's in your mouth?" Baskerville heard her say as they walked off, but he did not hear the boy's reply.

Baskerville made his way back to his car. By the time he drove up the driveway to his house, twilight had inched the day aside. The old farmhouse loomed dark against the evening sky. Baskerville walked slowly up the steps, then inside. He asked himself how he felt, but he got no answer. Without turning on any lights, he wandered through the rooms of the house, each one seeming larger than the last, each one full of strange and shifting shadows. His footsteps echoed. A mouse or chipmunk scurried through the walls.

Baskerville ended up in the living room. There had once been artwork on the walls, but it was all gone now. This room was more obliterated than the others—the only piece of furniture that remained was the old grey couch he'd had since his senior year of college. Cal had always hated that couch and threatened to throw it out, to burn it, to blow it up with dynamite or TNT or vitriol. The couch was bruised and scarred, certainly, but sturdy, a survivor, built to last. Baskerville stared at it for a moment, then, finally, not knowing what else to do, he sat down and enjoyed the ruin.

A Map of the Everywhere

Alfred worked in the sewer fields because all the other jobs he'd held had disappointed him. He was easily given to disappointment. A few days after his seventh birthday, his parents had stopped talking to each other, and soon they used only the smallest possible words with him, often communicating purely through grunts and snorts. Aching for more variety and another way to live, he apprenticed himself to a clockmaker when he was fifteen, but never quite learned the craft before running off to work for a potter, then a civil engineer, then a mason.

None of these jobs held his interest for long, he showed no talent for them, and though he disliked making decisions, he found the one decision that came naturally to him was the decision to move on. When he was twenty-two, he entered a mountain monastery, but he discovered his faith was thin, slippery, and easy to lose, and he found the daily routine of prayers and flagellations left many scars. He moved on to join the nomadic coffee pickers who wandered past the monastery every few days shouting out obscenities at the monks, who, legend had it, had once refused to pray for a picker who had plummeted to his death after reaching for a bean dangling off the side of a cliff.

Alfred enjoyed his time with the coffee pickers, enjoyed their ribald humor and earthy wisdom, but the constant exposure to coffee kept him from getting much sleep, and after a few sleepless years he found himself wandering farther and farther away from his colleagues in search of beans to pick, until one day he realized he'd lost his way and wandered all the way back to the city.

He did not want to be in the city, and so he walked down street after street, but the streets only led to other streets, all of which seemed to lead back to each other. He asked pedestrians for directions, but only one spoke to him, a small old woman with eyes obscured by a grey-green gauze of film. "Get yourself a shovel and dig," the woman said, then snorted dryly and blew a cloud of dust from her nose. Alfred would have been annoyed and distressed if he weren't so exhausted, but he did not have the strength to offer any response. He stumbled down a blind alley, curled up amidst a pile of outdated computer components dumped behind a pet shop, and fell asleep. He dreamed of roads leading toward treeless hills where wind scarred the soil and a grey moon cast shadows that looked like ancient pictograms written across the landscape.

When he woke, Alfred discovered he had been loaded into the back of a large pickup truck along with the computer components. He ran his hands over acoustic couplers, memory cards, logic boards, monitors with sentences burned into their glass, and bulky CPUs sporting little metal labels saying, "Made in China."

Soon the truck came to a stop at a junkyard. A plump man with a scraggly grey beard and a missing eye asked him who he was and why he was in the back of the truck. Alfred said he was looking for work, and the man said there was no work at the junkyard, but the sewer fields a few miles in that direction were always looking for workers with nowhere else to go, and Alfred thanked the man and began walking down the road.

He was still far from the sewer fields when he heard the clanks and groans of the refinery. Soon he could see the massive pipes and smokestacks silhouetted on the horizon, and then he saw the fields, the broad expanse of brown-black sewage oozing from the side of the road to the farthest horizon. He had heard about the sewer fields, heard terrible stories of the people who toiled in them, sorting through the waves of excrement in search of objects and materials that would please the field owners. Workers who were lucky could make quite a lot of money, it was said, but Alfred had never met anyone who knew a lucky worker—at least one whose luck had held out long enough to be enjoyed. Instead, he heard tales of Jack's friend Franco who got sucked up into the refinery engines and turned to smoke and ash, or Rosa's Uncle Hans who drowned in the sewage, or the ghosts that spoke in ways no-one understood.

Alfred, it turned out, was neither lucky nor unlucky, which is the best fate for a field worker. After only a few days in the fields, standing in chest-high sewage with a yellow plastic colander the foreman had given him on the first day, he stopped noticing the stench, stopped retching and puking, stopped thinking that at any moment he would collapse and end up like Franco or Uncle Hans. By the beginning of the second week, the refinery's gasps and screams and hums calmed him as he worked, lulled him into a pleasant state of half-dreaming, his mind lost in images of roads and of the words for roads, images that lasted just long enough to be erased as his hands held the colander and sifted through the sewage.

At first, Alfred spent his nights sleeping on the edge of the fields. He could have joined one of the camps of workers farther out, but by the time the sun set, he was too tired to talk. He ate roots and vegetables that grew plentifully near the fields, and enjoyed his solitude. It required no prayers or self-abuse, and it gave him time to think about the strange visions that filled his daydreams: visions of lollipop-shaped children and old men with mouths full of coins and cuckoo clocks that held midnight rituals to sacrifice pocket watches to the gods. He had never had such visions before. Before, the monotony of daily work would lull him into a blind and mindless state, letting time drift through him without notice.

One night, Alfred woke to the sound of whispers. A pair of gauzy eyes stared down at him from a face as craggled as the moon. "This is where I have come to dig," the voice (little more than a breeze) said from dusty lips.

Alfred stood up. He could not tell if it was a man or woman in front of him, wrapped in shreds of plastic, leaning on a rusty shovel. "What are you digging?" Alfred said.

"A hole," the creature replied.

"Why?" Alfred said.

The creature paused for a moment to consider the question, then said, "I must dig a hole to China."

Alfred tended toward grumpiness whenever he was woken in the middle of the night. He said, "Look, I already have enough surrealism in my life, and I really don't have the patience for more. Would you please explain to me why you have to be exactly here at exactly now doing exactly this?"

The creature spoke of pecuniary canons of taste, the conservation of archaic traits, modern survivals of prowess, and the belief in luck. Alfred didn't listen closely. The voice slipped more and more toward silence as the creature stood there, sweeping loose gravel with the shovel, until the voice disappeared in the scrape of rock and dirt against metal. Alfred feared that the creature was crying and not able to make a sound or shed a tear, its voice hollowed out, its ducts gone dry. Alfred shuddered. He walked away.

As the first bits of sunlight slipped over the horizon, Alfred stopped walking and looked out across the shadowy plains of the sewer fields, where he saw workers already sifting through it all and foremen riding motorized sleds from one worker to the next to note who had collected what and to prod them on with lectures about empowerment and the good life. Alfred fell to his knees, ready to pray for salvation, but then he remembered that he had lost his faith and lost his way, and so he clawed at the damp soil in search of something he could not name, hoping his luck might reveal itself if he just jostled the topography a bit, but he found only some berries. They were sweet and made him smile.

Behind him, Alfred heard soft footsteps. He turned around. Three creatures with gauzy eyes, craggled faces, and dusty lips, all wearing shreds of plastic, all leaning on shovels, stood staring at him. "You must dig a hole to China," one of the creatures whispered.

"I was digging for faith or direction," Alfred replied. "I have no interest in China. I couldn't even find it on a map."

"Then you have need of a cartographer," another of the creatures said. "I have known many cartographers."

"They are a strange breed, cartographers," another of the creatures said.

"They live in hovels and garrets," another of the creatures said. "They seldom shave."

"I have to go to work soon," Alfred said. "I need to find some more berries before I starve to death or start to eat the dirt. Excuse me—" He began to walk away, but the three creatures stood in front of him.

One of the creatures said, "The conventional scheme of decent living calls for a considerable exercise of the earlier barbaric traits."

One of the creatures said, "We are the scars of wounding words."

All three of the creatures thrust their shovels into the ground. Each pulled up a pile of dirt and held it in front of Alfred. "Choose wisely," one of the creatures said.

Before he could think about what he was doing or why, Alfred reached into the pile of dirt in the shovel of the creature to his left, and from the dirt he pulled a grey business card with a name and address printed on it. He flicked the dirt off the card with his finger and read what was written there:

> GÜNTHER P. LOPEZ
> *cartographer and mime*
> *17 Gough Square, Lichfield*

When he looked up from the card, Alfred for a moment thought the creatures had disappeared, but then he saw that they had positioned themselves along the side of the road with their backs to him, and they had commenced digging to China.

At that moment, Alfred realized the dawn had turned to day and he was late for work. He could not pull his eyes from the spectacle of the creatures at the side of the road. He was entranced by their gnomic greyness, his imagination inspired to build entire lives for them, lost lives—families discarded for the sake of indeterminate destinies, memories forgotten in quests that the years whittled down to simple syllables and empty gestures. Alfred pressed his fingers into his eyes. The creatures did not turn around. "Please…" he said, but they continued digging. Fury rose in his chest, he clenched his teeth, he tried to keep his feet from moving, but within a moment he had become so unwitted that he could not escape his old habit of moving on, and he ran and ran down the road.

It was, for a very long time, a straight road, utterly without curves or even indentations, basically a berm raised in the midst of the sewer sea, but after many monotonous miles, kilometers, and versts of unvarying straightness, the road curved, swerved, dived, and diverged into a web of tributaries radiating from a point, all labeled with flimsy metal signs indicating avenues and boulevards, lanes and highways, turnpikes, beltways, thoroughfares, underpasses, boreens, detours, post roads, and main drags.

By now, Alfred's anxieties had barnacled themselves to other possibilities, worrying him about where to go and what to do there or here or wherever he ended up, but he remembered the card of the cartographer and it eased his mind, giving him one direction to look for: Lichfield.

§

Alfred wandered down Lichfield Lane, going on the assumption that such a lane might lead to Lichfield, and for once his assumption proved correct. He emerged from the tree-lined lane in a small town with dirt streets and narrow wooden buildings raised on stilts. "Why the stilts?" he asked an old woman sitting in a rocking chair up on the porch of a supply shop for rocket scientists.

"Better circulation!" the woman yelled down at him, apparently assuming he was hard of hearing. Alfred was about to reply, but before he could issue any words, the woman got out of her rocking chair, fired up a jetpack, and flew off into the clouds drifting across the blue and summery sky.

It did not take Alfred long to locate Günther Lopez, whose office towered high above everything else in Lichfield. Not only were its stilts taller than any others, but it was the only lighthouse in town, although why a town so far from the ocean would need any lighthouse at all was (and remained) a mystery to Alfred.

"Ahoy!" Alfred called up to the lighthouse. "Günther Lopez!"

After a moment, a man with a bright white, clean-shaven face and sensitive green eyes peaked out of an open window toward the top of the lighthouse tower and called out, "Wie ist die Wetter Heute?"

"Excuse me?"

"No creo en los signos del zodíaco!"

"I am in need of a cartographer," Alfred said.

Lopez held his hands to his face and suddenly his entire countenance erupted with a bright, idiotic smile. He gestured for Alfred to ascend the iron stairs spiraling around one of the stilts.

The inside of the lighthouse was spare, a single round room with brightly-colored plastic chairs and a large glass table in the center. At the far side, a bookcase sprouted rolls of maps.

Lopez greeted Alfred by pretending to shake hands with him from across the room. Alfred watched with growing frustration as the man carried on a lively, silent conversation with himself. Finally, Alfred said, "Shi-gatsu ni Amerika e kaerimasu!"

Lopez froze when he heard the words. His face sank like wet clay. "How did you know?" he said quietly.

"How did I know what?"

"Don't be coy. My mother's ancestry is a precious secret to me. I had no idea anyone else knew she was Finnish."

"I have come here with a purpose," Alfred said. "I am allergic to *non sequiturs*, and I can already feel my nose stuffing up. Please, can we talk cartography?"

"Upland planetable rectification alidade bathymetry hachure monoscopic isopleth!" Lopez screamed, then fell to the floor, where he gasped and panted with great élan.

Alfred turned away so that Lopez would not see the tears welling in his eyes. This road, too, had led to nothing. The muscles in his back tensed, whipping memories across his skin.

From the vantage of the lighthouse tower, Alfred looked down at a clearing in the middle of a dense forest. On a rock in the clearing sat a man who rested his head in his hands. While the cartographer continued to chatter behind him, Alfred stared at the man, wondering if what he saw were alive or, instead, a particularly skilled sculpture. The answer came when the man glanced up at the lighthouse. Sorrow-laden eyes, indisputably alive, met Alfred's own eyes for one blink before the head returned to the hands.

Without looking back, Alfred climbed down the spiral stairs and walked away from Lichfield toward the forest. He trudged through the undergrowth and between the trees, pushing his way into the lightless woods. When darkness engulfed him he saw a sparkle of light coming from the clearing at the far side, and he made his way toward it.

The man still sat on the rock. Alfred looked at him and felt compassion growing in his heart. He wanted to speak, to offer words of consolation or sympathy or hope, but language seemed suddenly too blunt, too barbed, too barbaric. Gently, tentatively, he set his hand on the man's neck. The skin was soft and warm. The man turned and looked at Alfred. He had a dark face with a prominent nose and small green eyes, their whites crackled red, having run out of tears.

"I'm looking for a cartographer," Alfred whispered.

"My mother is a cartographer," the man said. "Her office is in the lighthouse. Her name is Günther Lopez. She is insane, but she is a good cartographer."

"She's not the kind of cartographer I need," Alfred said, but he wasn't sure why he said this or how he knew it was true, and so he decided to tell a story: "I once spent some time with a civil engineer, surveying places to put new roads and buildings, but I could not make the compass work and I could not draw straight lines. He stopped talking to me and would scream when anyone said my name. He accused me of being a poet, and he said that I would ruin him."

The man nodded. "When I was younger," he said, "I told my mother I didn't know where to go or how to get there, and she said she would draw me a map, because she hated to see me in pain. I followed the map to the edge of the world, and when I got there, all I found was silence. I wrote a play, because I thought that might alleviate the silence. It didn't help. When I dragged myself home, my friends stole the play and read it to each other and after they woke up they said well at least I'd learned to amuse myself."

Alfred leaned down and kissed the man. "My name is Zachary," the man said.

Zachary and Alfred sat together in the woods until the sun went down and the stars came up and the sky filled with old ladies wearing jetpacks, out for an evening flight. Zachary whispered words from his play into Alfred's ear, and Alfred laughed many times, amused.

§

Here is the last speech in Zachary's play:

> **ZEUS:** *Tales from the unpublished autobiography of Zeus, god of everything, part one. Ahemmm. When I was just a wee-little deity, crawling about in some ethereal nook or cranny, I found a map of the Everywhere, and I studied this map until the stars went out for the night. When light returned, the map was gone. No-one could tell me where it went. I was lost, destined to not so much wander as stumble from point to point, thing to thing, and where to where. Forever finding hosts of theres, never finding a single here. Waiting, always, for the stars to go out again, and for my map to find me, to press itself against my skin in the momentary darkness.*

§

By the clocks, it was tomorrow when they left the woods, and even the clearing was dark. The forest itself was so dense as to be more than dark, to be the very antithesis of sight, but Alfred and Zachary had four other senses left, and used them well to touch and hear and taste and smell their way back to Lichfield.

"Can we go anywhere other than the lighthouse?" Alfred asked. "I'm not sure I'm up for another encounter with..."

"My mother won't be there now," Zachary said. "She goes home at night, because the light bothers her."

Alfred looked up and saw a thick bolt of light swirling through the sky from the top of the lighthouse. It caught clouds and moon-dust in its journey from one side of the night to another, illuminating the way for the ghosts of unmoored boats potentially floating lost across the land.

Alfred said, "Let's go there then," and so they did.

In the round room in the center of the light, Zachary showed Alfred map after map: maps of fertile and infertile lands, maps of entangled roads, maps of divided continents and lonely islands, maps demonstrating the movement of authoritarian medical discourse from urban centers to rural outlands. "This is her favorite," Zachary said, pulling a small vellum map from the bookcase and unrolling it with care and respect on the glass table.

Alfred scrutinized the map, but did not know what it showed. The outlines of areas looked like towns of some sort, with hills and rivers between some of them. But none of the words made any sense to him. "What is it all?" he asked. He pointed to words: *gynecomastia, feminae barbatae, androtrichia, androglottia, gynophysia...*

"She said it was a map of the states of desire. Or maybe disappointment. I don't remember. I've never been able to understand it, myself, but I find it entrancing, nonetheless."

After looking at the maps, they lay together on the wooden floor and let the light spin around them. Zachary told Alfred about his father, a linguist, and how he was certain it was his father who drove his mother mad, filling her with words she could not mime, an entire ungesturable grammar. His father died in an act of conjugation soon after Zachary was born. Alfred told Zachary about his own parents, his father who had always regretted not dying in a war, his mother who became an architect after years spent studying accounting. He spoke of his apprenticeships and of his time in the monastery and his life with the coffeepickers and in the sewer fields, and he said he had come to Lichfield to find Günther Lopez because foreigners in plastic rags had whispered it would be best for him, and so he'd run down yet another road, and arrived here at this place that seemed to him more vivid and specific than any other he'd encountered, though he could not say how or why, and the mystery of it all pleased him and helped him feel, for now, alive.

Zachary said he had once had an older brother who was somewhat simple-minded, who got what jobs he could here and there depending on the season, now and then collecting some money from the worst sorts of labor, now and then stealing some pennies from their mother, but he seldom came home and mostly slept in barns and stables. Eventually, someone turned him over to the authorities, because someone had seen him in the clearing in the forest with a young girl, and the young girl had given him some caresses, the sort of caresses he had seen other men his age receive from girls not much older than this one, and that he himself had received when the bigger boys from town made him play the game they all called "curdled milk". The authorities brought Zachary's brother to a judge, and the judge indicted him and then turned him over to the care of a doctor, and the doctor gave the boy to other doctors, specialists, who asked Zachary's brother many questions and then wrote up a report that was published in a well-known journal. They measured his brainpan, they studied his facial bone structure, they inspected his anatomy to find degeneracy, and they made him talk and talk about his thoughts and ideas, his inclinations, his habits, his feelings. In the end, in terms only lawyers could understand, the judge pronounced Zachary's brother not guilty, but the doctors kept him for themselves. "He is still with them," Zachary said, "in their asylum, but we are told we cannot talk about it, that he no longer exists and never existed. I heard boys in the schoolhouse trying to tell the story, and the schoolmaster told them to watch their language and never talk about these things ever again, or they, too, would end up like my brother."

Alfred kissed Zachary's cheek. They lay side-by-side in silence. Zachary began to unbutton Alfred's shirt, but Alfred pushed his hand away. "Not while there is light," Alfred said.

"Why not?"

"My skin will repulse you," Alfred said. "It was ruined by the lash and by the sewer fields, by every place that I have lived and every person I have known."

Zachary looked into Alfred's eyes and smiled and kissed him, then continued to unbutton his shirt. Alfred began to object again, but stopped, and soon Zachary ran his hand gently over Alfred's chest and back, feeling the landscape of welts and scars, while Alfred sobbed. Zachary removed his own shirt, revealing smooth and perfect skin, a blank world. He pulled off his trousers and underpants, and Alfred did the same, and they lay together in the very center of the room, arms and legs entwined, breaths intermingling, skin against skin, while the lighthouse light swung around them, reaching out through the unmapped darkness to the stars.

§

Just before morning, a breeze blew through the room, and all the maps on the table, and many of the maps from the bookcase, danced into the air and settled on Alfred and Zachary's bodies. The sight might have horrified Zachary's mother, who prided herself on the care and organization she devoted to her maps, but she didn't come to the office in the lighthouse until the afternoon, because in the morning she woke from a dream of Zachary's brother with the sudden knowledge of how to reach the asylum, and so that morning she walked to the other end of Lichfield Lane to a perfectly square building made from obsidian bricks, and she spoke to an army of doctors and demanded that her son be released to her, and he was. The moment she saw her son, his mother began to unwrap the plastic the doctors had bound him with. She wiped his eyes and scrubbed his face and gave him water to bring back his voice, which, after years of breathing medical dust, had all but gone away. His skin was hard as sun-baked clay, but it softened slightly beneath her touch.

Zachary and Alfred spent the morning cleaning up the room and teasing each other, and by the time Günther Lopez arrived with Zachary's brother, the maps seemed to be unruffled and unbreezed.

"This is Muriuki," Günther Lopez said. "He is your brother."

Muriuki was a short, plump man with a bald head, perfectly round eyes, and exactly the same nose as Zachary. Günther Lopez said, "I am going to teach him to make puppets. We will be a family again. I will perform as a mime and cartographer, and you and Muriuki will put on a puppet show, and we will all be happy and world famous."

Zachary said, "Mother, this is Alfred. He and I are moving on from here and we will never return."

Günther Lopez said, "Well, wait till we get some puppets made. We can't leave until then."

Zachary held Alfred's hand and led him toward the door. "Goodbye," Zachary said to Muriuki.

"I'm sorry we didn't get to spend more time together," Muriuki said.

"You're welcome to come with us if you want," Alfred said.

"No," Muriuki said, "I think our mother needs me. But I'll send you postcards."

"Where will you send the postcards to?" Zachary said.

"The moon, of course," Muriuki said, his eyes wide, serious, and poetic. "He'll see you, wherever you go, and he'll write my words into your dreams."

Zachary and Alfred climbed down the spiral stairs and walked slowly through the town, letting each building inspire imaginary memories for them of where they might have first caught a glimpse of each other and where they might have first touched hands and where they might have first watched a movie together and where they might have first kissed.

As they passed a diner in an abandoned boxcar, Zachary said to Alfred, "You're too thin!"

Alfred said, "It's been a long time since I had anything to eat."

"We must eat!" Zachary said, and he led Alfred into the diner. They sat in a booth with wooden seats and a marble table. A waiter dressed in a tattered tuxedo brought them menus written on fig leaves and told them the special of the day was broiled anaphora. Zachary ordered a peanut butter sandwich and a cup of coffee. Alfred ordered a garden salad and a tofu burger.

"I've decided to become a vegetarian," Alfred said.

"I've been a vegetarian for a long time," Zachary said. "I don't like to hurt animals. They know more about the world than we do, but the knowledge disappears when they die."

"I just like being a member of minority cultures," Alfred said.

After they finished their food, Alfred said, "Where should we go from here?"

"I don't know," Zachary said. "We left all the maps back at the lighthouse. If you want, we can just sit here and look into each other's eyes forever."

Alfred blushed and bowed his head. "I can't stop moving," he said. "My life is a picaresque story."

Zachary put a finger under Alfred's chin and lifted his head. "But you're in a love story now."

"It can't last," Alfred said.

"Why not?"

"They never do."

"Some love stories are timeless," Zachary said.

"We'll fight. We'll misunderstand each other. We'll hurt each other's feelings with careless comments and selfish moments. We'll get old and wrinkled and sick. We'll fall out of love. I'd rather just keep walking…" He stood up, but Zachary stood in his way.

"Let's dance," Zachary said.

"There's no music."

The waiter pressed a button on the face of a cuckoo clock in a corner of the diner and the sound of a tinkly waltz filled the air.

Alfred said, "I'm a terrible dancer."

Zachary put his arms around him and began moving in time to the music.

At first, Alfred couldn't figure out where to put his feet, and he stepped on Zachary's toes and once even nearly fell over. But soon they were moving gracefully, their left hands clasped together and their right arms wrapped around the other's body, and they giggled and whispered, and while they danced the waiter carried all of the tables and seats outside, leaving the diner empty except for the music and the two dancers, who swung around and around, laughing and kissing and resting their heads on each other's shoulder. As dusk turned the entire world grey except for a warm yellow light inside the boxcar, Alfred and Zachary finally stopped dancing, and when they looked outside they saw a crowd of people sitting in the chairs there, watching them, a crowd of people dressed in rags of old plastic, their faces craggled and lips dusty, their eyes lively with childlike joy, and the sound of their applause carried through the night to the lighthouse (where Günther Lopez was trying to show Muriuki how to make puppets from paperclips) and then on and on to the sewer fields and to the junkyard and the pet shop and the monastery, where the coffee pickers stopped shouting obscenities at the monks just long enough to hear the strange sound filling the air, and the monks briefly ceased whipping themselves and praying, and somewhere even farther away Alfred's mother stopped designing a skyscraper and his father stopped looking at pictures in a book about war, and though they were too far away to hear the sound of the applause, they knew something had changed in the world.

Alfred and Zachary bowed to their audience and giggled with a bit of embarrassment, a bit of exhaustion. As the audience continued to applaud, the two men dashed out the back door of the diner and away, running through the dark until they collapsed together in a soggy ravine, where they slept through all of the day and most of the night. When they woke, they stood up stiffly, brushed off their clothes, and continued walking, hand in hand, Zachary humming a waltz and Alfred trying to remember some prayers. They would wander together through many more nights and days, and now and then they would utter occasional harsh words to each other, now and then one would withdraw or another would be selfish, now and then they would disagree about which road to follow or which restaurant to beg a meal from, but through it all they continued to talk to each other, to fight back disappointment together, and nearly every day brought a laugh or two, and they looked forward to reaching old age, when perhaps they might settle down somewhere and draw a map of where they'd been and what they'd seen, but for now, walking through the world, the last thing either Zachary or Alfred wanted was a map.

Lacuna

I heard this story from an acquaintance of mine a few years ago, and he claimed to have heard it from his grandfather, who heard it from the daughter of the man whose story it was. I have filled in gaps with my own best guesses for how certain events might have happened; as an amateur historian of 19th century New York City, I was able to draw on a significant amount of information accumulated over a lifetime of study. Nonetheless, I am painfully aware of how unlikely it is that everything happened as I tell it here.

I tried many times to write this story in as straightforward and objective a manner as possible, but repeatedly failed. There are too many lacunae. Therefore, I am taking the liberty of writing this story from the point of view of the person who is its main character. I have never written fiction before—its conventions are anathema to me—but I hope readers will forgive any awkwardness, for I do believe this is the only way I could accurately preserve what is, I hope you'll agree, a most remarkable history.

A Tale of the City

Let me call myself, for the present, Adam Wilson. My true name is not well known outside certain circles, but within those circles it is known too well, and the knowledge associated with it is more hearsay and fantasy than truth. Perhaps after my death, the truth of my life can be aligned with the truth of my name, but I do not believe such an event is possible while I am alive.

As a young man, I was passionate and indiscreet. I had been raised on a farm in northern New York, and had no knowledge of the world until I had nearly reached the age of maturity. My parents were taciturn country people, godfearing and serious, the descendants of Puritans who escaped England and helped found the colonies that became our Republic. Ours was a singularly unimaginative race of people, but stubborn and loyal. My childhood was not what I would dare deem a happy one, yet neither was it painful or oppressive; instead, it was a childhood of rules and routines, most of them determined by the sun and moon, the weather, and the little church at the center of the town three miles south of our farm, the church we traveled to for every Sabbath, holiday, festivity, and funeral.

As I advanced in years, I became aware of desires within myself to learn more about a world beyond the narrow realm of my upbringing. Ours was not a family given to frequent newspaper reading, but I had read enough to know that the life I lived was not the only possible life. I dreamed of cobblestone streets, tall buildings, and crowds of people. Now I know mine was a common dream, but when I was the dreamer, I thought my dream must be unique in the force of its import and portent. My fate was, I was certain, a great one.

With only the hope of my naïve yearnings to sustain me, I borrowed a few dollars from my parents and rode in the carts of merchants taking their wares toward Manhattan. I don't remember how many days it took to wind a serpentine way to the isle of my dreams. My memory of that time is obscured by all that befell me, for within a day of arriving I had been most violently shown the enormity of the chasm between my imagined city and the one to which I had brought myself. Desperate and hungry, I found what work I could, but I knew no-one and could rely on only the barest charity. Huddled by night in shadowy corners, trembling from cold and starvation and fear, I gave thought to returning home, of settling down to the simple life that seemed to have been predestined for me, but the very idea filled me with a nausea of defeat, for I would have rather thrown myself into the river's muddy torrent than retrace my journey. An evil luck brought me into acquaintance with a certain group of young men who showed me a way to profit from certain men's dark desires, and soon I did not have to hide myself on the streets, for I could afford a small room in a ramshackle building among the most disreputable of the city's inhabitants. It was here I lived and here I sold the only good that I possessed: myself.

After I had worked for a time in this most shameful of all employments, one of the men I provided services to asked me if I would like an opportunity to work in pleasanter surroundings, for a better class of customers and certainly more income than I might otherwise make in my debased and impoverished conditions. I was wary at first, having, after bitter experience, become something of a cynic, but this was a man who had been particularly kind to me, his tendency always toward gentleness, and I knew from his attire and mode of travelling that he was a man of means. Habit kept me obmutescent at first, but he persisted every time he saw me in saying how suited I was to the work, given my fair and feminine features, and I believed he was sincere when he said it pained him to see me in such low circumstances as then composed my life. Therefore, one Sunday morning late in the spring of 184—, after we dined together in my room, I accepted his offer and he provided me with an address at which I was to present myself two weeks hence.

During the time between that Sunday and the later night, I imagined countless and baroque possibilities for what this place might be. It was an address near Thompson Street, an area I knew well enough, though I did not frequent it, my haunts being more to the east, and in the fortnight between receiving the address and going to my appointment there, I carefully avoided the vicinity, for I have always been a superstitious man, and I feared some ill might punish my curiosity. The closer the moment came to present myself at the address, the longer the time stretched out and the more excited grew my imagination. I slept fitfully, my dreams alternately haunted by visions of great pleasure and nightmares of grotesque, delirious pain. Entire lifetimes seemed to pour themselves into the last hours before I set out from my gloomy little room.

Eventually, the waiting time dissipated and I found myself walking almost without awareness from street to street at dusk on the appointed day, the scrap of paper on which the address was written clasped in my hand, for though the address itself had long ago lodged in my memory, I conceived the paper on which it was scrawled to be a fetish, a charm against forces I could neither predict nor apprehend.

I arrived at the address as twilight gathered darkly and more darkly through the city streets. Though I had prepared myself to expect nearly anything, I was not expecting the address to lead to a few small, crude steps descending to a weathered grey door. Not knowing what else to do, I knocked.

This is one of the things I most dislike about fiction: the need to set a scene. Certainly, when writing a historical narrative there is context that has to be established, but it's not the same—here what we have

*is brazen lying. I know nothing about what the exterior of this build-
ing looked like. I don't even know that it was on or near Thompson
Street. It was somewhere on the island of Manhattan, I do know that,
but to be more realistic, I probably should have put it at one of the
more remote areas—maybe up north in the 12th ward somewhere.
I chose the location I did because once you move too far out of the
city as it was in the 1840s, you get away from the sorts of buildings
that could house the events that are central to the story. Honestly, I
expect it all actually happened in Brooklyn, but the person who told
me the story specifically said it took place in Manhattan, and so I
am sticking to that.*

*My mood is bleak today, and it's affecting my writing. Adam came
over to pick up some of his stuff, and inevitably we had to have a
Conversation. (I yearn for the days when our conversations were
lower-cased.) It ended when he asked me how I was doing and I told
him it was none of his fucking business. I regretted it immediately,
but regret is a useless emotion. He walked out. Just walked. Didn't
storm out, didn't slam the door, didn't break windows or anything
like that. Walked out. Again. Without a word.*

*Words. That's part of my problem: I'm trying to capture at least some
of the diction of this character, and spending hours with the OED,
looking up the histories of one word after another to make sure it's
historically accurate, or to find others that are more appropriate. It
took me all afternoon to write one paragraph. It's stilting the voice.
I can't go on like that. I just need to write and not worry about the
historical veracity of the vocabulary and syntax.*

*I'll never forget Adam unless I write this. The nights when we drank
cheap wine and played word games, the delirious night when we*

fell into each other's arms screaming our various pronunciations of "Ulalume" and "Angouleme," and the one glorious night when silence was enough. I loved his blue eyes, his wild blond hair, his crooked tooth. ("My own little Aryan," I called him.) We told each other stories of our pasts, and his were always full of adventure and excitement—because they were never true, and I knew it, and I loved him for it, and he told me I should loosen up and let go of myself and let my imagination play. I never could, and never dared try, and I hated him for it.

He accused me of being a slave to the facts, and later on, in the night-mare days, I accused him of writing potboilers. The worst nights were when he did more drinking than writing. "Great writers have writ-ten stories like mine," he said after half a bottle of Jack one night. I laughed at him and said, "Keep telling yourself that. Crappy writers always think they're great. And drunken assholes figure if they drink like Poe, maybe they'll write like him." He took a swig from the bottle and then spat it in my face. I can hardly blame him. I knew the nerve I was hitting. Still, I was angry. "You're a fucking hack," I said, "and your stories are pathetic and disgusting. They wouldn't scare a child." At the time, I thought it was the beginning of the end, but really, it was the middle. The truth is, I'd never liked his stories, even when we first started dating.

Anyway…

The door opened, no more slowly or quickly than any other door might, and a small man wearing the most ordinary clothes imag-inable stood there in front of me. I showed him the slip of paper I had brought with me, but he didn't look at it. Somehow, he knew I belonged here. He gestured to his side—his right, my left—and

I followed his gesture through a nondescript room and perfectly ordinary, if narrow, hallway, to another, and unmemorable, door. I knocked, but there was no answer, and so I turned the knob and opened the door, revealing a set of carpeted stairs leading down. I descended. The air grew musty and cold, the stairway became grey and then dark, and I felt my feet hit stone. I looked down, thinking I had reached some sort of bottom, but in the greyness I could make out more steps, now made of stone. Granite. Descending.

Eventually, light slipped through the darkness from candles set on shelves at the bottom of the stairs. I know now that the stairs were not miles long, but that is the impression they gave during that descent. Certainly, the caverns they led to were deep, and the edifice as a whole a marvel of architecture and engineering, but there was nothing supernatural about the place, at least in its design.

What the stairs led to was a series of small rooms with rock walls. Within moments of my arrival, a dark-skinned young man dressed as a servant brought me to one of the other rooms, a place filled with piles of women's clothing. In the dim light, the clothing looked expensive and impressive, but soon the young man held some pieces out to me and instructed me on how to wear them, and touching the fabric I saw that it was tattered, torn, and stained. I should say here that I had not worn women's clothing before, nor had much cause to examine it closely—a fact that had purely been a matter of chance, given how many of my compatriots were instructed at one time or another to unsex themselves for their men—and so I was awkward and required much assistance from the young man. His touch was gentle and soothing, as if he expected me to be frightened or disgusted, but given the circumstances of my hiring and the strangeness of the setting, I felt little surprise at the necessary attire. "What is your name?" I asked him. His smile was unforced and uncertain, as if it was the strangest query he'd encountered in many days.

"You don't need to know me," he said, averting his eyes.

I shifted my gaze to grasp his again, then took his hand in mine. "Necessity is the least interesting force in the universe," I said, parroting an aphorism once uttered by a priest who insisted on philosophizing whilst I pleasured him.

"My name is Charles," he said. "But please forget me. They'll call you to the stage in a moment, and you need to be ready."

"Will we meet again, Charles?"

I pulled him closer to me, but released his hand when I saw tears in his eyes.

Hands gripped my shoulders, spun me around, pushed me forward into light. Whiteness enveloped me, blinded me. I stumbled forward, knocking my foot against an obstacle. I heard chattering voices, the rumblings of impatient conversation. My eyes adjusted slowly, bringing shapes and colors into focus, and then I saw where I stood: a living room with a long couch, three chairs, and a low table. No—as my eyes accustomed to the light, I saw beyond it, beyond what I had taken to be walls and windows—beyond the whirlwind of lamps, mirrors, crystals, and smoke that obscured the view—I saw faces stacked in a small and narrow amphitheatre: the leering, lusting faces of men.

Breathless, my knees trembling with infirmity, I staggered to the couch and fell upon it. At that moment, a figure appeared from somewhere behind me. A man in a swallow-tailed black coat—his visage concealed by a black silk mask, his hands protected by white gloves—moved forward and presented himself to the audience. The men applauded vigorously.

I sat up on the couch and whispered, "Who are you?"

The masked figure rushed to me, his hand struck my face, and I fell back onto the couch. My cheek burned, my forehead ached, blood crossed my tongue. Ringing filled my ears, but then I heard the audience through the noise: their laughter, their rallying cries. His hands pulled me up, turned me to face him. The fabric of his mask was wet at the mouth and nose; his breathing made the silk pulse like a sail in a storm. Again his hand hit my face, and then the other hand, and then again, again—and all the while, the audience applauded, their claps in sympathy with each slap across my skin.

My abraded cheeks bled, my nose and lips bled, blood filled my mouth, I coughed. His hands grasped my throat and pushed me back onto the couch. Men whistled and stomped their feet. He tore the dress at the shoulder, snapping its seams. He wrenched it down. I pushed at him feebly, my arms and muscles moving by instinct, but he was stronger than I and easily held me back against the couch. His fists hit my stomach, my kidneys, then the bones of my ribs, knocking sense and breath from me. I keeled forward, and again he pushed me back, slapped my face, grabbed my hair. My eyes saw swirls of colors more than shapes, but soon I discerned that he stood over me and was pulling back his mask. I expected any face except the one I should have known would be there: The face of the man who had so gently implored me to come to this place. His eyes, which I had once, briefly, thought displayed a kind of love for me, now burned with contempt.

My recognition fired his fury. He rained more punishment upon me, and then, as I lay on the couch, my body throbbing, my eyes blurred with tears, he lowered his face to my chest, and the familiar tenderness there found its parody in his nuzzling kisses. The audience grew silent, their attention rapt, and yet soon there were stirrings—they became restless.

My tormenter paused. He now prepared the *pièce de résistance* of his performance. Holding me under the arms, he pulled me up to stand. The dress I wore sagged around my hips. He wrapped his right arm around my neck and with his left arm pulled—slowly but fiercely—the dress and all my underclothing down toward my knees. He could not hold my neck and further undress me, and so he pushed me forward—I braced myself with my arms, but fell hard on the floor, cracking a bone—and then felt myself hoisted backward as he ripped the shredding dress and all the rest from me until I was entirely naked in the hot fire of the lights and the hateful glare of all the men.

He retrieved his mask from where it had fallen beside the couch. He covered his face with it, sat on the couch, and removed his shoes. His feet bare, he walked toward me, then slowly, gently, took off each piece of clothing until only his mask remained. I glanced at him, not letting my gaze linger, for the pains coursing through my body demanded most attention for themselves. A quick look was enough for me, though, for I knew his strong, supple body well, and the sight of it above me now filled me with terror—the engorgement of his desire offered no thrill for me—rather, he seemed entirely grotesque, a demon, a force of unimaginable agony.

Even now, decades after the events, I cannot describe his actions without bringing myself to tears and raising aching memories across my skin.

I do not have the words to describe his final abuses, nor do I want to remember all he did to me or to remember the wild joys of the crowd.

I don't remember writing the scene I just wrote. I would never write such an absurd phrase as "the engorgement of his desire". It's disgusting and ridiculous. Those are not words I would choose. I should erase them now, I should get rid of this whole thing. And yet I know I won't. I've written those words there—"I should erase them now, I should get rid of this whole thing"—to let myself off the hook. I had no intention of erasing any of this. I've enjoyed writing it. I've gotten

out of myself, away from the shitstorm with Adam. I don't believe
a word of what I wrote above about responsibility. That's not true,
either, though. I believe in the idea of it. But it has no visceral mean-
ing for me. Because I really am writing this for myself. Really. It's an
escape, a bit of fun. Meaningless. Really. I don't need you to read this.
I don't need you.

(The memories rest as jagged shards, sharp and ready to freshen wounds.)

The light burns and stings its smoke into my eyes. My body moves, pulled over the wooden stage, splinters pricking my knees and legs. Darkness, then soft candlelight. Fingers trawl my skin. Cold water washes me. Charles won't meet my gaze. I realize why he had tears in his eyes. He knew. There are many words I would like to say to him, but my tongue is thick and my mouth dry. He dresses me carefully in the clothes I arrived in. Shadows shift in the room and take hold of me and drag me up the stairs and outside into early morning air, and I am carried around corners and dropped in an alley onto soggy newspapers and chicken bones and scattering rats. They toss coins at me.

I do not move. Movement is pain. I barely breathe.

(The subsequent memories are more dreamlike, less present, and they do not wound.)

The sun rose somewhere above me and distant voices fell and echoed through the air. A rat bit my leg. I coughed and yearned for water or, better, gin. I swept the coins from my chest and hid them away in my pants. My employer had been correct that this was more lucrative work for me—these were good coins, more than I would earn in a month usually—but the cost was too much.

I leaned against a brick wall and inched my way toward the street. Somewhere in this Herculean effort, I met my savior. He was a thin man, disheveled, and his attire making it seem that he, too, might have been dropped in an alley, but he sported no wounds to his bones and skin, just sunken, bloodshot eyes and an unsteady step.

I do not remember what conversation we had. I drifted from awareness to a kind of half-sleep where I was awake but uncomprehending. Somehow I told him the address of my room, and somehow he took me there. My first thought was fear: did he intend to add to my abuses? He seemed afraid to touch me, though, and so I did not long fear him. My second thought was embarrassment: at the squalor of my tiny room, at the weakness of myself. I had little reason for such feelings, though, for soon he had lain himself down on the floor and fallen asleep.

I woke in the night when he opened the door.

"Who are you?" I called, fearing I would never see him again, never see him when I was healthy enough to thank him for his tremendous kindness.

"A man who needs to piss," he said, and walked out. He returned some time later.

"I have a chamber pot," I said.

"I know," he said. "But you didn't have this." He held up a small bottle of whiskey.

"I have gin."

"I saw your gin. Indeed, I smelled it." He sat on the one chair in the room, a small wooden chair I had built myself from scraps I'd found near the docks. He opened his bottle of whiskey. "What you call gin is a fast road to blindness. I might consider using it to remove stains from my clothing, but I am afraid it would remove the cloth along with the stains."

"I wanted to thank you," I said, "for—"

"No need for thanks. My motives were entirely mercenary, and you still should receive the attention of doctors, especially given what looks to me like a broken bone in your arm. I have not called a doctor, however. I must leave that for you to do yourself. You were a useful excuse for me at a difficult moment. I needed to disappear from the vision of certain people for a few hours while they sought me out for debts I most surely do not owe them, and since you are a stranger to me, and we have no previous connection, it is unlikely anyone will think to look for me here. I trust you are sufficiently healthy to avoid immediate death, however, as I have no skill as a nurse. Also, I expect I will become insensibly inebriated within the next hour. I have been an advocate of temperance recently, and I intend to return to advocating temperance in the future, but in the present I desire nothing so much as the soft obliteration bestowed by this bottle." He drank deeply from it.

"I am still grateful to you. There is no telling what could have become of me."

After many more minutes and many more drinks, the man said, "How *did* you end up in this state, if you'll pardon my curiosity."

"I hardly know, myself. A poet might say I fell into a vortex of vice and infamy."

"A villainous vortex of vice. Or, perhaps, a villainous veritable vortex of vice. No, a vortex of villainy, a veritable vice of…" He sighed and swayed a bit on the chair. He emptied the bottle into his mouth, then carefully slid from the chair to the floor, his care undermined by his drunkenness, causing him to end up on hands and knees with little comprehension of how he got there. Eventually, he rolled onto his side and stared at me.

"Are you a thief?" he muttered.

"What?"

"You live in a thief's establishment."

"No, there are no thieves here. We are people of business."

He chuckled. "And what business is your business?"

I looked into his hazed and glassy eyes. "You won't remember anything I say in the morning."

He coughed fiercely, but somehow avoided vomiting.

"Men pay me money," I said. "And for that money, I pleasure them. I kiss them. I undress them. They kiss me and undress me. We pretend at love. Their tastes are, shall we say, Hellenistic. Some of them are strong men whose pleasure comes from dominating a weaker man. Some of them are weak men who fancy themselves women at heart. If they pay enough, I can give them any pleasure they desire."

"Do you enjoy…" he began, his words fading into gibberish.

"Sometimes, yes, I enjoy it," I said. "A shallow enjoyment, briefly real. I learned early to survive by trying to fall in love with them all. They pay better when I am convincing. They return. My best men seek my body's spirit, and they pay me for it, so I must… deliver it unto them."

He chuckled again, weakly, as he slipped away from consciousness.

In the morning, his body was so consumed with nausea and pain that the doctor I summoned to attend to my wounds spent as much time with him as with me. A few of my friends and regular customers paid a visit during the day, and while most of them assumed the man sprawled on the floor was an especially satiated customer, one of my favorite men, a lovely brute with mischievous eyes and a lady's lips, who worked among newspapermen, said he had seen my visitor around his own haunts and knew him to be disreputable and irresponsible, often a danger to himself but generally harmless otherwise, though he was said to have an acid tongue.

By evening, he had recovered sufficiently to depart, offering to return with provisions should I need them, but by that time my friends and colleagues had determined a schedule by which they fulfilled my needs in shifts, for though we may be lowly in our employment and circumstances, lowliness inspires fierce comrade-ship: my fate was one all my peers could envision for themselves, and though I knew of none whose experiences were as decorated with grotesque mystery as mine, few had escaped bruises, broken bones, and alley trash-heaps during their careers.

And so my savior departed, and I thanked him, and he seemed to remember nothing of our conversation, and I set my sails toward healing and forgetting.

I sent my customers away with apologies—the doctor had informed me that my body needed significant rest and tenderness, and my broken arm was going to be a problem for months. A few men offered me a penny or two for food and medicine, though most simply gave me a wary smile or hasty kiss before closing the door behind themselves. Many would never look at me with the same lust in their eyes as before, and most would pay someone else for their pleasures.

As the months passed and my body healed, if ever the terrible night left my mind, my dreams brought it back in monstrous night-mares. Shadow creatures tore all the skin from my face and chest and arms and legs—massive hands pulverized my bones—wild, full, liquid eyes flashed with red light across all my visions—and endless applause echoed through the maelström.

Many months later, as I undressed in darkness for a customer who sprawled naked across my bed, a shaft of moonlight illumi-nated my face more fully than he had seen it before, and he gasped and covered himself with the sheets. I knew then what I had first suspected when I saw him: This was Charles, the attendant to my nightmares. His face had grown more sallow, his body more angu-lar, but this was he.

I jumped atop him and held him to the bed. (In the moonlight, we perhaps resembled a strange etching of midnight wrestlers.) My muscles flexed with fury, and I wanted nothing so much as to tear him apart with my hands, not because he had himself abused me—he had been nothing but gentle and sympathetic—but because here, for the first time since that ghastly night, I held in my hands some physical representation of the misery that still terrorized my mind.

Leaning down close, I spat his name into his ear, enunciating it as a vicious noise, an accusation and condemnation, a curse. I held him firm, but gave him everything he had paid me for, and more than that—for though I always made sure to keep him pressed to the bed to prevent his escape, my every caress was soft, careful, loving. Malnourishment and maltreatment had faded his previous beauty, but its shadow remained, and it was the shadow I sought, the shadow I held in my imagination. This was a greater torture to him than any I could have inflicted with fists or whips or the manifold tools of so many Inquisitions. Once I recovered from my terrible night, I took to keeping my room quite dark, for certain scars and bruises never left my skin, and only a minority of customers are excited by damaged goods, so Charles had not been able to discern my features and had not known whom he was buying—his intent was as innocent as any such attempt could be.

After, as he lay nearly comatose from exhaustion and shame, I retrieved some rope from a corner of the room and bound him with it. He fought listlessly against me. I hauled him to the floor and dragged him up against the wall. And then I waited.

Though first he resisted and pleaded ignorance, then wept over the consequences his words would bring himself and his family, by mid-day, he had told me everything I hoped to know. He did not know names, or at least not useful ones (the names he knew were descriptive: "The Sailor", "The Old Swede", "The Painter", "Doctors D and F") but he knew times, locations, and pass-words. Though he wailed that he was certain things had changed since he had been unceremoniously relieved of his duties (for reasons he knew not), I thanked him and removed the ropes that bound him. I had brought a bucket of water into the room, and I cleaned him with it, and as I did so his tears subsided and his weeping gave way to stoic impassivity. I dried him with a small towel, then dressed him as if he were an invalid. I kissed him, but he did not respond. In the years since that moment, I have imagined many words that must have passed through his mind, but the truth is that he did not speak—he lifted his head high and walked away, a new force of will, or a newly willed force, propelling him from the room.

He had given me the address at which the malevolent club would meet, for they moved their meetings according to a strict plan, and he said it was always the third Thursday of the month, and that the revels began precisely at eleven minutes past eleven in the evening. That gave me one month to prepare, for Charles had visited me on the night of the third Thursday.

I spent the month perfecting my scheme and collecting the various items I would need to effect it. This required much cleverness and a certain amount of daring, for I had not nearly enough money to purchase all the items, particularly the clothing, and so I had to insinuate myself into places where such things could be acquired. My greatest luck came when a friend of a friend introduced me to an expensive card game in a building near Gramercy Place, and my experience with far less trusting competitors in far more complicated games allowed me to leave not only with what was, for me at that time, a small fortune in cash, but with what I had really come for: a fine hat, cape, and walking stick. (The other players were so amused by my encouraging them to wager their clothing that they insisted I return again in the future, as indeed I did many times, making the associations that would, in fact, send me toward the far more reputable sort of life I lead today.)

Thus it was that I was able to dress myself as a man of considerable means, and to secret on my person two pistols obtained for me by a faithful customer who was also an officer in the Navy, and who provided me with, in addition to the pistols, ammunition and numerous small sacks of gunpowder.

I began writing this as a way to, I thought—or I told myself—exorcise Adam. But that's not it.

Words are magic. That's what he said to me when we started dating. I loved his words, and I told him so, and he smiled and he said, "Well, words are magic." It's only when you're first in love with somebody that such banal and empty ideas seem profound. I should know better, but those first, rushing, blinding moments of love make everything seem profound, unique, consequential. I should know better. I've got a master's degree, I've studied philosophy and literature and art and history—and yes, my daily life is not glamorous, I work as a shipping and receiving manager at a warehouse, yes, I know I am not, as he said, living up to my potential (whatever that is!), but you don't think I'm as aware of that as anybody else? I've spent a lifetime being told how much potential I have, how brilliant and talented I am, what a fine mind I have. At the warehouse they call me "Professor" and "Einstein", but that's nothing compared to what people say to me when I get into a conversation with them about, for instance, the building of the Croton Water Aqueduct or the history of The Tombs and then they ask me if I've written a book or if I work at a university and I mumble and I shuffle my feet and I cough nervously and eventually, if they're persistent, I tell them, "Actually, I work at a warehouse." You should see their faces. You have seen their faces. And I've seen your face when you've seen their faces. It's not just that you think I haven't lived up to my potential, no—you're ashamed of me. At your book parties, at your conventions and conferences. You were always happy to be around anybody other than me. Remember the party where, after at least a couple of bottles of wine, you grabbed me and groped me and people gathered around, laughing nervously, and you yelled to them all, "Look, friends, at my Hop-Frog!" I should have grabbed a torch and hurled it at you and set you all aflame.

Words are magic.

No they aren't. I keep writing this, thinking of you, wondering what you would make of it, wondering if it would, somehow, be enough. Enough what? Enough magic.

Words are not magic. Words are echoes, shadows, ashes.

We tell stories because what else is there to do? This is a story. I am telling it. Summoning voices to keep me company through the night.

The entertainment that month occurred in a palatial private residence far north, at 52nd Street and Fifth Avenue. My card winnings easily paid for a fine carriage to carry me to the location, and though I had feared the pass-word system Charles taught me would have been changed, it was not, for I was admitted without a second glance from the masked and muscled men who guarded the inside of the door. From there, a very small man—a dwarf, really—dressed in an expensive (and miniature) butler's uniform led me through a corridor and up two flights of stairs to a kind of recital hall. It was a circular room, very lofty, and received the light of the moon only through a single window at top. A few dozen chairs stood in rows in front of a small stage, at the center of which had been placed a settee, and above which hung an immense chandelier dripping wax from its countless candles. Most of the seats in the audience were filled by well-attired men, and none of us looked at each other or spoke.

Within minutes, the man in the world whom I most loathed, the man who had first enticed me to attend one of these performances and then scarred and humiliated me so brutally, so publicly—this man now stood on the stage, directly in front of the settee, his face unmasked. His words echo through my ears as if I heard them mere minutes ago:

"Hello, my friends. Tonight's revelry is a singular one for us. It has been arranged to honor one of our most devoted members, a man who has been a friend to these festivities for longer than most, and who has provided us all with much continued pleasure through the imaginative chronicling of the emotional forces that are unleashed here every month. His is our true voice, his words the metaphors of our reality, his dreams the ones we share. He has, alas, fallen on hard times, as can happen to any man, and to lighten the burden of his days, I asked him what spectacle he would most like to see, and so tonight's pantomime is one that we should consider authored by our dear friend."

With that, the man gestured to a figure sitting in the front row, a figure who stood and acknowledged us—and it was at that moment that I nearly gave myself away, for I could barely stifle a gasp of shock and revulsion on seeing the face of my savior, the man who had rescued me after I had been subjected to such evil, the man who guided me home and stayed with me on the first night of my recovery.

I hardly had time to absorb the fact of his face before most of the lights in the room were extinguished, save for the chandelier above the stage, and a young girl stumbled forward, golden braids bouncing over her face. She looked confused and stunned. Before she could gain her bearings, the malevolent host strode forward and grasped her in his arms. She screamed, and a few men in the audience responded with laughs. The host lifted the girl onto the settee and then his hands performed a terrible dance upon her body. As her screams grew more desperate, the laughter in the room rose, and so, too, did sounds of encouragement and goading. I felt a psychic hunger course through the audience as the host held a dagger in his hand and, with great precision, sliced the girl's dress open slowly and methodically, then, after excruciating minutes of this, pulled the dress from her trembling body. It was then that we all saw that this was not, in fact, a young girl, but a young boy—and the men in the audience screamed their approval as the host slit and removed the last garments from the unfortunate boy's frame and then held him aloft like a prize calf. He held the boy before the man in the front row, who nodded his approval without touching the chaste, white, shivering body.

I was about to enact the climax of my plan when two men wearing masks of the *commedia dell'arte* style appeared, carried a small ivory casket onto the stage, and opened it. I stayed my hand because of a moment's fascination. The host then placed the naked and whimpering boy into the casket and closed it. The casket had been fit with locks, and the cover was thick enough to muffle the boy's terrified screams. The host gestured to the audience to enjoy the screams. It was what they had assembled for—not merely the sight of the boy being degraded and abused, but for the pleasure of his terror.

I couldn't keep watching. I stood, withdrew a pistol, and shot the host in the chest. The audience thought this was part of the entertainment, and they applauded and cheered. Only the man in the front row seemed to understand that something was wrong, and he stood up. I moved forward, keeping the pistol aimed at his head. "Do you know me?" I said. "Do you?"

He stared at me, and then recognition dawned across his face.

The pistol now pressed against his forehead, I repeated, "Do you know me?"

"Yes."

The shot would have cracked his skull open, but at the last moment my hand wavered and I merely fired past his ear—the shock and noise enough to make him fall to the ground, thick red blood oozing from inside his ear, but very much alive.

The men who had guarded the front doors rushed into the room, and the audience had now figured out that something was amiss, but they were paralyzed by shock and confusion.

I pushed the bleeding body of the host away from the casket, its ivory now decorated with blood. I sprung the locks, opened the lid, pulled the terrified boy out, and wrapped him in my cloak. "Hold onto my hand," I told him. "Don't let go."

As the guardsmen and the audience approached, I tossed bags of gunpowder toward the candles in front of them, bringing loud, acrid explosions that blinded them and robbed them of breath. I whisked the boy out of the room, down the corridor and stairs, and then outside, where my carriage waited around a corner. I attempted to hasten him into the carriage, but his terror gave him new strength, and he was unable to distinguish my care from the abuses of the men in the mansion, and so he struggled and fought until he was free of my grip and my cloak, and he ran, naked and screaming, into the night. I knew that the noise of my guns, perhaps, and the boy's screams, almost certainly, would alert neighbors and elicit eyes at windows, so I gave the boy no more thought and jumped into my carriage and we hurried away.

I learned much later that, shortly after I proved unable to shoot him in the head, the man I had previously thought of as my savior showed up drunk and sick in Baltimore, where he died. His literary work gained fame and notoriety in the following years, but I have always refused to read a word of it.

As I alluded above, I was able to make a new life for myself thanks to my own cleverness and determination, and to acquire something of a reputation as a philanthropist and an advocate for the preservation of Saxon strength through careful, deliberate habits of breeding—I am pleased that my pedagogical historical narrative *Hengst and Horsa, or, The Saxon Men* sold extremely well some years ago under one of my *noms de plume*. But I am an old and ailing man, now, and my time is limited, and as I have always devoted my life to the truth, I feel I must pen this manuscript, for fear that I will disappear otherwise into the vortex of time without having expressed the truths of my life—truths which, for all their apparent wonder and horror, I trust will speak their veracity to you, dear reader.

> "In me didst thou exist—and, in my death, see by
> this image, which is thine own, how utterly thou hast
> murdered thyself."
> —Edgar Allan Poe,
> "William Wilson"

It is not the ending I intended. I had been struggling with it for a week or so, failing to create the tone I wanted, trying out a bunch of things to give it both a sense of verisimilitude and drama, never achieving it—and then three days ago got a call from Ginny with the news that Adam is dead.

I was going to try to revise the ending, but why bother now? I secretly hoped he would read the story and like it, or even hate it but be amused. I thought he would see that I understood how hard he worked, how talented he was, the worth of stories and storytelling. Or something. I don't know. Maybe my intentions were less noble or naive. I don't know.

What I know is that now there is no point. Words are not magic. If there is truth, it lurks between the lines, unreachable, silent, lost like the truth of whatever happened to Poe in the last week of September 1849. Lost. We can imagine stories, but that is all they are: imagined.

I was writing this story for myself, I thought, but really I was writing it for him, and so I wrote it for nothing. It is here now, it exists, like me, alone, unfinished, a testament to nothing but itself.

I've read so many interviews with writers and artists who say they create to have a sense of immortality, of leaving something behind after they go. Adam said that sometimes. His stories, he said, were his children, his legacy, his history, his immortality. Even if he wasn't rich and famous, at least he had books on shelves and maybe one day in the future somebody would stumble on one in a library or a bookstore and his words would live in their mind. His work would live on. But what good is posterity? You're still dead.

Words are not magic. Stories are not truth; they are evasions, misdirections.

He took a couple Valium, drank most of a bottle of vodka, loaded his father's old Colt 1911 pistol, put it in his mouth, and pulled the trigger.

Those are the facts. End of story.

The Island Unknown

I have discovered a Victrola on the island. There is no other sign of civilization, just lots of sand and a few rocks and one big palm tree. And the Victrola, standing like a sentry beneath the tree. It's one of those cabinet Victrolas, one of the new ones, expensive. I opened the cabinet to see if there were any records, and there were. I put one on, but I didn't understand it, perhaps because sunstroke and dehydration were setting in, and I was still angry at the captain for declaring me a degenerate and marooning me here.

The noises coming from the Victrola sounded like a particularly enthusiastic and utterly out-of-tune klezmer band.

This was not to be my salvation.

When I saw the Victrola, I had thought I'd solved whatever metaphysical riddle my marooning posed, and that if I could just find the right record to play, an army of friends would arise from the ocean and carry me back to the ship, patting me on the back and sticking a cigar in my mouth, their own mouths issuing great waves of chortle.

But no, the only waves were the briny ones bumping against the beach.

"Be quiet!" I screamed at the waves. They would not obey, so I tore the record off the Victrola and threw it into the ocean as a warning.

I tried another record, but it was exactly the same.

They were all the same.

All the same.

I stared at each label, trying to divine differences and meanings, but the best I could come up with was that the labels were a deep red-purple color I decided should be called "maroon", and thus I had found my own label.

The words on the label were not English, nor the alphabet one I recognized—the precise, intricate letters looked like some sort of runes, but I know nothing of runes, having spent my few years of education learning to tie one thousand knots. I had hoped it would get me a wife, but women, I discovered, are more complicated than knots. I became a private investigator, and I roamed the shipyards, and one night I turned into a stowaway, because the divorce racket had grown depressing, and I figured some time on the sea would do me good. I hid in a box of toaster ovens, and then one day a swarm of turtles infested the hold and a long-repressed terror of animals with shells overtook my senses and sent me screaming to the top deck, where a bevvy of salt-scarred sailors tackled me and loved me and made me think I was one of their own. But I was not one of their own, which, had I been more perspicacious, I would have guessed from the Army helmet they stuck on my head, because I had seen all the old movies with John Wayne and Randolph Scott in which people of the land torment people of the sea, and vice versa, and their differences can never be overcome until combat in the last act, but we had no combat out on the empty sea, and the sea was endless, without act breaks or intermissions of any sort, and so we had no sacrifice and no reconciliation, and I was the landlubber, and eventually the sailors who had loved me so well and so tenderly fell into a routine of hour after hour and day after day throwing sand in my face and spitting tobacco through the bullet hole in my steel helmet, until one day they ran out of sand and tobacco and they took the helmet back and they tossed me to the island here, without even the grace of a box of toaster ovens for old time's sake.

The Victrola skips. Its needle bounces like a mosquito across the record. I begin to understand the sounds, I begin to hear their words: *The history of my life has never been read. A reckless, hard-hearted life I have lived. I leave my true love. I leave my true — my true — my love. I leave my true love to sorrow and pain. We'll meet I hope in the sweet bye and—*

No, this is not true. The Victrola tells the wrong story. It lies and lies and lies again!

I throw sand across the record, causing it only to skip more and issue more words I understand: *A story I tell of a sad rambling soul. He's lost, I've been told, on the Island Unknown.*

The history of life is the history of the dead.

I cover the Victrola with sand, until there is nothing but a mound in front of me, and the words have turned to soft, distant moans. I lean against the mound and let the sun slash across my skin, I let the dry wind sear my eyes, I wait to burst into fire or fall into dust.

I wait.

There is movement near my feet. Turtles climb ashore, lines of them, waves of them, endless numbers, and the sun explodes off the silver toaster ovens on their backs. They pile the toaster ovens around me like an igloo, and then they dig through the sand with their little claws and uncover the Victrola and clean off the record and set the song singing again.

I cannot escape the dark prison the turtles have built for me, I cannot destroy the Victrola. I hear the turtles out there, singing along and dancing.

It must be night now. The turtles sing louder.

The sound of the song and their singing echoes across the steel of the toaster ovens. *He's lost, I've been told, on the Island Unknown, he's lost, I've been told, he's lost...*

It is late now, but the turtles never tire and the Victrola never stops.

Listen!

Can you hear them? Can you hear them?

Please tell me I am not alone.

Acknowledgments

These stories were written over the course of fifteen years, and many of them would not have been written without the help and support of numerous family members, friends, and colleagues to whom I feel profound gratitude.

First, I must thank three teachers who allowed me to be a writer when I didn't even necessarily know that's what I was: Chris Finer, Rebecca Frame, and James Patrick Kelly. They've all known me since I was a weird little kid, and they let me be weird, which has meant more to me than I could possibly put into words.

At these stories' early, fragile stages, some first readers offered crucial support and advice: Christopher Barzak, Richard Bowes, Nathan Long, Njihia Mbitiru, Meghan McCarron, Katherine Min, Eric Schaller, Jeff VanderMeer, and especially Richard Larson, who read more drafts of these stories over the years than anyone else.

I've been lucky to work with some brilliant editors. Heartfelt thanks to the people who originally published and often helped shape these stories: Ann VanderMeer, Hannah Tinti, Nita Noveno, Thom Didato, Mike Allen, Jedediah Berry, Gavin Grant, Craig Gidney, John Joseph Adams, Peter Wild, John Klima, Bradford Morrow, Delia Sherman, Theodora Goss, Steve Berman, and Matt Williamson.

Black Lawrence Press has believed in the value of this book unstintingly, and I am immensely grateful to everyone there. Special thanks to Yvonne Garrett, who first thought the manuscript might be worthwhile, and to Diane Goettel, who called from Hong Kong to tell me I'd won the Hudson Prize, and who has shepherded these pages into print, helping me to realize a dream I've had since I was a child: a book of my own.

My life while writing these stories was rich with marvelous friends, colleagues, and students, too many to list here, but without them I would never have kept going, and my gratitude is profound.

To my family, some of whom did not get to see this book, but who live between its lines and flow through my blood: my grandparents Frank, Eleanor, Lois, and Ken; my aunts Meredith and Betty; and my father, the ghost in my machines.

My grandparents and all my aunts, uncles, and cousins still help this only child feel far from only.

And I have the best mothers in the world.